Jo Watson is the bestselling
Love to Hate You which has s
You Not; *You, Me, Forever*; *T*
Am. She's a two-time Watty *A* s
on Wattpad and 85,000 fo
Depeche Mode devotee. Sh

For more information, visit her website **www.jowatsonwrites.co.uk**, follow her on X and Instagram **@JoWatsonWrites** and find her on Facebook at **/jowatsonwrites**.

Love funny, romantic stories? You don't want to miss Jo Watson!

'The perfect choice for fans of romantic comedies' *Gina's Bookshelf*

'Full of pure-joy romance, laugh-out-loud moments and tear-jerkers' *Romantic Times*

'A masterclass in character development' *Hannah Reading Books*

'I love a good original love story and Jo Watson managed to surprise me over and over again. Her snappy writing style is refreshing, her main characters are endearing and dazzling and her book sparkles from beginning to end'
With Love For Books

'It was amazing, it was hilarious' *Rachel's Random Reads*

'A brilliant read from beginning to end' *Hopeless Romantics*

'I can't heap any more praise on this book, it just made me feel so happy! I laughed, I cried, I smiled, but most of all I LOVED!!'
Mrs J Tea

'A perfect read for fans of rom-coms' *Cheryl's Bookworm Reads*

'Jo Watson has found a fan for life in me' *Olive Book Reviews*

'Found myself frequently laughing out loud and grinning like a fool!' *BFF Book Blog*

'An addictive read, it is heart-breaking at times but ultimately a stunning heart-warming read' *Donna's Book Blog*

By Jo Watson

Standalone

Love To Hate You

Love You, Love You Not

What Happens On Vacation

Love At First Flight

Starting Over Trilogy

You, Me, Forever

Truly, Madly, Like Me

Just The Way I Am

Destination Love Series

Burning Moon

Almost A Bride

Finding You

After The Rain

The Great Ex-Scape

LOVE AT FIRST FLIGHT

JO WATSON

HEADLINE
ETERNAL

First published in paperback in Great Britain in 2024
by HEADLINE ETERNAL
An imprint of HEADLINE PUBLISHING GROUP

1

Cataloguing in Publication Data is available from the British Library

ISBN 978 1 0354 0052 2

Typeset in 11/14.5 pt Granjon LT Std by Jouve (UK), Milton Keynes

Printed and bound in Great Britain by Clays Ltd, Elcograf S.p.A.

FSC
www.fsc.org
MIX
Paper | Supporting
responsible forestry
FSC® C104740

Headline's policy is to use papers that are natural, renewable and recyclable products
and made from wood grown in well-managed forests and other controlled sources.
The logging and manufacturing processes are expected to conform to
the environmental regulations of the country of origin.

HEADLINE PUBLISHING GROUP
An Hachette UK Company
Carmelite House
50 Victoria Embankment
London EC4Y 0DZ

www.headlineeternal.com
www.headline.co.uk
www.hachette.co.uk

To all my neurodivergents out there.

Author's Note

I want to start off by saying that it takes a lot more than what I've put in this book to land a plane – so please, if ever attempting to do so, do not use my words! I had to paraphrase and shorten a lot of ATC commands for the sake of the story, and for this, I apologize to any aviation experts who may read this book!

But now that I've gotten that out the way, let me tell you another story. I've always been different and felt different my entire life. And as the years have rolled on, so I've accumulated many diagnoses, some absolute nonsense, and others totally accurate. But it wasn't until last year, when I was writing this book, that I finally got a diagnosis that made EVERYTHING I have ever experienced in my life, then and now, make sense.

Getting my autism diagnosis has been a massive relief to me, it validates a lot of my experiences, and also gives me a much better understanding of why I do what I do. In fact, I actually wanted to scream my diagnosis from the rooftops when I was first told, because I was so excited about having it. When I told my husband about my diagnosis, like Andrew, he burst out laughing and told me it wasn't exactly news to him. And when I told some other people who know me well, I got the exact same reaction. They'd all known or suspected. I know there are a lot of women getting these late-in-life autism diagnoses, because back in our day (I'm really showing my age now) we hardly knew what the word autism meant, and certainly not autism in girls.

When I started writing this book, I had no intention of writing Pippa as an autistic character, but when my diagnosis came in, I just decided to do it. I gave Pippa many of my traits, but also traits that are common to others on this very large and diverse spectrum. Some of the traits we share are a slight obsession with airplane crashes and synonyms (I always have my thesaurus open when I write and can spend way too much time scouring for an alternative word that usually lands up sounding wrong anyway, and then I delete it later), a challenge when it comes to maintaining connections with people like friends, social exhaustion hangovers and a terrible affliction to say what is always on my mind, and what springs to my mind in the moment. I've had some really awkward moments over the years with people when I've said something I probably shouldn't have, or info-dumped something that was probably not appropriate to be discussed at a dinner table.

My tone is not great, I practice conversations in my head, I pick my fingers and stim, touching my toenails makes me nauseous, touching certain textures makes me nauseous, certain sounds make me nauseous and very, very anxious. I can get lost down a Google rabbit hole for days with whatever my latest obsession is, as a result I have accumulated the most useless facts of anyone I know and can spout them at any given time. I mix up my idioms TERRIBLY, I do not understand jokes—even though I've been told I am very funny—and I don't think I've ever understood one of my husband's adverts. He's in advertising and has had to explain all of them to me. I'm petrified of bumping into people I know in public when I haven't prepared to see them and on most occasions have then tried to hide myself behind a pot plant, or duck into another aisle pretending I can't hear them saying 'Hello'.

Before my diagnosis I had no idea why I did half these things, but I'm really grateful to know that when I literally turn my back on someone and pretend I haven't seen them, it's not because I'm a rude bitch, but because the idea of having a spontaneous, unprepared conversation with a person that I was not expecting to see in that particular environment, fills me with such panic and terror, that I can't bloody cope. (I apologize to anyone I have done this to, it's really not you, this time it really is me!)

I am very new to my own autism journey, so am still discovering and uncovering things about myself. But anyway, that's the story, that's the reason I wrote Pippa like I did, and that's all for now.

Chapter 1

The phone was *still* beeping and I was *still* ignoring it.

It had first beeped at seven thirty as I'd eaten my breakfast, it had continued to beep as I'd brushed my teeth, and still, the beeping persisted as I drove to work. It was at this stage that I thought of muting the incessant noise, but as a law-abiding citizen and someone only too aware of the dangers of using a phone while driving, I did not. Instead, I tossed it to the back seat in an attempt to move the noise as far away from my ears as possible. The beeping was even more irritating from there. It was only when I'd gotten to work that finally I acknowledged I could no longer ignore it.

10-Year School Reunion WhatsApp Group

I moaned. You know when they assign a name to the chat it's going to be a very, very lengthy one.

Hannah (admin): Omg, I cannot believe it's been ten years, girls! I can't wait to see you all.

I moaned once more. I'd known it was coming. One didn't need to be a mathematician to calculate that we'd been out of school for precisely ten years. But now that it seemed to have actually materialized, I didn't know how to feel about it. But as I read on, my feelings became quite clear.

Emily: Ten years . . . and it's starting to show in the mirror ☺😉

Bianca: A whole decade! It's insane. And as you can see by this pic, I'll be coming to the reunion with a baby on board ☺

Lilly: Congrats!

Sarah: How exciting. I have two. Ben is 2 and Angie is only 4 months, so I won't be looking my best, girls . . .

Yanilla: Omg, me neither. My little one is only six weeks. I have permanent black rings under my eyes.

Lira: Concealer is a new mama's best friend.

Tracy: Omg, I'm also baby-on-board! When is your due date?

Emily: Concealer is also a bride-to-be's best friend. No one told me how stressful planning a wedding is!

Sarah: Congrats! When is the wedding?

Emily: In two weeks. I'm freaking oooooooout!

Lulu: You're kidding – my wedding is in three weeks!

Rachel: That's soooo cool. I love a spring wedding.

Hannah: This is so much fun! I literally cannot wait to see you guys. I just got married, so I'll be bringing hubby. Remember, partners are very welcome. The more the merrier. Champagne, girls!!! Yaaaaaaaaay!

I tossed my phone onto my desk as if it had electrocuted the palm of my hand. It continued to buzz and shake as if possessed by these bite-sized bits of communication. Winky face emojis and words with way too many vowel sounds. I wiped my hand on my pants; it was wet and sticky.

Just reading that string of upbeat messages was bringing back less than pleasant high-school flashes. It wasn't that I hated high school or the people in it per se, it was just that I hadn't fitted in there with them. I hadn't tried *not* to fit in though; in fact, quite the opposite. When I'd first gotten there I'd done everything possible to successfully integrate. I'd attempted to be exactly like them, observing their behaviours and imitating them. But the more I did that, the less I seemed to fit in. So after those unsuccessful attempts at social assimilation, I embraced my obvious differences and stopped trying to be someone I would never be.

After that, I willingly lurked on the edges of their effervescent social groups, choosing to sit in the library at break reading a book rather than sit in the quad talking with them about what dress they were going to wear to the dance, who was dating who, who liked who and whether it was okay to let him finger you after a few weeks of dating. At an all-girls boarding school there were three main things that occupied all conversations:

1. The opposite sex
2. Having sex
3. Having sex with the opposite sex

Nothing else seemed relevant. The Global North could be sending missiles off into the sky to entirely obliterate the Global South and they would probably still be talking about whether it was okay that Jessica was going out with Edward now, because she used to go out with Mike, Edward's best friend, and was that breaking the 'bro code'.

I've never really got it, this obsession with men. Don't get me wrong, I like men, although I have very specific criteria when it comes to engaging with them. But for the most part, I'm not averse to the idea of them at all. Not only were men absolutely necessary for the evolution of the human species, but they're also good for other things, apart from their ability to aid in the procreation process.

For example, I like to look at men. Not all men, obviously. But some men are so easy on the eye that one just can't help but look at them. Like that man on the giant highway billboard in that jeans commercial. There've been several occasions when I've found myself looking at him so intently, sweeping my eyes over that perfect symmetrical V-shape that runs across his abdomen and disappears into his jeans, that I've almost missed the off ramp. I emailed the Advertising Complaints Commission about this, suggesting that perhaps they find a more suitable, less distracting place for the billboard. They never got back to me, which I thought was terribly unprofessional.

I also like the way men feel. I like the way their skin is different to ours. I like the way that running your hands over a man's skin is almost like running your hands over a foreign creature. Did you know, a man's skin is twenty-five per cent thicker than a woman's because of the increased testosterone, and that's why it feels so unlike ours.

Although it should be noted that I'm not a fan of excessive body hair, especially when it culminates on the chest and back. I'd landed up in bed with a man some years back whose chest was covered in so much coarse hair – almost boar-like – that I broke out in a severe rash from the constant rubbing back and forth. I had to go to my doctor the next day for rash cream.

I usually liked the way men smelled too, except for that date I'd gone on with the man who smelled like a pack of freshly opened Vienna sausages. And then of course there's the whole sex part. Sex has always been somewhat of a mystery to me. The act is essentially the same in the way it's physically conducted, and yet it can vary so much from person to person. And it's impossible to pinpoint exactly what makes for good sex, and what makes for bad sex. And of course it's also impossible to gauge what sort of sex it will be prior to having it. I've often wondered why dating apps don't have some kind of rating system for that sort of thing. It would save so much trouble. Landing up in bed with someone who you're just not sexually compatible with can be a very unpleasant experience.

For example, had I known that one of my online dates was into dirty talk during sex I would never have slept with him. I'm not a fan of conversation in general; I find it awkward and hard to keep up with. But when paired with sex and the man you're with constantly describing in real time in graphic detail what he's doing to you and what he intends to do with you next, it's very off-putting. I shouted in his ear that he should 'shut the hell up', but this only seemed to encourage him, as he told me what a 'naughty, naughty slut' I was. I think 'slut' is a disgusting-sounding word.

But when sex is done correctly, when all those intangible elements come together, I enjoy it immensely, because it gets me out of my head. For a few blissful seconds the rampaging thoughts stop and the millions of conversations I have going on inside my head all at once, all the time, fade into oblivion. And for one moment, one amazing, glorious, awe-inspiring, blissful moment – *silence*.

Unfortunately, sex doesn't come around as often as I would like it to, despite the fact that I'm fairly attractive and pride myself on being sufficiently good at the act of sex. The sex isn't the hard part; it's the converting of a meeting between two people into sex which is the part I fail at almost every single time. I've never been good at dating. Sipping awkwardly on wine while making polite small talk in which you make very shallow attempts to grab at mutual straws just to be able to tick the box of 'getting to know each other'. This part always seems like the most ineffective use of time. Superfluous, unnecessary window-dressing that comes before the real undressing.

My thoughts dragged me back to one specifically disastrous sexual moment. The time I'd gotten my hair stuck in my date's zipper after being in that general area for longer than I would have liked to be. It's not that I'm against giving blow-jobs, but by the one-minute mark I'm always wondering why they can't hurry up, and by the five-minute mark I'm wondering whether or not I should defrost the ready-meal for dinner or eat the leftovers or give them to the dogs?

Although I'd put my phone on silent mode, it suddenly burst forth with a series of dramatic vibrations that increased exponentially.

I picked it up, swiped a few times and came face to face with the cause of said vibrations. A photo had been posted on the group. I enlarged the photo and peered at it. Class of 2013. I traced my eyes over the faces, trying to locate myself. It wasn't that hard. I'd stuck out, even though we were all wearing the same school uniform. Flaming-red hair always scraped back into a high, tight bun on the top of my head. Everyone else seemed to have wispy bits of hair that hung around their faces. In fact, I'd seen them purposely pull those strands of hair out of their ponytails in the mornings. I'd never understood this – surely you would want your hair out of your face for school. I'd also worn chunky, 'severe' glasses back then, as my mother had called them. Every holiday she'd tried to take me to an optometrist to buy a more delicate pair, but I liked the ones I had. They were very hard-wearing, and I often dropped them – or dropped myself, to be more accurate – my clumsiness was well renowned. I scanned the photo for my only friend, Jennifer. She also stood out with her dyed-jet-black pixie cut and her pale face (she refused to sit in the sun). Speaking of Jennifer . . .

Jennifer: Gggrrrr! The WhatsApp group!

Pippa: I know!

Jennifer: They'll all the same. Nothing's changed, other than the fact that they seem to be incredibly prolific breeders. And marriers.

Jennifer: In fact, one of them seems to be regaling us with a story of her water birth right now.

My phone vibrated again, and I saw the message Jennifer was referring to. I typed back quickly.

Pippa: She used the word 'enchanting'.

Jennifer: Last word I would have used. Mind you, I've never actually had a conscious water birth, or any kind of birth.

Jennifer: I wish I was there so I could go.

Pippa: You actually want to go?

Jennifer: Don't you?

Pippa: No!

Jennifer: Come on – morbid curiosity. Like slowing down at a car crash. You have to go and then tell me all about it.

Pippa: Why don't you go if you're so eager?

Jennifer: Well, I live on this little island called Australia – you heard of it?

Jennifer: Not to mention the fact that I'm currently in my psychiatry residency and am trying to douse the flames of a full religious war raging on my ward.

Pippa: The two Jesuses still there?

Jennifer: One of them thinks he might be Moses now. He's trying to part things. The poor nurses are constantly having to put the furniture back together.

Jennifer: Please go to the reunion . . .

Jennifer: I want to know what they look like now. In fact, buy one of those button cameras and stream it live to me.

Pippa: You seriously want me to go?

Jennifer: Yes!

Jennifer: Besides, it might actually be good for them to see someone whose sole purpose in life is not to give birth and walk down the aisle. Think of it as your duty as a fulfilled, single career woman.

Pippa: I'll think about it.

Jennifer: Aren't you even a little bit curious?

Pippa: I suppose I am, but school wasn't exactly a high point in my life, as you know.

Jennifer: And look at you now – a masters in aviation management and an air traffic controller on track to becoming a junior supervisor faster than anyone else because you flew through your training, doing one of the most stressful jobs in the world and already a legend in your field. First day on the job and you successfully navigated an emergency landing!

I wiggled in my chair. Compliments made me uneasy.

Pippa: I'd better get back to the screen if I don't want another emergency landing.

Jennifer: Come on, take the compliment, just a little bit . . .

Pippa: Fine. Taken. Thank you.

Pippa: Have to work.

Jennifer: Chat sometime then.

I turned my phone off and looked at the other screen in front of me. I loved this screen. I loved arriving at work and casting my eyes over it as if it were some great work of art. Which, to me, it was. My own personal *Mona Lisa*. Shapes and numbers, greens, blues and oranges. Identification, altitude, data tags, maps. Speed, origin, destination. All the information you need in order to track planes through the air combined together on one screen.

To the untrained eye, it might look like chaos. But to me it's a beautiful, intricate web of patterns. I've always seen patterns in things: licence plates, house numbers and streets – even in road maps. So this I could handle, but I wasn't sure I could handle a ten-year school reunion. I studied the screen until my eyes found my favorite plane. I waited eagerly for the familiar voice. I didn't have to wait long.

'Good morning, City Tower, this is Flightbird Six Zero Zero.'

I smiled at the sound. This was by far my favorite voice. It had an easy timbre to it. The pitch and tone were warm while the resonance was deep and full. The rhythm and pacing of his words were also pleasing. Not too fast, and not too slow.

'Good morning, Flightbird Six Zero Zero. How's the view today?'

'Beautiful sunrise from up here, City Tower. We are inbound to

Johannesburg Airport, heading over the golf course. Request vectors for ILS, please. Flightbird Six Zero Zero.'

'Fightbird Six Zero Zero, turn left heading two niner zero.'

'Copy, City Tower, turn left heading two niner zero. Flightbird Six Zero Zero.'

I waited with a sense of anticipation to hear his voice again. And as soon as I did I straightened in my chair.

'City Tower, this is Flightbird Six Zero Zero. Established ILS, runway zero seven left. My favorite runway.'

I smiled to myself. I'd learned that pilots were very superstitious creatures, and Captain Boyce-Jones was no exception. For him, his lucky charm seemed to be runway zero seven. I'd never understood superstitions. Especially when you looked at the word's synonyms, *irrationality* and *false belief* being just two of them. I'd noticed too that superstition wasn't just reserved for those airy-fairy, hippie types: very rational people, like pilots and my father – a surgeon – were superstitious. My father only ever wore blue socks when performing surgery. I have no idea why but he has an entire drawer at home dedicated to his 'operating socks'. In my opinion, there's simply no correlation between a color and your ability to perform surgery. That was down to your training and experience.

'Flightbird Six Zero Zero, you are cleared to land on runway zero seven left.'

I looked out of the tower window as his plane came into view. I knew so much about his aircraft – first developed in 1967, the best-selling commercial airliner in the world, 30 meters long, 28-meter wing span, fuselage height of 4 meters and maximum take-off weight of 115,000 lbs – but I knew nothing about the man who piloted it, even though we'd spoken almost every day for the past six months.

'How's the weather down there? Flightbird Six Zero Zero.'

'Flightbird Six Zero Zero, wind two fifty at ten knots. Should make for a smooth landing.'

'Copy, City Tower, wind two fifty at ten knots. My landings are always smooth. Flightbird Six Zero Zero.'

I wasn't going to admit that he was right but, of course, his landings were always smooth. I watched out the window as he glided the plane down to the runway. This is always a magical moment for me, to see a plane – an enormous, complicated piece of engineering and machinery – float effortlessly down from the sky. Rate of descent, reduction of speed and thrust. All these elements coming together perfectly like a well-conducted orchestra, enabling something so large to simply touch down elegantly and gently.

'Flightbird Six Zero Zero, this is City Tower, please vacate left onto Alpha taxiway and contact Ground Control on zero two zero point six.'

'Copy, and vacating left onto Alpha taxiway, contact Ground Control on zero two zero point six. Flightbird Six Zero Zero.'

This was the part of our conversations I hated. Despite not being a fan of small talk in general, I liked talking to Captain Boyce-Jones, and when he had to change frequency for Ground Control I always felt a little inexplicable pang in the pit of my stomach.

'Have a great day, City Tower. And happy spring day.'

'I forgot it was spring day.'

'Everything is already looking so much greener from the skies.'

'I must make a note to sow some seeds this weekend.'

'Are you a gardener, City Tower?'

'I wouldn't call myself a gardener, per se. But I do garden.'

I heard a small, breathy chuckle through my headset. I preferred this sound to his voice even.

'Bye, City Tower. Happy gardening.'

'Bye, Flightbird Six Zero Zero.'

Chapter 2

'So, who thinks I should go to my ten-year school reunion?' I asked loudly. The chatter around me stopped abruptly. Everyone lowered their cards and regarded me as if I'd asked the world's most confounding question, one that didn't have an easy answer. When, really, what I'd intended was a simple 'yes' or 'no'. I ran my eyes over the people sitting in front of me and then started to realize *why* my question had not been so straightforward after all.

'I can see I'm asking the wrong demographic here.' I looked back down at my cards.

'Does it look like any of us enjoyed our high-school experience and want to relive any part of it?' Zane asked with what was clearly sarcasm. That much was very obvious. Even I – who was not good at deciphering tones – was able to glean that.

I peered up from my cards again, taking in the faces of the motley crew of Pokémon players who gathered here every Friday night to battle each other's mythical monsters. As far as geeky subculture went, this was the epitome of it. We were the teens who didn't go to parties on a Friday night but stayed in and traded cards. Who got high on 'Donking', not drugs; 'Aurora energies', not alcohol. Each one of us was awkward in everyday conversations, but not the conversations here, where we got swept away in a fantasy realm and could talk about the new Origin Forme Palkia VSTAR until our vocal cords were completely worn out.

'Have none of you been to your high-school reunions?' I asked.

Everyone shook their heads, except for Sheila.

'It wasn't that bad, actually,' she said. 'In fact, a few of them apologized for bullying me. A lot changes in ten years – people change too. For me, I wanted to show them that I wasn't the same person I was back in high school. It was kind of cathartic.'

'Huh?' I looked at Sheila thoughtfully. She was a successful game designer now but, like me, she hadn't exactly fitted in at a mainstream school. Looking around the room, you could tell that no one here had fitted into the high-school mould, but we all fitted in here. This place was our sanctuary, a safe enclave separate from the scary world outside.

'I hated school,' Orion said, wringing her hands together nervously.

'It sucked,' Jono added, and Silent Abe, who never talked, nodded.

'I was homeschooled,' Anele added, 'but I'm pretty sure I would have hated it too.'

I looked back down at my cards and smiled. A mew VMAX with a choice belt, two fusion strike energies and four power tablets. A powerful combination. If I played this, I would defeat my opponent in one swift move.

'Take that,' I said, playing the card with a dramatic flourish. A few 'oooh's rose up from the crowd, and then my opponent, Zane, grabbed his head and shook it.

'No. Not mew VMAX.' He conceded defeat and I folded my arms and smiled. But as pleased as I was, I was also somewhat thoughtful. Maybe Sheila was right. I also wasn't that shy, softly spoken girl who sat on the sidelines any more. For goodness' sake, I steered planes to safety and won card games with one swoop. Maybe the reunion wasn't the worst idea ever.

I opened the WhatsApp group when I climbed into my car at the end of the evening. The reunion was next month in Cape Town at the old girls' school hall. It would be easy getting there: one of the perks of being an air traffic controller was discounted plane tickets.

It was also over a work-free weekend, so no need to put in for leave. The reunion comprised a series of events that I'd already familiarized myself with.

Day one was a champagne get-together, followed the next day by wine tasting and lunch in the winelands. Which left Sunday free for me to visit my two favorite places in the world: the aquarium and the air force museum. I could catch a late-afternoon flight back to Jo'burg and be back at work on Monday. The trip to the museum and aquarium almost made the reunion feel like something I could handle.

I've been obsessed with three things my entire life – fish, everything aviation and synonyms – although it should be noted that aviation has always been my first love. I think it started way before I was even conscious of it. Before I was born, my parents had been expecting a boy. But when I arrived without a penis the general medical consensus was that the angle of my genital tubercle (as they call it at that stage) had been misinterpreted in my scans. As my mom always says, 'Even before day one, I've pointed in my own unique direction.'

However, because they'd been expecting a boy, they'd decorated accordingly, down to the blue walls and airplane mobile that hung over my crib. They'd repainted the walls, but agreed that airplanes were gender neutral. Besides, I loved that mobile. In the beginning, I think it was the colors and movements that attracted me to it. But as I got older I became enthralled with it. I would stare at the planes and wonder where they'd been and where they were going. I'd wonder who was flying them, how many people were on board and how it was that they all spun around each other so perfectly without ever crashing into one another.

By the time I was ten I could name every modern plane in the sky and give you a run-down of their specs, not to mention name just about every single tropical fish there was. I had wanted to become a marine biologist or a pilot when I grew up. But after watching a TV show on air traffic controllers I decided that was the perfect job for me. It was the precise nature of the job, which left no room for error. A job that was full of patterns and directions and facts. There was also no impressing clients or making office small talk. The only talk was technical talk to pilots, which I could do.

But if I went to my school reunion I'd be forced to make the aforementioned small talk. The thought was so off-putting that the idea of the aircraft museum and aquarium the next day was almost not enough to push through it. *Almost* . . .

Chapter 3

One month passed by quickly, as months tend to do when you're older. Not that the nature of time has changed – that would be physically impossible – but rather your perception of time has changed. As I've gotten older, I've felt that days have gotten shorter and weeks and years even more so. When you were younger, an hour, especially if you were bored, dragged on like a never-ending day.

I left my shift the Friday morning of the school reunion and headed over to change in the business-class lounge. Another perk of half living at an airport: the receptionists in the lounges let you use the plush changing rooms and bathrooms to freshen up, when they aren't too busy, of course.

The name of the receptionist at Middle East Air's business-class lounge was Blessing. International tourists are always fascinated by his name, even though names like Blessing, Patience and Fortune are commonplace here. Blessing always tried to strike up a conversation with me whenever I came in. I was always relieved, though, when his idea of a conversation was a one-way monologue in which he gossiped in hushed tones about the goings-on of the airport. The airport really was its own unique ecosystem. Like a small city that has been shut off from the rest of the world, inhabited by an endless variety of people, from shop owners to security to cleaning staff to management staff, pilots, air traffic controllers and police. Personally, I've only gotten to know a few people over the last two years but, for some reason, Blessing seems to have fully immersed himself in the airport culture.

'Soooo.' He leaned over the desk and looked at me. I'd learned that this long and protracted 'sooo' was a sign that the gossip was about to commence. I was pleased that it was such a distinctive-sounding word, with such a distinctive tone and delivery; it made it much easier for me to read. I readied myself.

'Did you hear about the woman that gave birth to a baby midair last week?'

'Yes.' I nodded triumphantly. This I did know. I never knew anything he talked about, but this I knew, because Barry, a fellow ATC, had dealt with the emergency.

'She named the baby after the pilot – how sweet is that?' Blessing placed a hand on his chest and swooned. I hadn't realized he was so enamored with babies. Well, to be fair, I'd observed that most people had a fondness for babies and that when they spoke about them their voices usually took on a soft, sing-song quality and their pupils dilated somewhat. I did not harbor those same feelings about babies.

'I'm sure the flight attendant actually did more to ensure that baby's safe entry into the world. They are, after all, trained in basic first aid, including infant delivery, should the need arise,' I said. It was a very logical conclusion. The pilot would have been flying the plane, not attending to the baby. Blessing looked deflated for a moment and I realized the error of my ways. I went on, 'But I'm sure he landed that plane as quickly as possible and he would have radioed ahead for medical assistance.'

My response perked Blessing up again, and he continued.

'Did you hear about Louise at the coffee shop?'

'Which coffee shop?' There were twenty here.

'The Grind.'

'Aaaah, yes, next to Domestic Arrivals.' I knew it, even though it wasn't my coffee shop of choice, Express Espresso.

'Anywaaaaay' – another lengthened vowel sound – 'she's having a secret tryst with that waiter from the steak place at the international terminal.'

'Which steak place?'

'A Cut Above.'

I shook my head. *A Cut Above*. Another play on words. I'd noticed that this was an incredibly popular device when it came to the naming of restaurants, coffee shops, retail facilities and advertising agencies. I disliked names like these. I was also not a fan of restaurants called things like 'The Blue Olive' or 'The Singing Avocado'. Because, clearly, olives are not blue and avocados do not sing.

'I don't know anyone from A Cut Above,' I said. 'Nor have I ever been to A Cut Above.' And what cut were they referring to? What was their cut above? Sirloin, fillet, ribeye? There were many cuts. And so many unanswered questions.

'Well, anywaaaay,' Blessing continued, with another extended vowel, 'Angela from the Asia Pacific business-class lounge told me that late one night Lungile from Baggage Handling found them canoodling in the Lost and Found room.'

'What was Angela from the Asia Pacific business-class lounge doing in the Lost and Found room?' This seemed like the most interesting part of the story, to be honest.

'One of their first-class passengers lost their Montblanc pen. Apparently, it's some very rare limited edition. Ruby-encrusted or made out of unicorn ivory.' He rolled his eyes, and I did the same, even though I wasn't sure what he was trying to convey with that ocular gesture.

'Scandalous, isn't it?' he said, clapping his hands together.

I clapped mine together too, even though I took little delight in this story. Don't get me wrong, I really liked Blessing and appreciated that he wanted to tell me stories, especially because they involved the people around me. It did in some small way make me feel included and connected to something bigger than myself.

'Anyway, where're you off to today? You're looking a little too glamorous to be heading home.'

I blushed and touched my hair and face. I'd released my hair from its usual functional, pulled-backed bun. I'd then styled it into what the YouTube tutorial had called 'effortless waves'. It had not been effortless at all. In fact, I'd put so much time and effort into twisting that hair straightener back and forth to create those waves I was sure I had carpal tunnel syndrome in my fingers. I'd also done a full face of make-up on myself, a painstaking job that had taken far too long. Once again, the YouTube tutorial's name had been very misleading. The look was called 'The Clean Girl Look', and when I saw the finished product it looked as if there was hardly any make-up involved. But what I'd discovered midway through the arduous process was that trying to look like you were *not* wearing make-up actually required a lot more make-up than one expects. But, and I hate to admit to it, I wanted to look a little more 'put together' tonight, as my mom would say. My mother was always running late because she was busy 'putting herself together' in the bathroom, a phrase I'd found quite disconcerting as a child. I'd imagined her pulling on her arms and legs, maybe even screwing on her head.

A part of me wanted to impress my old schoolmates. Wanted them to see how I'd blossomed since school. Maybe even have them comment on it, even though that thought filled me with such awkwardness that I physically cringed at the notion. And I also wanted to feel good about myself tonight. I hadn't felt good about myself as a teen. I'd been rail thin, angular and gangly, my knees the biggest part of my legs. I was ghostly pale, with upper-front-teeth protrusions caused by excessive thumb-sucking as a child. My eternal clumsiness had also led to a crooked nose, from one of my many tripping accidents. Braces had corrected my teeth, my plastic surgeon father had fixed my nose at eighteen, exercise and the treatment of my hyperthyroidism had rounded me out nicely, and today I would say I was a solid eight out of ten. On some days, even a nine. The paleness, I could do nothing about – my mother's Irish roots, as she always said – but unlike her I'd refused to self-tan and had embraced my alabaster skin. In fact, I was very fond of it now, and the comparisons to Sophie Turner over the years were most pleasing, since *Game of Thrones* was one of my favorite TV shows.

'It's my school reunion, so I . . .'

'Say no more!' Blessing said. 'As a gay black man, I feel your obvious high-school pain.'

'How do you know I had high-school pain?' I enquired.

He eyed me up and down and then leaned against the reception desk. 'I just assumed, you know.'

'You know what?' I asked, not offended, but my curiosity definitely piqued.

'You didn't exactly fit in there, right?'

'No. I didn't. How did you know?'

Blessing shrugged. 'Call it the gift of intuition. I just get people. Always have. Maybe it's because I see over two hundred different people walk through these doors a day, or maybe I was just born with the gift,' he said with a smile.

'Huh,' I replied thoughtfully, grateful for this newly acquired knowledge. Perhaps, in the future when I had a personal, human-related problem, I could come to Blessing. 'I shall remember that,' I said to him as I walked out. But as I crossed the threshold of the lounge and the automated glass doors began to close behind me I got it. I swung around with a triumphant swoosh.

'Because the pen can't be made of unicorn ivory, because unicorns are mythical creatures. They don't exist!' I pointed at Blessing and let out a laugh. 'But you could have said narwhal tusk to make it more authentic. Nonetheless, got it!' I turned happily and headed for my favorite coffee shop.

CHAPTER 4

As I sat down in the coffee shop, my phone exploded with sounds. I didn't need to look down to know where they were coming from.

10-Year School Reunion WhatsApp Group

Katie: IT'S TONIGHT, GIRLS!!

Katie: I can't wait to see you all.

Yanilla: It's going to be so much fun.

Larissa: I'm sure we'll have so much to tell each other. The talking is going to go on sooooo late into the night.

Fabienne: We'll all lose our voices by the end of it.

Sasha: I'm sure my husband won't mind if I lose my voice for a day.

Who the hell were Fabienne and Sasha? I was so good at remembering facts that interested me, but when it came to remembering people's names my brain worked like a sieve. The conversation continued, with lots of 'LOL's after that.

Bianca: I wouldn't mind it if my kids and husband lost their voices for a day, I could do with the break.

Dominique: Haha!

Katie: Love this! It's just like old times!

Old times!

For some reason, this phrase made my palms sweat. Synonyms for *old* included *aged*, *decrepit* and *vulnerable*. Not comforting words at all. And the more I thought about it all, the more the sweat rushed to my palms as if someone had turned on an internal tap. My phone slipped out of my hand. I looked down as it collided with the floor, bounced, once, twice, and then skidded across the highly polished surface. I jumped off my seat and raced over to it. Panic and anger bubbled up so quickly and intensely when I saw that my screen had been damaged. A long crack cut it into two distinct parts. I dried my hands on my jeans, tried to push the panicky anger back down and took my place at the table once again. I hated it when things like this happened. Surprise things. Unexpected things. Things that deviated from my regular routine. Now I was going to have to take my phone to a repair shop, and those were always located inside loud, busy malls. And visiting malls was not something I ever did.

Old times . . .

I sat up straight as the veil of what had clearly been a very bad and poorly made decision lifted in a swoosh. *What the hell was I thinking, going to this ridiculous reunion?* I didn't want to talk all night, relive and rehash and reminisce. I didn't want to spend the night forcing laughter at jokes I was bound not to understand. Jokes about their husbands and kids. Those 'men are from Mars and women are from whatever the hell planet they are meant to be from' jokes. Everyone on the group seemed overly excited too. And there was going to be champagne! An explosive combination that was sure to make it even more rowdy. My skin itched as indecision took up space in my brain. I didn't like indecision. It was far too vast and endless. I wanted facts. Certainty. Black and white. Not this in-between color that flapped about in the air like an untethered form.

'Okay,' I said out loud, soothing myself by fluttering my fingers together three times under the table where no one could see. I would *not* go tonight if I received two more bad surprise signs; if two more unexpected things happened, then I was definitely not going. Not that I believed in the universe giving you signs. I wasn't one of these esoteric types that believed in signs and lucky trinkets. But there was something I *did* believe in: patterns. If two bad things happened in quick succession, then that was random, a genuine coincidence. But if three bad things happened, then that was a pattern. And patterns could not be ignored. Patterns were the very things that made up our entire existence. DNA and its double helix, the solar system, orbiting planets – everything was made of patterns. Patterns needed to be heeded.

'What can I get you?' a waitress who I'd never seen before asked.

'Iced cappuccino, almond milk, thank you.'

'Sorry, we're out of almond milk,' she said, and my heart dropped. Could this be surprise number two?

'Out . . . of . . . almond . . . milk.' I stretched the words out in disbelief. They'd never been out of almond milk. In all the time I'd worked here, I'd had an iced cappuccino with almond milk at least twice a week.

'We have oat milk,' she said casually, as if it wasn't a big deal at all.

'Oat milk is not almond milk,' I said.

'Indeed.' The waitress took a step back. Had I offended her? I was just stating a fact: oat milk was most certainly not almond milk. Despite their obvious physical differences – being derived from completely different food sources – oat milk gave me gas. Gas might be vaguely acceptable when in the privacy of your own home – after all, it was just a biological process – but the potential of flatulence on an airplane bothered me. I did not think it would be very polite to inflict my gas on strangers.

'I'll have a Coke then, in a tin, please,' I said.

The waitress smiled and walked off. I was not so terrible at interpreting facial expressions that I couldn't tell it was a forced smile. Forced smiles, I'd noticed, had less teeth involvement. They were usually just confined to the lips and often had a tight, pulled quality to them. As if the person had just had Botox.

'Here we go.' Moments later she put my Coke down on the table. I stared at it in disbelief.

'I asked for Coke in a tin,' I said, trying to infuse as much politeness into my tone as possible.

'Sorry, we only have it in plastic bottles.'

Number three. The third sign. This was it. 'I only drink Coke in a tin. I don't like the way it tastes in a bottle. So, no, thank you. But thank you for doing your job. Thanks.' I tried to force a smile at the waitress too, to communicate my appreciation and understanding. It wasn't her fault that they only had bottles. It wasn't her fault they were out of almond milk. That was clearly the fault of whoever's job it was to order stock.

'They taste the same,' she said, pointing at my bottle.

I shook my head. 'No, they don't.'

'The recipe is the same for a tin and a bottle.'

'While that might be technically true, Coke from the tin tastes sharper and more carbonated. The Coke from the bottle is never as fizzy or as cold.'

'I actually agree with City Tower on this one. Coke does taste different out of a tin.'

I swung around at the sound of the *very* familiar voice. 'Flightbird Six Zero Zero.'

The face in front of me smiled. 'City Tower.'

'Flightbird Six Zero Zero.'

'Finally, I can put a face to the voice,' Flightbird said, continuing what I could see was a genuine smile.

'Your face doesn't look anything like your voice,' I stated.

'What did you think I looked like?'

'Older. And less attractive.'

Flightbird let out a shocked-sounding gasp and the waitress next to me clicked her tongue. I wasn't sure what that was meant to convey, but I could see she was now very interested in what I had to say.

'Sorry, that was blunt. I'm blunt sometimes. But I am simply stating an obvious fact.' Because Flightbird *was* good-looking, and anyone could see that. His face was balanced and perfectly symmetrical. I liked symmetry. He had deep blue eyes which bordered on navy. No, not navy. Royal blue. Navy was too dark and dull for what his eyes were. Flightbird's hair followed the same symmetrical pattern. It was dark brown, apart from those flecks of golden brown which were in the exact same place on the left and right side of his head. He was proportional perfection personified.

'Your shoulders are also broad,' I said, beginning to admire his shoulder to waist-and-height ratio.

Flightbird laughed. 'Is that a compliment?'

'Broad shoulders have always been favored by females, since prehistoric times, when they were seen as a sign of strength and protection, which was what females primarily looked for in a mate. Just as wide hips were seen as favorable in women. I don't have wide hips though.'

Flightbird laughed. People often found me funny. That's what they said, anyway. People had told me I should become a stand-up comedian, due to this funniness I supposedly possessed. But what people didn't realize was that, first, I wasn't trying to be funny and, second, being funny and telling jokes are two totally different things. I didn't tell jokes. I didn't get jokes. Punch lines were a mystery to me, so if I happened to be considered funny, it really was only by sheer accident.

'Well then, in that case, I'm flattered,' he said when he'd finally stopped laughing.

'May I?' he asked, and pointed at my table. I looked down at it, wondering what he wanted.

'What do you want?' I asked.

'May I join you?' He began standing up before I'd even said yes.

Presumptuous of him. He must have sensed my reticence though, because he stopped moving. 'Sorry, if you want to be—'

'No! No, it's fine. You can sit,' I said, surprising myself with my reply.

He tipped his head at me and walked over. He pulled the chair out then lowered himself into it.

'Andrew Boyce-Jones. We've never officially met, even though I seem to speak to you more than anyone else in my life.' He reached out a hand for me to shake. I tapped it with my elbow, like we'd all been directed to do during the pandemic. It was a great way to touch a person without having to stick your whole hand into theirs, which was a feeling I absolutely hated. Flightbird looked at my elbow and then let out another small laugh. The waitress cleared her throat. I'd totally forgotten she was still standing there.

'So?' she asked.

'So what?' I replied.

She pointed at my Coke and raised her brows. I raised mine back.

'Do you want the Coke or not?'

'No, thank you. I'll have a glass of water though, please. Sorry. And thank you. Very much.' I was overcompensating with placating words. Too many placating words.

'Ice and lemon?' she asked.

'Ice, no lemon.'

The waitress walked off but, before disappearing, she shot me a glance over her shoulder.

'So what brings you to my newly favorited coffee shop?' he asked.

'This is my favorite one too,' I echoed. 'I've tested most of the ones in the airport, and this one definitely has the best coffee.'

'Totally agree,' he said.

'I was going to be flying to Cape Town on the 13:15 flight, but now I'm not,' I stated, looking down at my small suitcase, which was just the right size to be taken as carry-on.

'Flight A356?'

'Yes. That's the one.'

'That's my flight. I was getting a coffee before take-off. Why aren't you going any more?'

I put my hands under the table and fluttered my fingers together a few times to calm me down. I had not expected to bump into someone that I didn't know today, and I hadn't expected to now be having a conversation with that person in a coffee shop that did not stock the thing I usually drank. I hated bumping into people I knew when I was out and often pretended not to recognize them when they looked in my direction. I've mastered the art of quickly generating a sudden blank look in my eyes, as if I'm seeing through them.

'High-school reunion. But I've decided not to go.'

'Why? I loved mine. I'm still really close to my friends from school. In fact, we have our annual get-together coming up soon.'

I looked him over. 'You were popular in high school.' It was a statement, not a question. A man that looked like he did had no doubt been incredibly popular. A man that sat at a chair with such a sense of belonging and purpose, who spoke with ease and smiled so freely, he was the kind of person who'd enjoyed his high-school experience.

'I was fairly popular,' he replied with a smile he was clearly trying to hide, which I interpreted as an attempt at modesty.

'You loved school.' I took it a step further, and he did not disagree. 'I did not love high school, nor was I very popular. Not that I wanted to be popular, but I've observed that the more popular you are, the more you seem to enjoy your high-school experience. Don't you think?'

Flightbird took a sip of his coffee and stared at me over the rim, as if he was considering something. His stare made me uncomfortable, and I felt that swell of words in my brain. Those over-explaining words that I throw out into empty, quiet and awkward moments when I can't cope with the silence. The longer he kept quiet, the more I was going to be compelled to open my mouth and totally overshare, something I always regretted later. The words dropped out of my brain and into my throat. I could physically feel them wiggling around in my mouth, trying to come out . . .

'When you're popular, school is easy. When you don't fit in, it's not. And I don't really have anything in common with the girls I went to school with, not then and certainly not now. In fact, they couldn't be more different from me if they tried. They're all married and seem to be breeding like small rodents. Everyone seems to have a husband, or a fiancé, or a small human, and that is all they're going to talk about at this reunion. And they're going to ask me all sorts of questions, the kind of questions I hate – why don't I have a fiancé and a husband and a small human in tow? – and I will be forced to answer them and then be pulled into talk about how I should be on a dating app or they have a friend/ brother/cousin that maybe I would like. I'll be dragged into small talk. And I hate small talk. And there's going to be champagne, and everyone will be all "wine o' clock" – a saying I hate, by the way, but that I think is pretty apt here. And it's going to get very celebratory and loud and I'm afraid I'm going to be forced into some kind of drunken dancing and reminiscing, and then I'm going to feel pressured to say something worthwhile, and not just one of my awkward gap fillers, like this rant clearly is.' I took a breath, a quick one, and continued. 'I just hate this pressure, you know. To be in a relationship, get engaged, get married, have a baby, have another baby. You start to feel that there might actually be something wrong with you because you don't want those things, and without those things you just stick out even more. *Not* being in a relationship seems to have become an open invitation for others to tell you why you *need* to be in a relationship. Take my mother, for example. She's so desperate to throw me a wedding.' I stopped talking as abruptly as I'd started. I was about to say something else, something way too personal, and was glad that I'd managed to stop myself from saying it. *It was perhaps the main reason I hated being asked why I wasn't in a relationship.*

'There's nothing wrong with you for not wanting to be in a relationship,' Flightbird said.

'I know that logically, of course, but when everyone carries on and on about it, sometimes you feel . . .' I paused, not able to find the word.

Flightbird put his coffee down. 'I know exactly what you mean.'

'You do?' That was somewhat hard to believe.

'I have three sisters, all married, all with kids, and parents who keep asking me when I'm going to find someone to settle down with and have kids. It's their greatest disappointment that I haven't found a "nice girl" yet, and they remind me of it constantly. They're concerned that my career takes up too much time and energy and I don't put enough time and energy into my personal life.'

'That's exactly the same as my family!' I said.

'Sometimes I feel like I might crack under the pressure,' Flightbird said.

It was such an honest statement, and I liked it. I often found that people shied away from making statements like this that were brutally honest with no sugar-coating whatsoever.

I nodded at him.

'And the pressure only gets worse over weddings and holiday seasons and family get-togethers,' he added.

'Weddings!' I scoffed. 'My cousin, who is four years younger than me, is getting married in two months' time, and they're going to make me sit at the singles table, and everyone is going to say, "Shame, are you still not dating?" or something like that. As if not dating is some kind of disability at my age. As if *not* having a boyfriend or a husband is akin to missing a gallbladder or some other organ.'

He laughed again. 'Your wisdom teeth.'

'Appendix,' I added, and couldn't help smiling back at his face, which was so open and friendly. Familiar, even though I knew that to be impossible, since I'd never met him in the flesh before.

'My mom's sixtieth birthday is coming up. We're having this big family get-together and I know all I'm going to hear about is why I haven't found a lovely girlfriend yet and how my mother would like her only son to have a child before she is too old to pick it up.'

'My parents constantly remind me that I'm their only child, so their only way of becoming grandparents. Apparently, when you reach a certain age as a woman, your sole purpose for existence is to procreate.'

Flightbird laughed again. I liked his laugh. He had really nice white teeth too. They were dead straight, and I wondered if he too had had braces when he was younger, or if his teeth were thanks to what was clearly a *very* superior gene pool.

'My mother wants me to go to a gynaecologist to see how many eggs I have left, even though I've told her multiple times that I don't want to become a parent.'

Flightbird frowned at me.

'That was an overshare,' I said quickly. 'Sorry. I went too far on that one. If I'm not careful, I'll be telling you about my menstrual cycle next. Shit. Which I just did. Sorry!'

'Well, if you don't mind, I won't be talking about my sperm count, if that's okay.' Flightbird raised his coffee to his lips. He was clearly joking, although I honestly wouldn't mind if he told me about that. I never get embarrassed about those kinds of conversations; in fact, I preferred to have conversations about real topics and issues rather than trying to eke conversation out of generic small talk about the weather or the rugby or the state of the nation and its energy crisis.

'After forty, you'll naturally have a lower sperm count. How old are you?' I asked briskly.

'Not forty.'

'Of course, you also have to take things like sperm motility into account too. No point in having a good sperm count when they don't swim correctly.' I was just about to move on to why it's *not* advisable to put your laptop on your lap when he chuckled again.

'This is seriously turning into one of the most interesting conversations I've ever had.'

Synonyms for *interesting* were *intriguing* and *unusual*. Was that a compliment?

'It's also nice talking to someone who gets all the relationship pressure too.' He put his coffee down and rubbed a big hand across his forehead. 'It's a lot sometimes.'

I nodded in agreement. 'I wish there was something I could do to permanently get rid of all that pressure.'

'Me too,' he said on a long sigh. His sigh sounded defeated. I could relate to that feeling. 'I once thought of phoning up my ex-girlfriend and asking her to come with me to a New Year's party, just so all my friends wouldn't hassle me. But I didn't.'

'Why? That sounds like a really good idea.'

'Found out she was dating someone else, so that wouldn't have worked.'

'You could have gone as a throuple,' I said.

'A what?'

'A romantic relationship between three people,' I stated.

'I can't seem to get one person to date me, let alone two.'

'You don't strike me as a man who has problems getting a girlfriend. You're far too good-looking to have that particular issue.'

'Thanks, but you can't find something you're not actively looking for. It's the "not actively looking for" part that seems to confuse everyone around me. But I'm really just trying to focus on my career now.'

'Me too. I have so many career goals, a relationship would be terribly distracting.'

We both sat in silence, him sipping his coffee and me wiping the condensation off my glass of water, which had finally arrived. My attention was diverted by a woman sitting down at the table next to us. She'd overpacked her handbag and, as she sat, a book tumbled to the floor. I cast my eyes at it. The cover featured a shirtless man, his fingers looped through his jeans. He was pulling them down just enough for you to see what that 'V' would inevitably connect with. A hand with long red fingernails dug into his hard sixpack stomach and lust oozed from his eyes. The title caught my attention now. *The Dating Arrangement*. She picked it up quickly and the book disappeared into her bag once more, but as she did . . .

Part of a thought came to me.

It was hazy at first. Enveloped in misty brain fog. But as the mist started to dissipate the thought began to materialize and, when it did, I sat up straight in my seat.

'What?' Flightbird asked, clearly surprised by my dramatic move.

'Nothing.' I shook my head, trying to remove the thought from it. But it lingered.

The thought was logical. A plausible solution to our mutual problem, but would it work?

'No, seriously, what? You look like you've just solved an ancient mystery.'

'What if . . .' I started, but stopped. 'It might work, but . . . I don't know.'

'What?' he pressed.

'I'll be your fake girlfriend if you be my fake boyfriend.' I blurted it out.

'What?' Flightbird almost choked on his coffee. He put it down on the table so hard that some of it sploshed out. 'Sorry, what did you say?'

'Fake girlfriend and boyfriend.'

'You're not being serious, are you?'

I nodded my head solemnly, trying to convey the seriousness of my suggestion.

Flightbird wiped up the spilt coffee slowly. He looked like he was searching his brain for the right words to say back to me. 'So, how would that work, hypothetically, of course? Your suggestion?'

'Well, you would come with me to my reunion tonight – you'll be in Cape Town anyway, and you'll come with me to my cousin's wedding as well. I'll go with you to your mother's sixtieth and whatever other occasion you need me at. That way, we'll both be saved from the incessant relationship questions.'

'Huh. Interesting,' he mused.

'I have to warn you though, I'm not particularly good in social situations. I can't do small talk and sometimes I'm too blunt – some people say, anyway – but I'm sure I would make a fairly adequate fake girlfriend. At least you would have a girlfriend. That's better than not having one, isn't it?'

'It would certainly solve our respective problems for a while.'

'Exactly. And because it will be completely fake, there'll be no need for kissing. Not to mention all that phoning and messaging that takes up way too much time. And no sex.'

Flightbird choked on his coffee again and this time was forced to smack his chest. 'God, you *are* blunt.'

'I can try and tone it down if you want?' I offered.

'No. I like it. It's just . . .' He paused. 'Unexpected.'

I tapped my fingers on the table as another thought materialized. 'No. On second thoughts, it won't work.'

'Why not?' he asked.

'Well, because you are you,' I pointed at him, 'and I am me.'

'What does that mean?'

'You are *not* the kind of man I would date. And vice versa, I'm sure.'

'Still not getting you.'

'You're the cool, popular guy. I bet you played in many first-team sports with lots of big high-fives and had ten girls wanting to go with you to the end-of-year dance.'

'Uh,' he hesitated.

'Exactly! And I was probably one of those girls guys like you thought was a weirdo.'

'Guys like me? I think I'm offended.'

'No need to be. Just stating a fact. It's the way the world works. Social constructs. As my friend Jennifer would say – she's a psychiatrist, so she knows what she's talking about – much of our identity is formed through interactions with people and their reactions to us.'

'Wait, so you're just assuming what my reaction to you would be?'

I nodded.

'Well, you've got it wrong. That's not my reaction to you, and I'm not one of those guys.' He looked genuinely hurt by what I'd said, so I took that to mean that perhaps I'd misjudged him. If that was the case, I needed to course-correct.

'I'm sorry if I judged you incorrectly,' I stated. 'And if I have, then maybe this will work?'

'It's certainly an interesting proposal.' He picked the serviette up and dabbed the corner of his mouth. He had a good mouth. Lips that were neither too big nor too small. Positioned in just the right spot between his nose and his chin. 'So, I'll be your fake date, and you'll be mine?'

'Yes.'

'And you're okay with this? You don't really know me. We talk almost every day, but we've only just met.'

'Should I *not* be okay with you?'

'No, not at all. I'm not a criminal or anything.'

'Of course you're not. Pilots can't have criminal records. And pilots also undergo rigorous psychological evaluations to rule out any personality disorders or instability, and those are ongoing, so I also know you are psychologically sound of mind.'

He smiled again. 'Thanks.'

'Pilots also need to be in good health with no underlying chronic illnesses, so that's also a plus. You won't be falling over from a cardiac arrest mid-evening. Pilots also have basic training in CPR, which is excellent, not that I imagine it comes in handy very often, but having additional skills is always good. It makes you a more well-rounded individual, which is desirable in a partner. Also, in a recent study it was shown that a typical pilot is someone who displays low levels of anxiety, hostility and impulsivity, also good when choosing a fake boyfriend.'

'Wow! You know more about me than I know about myself.'

'Doubtful,' I said, and cocked my head to the side.

'I'm being sarcastic.'

'Sarcasm isn't my strong point either. But I suppose I can practice it a little if that's something that's important to you in a fake relationship.'

'Not at all.'

'I do have other very desirable qualities though,' I said.

'Like what?'

'Well, as an air traffic controller, I have excellent problem-solving abilities. Incredible levels of focus and very high ethical standards. Sense of responsibility and duty, excellent attention to detail. Only twenty per cent of students make it through training to become an ATC, so that also shows that I'm hardworking, have a high degree of intelligence, and once I set my mind to something, I always follow through.'

'Wow. That's impressive, but what about your personal qualities?'

'Personal?'

'Yes, qualities you possess that have nothing to do with work.'

I blinked at him. 'Wh—what do you mean?'

'Are you spontaneous? A loyal friend? What about hobbies? Good-humoured?'

'Uh . . .' I was stumped. Questions rarely stumped me, but this one did.

'Just trying to get to know my prospective fake girlfriend a little better, outside of work, that is.'

'Not spontaneous. I have few friends. I play Pokémon, the card game, and if you mean by "good-humoured" whether I'm a naturally genial person, then no on that too. But if you're asking whether I have a good sense of humour, then also no on that one.'

His lips twitched into yet another smile. 'I find you very friendly.

And so far, from what I've gathered, you have a great sense of humour. Unconventional, definitely, but not lacking, which I suppose are all good qualities for a fake girlfriend.'

'So does that mean you're accepting my proposal?'

He observed me for a while, which made me very uncomfortable. He looked at me like someone at a zoo might observe an exotic creature that they'd never encountered before. He probably hadn't. Not many people encountered someone like me, and I was acutely aware of that. People often told me that, and I was never sure if it was a compliment, or not.

'There's one thing I need to know about you before I agree to this,' he finally said.

'What?'

'Your name would be a good start.'

'Oh! Yes. That would be appropriate. I'm Pippa. Pippa Edwards. It often gets shortened to Pip, which I don't like at all. A pip is a fruit seed. Not a person.'

'Pippa, not Pip, nice to meet you. I'm Andrew Boyce-Jones, as you know. My friends often shorten it to BJ, which I absolutely despise.'

'Yes, I can see why that would be a very regrettable abbreviation. Why didn't they shorten it to Andy?'

'Because when your friends are adolescent boys, they tend to choose names like BJ over Andy.'

'Yes, teenage boys tend to be very obsessed with sex. It's all the hormones. It's very natural though. And then of course there's all the masturbating as well . . .' I tapered off, thinking about a statistic I'd once read about this particular activity, but was brought out of it by what sounded like another laugh-cough-choke combo.

'You okay?' I asked.

'Fine! Fine. But, wow. Only ten minutes in and we've discussed fertility, marriage and puberty. What's next?'

'You telling me definitively whether or not you'll be my fake boyfriend?'

'It is the most unconventional proposal I've ever been presented with—'

'So that's a no?'

'But it does have some strange kind of genius to it too.'

Strange genius. Another phrase I'd heard a lot in my life. And again, I was never sure if it was meant as a compliment. Synonyms for *strange* included *odd*, *weird*, *bizarre* and *alien*. And those did not sound like complimentary words.

'So it's a yes then?'

'Are you sure?' he asked again.

'The way I see it is that we both have the same problem. I don't like problems. I only like solutions, and I've found a solution to our mutual problem, so it makes sense that we should solve it together.'

There was a long interlude before he spoke again. 'Sure. Okay. Why not? I'm in Cape Town for the weekend anyway, so let's do it.'

Chapter 5

The plane took off very smoothly, and it was strange to hear Andrew's voice in another setting. I'd only known his voice through my headset in the air traffic control tower, not in a coffee shop, or inside a plane. Yet another surprise this day had delivered. I hoped there weren't going to be too many more. I'm not sure how many surprises a person like me can take in one day.

I checked my seatbelt once more and pulled my small notebook out of my handbag. Lowering the tray table, I opened it and poised my pen above the paper.

Small talk for tonight, I wrote, and underlined it.

I looked at the page and bit the tip of my pen. I always found it useful, before going into any social situation, let alone an unfamiliar, anxiety-ridden one, to have a set of small-talk questions in my arsenal, jotted down and memorized so they could be pulled out when the need arose. I always practiced conversations and found this very helpful. I tried variations of these conversations too, testing them beforehand like one might test a hypothesis. I lowered my pen to the page.

What do you do? This was always a good one, unless of course the person hated what they did, which would then throw the conversation into uncharted territory. I scratched that question off the list.

So what does your husband do? Ah-ha! This was a better one. This kept them talking about their husbands and their manifold delights. That was a question I could definitely use. And this time, when it led them to ask me what my boyfriend did, I could smile confidently and tell them he was a pilot. I sighed with relief. I could finally answer that question without it filling me with dread and anxiety. What I'd almost said to Andrew earlier, but didn't, was that the question of *why* I was still single didn't have that much to do with my career, after all. That played a part in it, but it was also something else. Something about me, intrinsically. But that was not something I would share with him, not something I shared with most people. It wasn't necessary in everyday dealings, but whenever relationships progressed to a certain stage I found that this *something else* was always the thing that tripped me up. That made it so hard for me, impossible even, to sustain any kind of relationship. But I didn't want to think about that now, so I thought of some more questions.

How many children do you have?

What grade are they in?

What do they like to do?

All excellent questions, and I quickly practiced the various responses in my head to make sure they sounded perfect.

Two, how lovely, what a perfect number.

How sweet, grade one is such an important year for their development. (Or, maybe I should google that?)

Video games! Did you know that almost twelve per cent of children who play games will become addicted? (Okay, that might not be the best response to that question.)

I put my pen down when I felt the stranger next to me bump my arm. I leaned into the aisle as far as I could go, without offending him. I didn't like touching strangers, I didn't like strangers in my space, and whenever I flew I took an aisle seat so I wasn't sandwiched between two people and could lean into the open. But the person next to me was a rather broad-shouldered individual and, in order to avoid him, I had to extend half my body at a very awkward angle all the way into the aisle. This had caused the air hostess to look at me oddly a few times.

I ran over a few more general pointers for tonight in my head.

Make eye contact, but not too much.

When they start looking around, they probably want to end the conversation.

Share, but don't overshare. (This one was very important.)

Don't just talk about yourself, ask questions.

Try to let the other person finish a sentence before jumping in and cutting them off.

Other people didn't need to remind themselves of how to have conversations, but I did. Other people seemed to find socializing and interacting easy; it came naturally to them. Me, I always seemed to miss those unspoken social cues, the ones that people made with their body language and vocal tones. I struggled with the interactive nature of a conversation too, and often filled the spaces between sentences with things that others found inappropriate. Things that flew out of my mouth before I was able to censor them. Teenage masturbation probably being a prime example of that.

But tonight I wouldn't do that. Tonight would be different.

Andrew glided the plane down for a very solid landing, despite the strong southwester, something the Cape was known for. The winds in Cape Town had caught many pilots off guard, making for plenty of go-arounds. But Andrew got it right first time, despite the very turbulent approach, despite the crosswinds that pushed the back of the plane out on the runway and caused a loud and dramatic skid as he slowed the plane down. He was a very accomplished pilot, but I'd known that. I hoped he would be an accomplished fake date too.

Chapter 6

'Okay, so I think we should set some ground rules for our arrangement,' I said as we ubered together to my hotel. The reunion was in two and a half hours and Andrew was conveniently staying at a hotel close to me.

'What kind of ground rules?'

'No holding hands. No unsolicited touching. No kissing.'

'I think that goes without saying.'

'And we will need a convincing back story. How we met. How long we've been together. I would prefer it to be as close to the truth as possible, since I'm not a very convincing liar.'

'We met a few months ago when I was a pilot and you were my air traffic controller. We talked to each other for months before meeting in a coffee shop by chance. We recognized each other's voices, and the rest, as they say, is history.'

'What history specifically?'

'I asked you on a date, and then another one. We share a lot of common interests, like our love for our jobs. We fell in love. We're even thinking of moving in together.'

'That doesn't sound like something I would do. Far too impulsive. I barely know you.'

'Do we at least leave toothbrushes at each other's houses?' He sounded amused.

'Well, that would mean we're having sex.'

'Aren't we? We've been together for a few months?'

I turned in my seat and scrutinized Andrew once more. He really was very good-looking and, realistically, if we were dating in real life, I would probably be having sex with him. 'Okay, fine. We're having sex.'

'The enthusiasm in your voice doesn't make me feel good about myself,' he joked with a smile on his face. 'Doesn't sound like it's particularly good sex.'

'I'm afraid you're only a six out of ten. But you are getting better,' I quipped.

'Good to know,' he said. 'But average sex aside, are we in love?'

I shrugged. 'I guess we have to be. Not that I know what that feels like.'

'You've never been in love?'

'Nope.'

'Why not?'

'I don't know, actually. I've been in, like, in obsession. In lust, even. But I don't think I've ever been in love.'

'Well, if this is going to work, we do need to look like we're in love,' he said.

'And how do we do that?'

'Some hand-holding might help.'

I instinctively looked down at his hands. He held them up for me to inspect.

'I do wash them,' he said.

'That's not what I'm looking at.'

'Then what?'

'I don't like it when people have fingers like King Charles – sausagey. It's very off-putting. But you have good fingers.'

'Uh . . . thanks. I don't think anyone has ever complimented my fingers before.'

'In general, people don't pay nearly enough attention to fingers as they should. But if you think about it, they may actually be one of our most important features. If it weren't for our dexterous opposable thumbs, our primitive ancestors wouldn't have started making tools and evolved into what we are today. If it wasn't for our thumbs, we would still be covered in hair and living in a cave.'

'So, is that a yes or a no to holding hands?'

'I'll think about it and get back to you,' I muttered thoughtfully.

'What if we call each other pet names?' he asked.

'I despise pet names.'

'But no one calls their partners by their real names. As soon as you're in love, real names go out the window.'

'Give me an example.'

'I could call you babe and you could call me dear.'

'Absolutely not!'

'What do you suggest then?'

'I suggest calling each other by our real names,' I said firmly.

'What about something more rooted in us?' he offered. 'I could call you City Tower and you could call me Flightbird. People would find that unbelievably cute.'

I considered this for a while. People did find this kind of thing cute. But the more I thought about it, the more it gave me intense, spine-curling cringe.

'How about we stick to our real names? City Tower and Flightbird would sound ridiculous outside of an airport setting.'

'I guess no arms around the waist then either?' he asked.

'Definitely not!'

'And it goes without saying that a quick kiss on the cheek would also be out?' he questioned.

'A quick kiss on the cheek, or even the lips, would definitely add to the authenticity of the moment. But no.' I shook my head. 'No kissing of any kind.'

'Got it. Anything else?'

'No, I think that about covers it for now. I'll let you know if I think of anything else.'

The Uber driver finally pulled up to my hotel. I'd booked myself into a fairly small one. I preferred them; there is nothing worse than standing in a line with people as they queue for a breakfast buffet and jostle for the last cold pancake.

'See you soon,' Andrew called as I climbed out of the Uber.

'In exactly two and a half hours.' I tapped my watch.

I checked into my hotel room and looked around. I hated new spaces, unfamiliar ones, but mostly I hated unfamiliar pillows. So the first thing I did, the first thing I always did when I checked into any foreign place, was unpack my pillows from home and pack their pillows away. The idea of resting my head on something that hundreds, possibly thousands, of heads had been on did not sit right with me. Besides, I also had a very specific pillow configuration that allowed for ultimate comfort and relaxation. I pulled out the dress that my mom had insisted I take with me. She'd come around to my place while I packed and sat on my bed making fashion suggestions. Her suggestions were always based on what garment would garner me the most attention, which would hopefully lead to a male admirer, hopefully leading to a wedding, a honeymoon and grandchildren.

'You have such a gorgeous figure. You should really show it off more.' She was always so fond of pointing this out.

She was right, of course, I did have a good figure, which I attributed to my daily swimming routine. I loved swimming. The blissful feeling of being enveloped by liquid, and the inevitable silence that followed. The world above you stilled and muted. I find the world very overwhelming: the sights, the sounds, the smells. But down there under the water, there's a kind of peace that I never get up here. If there was a way of living underwater permanently, I would. My dream has always been to live in one of those underwater floating villas in Dubai. I dream of waking up every morning in my underwater bedroom, looking out into the calm blue waters, hearing the soft sounds of water lapping at the sides of the house. But with a price tag of $3.3 million, that dream is perhaps a little far out of my reach, right now anyway. But it's always good to have something to work towards. Perhaps one day I'll be running the airport in Dubai – my ultimate career goal was to run my own airport – and then I'd be able to have as many underwater villas as I wanted.

I pulled the red – my mom had called it a 'bodycon' – dress out of my suitcase and held it in front of myself as I looked in the mirror. The red suited me; it accentuated my green eyes and contrasted with my porcelain skin. But it was tight. I did not like tight clothing, and that's why, much to my mother's despair, I spent most of my days in loose trousers and even looser tops. Tight clothes made me uneasy. The squeezing sensation always made my mind drift to a documentary I'd watched once on the African rock python. The video of it constricting and then eating an entire springbok in one fell swoop had always stayed with me. But despite thoughts of giant snakes, I'd promised my mother – and I always keep my promises. My phone beeped. Andrew and I had swapped numbers in case we needed to liaise further.

Andrew: Is this a formal thing? What should I wear?

Pippa: The invite says smart/casual.

Andrew: Can I wear jeans and a white button-down shirt? I don't have many clothing options. I wasn't expecting to go out tonight.

Pippa: Wear whatever you have. I'm sure it'll be fine.

Andrew: Okay, see you soon.

I put my phone down on the bed and slipped into the dress. My mom was right: it did accentuate all my good parts. I contemplated putting some red lipstick on but didn't want to look as if I was trying too hard. I put on a pair of comfortable flats. I never wear stilettos. Quite frankly, I was utterly terrified of them, especially given how eternally clumsy I was. I touched up my so-called 'clean girl' aesthetic and headed out.

Chapter 7

I sat in the back of the Uber waiting for Andrew to emerge from his hotel. I'd become acutely aware by this stage that this dress had a habit of creeping up my thighs when I was seated. And being a tight dress, it was hard to pull down to a more appropriate level. I bet my mother knew this when she packed it for me. I bet this was part of her plan: expose my thighs to attract a mate. I made a mental note to spend as little time sitting as possible, for fear that too much leg would show. Besides, I already had a mate, a fake one, so no need to attract a real one.

I peered up as Andrew walked – nay, strode – towards the Uber. His strides were wide and confident, with just the tiniest hip swagger that ramped up the catwalk sexiness of it all. He was an awfully handsome man, especially in the clothes he'd chosen to wear. His dark hair looked darker against the white button-down shirt. Muscular forearms were visible under the sleeves he'd rolled up. The black watch he wore made his wrists look larger than they probably were. You could see he worked out regularly; those sexy veins that ran from the back of his hand into his forearms told me so. His untucked shirt flapped open just enough in the front for me to see how his jeans fitted. Slightly tight, framing what was possibly something impressive inside. Not that one can make any assumptions about penis size based on the fit of the pants – after all, body builders stuff their trunks, and we all know what they say about body builders' appendages. Besides, even if he was boasting something impressive, I wasn't into impressive. I was into average. A perfect five to six inches was more than sufficient. Anything more was unnecessary. Not that I was ever going to have sex with him, of course, so this speculation about the size of his penis was utterly pointless. I willed my brain to stop the current tangent it was so happily galloping off on.

He bent down to open the door and, as he did, the light from inside the car flashed across his face, revealing once again those royal blue eyes. It was then that I noticed the only non-symmetrical thing about him.

'What's wrong with your left eye?' I enquired as soon as he was inside the car. Andrew didn't answer right away. 'Sorry, was that rude?'

'Not at all.'

'You have a brown stripe of color running from your pupil to the bottom of your iris.'

'It's a mild form of heterochromia. Some people have different-colored eyes; I just have this stripe. It's something I've had since birth.'

Without asking, I peered into his eyes. He accommodated me by opening them wider.

'It's very beautiful. Unusual.' I sat back in my seat once I was satisfied I'd studied this ocular phenomenon enough. I made a mental note to google this heterochromia later and do a thorough deep-dive into the subject matter. Now was not the time for it though; I knew from past experiences that suddenly googling something in the company of others, in social situations, can often be perceived as rude. But my fingers itched to pull the phone out and type that word into the search bar.

'Thanks,' Andrew said, sinking into the seat. 'You have lovely eyes too.'

'My eyes are just green. Nothing as interesting as yours.'

'You don't meet many people with green eyes,' he continued.

'Only two per cent of the population have green eyes, actually.' I lifted my phone to my face, put it on selfie mode and stared at my eyes.

'Moss green,' I finally announced, once I'd established the exact color of my eyes. 'Lichen green – they have some gray in them too.'

'Lichen? As in fungus?'

'Yes.'

I heard a small, soft chuckle next to me and turned to look at Andrew, holding eye contact for only a moment before looking away.

'What?' I asked.

Andrew shook his head and smiled. 'Nothing, you're just . . . surprising. That's all.'

'Surprising good, or surprising bad?' I wasn't sure what he meant, considering synonyms included *shocking* and *unpredictable*. Two words I didn't much care for.

'Good,' he said. 'I talk to you almost every day, and I guess I didn't imagine you being this funny.'

'It's not like I can showcase my humour while navigating a plane to the ground.'

'True.'

'Besides, I don't consider myself funny. I simply say what I say, and sometimes people find it amusing, even though most of the time it wasn't intended as such.'

'Funny, yet strangely informative too,' he said, continuing to smile.

'Sorry, I have a habit of bombarding people with information. Sometimes they find it useful; most of the time they don't.'

'Personally, I'm glad that I've been forewarned about my soon to be declining sperm count and been introduced to the world of throuples. Not to mention the importance of opposable thumbs.'

'Are you being sarcastic?' I asked, always unsure.

'Not at all. I mean it. Seriously. I don't think I've ever covered such a variety of fascinating topics in such a short space of time.'

I studied him until I was satisfied I believed him. 'Good, because synonyms for *sarcastic* include *mocking* and *ridiculing*, not to mention *contemptuous*, and *taunting* even.'

He tilted his head, bringing his eyes to mine. I immediately looked away. I hated the intensity of eye contact; it felt like such an incredibly intimate act, one that should *not* be done with strangers.

A long silence descended on the Uber. I shuffled in my seat, hoping to make some kind of noise to break it, even if the noise did sound like flatulence. I dreaded silences like these. Silences in the presence of others made me obsess about what the other person was thinking. I didn't like not knowing, and silences were the ultimate manifestation of not knowing. I'd long wished I possessed the ability to read minds; it would be so much easier for me to make my way through life if I was able to read people's thoughts. A few years back I'd research extensively if the human brain was indeed capable of such psychic feats. I'd even enrolled in a Udemy course that promised to 'unleash my innate psychic abilities'. It did not. And when I demanded a refund from the instructor, she told me that 'some of us are just not meant to be psychic'. I asked her why she hadn't known this before letting me enrol, considering she claimed to be psychic herself. She blocked all my emails, but not before telling me what a 'negative soul' I had.

'So, tell me a little more about what I'm walking into,' Andrew said, and I released an audible sigh of relief. 'Let's start by what school you went to.'

'Redford Girls Academy.'

'Wow. Fancy.' This was usually the response I got from people when they learned I'd gone to the most prestigious girls' school in the country.

'Lots of pearl necklaces and designer handbags,' I said, with a splash of disdain in my voice. I was thinking back to a particular event, where at Catherine's sixteenth birthday her parents had presented her with her first Hermès Birkin bag. I'd wanted a pair of binoculars for my sixteenth birthday so I could climb on the roof and watch the planes begin their descent towards the airport some kilometers away. Although our house was far from the airport, we were directly under a flight path, and I'd spend hours on the roof watching the planes fly overhead.

'I take it you do not own a designer bag?' Andrew enquired.

'No, they are a complete waste of money. A bag's ultimate function is to carry personal belongings in it, and I don't see why a designer label would do that job any better than a bag that costs a few hundred rand. A higher price does not equate to superior functionality.'

'I don't think people who buy designer bags are concerned with their functionality.'

Andrew's voice had a smile in it, so I assumed he was enjoying this conversation. So was I, actually.

'Although having said that, I did read an article about the Birkin bag being a better investment than gold and the stock market,' I added quickly.

'So perhaps Catherine's parents were on to something.'

'Perhaps,' I muttered, seriously considering whether I should sell some unit shares to invest in a Birkin bag. I made a mental note to google how much one cost and where to get it from.

'So, what else? What are your interests? What are your hobbies?' Andrew asked.

I turned in my seat. 'What's that got to do with anything?'

'I'd just like to have a little more personal info on you, in case the evening calls for it.'

I thought about it. I only had a few hobbies and interests. Well, 'obsessions' was really the only word for them. 'I like fish. I like swimming. I like my job and planes. I like synonyms.'

'What kind of fish?'

'Tropical fish are my favorite. I like their colors. I'm an aquarist.'

'A what?'

'Aquarist. I keep fish,' I explained.

'Huh,' Andrew said thoughtfully.

'Is that helpful?'

'I'm not sure yet,' he admitted. 'I can't quite see how to slip that into conversation. But you never know.'

The Uber delivered us to our destination, and soon we were standing outside my school, looking up at its ivy-covered walls. I stared at the grand entrance and read the Latin words sprawled across the top of it. Our school motto.

Sapientia et veritas. Wisdom and truth.

I was perpetually baffled by this continued usage of Latin terminology in the modern age, especially here in Africa. It seemed utterly irrelevant and out of place. It would be so much more appropriate if 'wisdom' and 'truth' were in one of our vernacular languages, not a language that hadn't been spoken since the sixth century. I'd suggested this once to the school's governing body. It had not gone down well, even though my argument was a very solid one.

I kept staring at the school entrance. *Why did it suddenly look so foreign and strange?* I'd seen this entrance and stood outside it so many times before, and yet tonight it felt like a place I'd never been to in my entire life.

'I think this was a bad idea.' I took a step back. 'I get these sudden ideas that I don't quite think through sometimes. Or I do think them through, but when tested in the real world they fail to live up to the expectation I had in my head.' I pulled the hem of my red dress down again; it was creeping up. 'Besides, my dress is too red and too tight and too short.' I yanked at the fabric around my stomach to see if I could stretch it a little, so it didn't cling like a second skin. 'I will never let my mother pick out my clothes again.'

Andrew threw me a sideways glance. 'Your mother picked that out?'

'Apparently, if I wear sexier clothes, my chances of attracting a mate are much higher.'

'Aaah,' he muttered.

'I feel like how one of those birds of paradise in a David Attenborough documentary must feel, dressed in my most alluring plumage and ready to perform for everyone.'

Andrew laughed. 'I feel so sorry for those birds. Can you imagine building nest after nest only to have them ripped up over and over again?'

'I think the birds have it right, though. Their society is a matriarchy. The women always have the final say, and I think that our world would be a much better place if women were in charge.'

'Sounds like home,' Andrew said.

'Did you grow up in a matriarchy?'

'You better believe I did. I still feel sorry for those birds, though,' he said as he moved towards the entrance. I didn't follow him. He stopped and turned. 'You coming?'

'I kind of wish I wasn't, to be honest.'

'I think it's a little too late to change your mind.'

'Is it?' I heard the desperation in my voice. It was not something I was proud of.

'Come on, you can do this. We flew all this way.'

'We did.'

'And if it's awful after thirty minutes, we'll leave.'

'True. No one will notice me anyway,' I said, pulling at my hem again. 'It's not like they noticed me in school.'

'Mmm, I'm not so sure about that. Not in that dress, anyway.'

'Is it completely inappropriate? Should I go back to the hotel and change?'

'Not inappropriate, but it is noticeable. You'll definitely turn some heads.'

'I don't think I want to turn heads,' I said.

Andrew walked back towards me. 'You know the best way to get over a terrible high-school experience?'

'No?'

'Make them all jealous as hell. Well, that's probably what one of my sisters would recommend anyway.' He swooped his arm in front of me, like a maître d' might when ushering you towards your table. He started walking again and, this time, I followed.

'That makes no sense. Why would making them jealous make up for what happened ten years ago?'

'Just trust me on this.'

'Trust you? I hardly know you.'

'And yet here we are. Ascending a staircase together to your school reunion.'

Chapter 8

Only they did notice me. I don't think I'd ever been noticed with such intensity before, and it was truly unsettling. Their eyes moved up and down my body as they scanned me like someone running groceries through a barcode scanner might. And then, once I'd been sufficiently scanned, they turned their laser-like eyes on Andrew. Many of them spent a lot of time looking at him. Inspecting his packing, checking his price tag, expiration date, et cetera. Some also looked at him as if they were so starving they couldn't wait to leave the grocery store, tear the wrapper off and sink their teeth into him as soon as possible. I noted that their husbands looked at Andrew in a very different way. In fact, every time he came near a fiancé or husband, said fiancé or husband suddenly grew a few inches taller. Their shoulders and chests seem to broaden too.

'You just look stunning. I mean, *stunning*,' Hannah gushed. Hannah had been our all-round over-achieving head girl, general teacher's pet and hander-out of detentions and enforcer of rules. This was about the tenth time one of them had used the word 'stunning', and I was tempted to jump in and offer up some alternatives.

Brilliant.

Dazzling.

Gorgeous.

And my personal favorite: beauteous. I liked how many vowels it had. I liked the way it sounded too, in fact . . .

'Thank you, Hannah, you look rather beauteous yourself this evening.'

Silence.

Everyone around me stopped talking for a moment, and then laughter ensued.

'I forgot how funny you were!' Hannah commented, and a few of the others nodded in agreement. I was about to point out that that was in no way meant to be humorous, but left it. Humour, I've learned, is an incredibly subjective thing. And I'm still at a loss about the sheer amount of mirth that people seem to derive from the things I say. I've noticed that my statements seem to elicit two types of laughter from people. The first comes out fast and loud and involves the entire body. But the second one comes out slowly, tentatively, usually after a very long awkward pause. This laughter was *not* the latter.

'Beauteous?' Andrew whispered in my ear as we walked around the room greeting more people. There were people everywhere!

'It's a perfectly good synonym for *stunning*.'

'That hasn't been used in common conversation for over two hundred years.'

'They'd used the word *stunning* too often.'

'I agree with that. But *pretty* or *nice* would probably have sufficed just as well.'

'Pippa!' A voice interrupted us, followed by two faces I did not recognize.

'Hi, I'm Andrew.' Andrew stuck his hand out and intercepted the woman before she was able to launch herself at me and pull me into another one of those death-clutch hugs that everyone seemed to be dishing out tonight.

'It's me. Meg. Do you remember?' She placed her hand on her chest and looked at me. I got the feeling that if I *didn't* remember her, she would be deeply, deeply upset, and then I would be pulled into a long conversation where she would go about telling me how we knew each other, what classes we'd taken together, what extra murals, borrowed pens, et cetera. I knew I needed to feign enthusiasm.

'MEG!' I exclaimed. Too loudly. Too, too loudly. I knew this because everyone nearby swung around and stared at me. God, I was so bad at this. I was either too big, or too small. Too soft, or too loud. Why couldn't things come out of my mouth naturally, with the right tone and volume? Constantly moderating my words and their delivery was exhausting. I coughed. Beat my chest a few times and then tried to readjust my volume.

'Meg. Of course. So delighted to see you. Thrilled and ecstatic. How are you?' I asked, tilting my head to the side and widening my eyes in what I hoped looked like genuine interest. (At the same time also reminding myself to stop adding so many synonyms to my sentences.)

'Wow. You look stunning, Pippa. Stunning!' she said, and Andrew grinned at me.

'You look very pretty too, Meg,' I said awkwardly, even though I didn't much like what she was wearing at all, but it was never polite to point this out.

And then she turned her attention to Andrew.

'Andrew.' He held his hand out and she immediately grabbed it. She seemed to shake it for several seconds too long, and then suddenly, with an almost inaudible apology, let go of it. And that's when it dawned on me. Andrew was, by far, the most attractive man in this room, and that's why everyone was looking at him like that. Holding his hand and his gaze for too long. Meg cleared her throat and stepped away from him.

'Sorry! This is Christopher. My fiancé. *Christopher.*' Christopher gave her a displeased look, and I wondered if he'd notice the two-seconds-too-long hand hold. 'And you two? Engaged? Married?' she asked me.

'We're—' I started. But she clearly wasn't interested in my answer, because she cut me off by thrusting her hand in our faces. It was such an unexpected gesture that I jumped back in fright and almost fell backwards.

'Christopher and I just got engaged!' Her voice was high-pitched. Almost too high-pitched for human ears, and I was sure I heard the distant howl of a dog responding.

'Congrat—'

She cut me off again.

'It was soooo romantic. He took me to our favorite restaurant and, at the end of the meal, all the staff walked towards the table, and one of them was holding a silver cloche, and then Christopher got down on one knee, right then and there in front of the whole restaurant, and proposed. I swear, when the waiter opened the cloche my heart almost missed a beat. I mean . . . Look at it . . .'

She looked down at her ring and we all followed suit.

'Princess cut. Three carats.'

I nodded. I had zero idea what a three-carat ring versus a one-carat one was all about. Obviously, the three-carat was superior, but I had no idea what criteria that was based on. Nor did I know what a princess cut was. I should google it. But not now.

'It's stunning,' Andrew said, and then gave me the tiniest nudge, as if trying to convey that we were now sharing some kind of private joke. Which, I guess, we were.

'Very . . .' I paused. The stone was way too bright for my liking. And when she turned her hand the lights caught its sharp facets and sent what felt like laser beams directly into my eyes. 'Luminous,' I managed.

And so it went on like this. The next couple we met were Yanilla and Marcus. She was pregnant, and they'd just had their gender-reveal party, where one hundred helium balloons had been released into the air from a skyscraper in Sandton. I was about to open my mouth and remind her of the deadly and devastating consequences balloons had on wildlife, but I didn't. Instead I asked the more appropriate question.

'So what color were the balloons?'

'Pink,' she said, clutching on to Marcus even tighter.

'Because it's a girl,' I stated, and nodded, even though I'd never really understood this need to assign colors to the sexes. It all seemed like a rather archaic ritual, if you asked me. Mind you, when it came to babies and the rituals surrounding them, it was all rather archaic. At the only baby shower I'd ever been invited to, the mother and father had willingly eaten melted chocolate out of a diaper while everyone hooted with laughter and cheered them on.

The next encounter was very much like the previous two, except this time we'd had to endure a very long story about a wedding that had taken place in Iceland under the Northern Lights. The story had been so extravagant that I'd almost expected them to conclude it by saying that a trained penguin had waddled up the aisle carrying a ring on his little wing stump. The next story was even more elaborate, featuring a hot-air balloon and the words 'Marry Me' mowed into a large wheat field. Granted, the husband's family did own the farm. It wasn't as if he'd driven his lawn mower into some poor unsuspecting farmer's crops.

These couples we met all jumped straight into stories of their engagements, weddings, gender-reveal parties and even births, much to my horror. I was starting to look at each one of them as a story, and not two humans. It was as if whatever story they told had somehow became their personality. But it all fell apart when the fifth story asked a question that they actually *did* want answered.

'And what about you guys? Any plans to tie the knot?' A woman who I'd totally forgotten named Nobuhle asked.

'Well, that's so strange you should ask,' Andrew said quickly, before I could set the record straight. 'Strange, because we've actually just gotten engaged!'

'We have?' I couldn't disguise my obvious shock.

He let out a slightly strange-sounding laugh and then pointed at me. 'It only happened a few hours ago, so she still forgets.'

I glared at Andrew. 'I don't forget things.'

'Usually you don't, but we were both just so overcome with emotion when it happened. It was a very intense moment.'

I turned back to Nobuhle to tell her he was lying but didn't have the chance to as Andrew launched into the most far-fetched story I'd ever heard.

'It happened so spontaneously. In fact, it was so spontaneous that I haven't even gotten her a ring. It was very spur of the moment. But when it feels right, it just feels right, you know.'

There were some breathy sighs at this point and, much to my horror, Andrew continued. 'We'd just taken off in the plane. I'm a pilot, and the weather couldn't have been more perfect. Crystal-clear skies and no wind whatsoever. And I remember thinking that there was just something special about that day. And then, this massive. beautiful dam came into view, and the sun was casting a glow on it, making it look silver, and I immediately thought of Pippa. Because it was one of the most beautiful things I'd ever seen, and because silver is also her favorite color. And that's when this moment of clarity hit me. I knew I wanted to spend the rest of my life with her, and so I picked up my intercom and, right there and then, flying over the Free State at thirty-one thousand feet, with a cabin full of passengers and crew, I asked her to marry me.'

Nobuhle let out a soft 'aaaah' sound and put her hand to her heart. A few others had moved towards us during Andrew's very tall tale. Did they actually believe this nonsense that he was spouting? And here I thought he was a pilot, not a romance writer.

'On the intercom!' Katie said on a long, loud exhale that at the end went breathy and silent and melted into the air around us. 'That is the most romantic thing I've ever heard.'

'That's so romantic,' one of the other Katies cooed – or was she a Chloe, or a Cath? – it was hard to tell. But she did coo. That was really the only way to describe the silly thing her voice did. A dove-like murmuring that I found, frankly, disconcerting.

'I thought so too,' Andrew said, and then faced me. 'What did you think, my angel?'

'Uh . . .Uh . . .' I stumbled, I'd never been good at lying, and now everyone was looking at me expectantly.

'Sweetheart, are you lost for words?' he asked.

I nodded, and spoke the first bit of truth that had been uttered in the last few minutes. 'I don't have words for it at all,' I concluded.

More 'aaaah's rose up from the crowd and I forced a smile. Maybe if I smiled, I wouldn't be required to talk again. I could just fix my mouth like this permanently. So I arranged my lips and teeth into something that I hoped conveyed the depths of my supposed emotion. I wasn't sure if I was making the right smile for this moment, though. But there was certainly no guide called 'How to smile when a man you barely know tells a room full of your ex-schoolmates that you are engaged when, in fact, you're not.'

'So what happened next?' someone asked. I looked at Andrew for this one, because of course I had no bloody idea what had happened.

'Well, when you're at cruising altitude, the pilot is allowed to leave the cabin, so I turned the plane over to my trusty co-pilot and walked down the aisle towards her. Everyone was watching. I got down on one knee and because I didn't have a ring with me, I tied a small piece of thread around her finger and I promised to love her for ever.'

People looked down at my empty finger.

'Needless to say, it fell off in the bath,' he said quickly. 'But I'll get you a real ring soon, love.'

More people had gathered around, and all of them were concurring that this was indeed the most romantic thing that anyone had ever heard. Personally, I wasn't sure why this was so romantic; I could think of nothing worse and more cringy than sharing your feelings publicly like that in front of a flying cylinder full of strangers. But I smiled and nodded, and this seemed satisfactory. Andrew then embellished the story even more, telling them that as soon as we were back home he was going to be giving me his beloved grandmother's ring, a ring that she'd bestowed on him on her deathbed. More 'aaaah's were made – apparently me receiving a dead person's ring was also considered far more romantic than a store-bought one. But he took it too far when he told them that I'd always dreamed – since I was a little girl – of getting married in a glass-bottomed boat while floating over a coral reef. That was the last straw for me, and as soon as I could I pulled him away from the crowd, out the hall, down the corridor and into my old science classroom.

'What the hell are you doing?' I said, closing the door behind us.

'I know! I know. But I couldn't take it any more. They were driving me nuts with all their stories about gender-reveal parties, exorbitant engagements and weddings. And they were all trying to one-up each other – I mean, this one had a three-day baby shower and the other one had a bachelorette party in Barbados or Greece or whatever. And I'm competitive, and I'm sorry, I cracked. I couldn't look at one more blinding engagement ring or listen to one more story of tears on bended knee.'

'Yes, it was getting pretty sickening,' I admitted, walking over to my old desk and running a hand over its wooden surface.

'God, now I understand why you didn't want to come to this alone.'

'Exactly. Hence the need for this arrangement,' I concurred, flopping down in my old chair. It felt different. Or maybe I was different. Bigger? 'But still, you took that way too far.'

'I know. Sorry. But like you said, you're never going to see any of these people again, at least for another ten years, so it's not like we have to carry on this pretence. And in ten years' time most of them will be divorced and on their second marriage, and you can be divorced too. You can all bitch about your ex-husbands together. You can tell them all how awful I was.'

'I doubt they'll believe me. You seemed to have charmed them all.'

'And did you see how jealous Meg looked when I told her how I proposed? I could see her side-eyeing her fiancé, as if his bended knee at their favorite restaurant paled in comparison to my mid-air declaration.'

I smiled to myself. The smile grew and I put my hands on my cheeks. They felt warmer. 'Okay, I admit it, that did feel good.' I giggled to myself and finally understood what he'd meant about the satisfaction I was deriving from making them all a little jealous with my gorgeous, romantic fake fiancé. It was also a little exhilarating, this lie. Delicious and naughty and so not something I would normally do and, until now, not something I'd ever thought I would have enjoyed. Did that say something about my character? I wasn't sure. And I wasn't sure whether that was something I could google.

Andrew walked up to me. 'Is this your old desk?'

'This was my science class.'

'I bet you were good at science,' he said, sitting down in the chair next to me, the chair that Katie used to sit in.

'I was. I bet you were too.'

He smiled. 'I was. What was your mark for matric?' He folded his arms and looked at me.

'Ninety-two. You?'

'Shit! Eighty-seven. You beat me.'

'You really are competitive.'

'Sometimes it's an asset, sometimes not so much.'

'Mmm,' I mumbled in agreement.

'So . . . shall we go out there and make some more of them jealous?'

I narrowed my eyes at him. 'But no more glass-bottomed boats and coral reefs.'

'So I shouldn't tell them that after the wedding ceremony we are both skydiving from a plane together to seal our love at altitude.'

'Definitely not!'

'And I shouldn't tell them that a specially trained dolphin is going to preside over our wedding service?'

'No! Absolutely not!' I stood up and wrestled with my defiant, leg-creeping dress. 'We only have another hour to go of keeping this up.'

'We should make it count then,' he said.

I looked down at my hand, thought for a moment and then held it out for him. 'You may hold my hand for the rest of the evening,' I said. 'But only if your palms do not get sweaty and moist.'

Andrew took it tentatively. 'My palms never sweat.'

'Fine. And . . .' I paused. I could not believe I was about to say this. 'And once, *only once*, and only if it is absolutely necessary, you may kiss me with closed mouth on the cheek or the lips. But briefly. No lingering and absolutely no tongue.'

Andrew looked like he was trying not to smile. 'Got it. Only once. No lingering tongue and only when necessary.'

I nodded and he tightened his grip around my hand. 'I don't like my hand to be held with so much pressure. Less pressure, please.'

He was no longer holding back his smile. 'Sure.' His hand loosened around mine and it didn't feel as awful as I thought it would. 'This okay?'

'I don't hate it as much as I thought I would.'

'Wow, between our mediocre sex life, the no-tongue kisses and the fact you only just don't hate holding my hand, it's a miracle we've made it this long.'

'I did say the sex was improving,' I said, playing along, because I liked the way it felt to joke around with him. 'But only marginally,' I added, and dragged him towards the door.

Chapter 9

'And then I heard his voice over the intercom and he asked me to marry him,' I'd just finished the story again, and Larissa and her wife, Jules, smiled at me.

'And do you plan on having any kids?' Jules asked.

'Oh, absolutely,' Andrew said. 'We both want at least four kids. Isn't that right, lovie?'

I forced a smile. He was still playing it up, maybe even more so this time, with all the pet names and hand-holding. And each time we talked to someone else, he added a new future child to our family. We'd started out with one – apparently Andrew had always wanted a son – and now we were going for a soccer team.

'Let me show you ours, she's only three months,' Larissa said, pulling her phone out and turning the screen on. She held up an image of a toddler with her blue eyes. I leaned in, because it was the polite thing to do. Honestly, I never knew what to say when people showed me pictures of their kids. I have absolutely zero interest in seeing other people's children; it just does not appeal to me at all. And all babies look the same. I would have preferred it much more if I was looking at a picture of a Labrador puppy, or a kitten or cockatoo. Preferably all of them together.

'Isn't she cute?' Larissa asked the dreaded question.

'Mmmm,' I said, nodding vigorously. There wasn't much to see really: the child had its entire fist in its mouth and drool was dripping down its arm and chin. 'She has your eyes,' I stated. This *was* true.

The two of them smiled. Clearly my statement had landed with them in the right way.

'Thank you,' Larissa said. 'Jules is going to do the pregnancy next time round. I hated being pregnant.'

'Having two wombs in the family has its advantages,' Jules added, and this got me thinking.

Questions began flooding my brain. Will the fathers be the same? Did you use an anonymous donor's sperm? How did you choose the father? How long did it take to become pregnant? Was it IUI or IVF? I kept my lips tightly closed though. I knew from past experiences – many, many past experiences – that even though these were legitimate questions, it was not always good to ask them.

'It's not always appropriate to ask the first question that comes into your mind,' I could hear my mom saying after an incident in a shopping queue in which I'd asked the man standing in front of me with only one arm how he'd lost it and had it hurt. To me they were perfectly logical questions, but apparently that wasn't the point. The point was, it could cause offence.

We moved on from the baby photo. We told our story again to someone else, and this time it led to us having five kids. Andrew had always wanted twins now too. He upgraded the lie even more when he added two cocker spaniels and a parakeet who could repeat basic ATC commands like 'You are cleared to land on runway zero seven left.'

'You guys make such a gorgeous couple,' Sindiso had said. She was in her residency to become an orthopaedic surgeon, and on her arm was the most beautiful Italian man – almost as beautiful as Andrew – also in his residency to become a neurosurgeon. They were planning on getting married after they'd completed their residencies. She had always wanted a big traditional wedding. I told her that I too had dreamed of a traditional wedding.

'What tradition exactly?' she asked, and I realized my faux pas. She was referring to a *real* traditional wedding, a Zulu wedding.

'Irish!' I said quickly, surprised at how speedily the lie had managed to come out of my mouth. It was a semi-truth, though.

'I'll have to wear a kilt and we'll walk down the aisle to the melodic sounds of the wedding march played on bagpipes,' Andrew colored the story in.

I nodded and smiled. 'And I'll have to carry a horseshoe with me all day. It brings good luck.'

'Photo time!' someone exclaimed loudly, and jumped in front of us with a cell phone.

'Uh . . . No, thank you!' I hated having my photo taken. I never knew how to stand, where to look, what to do with my arms or how wide to smile.

'You have to!' She was insistent, brandishing the phone around as if she might cause someone a concussion. 'You guys look stunning together.'

The word hit me like a ten-tonne truck again. I hated repetition. I hated hearing the same word or sound over and over again. It grated on my senses. It made my skin itch and I just couldn't help it.

'I think we look resplendent, actually!'

'Oh my God, you do!' the phone-wielder said. 'That's why I *must* have a photo of the splendid couple.'

'*Re*splendent,' I corrected her.

'Exactly! Now put your arm around him. Move closer, closer . . . come on now, closer.' She waved her hand at us, and I shuffled towards Andrew.

'Put your arm around her,' she called, and I heard Andrew ask if it was okay from next to me. I nodded and readied myself for the feel of his arm. His arm slinked around my waist, and I wondered where he was going to choose to settle his hand. On the small of my back? My waist? His arm stopped slinking and I waited for the hand to connect, only it didn't.

'Where should I put my hand?' he whispered through gritted teeth.

'I don't know. You choose.'

Andrew's hand poked out from the side of my body, hovering suspiciously above my hip like a UFO over a cornfield. I waited for it to land. It didn't.

'Oh, for God's sake!' I grabbed his hand and flattened it to my waist. His hand was big, and my waist felt tiny beneath it. His fingers felt like they stretched on for ever, like they could wrap around my entire body, even though I knew that was impossible.

'Smile!' the Apple iPhone photographer said. I attempted a smile and she burst out laughing. 'You're so funny, Pippa!'

But there was nothing funny about what I was doing: I was genuinely trying to smile. If I'd known beforehand that I was going into a situation where I needed to have my photo taken, I'd have practiced my smile in the mirror. But today I had not done that. I tried again, and she laughed once more. But when I tried for the third time and she didn't laugh, I think she finally realized I wasn't joking.

'I'm not good at smiling on cue!' I said. 'Sorry.'

'Okay, no problem. Why don't you put her out of her misery and kiss her instead. That'll make a great picture.'

The word 'kiss' felt like it punched a hole in the air between us. Andrew and I looked at each other. This seemed like a necessary moment. In fact, I would rather kiss him than attempt another disastrous smile. Andrew raised his brows, and I gave the most imperceptible nod. We leaned towards each other slowly, and I tried not to grimace, or something equally off-putting. Our noses touched briefly, and then our lips. I heard an 'aaaah' from the amateur photographer.

'Perfect. Hold it for a moment,' she said.

I kept my lips pressed to his.

'Hang on. I need to turn the flash on – hold it!' she said.

We must have looked ridiculous like that, standing next to each other, lips pressed together but not actually kissing.

'Another second! I turned on the torch instead of the flash. Can you believe it?' She laughed, and now this situation was just farcical. How much longer did we need to pose like this?

'Oh, for heaven's sake,' I said against his mouth, and then I kissed him. Properly. Not a silly lip press but an actual kiss. Slow, soft, lips slightly parted. I could taste and smell the champagne on his lips. I felt warm pressure on my waist as his hand tightened. His mouth followed suit and then, for a second, a warm, wet, glorious second that sent a bolt down my spine, the tip of his tongue grazed my lip. A light flashed around us and I pulled away.

CHAPTER 10

'You kissed me with tongue,' I said to Andrew as we got into the Uber and drove back to our hotels.

'You kissed me back with tongue! And I didn't intend on using tongue, but when you opened your mouth like that—'

'I only opened my mouth because we weren't really kissing and I thought it was starting to look strange,' I said.

'You opened your mouth to make it look more authentic?'

'Exactly,' I concluded.

'Sorry. I didn't mean to use my tongue – it was just . . . muscle memory.'

'What?'

'Like riding a bike, or . . . you know what I mean.'

'I don't actually,' I said.

'When you opened your mouth, it signalled to me that a real kiss was happening. So my tongue kind of joined it, without really thinking about it. Besides, it's not like I stuck my entire tongue in your mouth. It barely grazed your lip.'

He was right, of course. It had just grazed my lip and, perhaps like him, my tongue muscle memory had kicked in too, because the tip of my tongue had somehow reached out and brushed his lips as well.

Andrew sighed next to me. 'Sorry. I apologize, I know we said no tongue.'

It was my turn to sigh. 'I tongued you back,' I said, and we sat in silence for a while. The Uber driver eyed us in the rear-view mirror and I narrowed my eyes at him disapprovingly.

'You're a really good kisser,' I stated. 'It was quite hot, actually.'

'Uh . . . thanks.' He wriggled in his seat.

'Did that make you feel awkward?' I asked.

'No. Sort of. I mean . . . just a little.'

The Uber driver looked at us again.

'Hey! Eyes to the road,' I said, and pointed at him. 'Please,' I added quickly, in case he thought I was rude and now wanted to throw me out of the car or, worse, leave me a bad review, which had happened before, after I'd told an Uber driver that his car stank.

'You're a good kisser too.' I almost didn't hear Andrew say that, it was so soft.

'I know,' I said, because I was a good kisser. I'd practiced a lot to become one. 'But let's not kiss again. Kissing usually leads to sex, and I don't want to have sex with you! Even if the kiss does indicate we would probably be sexually compatible.'

'Uh . . . sure!' Andrew said. His cheeks had gone red. I never understood why people became so shy and strange when talking about anything sexual. But they did, and I always had to remember that. It was a pity one couldn't just have frank conversations about sex with people. It would make it all so much easier.

That night in the hotel room, after I'd slipped out of the red dress and into a warm bath, I found my mind drifting off towards that kiss. I searched through my memory banks, running over all the information I'd gathered over the years about kissing, to pinpoint exactly what it was that had felt so good. But I couldn't quite find it. I think it was that mysterious, intangible thing at play again. The technique had been so simple: lips parted, tip of tongue making gentle lip contact. Nothing special. But it had definitely felt special. Completely different to all the other kisses that I'd had.

I climbed into the large hotel bed and nestled my head into my special pillow nest. My pillows always smelled good; I sprayed a lavender essential oil on them. I found that aromatherapy really did calm you. It engaged one of your senses in a pleasant way, making it easier to calm the other senses down. I took a deep whiff of my pillows: tonight had gone well. Better than expected. In fact, in some ways, I had even enjoyed it, which I'd not expected. I took another deep breath, put my AirPods on, turned on the relaxing rain sounds I listened to most nights and fell asleep.

CHAPTER 11

The winelands are always beautiful. Their beauty is a predictable one, though. Chocolate-box, postcard predictability. Everything looked so perfect out here, as if it had all been curated and stage-directed this way. As if there was a stylist responsible for this entire area, making sure all of it, every last component, conformed to an aesthetic standard. I liked that. I liked predictable patterns that were aesthetically pleasing. So I understood why people came here, why whenever someone had a special party, a wedding, an engagement or a reunion in the Cape, they flocked to the winelands for the event. Well, there was also the wine, of course – another attraction for most people, although, for me personally, wine had never really held much allure.

My father loves wine, and for one of his birthdays my mother had invited all their friends around, as well as a famous sommelier. Too young to drink, but intrigued by it all, I'd listened to this man extol the aromas of herbs, subtle florals, notes of spring fruits. Roasted nut, old tobacco, autumn leaves. Spicy, velvety, earthy, waxy, silky and suede. His descriptors were endless and had transported me into the depths of my imagination, where I'd pictured textures and flavors I'd never experienced before. When the party was over and my parents were asleep, I found myself in the kitchen with all the used glasses of wine. I'd imagined sipping the leftovers and my pallet exploding with the most exotic flavors imaginable: the butterscotch, pine and aniseed. It had all sounded so incredible and my curiosity was piqued. I poured the first drop of blood-red wine on my tongue and was sure it must have been a mistake. It was horrendous. Like cork and coal, and it felt sharp and bitter in my mouth. I raced to the kitchen sink and washed my mouth out, confused by the terrible letdown. I was convinced I must have chosen the only bad one. I dipped my finger into the next glass and brought it to my tongue. Again, sharp, vile, nauseating. Where was the orange blossom, the violet and nutmeg? I was utterly perplexed. None of what I was tasting was lively, delicate or austere. It was not well structured and harmonious. The man had clearly used the wrong adjectives. I was so disappointed that night that I'd hardly ever drunk wine again and considered it to be one of the greatest culinary cons. I'm convinced that people just pretend to taste what they're told to taste.

The driver dropped us off and we found ourselves at the bottom of a long, cobbled driveway. We walked up to the old Cape Dutch house, the long driveway flanked on either side by rows and rows of precisely planted grapevines. I stopped to look down one of the rows and was met with a perfection that even I was taken aback by. These vines were in dead-straight lines and, as I walked past their neat rows, a sense of calm settled in me.

The white Cape Dutch house in front of us rose up out of the greenery like a sculptural piece of art and, behind it, the mountain was draped in white cloud. This was the thing about Cape Town, its defining characteristic if you like; the thing that made it unique and special was always the mountain. And no matter where you went in Cape Town, like a lighthouse guiding you to safety, it was always there.

On the terrace of the house, red and white umbrellas stood side by side – our school colors. At every cultural or sporting event, those exact umbrellas had been dragged out and stuck in the ground. Underneath the umbrellas, like something that buzzed and bustled, were all the girls and their partners. I hoped that no one would see us coming and we could slip into the crowd unnoticed. But alas.

'Pippa! Andrew!' someone shouted. A chorus of what were clearly already slightly inebriated 'hellooooo's with long 'o' sounds rung out. I followed Andrew's direction as he gave everyone a casual-looking wave. He was so comfortable; how did he do that? How did he wave so unself-consciously, so effortlessly, when it felt so awkward and disingenuous to put my hand up in the air in that manner and flap it about?

'Hurry, we're already on the second wine pairing,' called Palesa, beckoning us over with her bejewelled hand. Palesa was one of the people I'd remembered easily. She was, after all, a descendant of the Sotho King, and thus royalty. You don't easily forget having a member of the royal family in your maths and science classes.

'You ready for this?' Andrew asked, clearly sensing my obvious apprehension, since my body had stiffened like an ironing board.

'Absolutely not,' I said, but continued walking towards the terrace.

'Don't worry, it'll be fine,' he said, and I gave him a small nod.

'Thank you,' I replied softly.

'Hey, what are fake fiancés for?' He held his hand out, but then quickly pulled it away. 'Wait, are we holding hands today or not?'

I inspected his hand. It looked clean; his palms looked dry.

'Mmmm, I don't know. Maybe. But no kissing.'

'My lips are sealed.' He held his hand out again and I slipped mine into his.

'Well, technically, they're not. You're talking.'

Andrew chuckled. 'I can't argue with that.' We walked up to the terrace hand in hand and were met by a long table with wine glasses and charcuterie platters on it, and sommeliers in black suits. And then we were inundated with hugs and greetings as if we were all long-lost friends, even though I hadn't seen any of them for ten years. It was difficult to explain their sudden interest and enthusiasm in me, although I'm sure it had less to do with me, actually, and more to do with the man I had on my arm. I think Andrew gave me a kind of status I'd never had before. A kind of status I never thought I'd ever be able to achieve. And then, the first of the wine glasses was thrust into my hand.

'And what imaginary things am I supposed to taste with this one?' I asked the sommelier.

'It has notes of pineapple, ma'am,' he said enthusiastically.

'Really?' I raised my brows at him. 'And is it full-bodied?' I asked, and a few of my old classmates let out amused sounds.

'No, it's actually light-bodied with a floral bouquet.' He looked less enthused now.

'A floral bouquet,' I repeated, bringing the wine to my nose and smelling it.

'It's a crisp wine with a lively, fruit flavor,' he added.

'Of pineapple?'

'And some secondary notes of vanilla and a hint of truffle on the palate.'

'Would that be black or white truffle?' I asked, and heard a few laughs, even though I wasn't trying to be funny.

'White truffle. With an ample mouthfeel.'

'Is it buttery?' I asked.

'No, actually, it's supple and very easy drinking.'

'Give me one of those glasses.' Palesa held her hand out. 'You have me intrigued now.'

'Me too.' Yanilla joined in, and soon more glasses were handed out.

'Would sir like a glass too?' he asked Andrew. I couldn't tell whether the sommelier was angry, but there was a bite in his tone, that's for sure.

Andrew accepted the glass, and a few more people asked for glasses as well. A small crowd had now gathered around me and the sommelier. As if we were about to have a boxing match.

'Well, who's going first?' Yanilla asked, raising the glass to her mouth.

'I think Pippa should go first,' Andrew said.

I took a sip of the wine, trying, this time, to keep an open mind. Even though I believed it to be utter nonsense. A few others took sips, but no one said a word after we'd all swallowed.

'Well?' one of the Katies asked me.

I wasn't sure when this had become *my* wine-tasting event.

I looked up at the sommelier and shook my head. 'Nope! None of that. No pineapple and liveliness, and how on earth can a liquid be supple?'

Everyone around me started laughing. It seemed like a nervous laugh at first, but grew.

'I'm so glad you said that. I thought I was the only one who didn't get it,' Yanilla said.

'It tastes great, but I also don't get the pineapple,' Palesa added.

'I've always felt like such an idiot because I never got it either,' Katie said, polishing off the entire glass.

The sommelier's face dropped and I felt bad immediately.

'But you're doing an excellent job. You're very knowledgeable,' I quickly added, but then realized how patronizing that sounded. 'It's probably us – our palates are not sophisticated enough, our olfactory senses are clearly inferior to yours.' He looked at me blankly. 'It's delicious. Really, very tasty and' – I took another sip – 'and maybe, now that I think about it, perhaps I can taste pineapple.' I made eye contact with the sommelier. 'Sorry, now I'm just lying. I cannot taste any fruit.'

'I taste the pineapple,' Andrew said, and the sommelier turned his attention to him. 'And something else, like lychee?'

'Yes! Exactly, there are hints of lychee in it,' the man confirmed.

'Well, there you go!' I pointed at Andrew now, delighted for the sommelier's sake that someone had tasted something. 'He gets it!'

'Did you *really* taste the lychee?' I asked Andrew when we were alone.

'No, but while everyone was distracted I googled the wine. I felt sorry for the guy.' He smiled at me.

'Was I mean to him? Should I go and apologize?'

Andrew shook his head, his smile growing. 'You were honest. You say what other people are thinking but are too afraid to say.'

I didn't respond. I'd heard that a few times in my life before, but usually I interpreted that as negative. But this time, that wasn't how it felt.

Alcohol has always done one of two things to me. One, it makes me want to run away, find a soft corner, curl up into it and drift into a warm, relaxing sleep, or two, it knocks down all my social inhibitions, all my awkwardness, and suddenly, like a butterfly emerged from a cocoon, I turn into a social creature who moves and glides through the crowds with an ease I do not possess in a sober reality. I'm not sure how I feel about this socially lubricated version of myself, though. I find her somewhat embarrassing, but others seem to like her. They certainly want to talk to her more than they want to talk to me under normal circumstances, where I've been described as 'prickly and standoffish'.

But today I was none of those things. I'd become the most socially amenable version of myself that had ever existed.

'Why didn't we ever hang out at school?' Palesa asked me. She'd draped an arm through mine after the wine-tasting incident and seemed to have attached herself to me. Normally, I would have hated this, but today, social Pippa was going with the flow.

'I guess we moved in different circles,' I offered.

She let go of my arm and stood in front of me. 'Isn't that so stupid? How we all did that? Cluster into these little groups and never get to know anyone outside of them. It's so ridiculous, looking back on it ten years down the line.'

A few others joined in the conversation and agreed.

'I'm going to be honest,' Yanilla said to Larissa, who had also joined us. 'I was always so intimidated by you at school.'

'What?' Larissa looked taken aback. She and Yanilla had shared a dorm room.

'You always seemed so sorted. Nothing ever fazed you. I remember, my first night there, I went to hide in the bathroom to cry, and you always seemed so strong. I never wanted you to see how much I missed home.'

'Oh my God, seriously!' Larissa pulled Yanilla into a hug, and the hug seemed to grow as more and more people joined in and agreed with the sentiment, that we'd really not gotten to know each other properly at school. Everyone, including myself, started promising all sorts of things out loud that I knew I would *never* be able to deliver on, like keeping in touch and getting together more often. In that moment, though, I'm sure I *really* meant it.

As more wine flowed, so my lips loosened. I retold the story of the emergency landing that I'd had to deal with, much to the delight of all the people at the table. Andrew and I fielded questions about how many times we encountered emergencies. And when I'd told them just how many planes I handled in an hour, how many planes were up there all at once and how close they were to each other, they all gasped, shook their heads and vowed that flying would never be the same again. Andrew and I had become somewhat of a fascination, and for a moment I felt what it must have been like to be one of the popular kids at school. God, it was utterly exhausting, and I'm sure even more so when one didn't have a spiritous liquid running through one's veins.

But my new-found social freedom didn't stop there. I laughed at their jokes – even though I didn't understand most of them – I engaged in conversation about their children, congratulating them on their amazing ability to juggle the pressures of motherhood and work, and shaking my head and saying things like 'I just don't know how you do it all.' They congratulated me on my amazing career and marvelled at how, on top of being an air traffic controller, I'd received my Bachelor of Science in Aeronautics and Aviation Management and wanted to run my own airport one day. They said things like 'Well, you were always the smartest at school,' and Katie even admitted to sitting next to me in maths so she could copy my work. In fact, she'd thanked me profusely, as I was the only reason she'd passed maths.

Sober, I would have found this admission appalling but, like this, alcohol surging through the wiring of my brain, I only laughed and held my glass up for her to clink. We toasted and laughed and reminisced about things I could not remember but laughed along to anyway, because I was that way inclined. And Andrew played his role to perfection, like an actor delivering just the right lines at just the right time. He'd pulled my chair out when I'd gotten up to go to the toilet, and picked my bag up when it dropped off the table – all the things I imagine a real fiancé might do. And I was so grateful he was here with me.

With Andrew by my side, who had such an ease and lightness around people, I felt like I could be some other version of myself, and for those few hours while there, I quite liked this version, even though I knew I would pay the price of exhaustion afterwards for all this socializing. Socializing had that effect on me. It wasn't that I didn't like it all the time; sometimes (in small doses), it was enjoyable. But it was the after-effects that were hard to handle. Socializing left me with an energy hangover that could last anywhere up to a week.

At the end of what had turned out to be a very, very long afternoon, we began walking back towards the Uber. My head was spinning, especially when I closed my eyes, and my legs flapped about and wobbled like . . .

'Sheets in the wind!' I stopped walking and said triumphantly.

'What?' Andrew asked.

'I am like a sheet in the wind! Well, three sheets, to be exact.' I burst out laughing – I finally got it. I had a sudden urge to call my mother and tell her that I finally understood what she'd been talking about when she described Aunt Lulu as someone who was always 'three sheets to the wind', but didn't.

'I think it's best to get the sheets home then,' he smiled,

supporting me by the elbow as I navigated the uneven paving of the driveway.

'Was this driveway like this when we got here?' I asked, astounded that I hadn't noticed how uneven it was before. 'I think I might have drunk too much,' I said, my neck feeling less like it was able to support my head. 'But it's very deceptive. They bring you so many of those big glasses with tiny sips at the bottom and you don't think you're drinking that much until—' I hiccupped mid-sentence, and Andrew laughed.

'You're a hiccupping sheet in the wind?'

'Exactly!' I stopped walking and looked at Andrew as seriously as I could, although there did seem to be two of him. 'I feel bad for lying to them all. They were all so nice, and I was lying to them the whole time.'

'That was kind of the point,' he said.

'I know. But now I just feel terrible. I hate lying in general, and I just lied to everyone there. And they were all soooooo nice.'

His lips curled into a small smile. 'You've had a lot to drink.'

'You know what I have to do . . .' I pushed past him with a sense of purpose.

'Wait, where are you going?' Andrew followed me.

'I have to tell them all. I have to go there and tell them all that I was lying, that we were lying, that we don't even know each other, that this was all a giant deception.'

'No, no, nooooo.' He ran in front of me and blocked my approach. 'Don't. Trust me. You'll regret it when you wake up.'

'I'll never regret telling the truth.'

'Well then, it wasn't a lie.'

'Yes, it was!'

Andrew fell down on one knee. 'Pippa, marry me?' He took me by the hands.

'What?'

'Quickly, say yes, and then it won't be a lie.'

I scrunched my face up at him. 'That makes zero sense.'

'I'll take that as a yes.' He leapt up and then started walking me down the driveway again.

'We are not engaged!' I struggled to keep up with him as he scurried down the uneven road. 'I need to go back and tell them.'

'Trust me, you don't.'

'How do you know?'

'Let me be that friend who stops you from doing the equivalent of a drunk dial,' he chuckled.

'What's a drunk dial?'

'Haven't you ever phoned an ex you shouldn't have after a few too many drinks?'

'No!' I said. 'I don't drink this much, and I hardly have any exes to call. God, I feel sick!' I stopped walking, moaned and clutched my stomach. 'My head is spinning and I feel sweaty in these stupid clothes that my mom chose for me.' I lifted the hem of my dress and flapped it up and down, trying to force air up. The cool air rushed in and brought the temperature of my skin down a few degrees.

'You clearly need to stop taking fashion advice from your mother,' Andrew said, taking my elbow again, which I was grateful for, because I'd almost tripped on the garden tool that the nearby gardeners had left in the road.

'But she's so persuasive. No, *persuasive* is not the right word, a better synonym is *forceful*.' I lifted the hem of my dress and flapped it again. This time, though, I flapped it way too high and, without any kind of warning, Andrew's free hand shot up and pushed my skirt back down.

'Let's get into the Uber and put the aircon on,' he said.

'Do you think the gardeners saw my panties?' I asked Andrew, pointing at the men trimming the hedge. They quickly looked away.

'I think it's safe to say that everyone nearby saw your panties!'

I laughed. 'At least I look smouldering hot in them.' Because I did. I always prided myself on wearing the best underwear. In fact, buying underwear was probably the only unnecessary purchase I ever made. Instead of buying a sensible pack of cotton panties, I bought mine from a lingerie shop. Totally overpriced, but worth it. I liked wearing lace; it allowed for breathability. I did not wear G-strings, though. I only wore non-underwired bras, and it all needed to match. I disliked things that were mismatched, and today I was wearing one of my favorite sets, a Lilac Rose lace set from La Perla, pleasing on the eye to anyone.

'Did *you* see my panties?' I asked.

'Like I said, everyone nearby saw them.'

'They're one of my favorite sets,' I said as my foot slid across a stone. I tried to stop the slip, but my ankle twisted and my entire body wobbled.

'Shit!' I hissed as the forward momentum carried me. I swung my arms in the air but wasn't able to stop myself from falling into the lavender hedge.

'You okay?' Andrew tried to pull me out of the hedge, but my body was sinking lower and lower into it. 'Grab my hand,' he said. I thrust my palm into his and in one swift move he managed to pull me back onto my feet.

'You're strong!' I said, straightening my dress once I was upright again. I touched my head. A few lavender twigs had lodged themselves in my hair, and I pulled them out. I looked back at the once neatly trimmed, symmetrical hedge and realized I'd put a massive dent in it.

'I'm sorry,' I shouted over to the gardeners, who were both now staring at me. 'I didn't mean to! I can help you fix it!' I started trying to pull the lavender back up, but each time I did it flopped back down. I'd snapped all the stems.

'Stop, stop.' Andrew took my hand gently. 'You're making it worse.' He began pulling me away again.

'Am I? I didn't mean to.'

'I know you didn't,' he said. 'Look, there's our Uber.' He pointed at the car waiting at the bottom of the driveway. 'Nearly there,' he said, walking so slowly that I was sure we were almost at a standstill. When we finally reached the car he held the door open for me and I climbed in. The Uber driver was also staring at me.

'Did you also see my panties?' I asked him. His uneasy look away told me all I needed to know.

'Sorry for exposing myself like that. I don't usually do that, but I was just trying to cool down. It's very hot today, isn't it?'

'Shall I crank up the AC?' he asked.

'Yes! Thank you!' I sat back in my seat and, as I did, my stomach let out a loud noise. 'I'm hungry. I didn't eat enough. How are you supposed to line your stomach adequately with food when they only bring you tiny blocks of cheese and chocolates and little dried fruits? No wonder I feel so inebriated. Are you inebriated?' I looked at Andrew and my eyes quickly drifted down to his lips. I usually talked to people's lips. I found that people didn't really notice you weren't making direct eye contact with them if you talked to their lips. I could describe everyone's lips and teeth to utter perfection but could hardly recall what color eyes they had, except Andrew, of course. His were so startling it was hard to miss.

'I have definitely had one too many sips of wine.' He smiled at me. 'But I stopped when they started bringing out all that dessert wine with the baked cinnamon apple pies and mini crème brûlées.'

'Maybe I should have stopped there too,' I lamented, feeling sorry for myself that I had sipped that Moscato and too-sweet port. 'I have regrets,' I moaned again. The car started moving and my regrets increased as the motion made me feel even worse. I tried to distract myself by looking out the window, but the scenery felt like it was flying by faster than what was normal. My regrets were increasing exponentially.

'I hate feeling like this.' I clutched my head and moaned once more.

'Not to eavesdrop,' the Uber driver said, 'but would you like me to stop so you can' – he paused and looked like he was searching for the words – 'get some fresh air?' I realized he was trying to use a euphemism for 'throw up' or something equally horrific like that, something that if I landed up doing, I would feel utterly mortified about for the next year, at least.

I nodded at the man in the mirror and was soon standing on the side of the road. I took big gulps of fresh air, but it did little for my spinning head.

'I don't usually do this,' I said to Andrew as I sat down on a rock feeling violently embarrassed for myself. 'I really, really don't do this!' I insisted. For some reason it had suddenly become important to me that Andrew didn't think I was the kind of person who became unreasonably drunk at social events, flashed everyone their underwear, fell into bushes, acted like a fool and sat on rocks on the side of the road clutching their heads.

'I believe you,' he said.

The small road I was perched on like some kind of a rock rabbit was surrounded by more vineyards. The mountain, once again, rose up behind the fields and, with the sun setting behind it, patches of orange glowed against the rocky outcrops. The air was cool and crisp and I inhaled bucket-sized gulps of it, hoping that by some miracle of science that was yet to be discovered oxygen was able to counteract the effects of alcohol in the bloodstream.

'I'm so sorry,' I apologized to the Uber driver, who was sitting in the car. 'For this, and for the underwear.'

'Take as long as you need – as long as you know you pay a waiting fee.'

I shot the man a thumbs-up as the taste of bile crept up the back of my throat. This was so undignified. So terribly, terribly undignified.

'This might help.' The Uber driver produced a small bottle of mineral water and passed it over to Andrew. I ripped the lid off with gusto and took three large sips.

'I really don't do this,' I moaned, at the driver now.

'Honey, this is the winelands. No one makes it out of the winelands in one piece. You are not the first, and you will certainly not be the last, and as for you flashing me, trust me, I've seen a lot worse. A lot!' His admission went a little way in curbing the feelings inside.

I continued to sip the water and gulp in the fresh air, and after a while I felt my sense of gravity return and the spinning began to subside. I heard a noise overhead and looked up.

'Embraer Legacy.' I pointed at the sky.

Andrew looked up. 'Only one of the best jets in the world,' he added.

'Have you flown one?' I asked.

He shook his head. 'Not yet, but it is on my list of planes I would love to fly one day.'

'It's good to have a list of things like that,' I commented.

'You seem to have a very impressive list too, like running your own airport one day?'

I smiled at the thought of it.

'You'd be amazing at that,' he said.

I looked up at him and almost cried. I think that was the best compliment anyone had ever given me, and I was about to say something when my stomach let out a loud rumble. 'I feel much better, but now I'm starving.'

'I have an idea,' Andrew said, pulling me up off the rock. 'It's the perfect cure for too much to drink.'

Chapter 12

We sat on the bed together, our endless room-service bounty stretched out around us. And with every single bite of fatty, gooey, salty food, I felt the alcohol in my blood system dissipate. Andrew had been *so* right: this was the only way to douse the alcohol in my stomach. I stuffed my face with many a marvellous food while we flipped back and forth through the stations, until we both exclaimed at once:

'This is my favorite TV show!'

'Me too!' we said, again in unison, and laughed.

'And this is my favorite episode too,' I said, pointing to the screen. I was about to stuff a handful of fries into my face, when I stopped. 'Maybe "favorite" is not a good word. It was very tragic, of course – many people lost their lives – so I don't mean I like that part of it, but—'

'I know exactly what you mean,' Andrew said, reassuring me that 'favorite' had not been the most insensitive choice of word. The crash had happened in 2005 and I remember being glued to the news. I'd cut out all the newspaper clippings about it and put them all in my aviation scrapbook. A scrapbook that I'd started at an early age, when I'd decided that I was going to have a career in aviation.

'Air Traffic Control couldn't contact the plane for two hours,' I said. 'Can you imagine what that would have been like?'

'You wouldn't have panicked though,' Andrew said casually.

'No, I never panic,' I stated. 'They sent two fighter pilots up to see if the plane had been hijacked,' I added to the story, even though I could tell that Andrew knew it well. Everyone in aviation knew this story. It was the story of the plane that had crashed into a hillside in Greece, sadly killing all souls onboard. Andrew and I watched transfixed as the re-enactments of the flight began. The passengers boarding the plane in a festive holiday mood, oblivious to what was about to happen next. After take-off, a loss of cabin pressure had incapacitated the entire crew, leaving the plane to fly unmanned and on autopilot until it simply ran out of fuel. It had flown in the air like a ghost plane for hours before crashing, making it one of the most mysterious airplane disasters in history. By the end of the episode, Andrew and I had consumed our entire room-service feast and I was feeling full and tired and, thankfully, no longer drunk. It was only at this stage, with less alcohol in me, that I became aware of my physical body in space and, as a consequence, Andrew's too.

Our shoulders and outstretched legs were almost touching as we both rested our backs and heads against the headboard. He'd rolled up his sleeves and kicked his shoes off. This casualness made me feel incredibly attracted to him, for some inexplicable reason. His forearms were sculptural and, like this, with his trousers pulled tighter against him, a muscular thigh could be seen bulging through the fabric. I stole a sideways glance at his face. He had the perfect profile too. Sharp nose that was neither too big nor too small. A jawline that looked like it could cut through sheets of glass – nah, chisel down blocks of concrete. His face was perfect from every angle. This man would probably still look good if he was dangled upside down and all the blood rushed to his head and made his eyes bulge.

I felt warm again, as if the alcohol had gotten a second wind. But it wasn't that. It was Andrew's very obvious physical attractiveness and closeness that was making me feel like this. I shuffled right, trying to move as far away from him as possible without making it obvious. But in trying to move, my leg bumped his and a strange feeling settled in my stomach. I stole another glance and watched as his Adam's apple bobbed up and down in a manner that told me he'd just swallowed hard. I bit the inside of my cheek.

Shit, I was being such a pervert! Side-eye gawking his face and legs and neck. Some less than flattering synonyms for *pervert* floated through my mind: *devious*, *weirdo*. But Andrew was seriously the most attractive male I had ever laid eyes on, and being this close to him, I simply couldn't help what was clearly some biological reaction to him. Perhaps he was giving off a pheromone that I was unable to resist. I felt him shuffle next to me and hoped he didn't know what I was thinking. But what he said next led me to believe that maybe, just maybe, he did.

'I'd better get back to my hotel,' he said, and stood up more quickly than he needed to.

He knew!

'Yes. Of course. Late.' I fake-looked at my watch and wondered if I should attempt a fake yawn. I decided against it.

He started moving for the door. I stopped him.

'About tomorrow, the air force museum and aquarium. You don't have to come if you don't want to. But I'm going,' I said quickly, not wanting him to feel obliged or awkward.

'Are you kidding? I'd love to come.' He smiled, and I could see that he absolutely meant it. I smiled back. I couldn't remember the last time someone had actually wanted to do anything like this with me. It wasn't often that I met someone with such a shared passion for my narrow set of interests.

'By the way, what did you think about my incorporation of fish into last night's conversation?' he asked, grinning even more.

'I thought it was a little over the top, actually.'

'A wedding on a glass-bottomed boat floating over a coral reef?'

'Although I suppose it would be beautiful,' I said, trying to imagine what it would be like, saying your vows under a bright blue sky, tropical, crystal-clear waters below, a coral reef teeming with color.

'You're more than welcome to use that idea for when you do get married.'

'I doubt I'll ever be getting married,' I said matter-of-factly.

'Me neither, probably. Not that I don't *want* to get married one day, but it would have to be someone very understanding of my career. I'm already married to my career.'

'Me too!' I said, and quite liked the sound of that saying. It gave my career the kind of gravitas I think it deserved. It wasn't just a job to me, it was a spouse and, as such, I invested a lot of time and energy into it.

'My wife would need to be very understanding. Last year I flew over Easter, missed two of my sisters' birthdays and Christmas Day.'

'I also worked Christmas Day last year,' I mused. We were both silent for a while, and I wondered if he was weighing up his chances of ever finding someone who would put up with that kind of an arrangement. But, for me, a husband that was away for long periods of time would be ideal. In fact, it would be perfect.

If I ever did find someone, I'd like to find someone exactly like that. Someone busy who had their own life, so I would get to pursue mine. Someone who wasn't always there so I could still have alone time, something that was very, very important to me. I don't think I could ever be in a relationship with someone who was always in my space, I needed a reprieve, a moment to breathe, and having a partner who travelled a lot would do just that. So, in many ways, Andrew was the ideal boyfriend for me. If this was real, of course.

'Anyway, goodnight,' he said.

'Wait.' I got up off the bed. 'I think I acted like a total fool tonight.'

He smiled. 'Not really.'

'I was flapping my dress around, having to sit on rocks and falling all over the place. I'm very embarrassed.'

'Don't be. It wasn't as bad as you think.'

'Are you sure?'

'You were totally fine.'

'I think you're trying to downplay it now.'

'Not at all. You were actually great tonight. Everyone else thought so too. Didn't you notice how they all flocked to you?'

'I suppose,' I said.

'Anyway, goodnight.' He gave me a small wave and then closed the door behind him.

CHAPTER 13

'How are you feeling this morning?' Andrew asked when I appeared downstairs in the hotel lobby the next morning.

'Better than I thought I would, actually,' I confessed. 'I'm looking forward to the museum and aquarium.'

'Me too. And I've been to the museum a hundred times.'

'Me too!' I confessed.

We climbed into another Uber. Usually, I didn't like taking taxis. I preferred driving myself; I always feel that you have more control over a situation if you do, but it had been okay here. When we pulled up to the museum I couldn't wait to get inside and had to physically stop myself from running. I could feel Andrew right behind me, and I could see that he wanted to get in as much as I did. We couldn't pay fast enough and then, when we walked inside, we both exhaled slowly. I suppose some people might do that when walking into a holy, sacred space like a church. This was our church today. We entered the giant warehouse and, laid out in front of us, in a manner that felt like candy in a candy store, were dozens of historic planes. Some on the ground; some suspended from the ceiling, as if flying. I flapped my fingers at the side of my body. Sometimes I did this when I was excited too. When the excitement felt so large that it needed a physical outlet.

'Wow!' Andrew's voice had a reverence to it. Very different from the reaction that other people gave when I brought them here. Whenever my parents came to visit me on a weekend, I'd drag them here. The sincerity of their 'wow's diminished over the years, becoming less and less enthusiastic, but mine hadn't. Every time I came here, it was as if I was seeing it for the first time all over again.

We ambled around, weaving in and out of the old World War planes. It was incredible to imagine that, once upon a time, these very planes had seen war. I think war is such an unnecessary part of the human existence. War isn't productive. All it causes is suffering, and in my opinion there's always a more practical way to deal with disputes.

'I hate to think that these planes were involved in war,' Andrew said, as if thinking the exact same thing I was.

'War is so illogical,' I replied.

'Completely unnecessary,' he added, walking towards my favorite plane.

'The Vampire 277,' I said on a long, slow out breath.

'My favorite fighter jet.'

'ME TOO!' Shit, I'd said that way too loudly, but the sudden and overwhelming elation of having my sentiments echoed by someone else was just too exciting.

'It's the twin tail for me,' I said, pointing at the craft's unusual tail.

'I like the name too,' Andrew added.

'Vampire. It's a good name,' I agreed, and we smiled at each other. It felt like I could physically feel his smile. It gave me this hyper-awareness of my own lips and facial muscles. As if all I was as a person was a lump of lips and facial muscles. It felt strange and somewhat disorientating to be paying this much attention to my lips.

'Let's go outside,' I stuttered, which was very unlike me, but my lips were not doing what my brain was telling them to do. We headed outside to look at the truly large planes, the ones that could not be fitted inside a warehouse. The sun was shining, no clouds in the sky, and the planes glinted in the light as if covered in glitter. I could imagine what they would have looked like flying overhead: silver birds. And the sounds they would have made! Planes are far quieter today, but back then they would have roared as they raced through the sky, shaking the ground beneath you as they passed overhead with their turbo jet engines. I liked that, the overly dramatic noises that some planes make, and sometimes on weekends, I packed a picnic and drove to one of the small airfields that light planes took off from. I sat and ate my food while watching and listening to them. The violent noises that the small Cessnas made as they took off, almost sounding like their engines were about to explode. I always held my breath in anticipation as they climbed, and only breathed again when I was satisfied that their engines remained intact. Andrew and I walked around outside for about an hour, before the heat became too sweltering to handle.

'Don't know about you, but I could do with some aircon and a cool drink,' he said.

'Shall we go?' I asked.

'If you're done? I could carry on, but the heat is getting a little intense.'

I looked up at the sky again, shielding my eyes from the sun. It was the start of summer and the temperatures were soaring.

'I love summer,' I said, without thinking.

'Me too.' Andrew slid up to me and also looked into the sky. 'Are we looking for something?'

'Not really.' A thought popped into my head. One of those random ones that I always felt compelled to share when they came to me.

'Do you believe in UFOs?' I asked.

Andrew stepped back. The move was so sudden and decisive that it caught my attention immediately.

'What?' I asked quickly.

'You'll think I'm talking crap.'

'No, I won't. What?'

He paused for a moment and looked at me solemnly. As if weighing something up. 'Okay, I'm not making this up. I'm being serious.'

'I believe you,' I replied.

'So, I was doing a night flight to Cape Town a couple of years ago and we were flying over the free state – I remember exactly where we were. We'd just flown past Beauford West in the Karoo and . . .' He paused for a moment and closed his eyes, as if trying to find something in his mind. 'There was this light. It looked like it was on the horizon, which I thought was really odd, because I knew there were no towns or settlements there. We were flying over the open desert. I looked down at my instruments for a moment, and when I looked back up, the light had moved. But it had moved kilometers in a few seconds. Impossible, right? No plane I know can move that quickly, not even a military jet.'

'Did you call ATC to see if there was anything on radar?'

He nodded. 'Nothing. They said there was nothing there.'

'Which is impossible,' I added, as the hairs on the back of my neck bristled.

'Look, I don't know what it was. I'm not saying it was an alien spacecraft from another galaxy, but it was definitely an unidentified flying object.'

'Huh.' I looked back at the sky thoughtfully.

'What would you think if you saw something like that?' he asked.

I looked back at him and thought about it for a while. 'There are a hundred billion stars in our galaxy. One of them, the sun, supports life. There are possibly two hundred billion galaxies in our universe, and one galaxy, the Milky Way, supports life. Unless our solar system is a total anomaly among hundreds and hundreds of billions, then I doubt we are alone in this universe. Whether other life forms possess the advanced technology for intergalactic travel, I can't say. But if you're asking me if I think it's possible that what you saw may have been a visitor from another planet, then I would say it's definitely *not* impossible.'

'So you don't think I'm crazy?' he asked, looking genuinely relieved.

'I think it would be crazy to discount what you saw, and crazy not to investigate whether or not there was a scientific answer for it.'

The sun was directly in his face, and it was hard to make out what his gestures were doing in the harsh glow, but I was sure that he was smiling at me.

Chapter 14

An hour later, after a cool and contemplative car ride, during which I'd googled stories of pilot UFO sightings and relayed them to Andrew – they happened far more often than I thought – we arrived at the aquarium. I was so excited again and, this time, I didn't hold back and broke into a speedwalk to get to my favorite place. And when I was there, I did what I always did: I pressed my face to the glass and stared into the waters of the enormous tank.

Its interior was designed to mimic one of the underwater kelp forests that were common in the oceans around the Cape. Huge tree-like structures of brown kelp swayed in the water. The slow, repetitive movement, left to right, left to right, was hypnotic and, watching it, I felt this immediate sense of relaxation. This was what I loved about fish and being underwater: everything was slower and more rhythmic there, governed by repetitive patterns that were predictable and reliable, the current and the tides. The underwater world was also less sharp, less bright, less frantic and certainly less noisy.

A number of different fish moved slowly through the watery forest, weaving in and out of the giant swaying plants. They glided, as if not putting any effort into their movements at all. Their languid, smooth moves mesmerized me, and I wanted to submerge myself in the tank with them. The tank was huge; it filled the entire amphitheatre and was open to the sky above. This allowed sunlight to trickle into the water and, because most of the fish were silver, the light danced off their scales. Much prettier than a diamond ring, if you ask me. I put my hands on the side of my face, blocking out any peripheral vision I might have of the people around me, so all I could see was the water and the fish and the dancing, dappled light. I felt Andrew move closer to me and was vaguely aware that he too had put his face up against the glass. We stayed like this in total silence. The chatter and movement of the other people in the room disappeared. I loved this. This moment right here. The calm. The silence.

'I can see why you love this,' Andrew whispered, just loud enough for me to hear.

'It's relaxing,' I whispered back.

'Our jobs are so stressful it feels good to take a moment like this.' He turned to face me, and I surprised myself once more by looking back at him. The light from the tank cast rainbow-colored prisms on his face, and they moved over his features like lights on a dancefloor. I didn't think I'd ever seen anything more beautiful and started wondering what he would look like if he was a merman – obviously merpeople didn't exist – but suddenly the vision of Andrew gliding topless through the water floated through my mind. I ran my eyes down to his bottom half, then shook my head and laughed out loud.

'What?' he asked.

'I was just imagining what you would look like as a merman.'

'WHAT?' Andrew dissolved into a rather loud peal of laughter. 'You know mermaids don't exist, right?'

'Obviously not, and even if they did for a moment in time, they'd be extinct by now.'

When he finally stopped laughing, he crossed his arms and leaned against the tank. 'I'm very much looking forward to hearing your theory about why mermaids would be extinct.'

'They have no sex organs!'

'Wh—at?' Andrew spluttered through another laugh.

'Haven't you ever wondered about that?'

'Can't say I have.'

'Where are their sex organs? There's no sign of either piscine or mammalian sex organs. Unless they can pull their tails down like a pair of pants and there's something underneath? But that doesn't seem practical, to have to take your entire tail off every time you want to have sex. Or does the woman lay eggs and then the male fertilizes them? That doesn't seem right either, because then a parent would have to look after five hundred or so merbabies. And I still have no idea why the principal called my mother into school after I pointed this out to the class when we watched *The Little Mermaid*.'

'No idea?' he asked, but it seemed rhetorical.

'It's a perfectly logical question. How do they have sex?' I threw my arms in the air in frustration. This question had plagued me for many years. The answer was still unresolved and Google did not provide any adequate answers either, since it was all hypothetical. The only answers it provided were various Reddit speculations, which I did not put much stock in.

'Do you mind,' someone hissed. I turned in fright and came face to face with a furious-looking older woman. 'There are children here!' She narrowed her eyes at me and pointed to a boy next to her.

'What?' I asked, taken aback.

'You cannot talk about' – she leaned in, her eyes narrowing even more and her face becoming very twisted and ugly. I leaned back – 'stuff like that in front of children.'

'Stuff?' I asked, still not getting it. 'Oh, you mean mermaid sex?'

'Ssssshhhh!' she hissed again. Her face had become even more twisted, so twisted in fact that it looked like her features might actually fall off her face if she continued this current display of facial expression.

Andrew leaned in and graced the angry woman with a huge smile. Her lips and eyes unknotted themselves. 'We were just leaving, actually,' he said, and held his arm out for me to take. 'She didn't mean to be inappropriate around the kids, she—'

'I was hardly inappropriate.' I cut him off and looked at the child. 'How old is he, anyway? Eleven, twelve. Surely he knows the basics of reproduction by now. If not, then I think you've been pretty remiss as a caregiver. Children are engaging in sexual activity at a much younger age now, and knowledge about—'

'OKAY!' Andrew said, and started pulling me away as the woman's face began to twist again. 'Come, sister. Come, come.'

I jumped in with an immediate objection. 'I'm not your—'

'She's from the Netherlands. They're much more liberal there with that sort of thing,' Andrew said as he pulled me away by the arm.

'I'm not from the—'

'Amsterdam! Red-light district and coffee shops, you know,' he said over his shoulder as we disappeared around a corner.

'Hey, what was all that about?' I asked when we were out of Karen's earshot.

'Mermaid sex? Seriously?' He was obviously still amused. His non-stop chuckling was a dead giveaway.

'It's a genuine question. It wasn't meant to be funny.'

'Mermaid sex!' he repeated, and continued with his chortle. 'Amazing, truly amazing.'

'What's so amazing about mermaid sex?' I asked, which seemed to cause his laughter to escalate. 'Other than the fact that it's obvious they *can't* have sex.'

'Mermaid sex,' he said again, almost to himself, and then walked off into the next room, chuckling and shaking his head. I followed after him and was about to demand that he stop and explain all his chuckling, but the next room was my favorite one and I quickly forgot all about his laughter.

It was dark, filled with tanks illuminated by pink, blue and purple UV lights. In the light, translucent jellyfish swam up and down in tall glass tubes.

'Wow!' Andrew walked straight up to the nearest tank. In it, a school of ghostly looking transparent creatures moved jerkily through the water, expanding and contracting their see-through, gelatinous bodies. We strolled from tank to tank watching the mysterious creatures until we came to my favorite one. The box jellyfish. So small, and yet so deadly. Its long, thin tentacles floating behind it like a veil. The tentacles looked so small and thin, so harmless, but they weren't. We moved through the room together slowly, Andrew reading all the information on the tanks. Which I appreciated; not many people read the information in museums or zoos. However, every now and then he would whisper a 'how do they have sex?' and then laugh all over again.

I watched him while he moved from tank to tank, the odd burst of laughter here and there, and it dawned on me that he was the first person I'd ever brought here. I'd come here often while living in Cape Town, but I'd never brought Jennifer, or even my parents. I'd always thought of this place as my own quiet sanctuary. In my head, the addition of someone to this space, *my space*, would ruin it in some way. Only, today, it hadn't. Andrew seemed to fit here so easily. If anything, he seemed to enhance it.

Chapter 15

We stood at the airport, bags in hand. We were going to be on different flights, so this was our goodbye. I hated goodbyes. I never knew how much to say to someone and, worse than that, whether to hug or not. And of course there's the dreaded 'to kiss or not to kiss' issue. And far too many times I'd read the signals completely wrong. Someone comes in for a handshake, and I've gone in for a hug, their extended hand jabbing me in the boob as I force my body onto theirs. It's all so confusing and anxiety-ridden. Jennifer once told me about swingers' clubs, and how at these clubs they have a color-coded bracelet system that tells others what you're prepared to do. Red: no touching. Green: yes, but still ask. Blue: blow me! I wished there were colored bracelets for goodbyes. Red: I only hug. Blue: I kiss on both cheeks; et cetera.

'I think that was quite a successful weekend,' Andrew said.

'I agree.' And then I hesitated before I said what I wanted to say next. 'I . . . had fun.'

Andrew's lips twitched into that perfect symmetrical smile. 'I had so much fun! It was great, actually. It's not often that I meet someone with such similar interests.'

'Me too!' I agreed.

'So what's next in our arrangement?'

'I have my cousin's wedding in two months. I'm actually one of the bridesmaids,' I lamented.

'I have my mom's sixtieth in a month, then that get-together with old schoolmates, and then, not sure how you feel about Christmas holidays?'

'We always do a big family Christmas and it would be great having a boyfriend to keep the aunts at bay.'

'Boyfriend. I thought I was your fiancé?'

I laughed. 'Yes, I forgot about my mid-air proposal.'

'How can you forget? It was very, very romantic! In fact, I heard someone call it "the most romantic thing they'd ever heard", or something to that effect. And you know, when our wedding comes along, we could have it in that amphitheatre at the aquarium.'

'Oh my God, I love that,' I said, suddenly getting very excited about my fake upcoming wedding.

'The photos would be beautiful.'

'God, wouldn't they!' I drifted off a little, imagining what it would all look like, but then came back to reality. 'But I do think we should drop the engagement story. Go back to just being fake boyfriend and girlfriend.'

Andrew nodded. 'Agreed.'

I stuck my hand out abruptly. 'Well, thanks for this.'

Andrew looked down at it questioningly. *I got it wrong again!* He was expecting a hug, wasn't he? Maybe this was a hugging moment, especially after everything we'd shared this weekend. I quickly removed my hand and then almost threw myself at him with outstretched arms.

'Ouch!' I pulled away when his hand jabbed me in my stomach.

'Sorry, I thought we were shaking,' he said apologetically.

'I changed my mind at the last minute.'

'You okay?' he asked.

'Fine, you have a very firm handshake though.' I patted my stomach.

'Should we try that again?' he asked, and held his arms open.

'Uh, sure.' I leaned forward and put my arms on his shoulders awkwardly. Then I brought my chest to his, patted his back and pulled away.

'Was that a hug?' he asked.

'Yes,' I confirmed.

His lips curled into that smile again. 'Okay. Bye, Pippa.' He turned and walked away.

When I arrived back in Johannesburg two hours later and walked through the very familiar airport – the one I'd walked through so many times before – it looked and felt different. I couldn't put my finger on what made it feel different; all I knew was that it wasn't the same as it had been two days ago, when I'd taken off for Cape Town.

When I finally climbed into my car, I pulled my phone out. My finger hovered over Jennifer's name in my WhatsApp. I didn't quite know what to say to her. How on earth did I go about explaining all that had happened this weekend? All she knew was that I was going to the reunion, not that I was going with a fake boyfriend – nah, fiancé (apparently). I started typing up my explanation, but it was far too long, so I deleted it.

Keep it short and snappy.

'Right!' I said out loud, psyching myself up.

Pippa: I went to the reunion. Wasn't as bad as I thought it would be. They were all strangely nice to me. But I think that had less to do with me and more to do with my hot fake boyfriend. I have a fake boyfriend now. Well, actually, fiancé, sort of. It's a long story, too long for WhatsApp. I'll tell you all about it when we chat. But . . .

I paused and bit my lip.

Pippa: Thanks. For talking me into going. It was fun. Which I never thought I would say.

CHAPTER 16

The phone call sent me flying out of bed. I looked at the time. It was two thirty in the morning, and there was only one person I knew who called at such an odd time.

'Jennifer.' I picked the phone up without even looking at the screen.

'I literally have five minutes before my rotation starts. Fake boyfriend, or fiancé, or something . . . go!'

'I'm barely awake.'

'Four minutes thirty seconds.'

'Okay, okay!' I sat up quickly, hoping it would wake me up. 'I met this guy – well, I know him, he's a pilot. And he and I started talking and we discovered we have the same problem.'

'That you're both absolutely nuts?'

'This story has nothing to do with nuts! Rather the fact that we're both under pressure from friends and family to get a boyfriend, or girlfriend. Especially for events, like birthdays, weddings and school reunions.'

'Aaah, so you guys decided to be each other's fake date.'

'Exactly. Perfectly logical.'

'Perfectly mad!'

'Well, it worked,' I said.

'I know, I had the only two other people I'm still in contact with from school tell me what an amazing FIANCÉ you have. I had to pretend that I knew what they were talking about.'

'It wasn't meant to go that far. He was just supposed to be someone to have on my arm so I didn't have to field all those questions about why I'm not married and why I don't have a date.'

'Apparently, your fake fiancé is quite the catch. What did Cheryl say? It was something crass, like "He gave me a girl boner."'

'That's revolting,' I said.

'Does he give you a girl boner?'

'Stop saying "girl boner"!'

'Look, I don't blame you if you did. The picture of the two of you kissing is totally hot.'

I stood up. 'What photo of the two of us kissing?'

'The one they posted on the WhatsApp group, along with all the other pictures, and I see your fake boyfriend, or something, seems to feature in quite a few of them.'

'I'm phoning you back!' I shouted.

'I have to go anyway. But don't worry, I'll phone you back. I must hear more. Bye!'

Jennifer hung up, and I clicked on the school group as quickly as I could. Over a hundred photos came up. I began scrolling through them frantically, until I found what I was looking for. I'd completely forgotten about this picture. It was very poorly taken, if I do say so myself. But it *had* been taken, and now it was up on a group chat, probably for ever! I zoomed in.

'Mmm!' I was impressed. We did look like a real couple. And the kiss was exceedingly hot. I zoomed in and examined it closely. We fitted together so well – the shape of our faces, the angle of our jaws and the size of our noses. It was as if we were designed to kiss each other. I swapped across to my chat with Jennifer.

Pippa: It is a hot kiss!
Jennifer: That's what I'm worried about.
Pippa: What are you worried about?

Jennifer: I'm rushing around now, but let's chat later. I just don't want you getting hurt.

Pippa: Why would I get hurt? This is a purely fake and mutually beneficial arrangement-slash-relationship.

Jennifer: Famous last words.

Pippa: What do you mean?

Jennifer: I'll chat later.

Jennifer disappeared, and I sat there in the dark, wondering what she'd meant by all that. Why on earth would she be worried that I could get hurt? And what about 'famous last words'. What words?

I lay back down in bed and opened the reunion group again. I started flipping through the photos that various people had taken over the two days: the group photos, the individual photos, the couple photos; and wine glass and food photos; and the many, many – *wait, many* – photos of Andrew. I sat up again. He could be seen in almost all the bloody photos. The back of him, half his face in the corner, his arm in the shot, his profile and shoulder poking in on the left, his laughing face in the corner of another photo, and I'm sure that someone had gone to great lengths to include a photo of him bending over, his ass in the air, in the background of a rather irrelevant photo of a table setting. I zoomed in on that photo too. He did have a remarkably good ass. I felt a strange little surge of pride, even though that was irrational. My fake fiancé with a fantastic backside! I put my phone down on my bedside table and smiled to myself as I drifted back off to sleep.

Chapter 17

'Good afternoon, City Tower, this is Flightbird Six Zero Zero.'

'Flightbird Six Zero Zero, this is City Tower. Hi! Go ahead.'

'We are inbound to Johannesburg Airport, flying over the pylons, requesting vectors for ILS, please. Flightbird Six Zero Zero.'

I flushed at the sound of the voice I could actually put a face to now, not to mention an arse to. It had been the last thing I'd thought about before falling asleep last night, and now I was thinking about it again! I quickly pushed it out of my mind. I could not let things like that distract me at work.

'Flightbird Six Zero Zero, turn right heading two zero niner.'

'Copy that, City Tower, turn right heading two zero niner.'

I waited. My enthusiasm to speak to him had increased ever since our weekend away. I'd seldom been described as an enthusiastic individual and, in most of my school reports, teachers suggested that I should try display more enthusiasm for group activities, but these days I felt rather enthusiastic indeed. I seemed to have a little 'pep in my step', as my mother would say. And this morning when I'd come to work, I'd even smiled and said good morning to my co-workers. Something I never do. Not because I'm trying to be rude, but because I'm terrified I'll be dragged into small talk with one of them and have no idea what to say. I dealt with some other landings while waiting to hear back from Andrew.

'City Tower, this is Flightbird Six Zero Zero. Established ILS, runway zero three left. Not lucky number seven today, unfortunately.

How's the runway looking? Wind seems gusty from up here and visibility is low.'

'Wind is three forty degrees at eighteen knots. Safe for landing, but it will be a little bumpy.'

'Copy that, City Tower, wind is three forty degrees at eighteen knots. The passengers won't enjoy this. Flightbird Six Zero Zero.'

'Flightbird Six Zero Zero. Cleared to land on runway zero three left. Good luck.'

'Ha! Ha! I don't need luck, City Tower, cleared to land on runway zero three left.'

He stopped talking and, as soon as he did, that sense of anticipation flooded me again. The more time I spent talking to him, the more I wanted to talk to him, and over the last few weeks I had found that anticipation growing tenfold. Synonyms for *anticipation* included *expectance*, *expectancy* and *expectation*. Andrew had become an expectation, one that I waited for. I stood up and watched his plane land, something else I enjoyed doing more than I understood why. From here, it looked like the plane was being bounced around in the air on invisible springs. The passengers were probably all on the edge of their seats, gripping chairs with white knuckles. If only they knew what capable hands they were in, they wouldn't worry at all. He landed the plane relatively gently, despite the unrelenting winds pushing it out at an angle.

'See, perfect landing, City Tower. Flightbird Six Zero Zero.' His voice came through my headset again.

'I'd give it seventy per cent.' I tried to hold back a laugh, I knew how competitive he was.

'Seventy! I don't think so.'

'Flightbird Six Zero Zero, vacate right onto Bravo taxiway and contact Ground Control at one two one point six.'

'At least an eighty, City Tower. Vacate right onto Bravo taxiway and contact Ground Control at one two one point six. Flightbird Six Zero Zero.'

'Fine – seventy-five.'

'What?!' He was feigning shock, and I was trying to hold back a laugh. His plane was guided into the parking bay and came to a stop. I hadn't expected to hear his voice again. But I did.

'You working on Friday night?'

'No.'

'So you're free?'

'That depends on what time?'

'Around eight?'

'Why?' I asked.

'I'll message you a little later, but I think I need you on Friday night.'

Need me. The phrase struck me as so odd I almost fell out of my chair. No one had ever needed me before. I was so shocked by the phrase that I must have kept silent for too long.

'You there?' he asked.

'Copy that, Flightbird Six Zero Zero. Chat later.'

'Can't wait, City Tower.'

Can't wait? Was that a literal 'I can't wait to talk to you, do it right now' or a more figurative 'I can't wait to talk to you later'?

I guess it was the latter, because later that night when I was tucked in bed after completing my evening ritual, Andrew messaged me.

Andrew: Hey, about Friday night. I have a dinner with friends. They're one of those couples who can't stop extoling the virtues of marriage and then move on to the old 'why am I not married yet?' thing. I could really use a wing-woman there.

Pippa: What time?

Andrew: Dinner at eight.

Pippa: That should be okay. I have a Pokémon tournament at six, but it should only go on for an hour or so.

Andrew: You play Pokémon tournaments?

Pippa: I'm Gauteng's top player.

Andrew: I wouldn't expect anything less ☺

Andrew: How about I come with you to your tournament and then we can leave together and go to dinner?

Pippa: You want to come with me to a tournament?

Andrew: If that's okay.

I paused. Was it okay?

Pippa: I've never had an audience before. I don't know.

Andrew: Think about it. No pressure.

Andrew: Sleep tight.

I rolled my eyes. That was one of my least favorite sayings. Tight? How? How does one sleep tight? Are your eyes tightly shut? Is the blanket tight around you because you're tucked in? Synonyms for *tight* include *compact*, *cramped*, *rigid* and *narrow*. I had no idea what those had to do with having a good sleep. But I went with it.

Pippa: You too.

Chapter 18

I walked into the comic shop with Andrew right behind me. For some reason I felt abnormally apprehensive about bringing him into my world. I liked things compartmentalized. Work, recreation, family, and the drawing of perfect lines between all those things. But Andrew had been crossing those lines, rapidly, like at the aquarium. His presence was starting to blur all the lines in my life together; nothing felt as simple and separate any more. We walked through the shop to the lines of chairs and tables at the back where all the Pokémon, Yu-Gi-Oh and Magic games and tournaments were played. As I walked in, everyone looked up and greeted me.

'Hi, guys.' I turned to Andrew. 'This is my fake boyfriend that I was telling you all about – Andrew.'

Heads nodded in acknowledgement.

'He wanted to watch the tournament.'

Sheila honed in on Andrew immediately. Since telling them all about my arrangement during one of our previous games, she'd had so many questions.

'Do you rent your services out?' Sheila blasted forth, with little effort at subtlety. She, like me, struggled with things like that.

Andrew blinked at her, looking off-kilter at the sudden outburst.

'I might also need a fake boyfriend for a family function. They ask me constantly why I don't have a boyfriend yet, blah, blah, blah, et cetera. They never bloody stop!'

'Um . . .' Andrew looked stumped.

'Do you think you can pretend you're also into game design? They know I would never be in a relationship with anyone who wasn't equally obsessed with it.'

'I . . . I don't know anything about game design,' he muttered, still wide-eyed.

'Andrew doesn't rent his services out,' I said. 'He's an airline pilot, not a professional fake boyfriend.'

'If he was a professional fake boyfriend, he'd be an escort,' Sheila said, and then giggled.

Everyone at the table laughed at this, including Andrew, who seemed to have relaxed a little now.

'Well, I'm definitely not an escort,' he said.

'You should be,' Sheila said. 'You'd probably make a lot of money. You're very good-looking.'

'Very good-looking,' Orion echoed, and a few other heads nodded in agreement.

'Thank you, I'm very flattered,' he said.

'You have good hair,' Zane said, eyeing Andrew's full head with intensity, or maybe it was jealousy. 'Do you use any treatments?'

Andrew ran a hand through his hair. 'Can't say I do.'

Zane's shoulders slumped in disappointment.

'Mind you, if I brought an airline pilot home who was this good-looking, maybe my parents would leave me alone for five minutes about getting a boyfriend. You sure you don't rent your services out? I would pay well,' Sheila asked again.

'She's got lots of money,' Orion added.

'I make a lot of money.' Sheila nodded. 'More than you.'

'She makes more than all of us put together,' Zane said.

'I designed a gaming app. It's been downloaded over twenty-five million times.'

'Okay. Wow! That's impressive,' Andrew said.

'Impressive enough to be my fake boyfriend?' she asked.

Andrew looked around the table first, and then his eyes settled on me. 'Well, if Pippa doesn't mind, and I wasn't busy, I mean . . . I could come. If it would help you?' He raised his eyebrows at me. I looked at him blankly and then clicked.

'Oh, you're asking me if I mind you being Sheila's fake boyfriend too?'

He nodded.

'No . . . of course not. Why would I mind?' But as those words came out of my mouth, I realized that I did mind. An unexpected feeling made my stomach churn. I wasn't sure how to interpret it.

'The function is next week Friday.' She perked up as Andrew pulled his phone out and started scrolling.

'Sorry, I'm flying to Durban that night.'

Sheila slumped again. 'It's okay. Thanks for the offer.'

'I'll be your fake boyfriend.' Zane sat up straight in his chair.

Sheila did a double-take. 'You?'

'Why not?' he asked.

'You?' she repeated.

'Me.' He puffed out his chest.

Sheila stared intensely at Zane as if she'd never seen him before. 'Okay. But you can't wear clothes like that. You need to look smarter. And you have to brush your hair . . . or what hair you have left,' she said, looking at the bald patch at the top of his head that had been spreading rapidly this past year. He was usually so self-conscious about any mention of his hair, but he didn't seem to mind this time. On the contrary. He smiled at Sheila, for so long that I wondered if his lips had gotten stuck to his teeth, and then he quickly looked back down at his cards.

I landed up winning the Pokémon tournament, obviously. Zane and I had battled in the final, an intense match where our best decks squared off. My deck emerged triumphant though. Andrew had watched the entire tournament as if he was really interested; I could hear him asking questions as we played. They seemed like genuine questions, the kind that you ask when you really want to know something, not the kind you just throw out when you want to fill an empty space.

After the game, I found myself in Andrew's car driving off to meet his friends.

'That was really interesting,' he said. 'I've never seen a Pokémon game before. I liked it. Lots of strategy and details. I like that kind of thing.'

'Me too.'

'And the people there are cool. And I think Sheila and Zane will probably have something to announce soon too.'

'What do you mean?'

'Zane is totally into Sheila.'

'How do you know?' I was taken aback by this information.

'Didn't you notice his smile when she agreed to let him be her fake boyfriend?'

'And seeing that smile leads you to believe that he likes her?'

'Definitely.'

'Huh,' I said thoughtfully. I'd never thought about it before, but Zane often smiled at Sheila. He often brought her favorite coffee and chocolates and offered to take her home, since she only ever Ubered. I'd just never put two and two together. Mind you, liking or not liking someone; these kinds of subtle non-verbal communications that wafted invisibly through the air between people, were often missed by me. I was always fascinated when others were able to pick up on these invisible alerts that people apparently gave off. They moved like unseen radio waves, but no one had ever given me the correct frequency to tune in.

'I'm a little nervous about tonight,' I blurted out, after a protracted silence.

'Me too, to be honest. I'm dreading going.'

'Why are you going then?'

'You know those friends you've had since early school days that you've totally grown apart from but still feel obliged to see because of your shared history, even though your lives are completely different and if you had to meet them today, you probably wouldn't be friends?'

'No,' I said straight away.

'Well, you're lucky then. They live in England now, but come to South Africa once a year, so I do dinner with them. They're high-school sweethearts who got married right out of school and have produced a set of blonde twins. They seem to think I should be doing the same. Always telling me I don't want to be a sixty-year-old at my future children's graduations.'

'How old are you?' It hadn't occurred to me to ask him.

'Thirty-two. You?'

'Twenty-nine. My parents want to throw me a massive thirtieth-birthday party. My mom says if she can't plan a wedding, I should at least let her plan a party.'

'Maybe she can plan a wine-tasting evening,' he joked.

'No. Never again. I've decided that I'm never going to taste wines again. It seems like such an innocent thing to do – take little sips – but it's not! Before you know what you've done, you've consumed two bottles of wine and are sitting on a rock on the side of the road. I consider that a very low point in my life, dignity-wise.'

'If that was a low point for you, then you've managed to get through life pretty unscathed,' Andrew said.

'What was your low point?'

'There were many. But one that sticks out is when my friends and I graduated as pilots. Picture the scene: we all got very drunk, stripped down to our underpants and stood behind the engine of a jet and let it fling us into the fence.'

'I see.'

'Imagine grown men in their underwear pinned to a fence.'

'That is incredibly undignified!' I said, but couldn't help my smile, and then couldn't help imagining what Andrew might look like in his underwear.

'What underwear?' I quickly asked, in order to add detail to the mental images I was currently building.

'What?' He tilted his head to look at me.

'Briefs? Boxers? G-string?'

'Um . . . definitely not a G-string! Why?'

'I'm trying to picture the scene accurately.'

Andrew laughed. 'Would you like me to tell you what color they were?'

'That would be useful.'

'I was joking. I couldn't tell you what color my underwear was that day if you paid me.'

'Unfortunate,' I said. 'What about the gym? Were you going to the gym as much as you do now?'

'What?'

'I mean, your body. Did it look like it does now?'

'What does it look like now?' He turned in his seat and raised his brows at me.

'Well, you obviously work out regularly. And judging by your physique, I would say with an emphasis on strength training.' He definitely went to the gym; that much was obvious. But other things weren't that obvious, like, did he have a six-pack? I loved six-packs. The ones where you were able to see the outlines of all the muscles perfectly. Like a study that Da Vinci might have done of the human body. I loved it when you could see the veins that ran into the groin area, the sinews between the ribs as they turned their torsos. I liked bodies like that. Bodies that revealed the intriguing structures below the surface. That revealed the inner, fascinating workings of the musculoskeletal system. Not that I'd been with many men who looked like that; in fact, I'd started considering bodies like those to be somewhat of a fantasy. Most of the men I'd been with were a little squishier around the middle; not that I minded squishy, but my fantasy had always been *David* (preferably with a larger penis though).

'You're very quiet. Are you still trying to picture it?' Andrew asked, and because he'd caught me off guard, and because my mind had gone off on another one of its tangents . . .

'Did you know that in ancient Greece and Rome, a large penis was actually frowned upon, and a smaller one was considered to be a sign of intelligence?' I said casually.

'*Sorry, WHAT?*'

'And further to that, an erect penis wasn't seen as a sign of power or strength either. A small penis was considered to be the ideal male beauty standard. In fact, that's why you'll often see ancient Greek and Roman statues of men with very small penises.'

'Wow, that was . . . I was . . . not expecting you to say that. At all!'

'Well, you did tell me to picture the scene.'

'So you pictured my penis?' He laughed again.

'No, I didn't. But I did picture something that led me to ponder the representation of male genitalia in ancient Greek and Roman art. I was not picturing yours specifically.'

His laughter continued and I was worried that it was distracting him from driving.

'You shouldn't laugh so much while you're driving,' I said. But this didn't seem to have the desired response, as his laughter just continued.

'We're here,' Andrew said, pulling into a parking space that was right outside the restaurant. I loved it when I found a parking space right outside the place I was going to. I hated going to places in general, but when I knew my car was parked right outside it always made me feel safer. Something familiar was close by, keeping me company in some way. I climbed out of the car and immediately tripped.

'Shit!' I found myself on my hands and knees on the pavement.

'You okay?' Andrew ran round the car to my side.

'Fine, fine.' I stood up and dusted my knees off.

'You're bleeding,' Andrew said, pointing at one of the big, ugly grazes.

'It's not that bad. I think an old scab must have come off in the fall.'

'Old scab?'

'I tend to fall a lot,' I said, reaching into my handbag and pulling out my small first-aid kit. I took out two antibacterial wipes, wiped my knees clean and then dabbed them both with cream and stuck two plasters over the wounds. All the time, I could sense Andrew watching me.

'You seem prepared for this,' he said when I'd finished.

'Like I said, it happens a lot.' I pointed at the bruise on my arm. 'Walked into my doorhandle yesterday.' I pointed at my other arm. 'Scratched this on a branch when I was playing with my dogs.'

'Sorry,' he said softly.

'Sorry for what?'

'Sorry that you always accidentally hurt yourself.'

I sighed. I hadn't mean to, but suddenly I felt a little sad. 'It's just something that I do, I guess,' I said. 'Something that I do' was an understatement though. Broken arms, sprained ankles, knocked-out teeth, broken nose. I went through life feeling that I had no control over my body at all, that I was disconnected from it. My body did what it liked in the world, and I had almost no say over it. And it was always hurting me.

'Do you like Indian food?' Andrew asked, changing the subject.

'I actually hate it. Don't like the flavor of curry.'

He laughed all over again. 'And curry underpins literally every dish.'

'I always order butter chicken if I'm forced to come to an Indian restaurant,' I said. I always had a plan for restaurants. I knew exactly what kind of food I would order in certain restaurants. At a seafood restaurant, I always ordered calamari, but not the one with the heads still attached to it. Chinese, always chicken fried rice. Sushi restaurants, cucumber maki. I could not abide the idea of consuming raw fish, and avocado was too squishy in my mouth. I'd also once read an article about how a parasitic worm had made its way into a man's brain after he'd ingested a sushi platter. I had enough going on in my head. The last thing I needed there was also a worm.

We walked into the restaurant, and the first thing to hit me were the sounds. Pots and pans, a coffee machine, chatter, rushing waiters. Sounds like these, so many different types all at once, especially when in public, often triggered my anxiety. They never just blended together into the background like they did for most people; instead my ears seemed to be tuned into each and every separate sound: the clank of knives and forks, doors opening and closing, the change in songs. I reached into my bag and wrapped my fingers around my ball of fidget toys. It was a selection of bits and bobs that I'd collected over the years and stuck onto a key ring. When I fiddled with them, they made me feel a little better.

We rounded a corner, and as we approached the table at the back two people jumped up at once. The woman, Melissa, made straight for me. And then, like a verbal avalanche, words dislodging themselves like giant chunks of snow, her mouth opened and stuff flew out. It was difficult to keep up with the words because there were just so, so, so many of them.

'Pippa? Right? I was so excited when Andrew told me he was bringing someone. And look at you, you're so pretty. Isn't she pretty? I'm Melissa, but you probably know that. It's just so nice to meet you. I can't tell you how excited I am to be finally, finally, meeting a girlfriend.' It went on like that for a while. Melissa was an excellent talker: she talked and talked and talked. If there was a competition for professional talking, like they have for professional eating, Melissa would have won it. I fixed my features into a smile and nodded my head up and down, as if I was listening to her. But she was talking way too fast, way too loudly and way too enthusiastically. I was officially lost. The words had swallowed me whole and I was drowning in them. When I find myself in situations like this, I often squint my eyes together in a way that makes the world around me blurry. And if I squint really hard, I can even make the person in front of me disappear. But Melissa was undisappearable. She was like looking directly at the sun. No amount of squinting made her go away.

Her husband, Eddy, seemed just as enthusiastic as she was. He slapped Andrew on the back and said it was 'about damn time' a few times, while looking at me. Eddy and Melissa were perhaps one of the most enthusiastic couples I'd ever encountered. They looked like the kind of people who might go to the gym together on Sunday mornings wearing matching active wear and high-five each other after each set or, worse, cycle on a tandem bike. Their loud enthusiasm knew no limits. Synonyms for *enthusiastic* include *crazy*, *impatient* and *wild*. I didn't like those words. Not one bit.

I sat down and tried to make myself comfortable, but the chair felt like it was made of something that had been designed to make me itch. I wiggled back and forth in an attempt to get settled. More loud chatter, a loud toast after the wine was ordered, and then much loud and enthusiastic menu-flipping as Melissa and Eddy turned deciding what to eat into a stage performance.

'They have mussels, dear.'

'Oooh, I love mussels. But I don't think they will be nearly as good as the mussels we had in France.'

'Have you been to France, Pippa?'

'You must go. Look, they have braised lamb shank here too.'

'Mmm, too rich for me. Remember what happened last time I ate lamb shank.'

'Oooh, yes. I remember. Had to rush you off to the doctor the next day.'

'And it was my birthday! What a terrible gift, right? But everything was just going all the way through me, if you know what I mean. When is your birthday, Pippa?'

'Chicken and mushroom risotto?'

'Does it have dairy in it? I'm lactose intolerant now. Just awful really. No more ice cream for me.'

By the time we were ready to order I felt so strange and nauseous, after having the entire menu read to me and imagining each and every dish, that I had to excuse myself to go to the bathroom. I sat on the closed toilet seat for a while, trying to push the thought of what lamb shank and ice cream would taste like together when my phone beeped.

Andrew: You okay?
Pippa: Just taking a small moment.
Andrew: They are a little intense. Sorry.
Pippa: Fervent. Zealous. Manic.

I offered up some alternative synonyms. I'd been sitting here thinking of the perfect ones for them.

Andrew: Haha. Those too.
Pippa: Where are you?

'Right here?' The sound of Andrew's voice shocked me. I stood up on the toilet and peered over the door to find Andrew standing with his back up against the long vanity counter and looking in my direction.

'What are you doing here?'

'I also wanted to take a moment. I kept imagining "everything going through" Melissa and I needed a break. The toilet is unisex, in case you're—'

'I know,' I said. It was the first thing I'd noticed about the bathroom. I opened the door, walked up to the sink counter and rested my back against it like Andrew was doing.

'Why are you still friends with them if you don't enjoy their company?' I asked.

'I like them. We have such a long history together. They're just very—' He lifted his eyes to mine. 'Wait, are you a walking thesaurus or something? First there was "stunning" and now "intense"?'

I inhaled and paused. Did I tell him that as a child I'd spend hours sitting in the treehouse in the playground at school reading and memorizing the thesaurus while other kids had been playing? That, for fun, I wrote down the synonyms of commonly used words. This was one of those 'quirky' little things about me that people seemed to find endearing and amusing when they first got to know me, but which quickly turned to irritation when I began suggesting alternatives for them. I started a slow nod. 'I like synonyms.'

'You said that, but I hadn't realized that you could recite them at a moment's notice.'

'Give me a word and I'll give you a synonym,' I said.

'That's easy – *verbose.* Melissa and Eddy are rather verbose,' he said. I was impressed by his choice of word.

'*Wordy*, *long-winded*, *loquacious* or *garrulous*.'

I registered another smile on Andrew's face, and then he bumped me with his shoulder. It seemed like a purposeful bump, not an accidental one. I wasn't sure whether to bump him back.

'They are certainly that. Not to mention very enthusiastic,' he added.

'*Exuberant*, *vigorous*, *ardent* and *spirited*,' I recited.

'Indeed.' Andrew sighed, long and loud, and then pushed himself off the counter. 'Come on, let's go. They might get the wrong idea if we stay in here for too long.'

'What wrong idea?'

'You know.' He grinned at me and I shook my head.

'That we're, you know, engaged in some bathroom-stall shenanigans.'

'And by "shenanigans" you mean sex?' I asked, catching on.

'You really don't beat around the bush, do you?'

'I like to call things what they really are. And I also don't like sayings like "beat around the bush" either. They also don't describe things accurately.'

'Well, in that case, then, yes, *sex*. That we're having sex in the bathroom stall.'

'I would never have sex in a bathroom, ever,' I said, heading towards the door. I pushed it open and stopped walking. 'And I'm certainly not having sex with you in a *public* bathroom! That's even worse than normal bathroom sex.'

'Beg your pardon?'

I swung around at the voice and came face to face with an older-looking man. His eyes were wide, and he flicked them from me to Andrew and back again.

'We weren't really talking about having *actual* sex in the bathroom, by the way,' I quickly clarified. 'It was more a hypothetical conversation about bathroom sex in general, as opposed to a specific conversation about the act of sex.'

'I, um . . .' The man put his hands in the air and crab-walked past me as if he didn't want to touch me. 'No worries. Didn't mean to interrupt the . . . Anyway, whatever floats your boat, right?' He looked at Andrew strangely before disappearing into a cubicle.

'My boat wasn't floated,' I called after him. 'No one's boat was floated in this bathroom, I can assure you of that.'

The man did not reply, and I was just about to walk up to his door, knock and ask him to respond, when I felt an arm slip through mine.

'Let's go,' Andrew said, pulling me away, much like he'd done in the aquarium.

'But I don't want that man thinking I was going to have sex in the bathroom with you—' We almost bumped into someone else as we exited the door. This time, the person was a woman.

'We didn't' – I quickly said to her, and gestured back to the bathroom – 'have sex in there, in case you were thinking we did have sex, and—'

Andrew gave me another tug and led me out the bathroom.

'Oh my God, what's with you talking about sex in public and always getting caught! Mermaid sex, bathroom sex, what's next?'

'I'm not purposefully talking about sex,' I argued.

'I know, and that's what makes it even funnier.' He led us back to the table and, as soon as we got there, Melissa was on our case.

'Someone was in the bathroom for a very long time.' She drew out the words in a strange tone while winking her right eye at me.

'We did not have sex in the bathroom,' I said on an exasperated outbreath. 'Why does everyone think I'm having sex in the bathroom, with you?'

Andrew laughed, and I swung around and gave him a look. He stopped laughing immediately. 'We did not have sex in the bathroom, I can confirm that!' he said, laughter gone but still smiling. 'No boats were floated at all.'

'Sounds like you guys are protesting way too much,' Melissa said.

'Sounds like it,' Eddy echoed his wife.

I shook my head, reached for Andrew's glass of wine and took a sip.

'What happened to never, *ever* drinking wine again?' he asked.

'I feel the evening now requires it.' I took a second sip as I sat down.

Andrew sat too, and, as he did, his knee bumped mine under the table. I looked over at him and his smile grew. This was the second time he'd bumped me, and I was now quite convinced the bump meant something. A secret handshake of sorts. Were we sharing an in-joke maybe? Were we part of the same team? I liked the knee bump. The knee bump felt good. I was not opposed to the bump.

When dinner was over, I found myself back in Andrew's car.

'What kind of car is this?' I asked, running my hand over the dashboard.

'It's a 1996 Porsche Boxster. First and best Porsche Boxster.'

'It's not a very practical car.'

'No, I guess not.'

'It has no back seat. What's the trunk size like?'

'It's big enough for a small overnight suitcase, which is all I need.'

'It has a CD player,' I pointed out.

'It's a classic.'

'Why not at least buy a newer version of this car? One that doesn't have so much mileage.' I read the odometer in shock. 'A newer one would probably come with a maintenance and service plan? If this thing broke down, the parts are probably impossibly hard to get.'

'But where's the fun in that?'

'Where's the fun in breaking down and not being able to get parts?'

'When I was about twelve or thirteen years old, I was riding my bike around the neighborhood with my friends. We didn't grow up in a particularly wealthy part of town, and I remember, at the time, my mom drove this old Toyota with a battery that needed to be jump-started on cold days. I was out with my friends when this guy came driving around the corner in this exact car. None of us had ever seen a car like that before, let alone in our area. I'd never seen anything so fancy in my entire life, and I remember thinking that the guy driving it must be so damn cool, like Vin Diesel from *The Fast and the Furious*.'

'You wanted to be Vin Diesel from *The Fast and the Furious*?'

'Which kid didn't? Racing cars, beautiful woman, danger.'

'So when you got older you bought yourself this car. And do you feel like Vin Diesel driving it?' I asked.

'Do I look like Vin Diesel in it?'

'Absolutely not. You look nothing like him. You're much better-looking than him, I prefer a full head of hair.'

'Well, thanks.' Andrew laughed again.

'Besides, you're almost too tall for it.' I pointed at his head, which only had an inch or so to go until it was touching the roof.

'What car do you drive? I bet it's very practical.'

'I drive a gray Toyota Prius. With rising fuel costs, it's very economical. Toyota is also the most reliable car in the country, it has a five-star safety rating and gray is the easiest color to clean.'

'But can it do this?' Andrew asked. My head flew back into the seat as the car lurched forward with what could only be described as a ferocious roar.

'Oh my God!' I screamed as the car flew for a few seconds before returning to a normal speed. My heart pounded in my chest and, as soon as I was able to catch my breath, I laughed.

'Do that again!' I gripped the sides of the seat this time, bracing myself for what I knew was about to follow, which, I must say, I had enjoyed very, very much. It had filled me with a sense of sheer exhilaration!

'Why don't you do it?' Andrew pulled in to the side of the road and turned his hazards on.

'Me?'

'Yeah, why not?'

'I don't know. I don't think I've ever broken the speed limit.'

'I didn't break it either, just did a very quick acceleration and release. Or have you forgotten how to drive a manual?'

'I know how to drive a manual,' I said, looking down at the gear shift. 'Um . . . clutch,' I muttered, trying to refresh my memory, since the last time I'd driven a manual was for my driver's test over ten years ago.

'Yes, the clutch,' Andrew echoed.

I undid my seatbelt, but stopped. 'Wait, are you sure you trust me driving your car?'

'I trust you to help land my plane.' He smiled.

'Good point.'

I walked over to Andrew's side of the car and climbed in. The seat needed a lot of adjusting, considering Andrew's substantial height and remarkably long limbs. When the seat was comfortable, I tapped my feet on the pedals, reminding myself of the manual set-up. Clutch in, clutch out, brake, accelerator.

'Mmmm,' I mumbled as I looked down at the gearstick and the numbers on it.

'Pretty standard,' Andrew assured me. 'Six-speed gearbox. Clutch needs a bit of a heavy foot, but other than that, it drives very well.'

'Okay, here I go.' I lowered the handbrake and tried to manage the clutch-to-accelerator ratio as I pulled off. My ratio wasn't good, too hard on the accelerator and not smooth enough on the clutch. We jerked forward uncomfortably, and repeated that a few more times as I climbed up the gears. But the car was like a wild beast beneath me; it seemed to want to run away from us. After a few minutes I got the hang of it though, and soon I was comfortably cruising down the road at sixty kilometers an hour. But the car wanted to go faster. It told me so with its low, rumbling growls.

'Do it. Put your foot flat,' Andrew said.

I studied him. He was cool, calm and clearly trusted me. I checked the road: it was clear, which was good. I would never do anything to endanger anyone's safety.

'Okay.' I put my foot flat and the car surged forward with unrestrained energy. My head flew back, my spine melted into my seat and the speedometer flew up as the car rocketed forward.

'Oh my God!' I shouted as the rush hit me. When the speedometer hit 120 kilometers per hour, I eased off, not wanting to break the speed limit. The car slowed down and the noise of the engines subsided enough to hear another noise that I hadn't been aware of until now. I was laughing.

'That was so fun! Again!'

I did it again. I loved this feeling! Of being completely in my body and out of my head. There were only a few things that did this to me, and this was one of them. And in that moment, I got it. The need for speed. It was exhilarating, or perhaps another synonym described it better: *breathtaking*. Because that's how it felt; my breath pushed out of my lungs and every single nerve ending in my body fully charged. *Mind-blowing*, *heart-stopping*, *hair-raising*. Never had synonyms been so right about anything before. This moment was all of those things all at once, and maybe even more.

'You know what will make this even better?' Andrew shouted over the rumbling engine.

'What?'

'Pull over.'

I edged the car onto the shoulder of the road and, when I did, Andrew pressed a button and the roof of the car lifted. I tilted my head back and looked straight up into the sky. Stars, some white clouds like ghostly figures and a sliver of a moon. Without the roof over our heads, I felt connected to the sky above me in some way. I raised my arms into the air, and a cool breeze blew through my fingers.

'You ready?' Andrew asked, with what was clearly a mischievous look plastered across his face. I nodded and pulled back onto the road again. This time I kept the car at a lower speed, so the flat-out acceleration would feel even faster. And when I did it this time, it felt so, so much better. With the roof down, the wind pulled at my face and hair and clothes, heightening the experience even more. It was as if the entire world and all the elements were involved in this moment: the stars and sky and clouds and wind and engine roar.

'It's amazing!' I yelled over the sounds.

I began to slow down, and when I had I stuck my hand out the window and rode the wind, curving my hand up and down, as if surfing an invisible wave in the air that only I could see and feel. I was sad when the whole experience was over and Andrew pulled into the parking lot of the comic shop where I'd left my car.

'You good to drive home?' he asked.

'I had three sips of wine,' I replied.

'No, I mean, you want me to follow you or something? Just until you're out of this area; it's not the most savoury, especially at night.'

'Not to worry. I have mace in my car. My insurance company also has a panic button on my phone which I can activate at any time, and I have a black belt in karate.'

'Wow! Okay, remind me never to try and hijack you,' he laughed. 'Have you ever had to pull karate moves on anyone before?'

'Once, when I was in a nightclub – my friend dragged me out to one – a guy pinched my bum as I walked past and I palm-struck him in the face.' I thought back to that incident. I'd felt so violated by the unsolicited touch, and when I'd turned to see who'd done it and he'd given me a lascivious, drunken wink and then beckoned me with his dirty 'come hither' finger, I was overcome with fury. 'And I was the one who got thrown out of the club – can you believe that? The asshole even tried to press charges for battery. But he'd touched me without my permission! I never understood that.'

'My mom would call that male privilege and the culture of toxic masculinity. Unfortunately, it still exists.'

'So you'd never pinch a girl on the bum if she walked past you?'

'God, no! No!'

I squinted my eyes at Andrew, sizing him up. 'That's good to know,' I said, and then started climbing out of the car.

'Thanks for tonight. It was a big help,' he called as I walked to my car. 'I think my friends really like you.'

'It's my pleasure,' I said, and surprised myself when I realized that statement was in fact accurate. It had been my pleasure. Synonyms for *pleasure* included *enjoyment* and *contentment*. And right now, I felt very, very content.

CHAPTER 19

'A very good early, early morning to you, City Tower. This is Flightbird Six Zero Zero.'

'Flightbird Six Zero Zero, this is City Tower. It is an early morning.' I looked at my watch; it was coming up for four-fifty a.m.

'We are inbound to Johannesburg Airport, flying over the golf course. Sun is just starting to rise, beautiful actually. Requesting vectors for ILS, please. Flightbird Six Zero Zero.'

'Flightbird Six Zero Zero, turn left heading two zero eight.' I stood up and looked out of the window. The sky was navy blue and, in the distance, the first rays of warm light were shooting over the horizon. 'I'm sure we're in for a beautiful sunrise,' I confirmed.

'Copy that, City Tower, turn left heading two zero eight. I'll let you know what it looks like from up here.'

His voice disappeared again, and that same feeling I got every single time I talked to him now – an itchy, restless anticipation – took up residence underneath my ribcage. I was distracted by a few other landings, but all the while I felt effervescent. Synonyms included *frothy*, *bubbly* and *sparkling*.

'City Tower, this is Flightbird Six Zero Zero. Established ILS, runway zero three left. Not lucky number seven today. How's the runway looking?'

'Perfect weather. No wind.'

'Copy that, City Tower, no wind and looking forward to my

perfect landing. The sun is up over the horizon. Looks amazing from up here. This is why I fly. You cannot beat this view!'

'Wish I could see it, Flightbird Six Zero Zero. Cleared to land on runway zero three left.'

'Thank you, City Tower, cleared to land on runway zero three left. I'll take a photo for you. This is Flightbird Six Zero Zero.'

I stood up and watched his plane glide down, the morning rays now brightening the sky. It was a beautiful sight from here too, one of my favorite sights in the world. Andrew's favorite sight was the view from above; mine was the view from below. There's nothing better than watching a plane float smoothly to the ground with grace and elegance. And so many things needed to align perfectly for a plane to do that. Air speed, head and tail winds, angle, thrust, drag. I kept watching until his plane hit the tarmac, back wheels first, the front wheel and nose kept up until the very last minute, like a gymnast performing a precise routine and ending with the perfect dismount.

'Flightbird Six Zero Zero, vacate right onto Alpha taxiway and contact Ground Control at one two one point six. That was the perfect landing,' I said.

'Vacate right onto Alpha taxiway and contact Ground Control at one two one point six. Flightbird Six Zero Zero. Thanks to you too.'

'I don't think I did that much; you do all the hard work.'

There was a long pause, so long in fact that I wasn't sure if he was going to say anything back. But he did.

'You do more than you think for me.' And then he was gone again.

I'd just finished swimming at the gym when a message lit up my screen. I knew instantly who it was. I opened the message and a photo filled the screen.

Pippa: It's beautiful.
Andrew: It was pretty spectacular.

'Spectacular' was possibly an understatement for the image of the sun peeping over the horizon, tie-dyeing the sky in the most vibrant array of oranges and pinks.

Andrew: Are you still okay with going to my mom's sixtieth next weekend?

Pippa: Yes. What gift should I bring her?

Andrew: You don't need to bring a gift. I've got her something. We can sign the card from both of us. After all, that's what boyfriends and girlfriends do ☺

Pippa: Are we giving mutual gifts now too?

Andrew: We're a 'we'. That's what 'we's do, or so I'm told.

Pippa: What else do 'we's do?'

Andrew: I had an ex once that liked popping my pimples.

Pippa: WHAT? That's disgusting. I don't ever want to be a 'we' if I have to do that!

Andrew: I won't make you pop my pimples, promise.

Pippa: And no blackheads either!

Andrew: Definitely not. I would never dream of it.

Pippa: My mom waxes my dad's back once a month because he's too embarrassed to go to a salon.

Andrew: If I had back hair would you wax my back?

Pippa: No! If you had back hair, we wouldn't be a 'we'.

Pippa: Wait, do you have back hair?

Andrew: Haha! No, I don't.

Pippa: Thank God.

Andrew: What gross things did you and your exes do?

Pippa: What do you consider an ex?

Andrew: What do you mean?

Pippa: Most of my relationships have only lasted for a few weeks. If that. So we never really graduated to the 'we' stage. In fact, you're probably my longest 'relationship'.

Andrew: Seriously, I'm flattered.

Pippa: Weird, my longest relationship is a fake relationship. What does that say about me?

Andrew: What does it say about me that my best relationship is a fake relationship?

Pippa: This is your best relationship?

Andrew: Without a doubt.

My cheeks did that thing again for no external reason whatsoever – they warmed. The warmth came from the inside and, to cool them, I fanned myself with my hand. And then I typed again.

Pippa: Me too.

Andrew: This fake-relationship thing is great! Why don't more people do it?

Pippa: Maybe we should start a business offering fake relationships.

Andrew: We'd make a fortune!

Andrew: Okay, I have to go. Flying soon.

Pippa: Have a good flight.

Andrew: Blue skies and tailwinds.

Pippa: What's that?

Andrew: That's how you wish pilots good luck.

Pippa: Like 'break a limb' to actors.

Andrew: Leg. But same principle.

Pippa: I'll remember that.

Andrew: I wonder what one says to an ATC?

Pippa: I don't know.

Andrew: I'll have to think about it. Chat soon.

Even though Andrew had said not to buy his mother a present, I knew that *my* mom would be horrified to find out I'd arrived at a party without bringing a gift. To her, that would be sacrilege. Gifts, gifting, buying gifts and wrapping gifts were some of my mother's favorite pastimes. And she always chose the perfect, most thoughtful gifts. She had a real gift for giving gifts; it was a talent. Me, on the other hand, I was a terrible gift-giver. So much so that now I just gave people gift vouchers and let them choose their own presents. I'd thought about what to get Andrew's mom all week, but nothing felt right until I walked into the pet shop to stock up on fish food. That's when I saw it. Hidden away at the very back of the shop, alone and isolated in a tank. I walked up to the tank. Something about this lonely, segregated fish intrigued me. I felt drawn to it.

'Why is this fish alone?' I asked Adam, the shop assistant, who knew me well.

'He's in recovery. He has a bacterial infection, we're giving him anti-bacterial drops.'

I leaned in to inspect. The poor fish had tail and fin flop. His sides were covered in white patches, but then I saw it! I wasn't sure I was seeing correctly, so I pushed my face right up against the glass.

'I know. Interesting markings,' Adam said. 'Looks like two eyes on his back.'

'No! Looks like the number sixty.'

Adam cocked his head to the side. 'Oh my God, you're right. How about that. Sixty.'

'I'll take him!' I said.

'He's not for sale. Not until his infection clears.'

'But you know me. I have lots of experience looking after fish.'

'Fine, but I can't guarantee he'll survive.'

'That's okay. But he will survive!'

I walked out of there ten minutes later with what had to be the best present ever.

A few days later, I was back in Andrew's car. His parents lived about an hour outside of the city, and I was looking forward to the drive. Andrew had put the roof down and the weather was warm and sunny. Synonyms included words I loved, like *luminous*, *radiant* and *brilliant*. The day was brilliantly luminous and I felt radiant. We'd driven the entire way with the roof down, wind blowing in my hair and face and rushing over my ears so it sounded like I was on a roller-coaster. I loved this, and every now and then I'd squeeze the fishbowl tightly between my thighs and put both hands in the air. I splayed my fingers and kept them loose, allowing the wind to move them back and forth, as if playing a jazzy tune on an invisible piano in the sky. And whenever I did this, Andrew would turn and smile at me.

His parents' house was very different to my parents' house. It was small and humble, and the garden was absolutely crammed with Wendy houses, slides and swings. So much so that I wondered if he'd forgotten to tell me that his parents ran a day-care centre from their home. We parked in the street and climbed out. My nerves buzzed and hummed as I clutched the bowl. I looked down into it; Sixty looked a little shaken up, but not seriously. The bright sunlight brought out his golden sheen and the red in his now fully healed tail and fins. He was a beautiful fish, and a part of me was sad to let him go.

'You ready?' Andrew asked.

I nodded as he opened the gate and we walked into the small garden. I almost tripped over a small black plastic bike. It was the kind that small children rode on while making zooming noises, a game I'd never understood as a child. Making imaginary sounds on what was clearly *not* a real bike was beyond me. Did they know how silly they looked, playing this imagined game? I hadn't liked imaginary games when I was young; I'd much preferred having discussions with people, usually older people, and doing something practical, like reading, or drawing. Hide and seek was probably the only game I'd enjoyed, but only because I was so good at hiding that no one ever found me, which meant that I was free to enjoy some very long peaceful moments alone in a box, or up a tree, or sandwiched between the back of the school piano and the wall.

I almost bumped into a swing as I navigated the toy maze that was this garden. I could only assume that all of this stuff was for the many nieces and nephews that Andrew had warned me about. And as we got closer to the house, I heard the noise. No, it was more than a noise, so much more: it was a boisterous cacophony. Those were the right synonyms, weren't they? Or was the right one more in line with *caterwauling*.

'Sounds like the family is here,' Andrew stated casually. *The family?* A family of what? Of laughing hyenas. There were loud pool splashes, the shriek of children's laughter, the laughter of adults, the sizzle of meat cooking on a barbecue and the barking of what sounded like a very small dog. One of those grumpy chihuahuas that always thinks it can attack my much larger dogs. The front door was open, and Andrew made a beeline for it. I, on the other hand, froze.

'Uh . . .' I looked around frantically and then gazed down at Sixty. He looked relaxed, not like me. He was lazily swimming through the water, totally oblivious to the noise of this new environment. He was in the same, safe environment he'd always been in. I wished that I could somehow move through the world like that, inside a protective and familiar bubble.

'You okay?' Andrew asked.

'I think I just need a moment,' I said softly.

'Sure.' Andrew led me to some chairs on the veranda. They were old, plaited-wire chairs, the kind that had been very popular in the eighties but that you never saw any more. I put Sixty's bowl down on the table; it was also old. It was obvious that the chair leg had been repaired many times over. His home was the opposite of mine, but not in an unpleasant way at all. I scanned the garden. In the only flowerbed was an old, chipped garden gnome with one arm and a rusted watering can that looked like it had been lying in the sun for twenty years. The postbox, too, was worn and rickety and looked as if it had been repaired dozens of times. There was no grass on the lawn, only sand; I assumed from the usage of the many playthings.

In the shade of a tree, the only tree in the garden, a dripping tap had caused a flourish of strange grasses and weeds to grow up underneath it.

'My parents don't believe in throwing things away,' Andrew said as I fixed my gaze upon a wheelbarrow with a too-big tricycle wheel attached to it. 'They believe in fixing and repurposing things until they cannot be used any more.'

'Reduce, recycle and reuse,' I said. 'I'm a big proponent of that. That's why I buy most of my things second hand. Not my clothes, though. I don't like the idea of wearing someone else's clothes. But furniture and electronics.'

'It used to embarrass me when I was younger. All my friends had new things.' He shrugged. 'But now I like it.'

I was about to open my mouth when a woman stuck her head around the door.

'I thought I heard voices!' she said, beaming. Andrew jumped up and hugged her.

'Mom!' They rocked from side to side in one of those really big hugs that people give when they truly like each other. I hoped she wasn't going to give me a hug like that.

'So happy you're here!' she said, releasing him from her grip. I didn't want a hug, so I stood up quickly and thrust the fishbowl out in front of me, blocking any kind of approach.

'Happy sixtieth, Mrs Boyce-Jones. This is your present. I hope you like fish. I found him all alone in a tank at the back of the pet store; he was sick. But don't worry, I've been medicating him and he's doing much better. But if you look at his back, it looks like there's a sixty on it, that's why I got him. His name is Sixty!' I finished my preamble and pushed the bowl into her arms so enthusiastically that some of the water splashed out onto her shirt. I hadn't meant that to happen. That wasn't good. But she seemed oblivious to the water or, if she wasn't, she was pretending to be. She looked into the bowl and laughed.

'I don't believe it. It's a sixty. Look at that!' She graced me with a massive smile. Her face was make-up free, wrinkled, and her hair was unstyled and poofed up in places, as if she'd been sleeping on one side of it for so long that the hairs no longer flattened there.

'But you'll have to give this to the real birthday girl. Not me,' she said, pushing the bowl.

'But you're Andrew's mom.'

'I'm only one of his moms. And call me Grace. It's so lovely to finally meet you, Pippa.' Unperturbed by the bowl, she reached right over it and pulled me into a half-hug. I stiffened a little but forced myself to hug back with my one free arm. When she pulled away, she looked back down into the bowl and laughed again.

'Isn't that amazing. It's a sixty. As clear as daylight. Your mom is going to love it,' she said to Andrew, and then walked inside.

'I'm confused,' I whispered, following Andrew inside.

'I forgot to tell you. I have two moms.'

'Two moms,' I said thoughtfully. My brain was taking ages to compute. I'd had an expectation when he'd said 'parents'. I'd imagined a mom and a dad. Whenever an expectation of mine wasn't met, it always took me time to readjust, time to understand the new parameters. We walked through the lounge and headed for a door at the end of it, and as we approached it . . . 'OOOH! I see.' I smiled at myself, pleased that it hadn't taken me that long to get there. 'My best friend, Jennifer, she's also a lesbian – *shit*.'

I stopped dead. The noise around us stopped too, and suddenly what felt like a million pairs of eyes were blinking at me.

'Um . . . Unless you find the term "lesbian" offensive?' I asked the pairs of eyes. 'Gay? Homosexual coupling? Or was it that I just assumed your pronouns? Uh—' The eyes continued to blink. 'I have a fish,' I said, thrusting the bowl out again so enthusiastically that a huge splash of water landed on the floor at my feet.

I felt an arm come up around me. 'This is Pippa, my girlfriend. She's brought a fish and her best friend, Jennifer, is also a lesbian, and she makes really loud entrances that may or may not be offensive.' He squeezed my shoulder in a way that felt playful and caring.

I grimaced and shrugged. 'Sorry,' I said. The eyes had stopped blinking now, and instead a group of faces with growing smiles all looked at me.

'God, it takes *a lot* more than that to offend us, dear,' one of his sisters said, breaking the ice.

Chapter 20

I was engulfed. That's the only way to describe the feeling of people wrapping me up in hugs and passing me around. It was never-ending, non-stop and relentless, and all I wanted was for the wave to die so I could stop riding it. Mass hugging like this made me so uncomfortable, and coupled with the fact that I didn't know these people and was in an unfamiliar environment, I wanted to crawl out of my skin. But I bore it as best as I could until finally the wave did hit the shore and fizzled. I found myself standing in front of Andrew's other mother, Rebecca – Becca for short. She was the only person I hadn't hugged yet, and I intended on keeping it that way.

'His name is Sixty,' I said, passing her the fish as quickly as I could.

'I can't believe it,' she gushed, and looked around at everyone. And then a new wave descended, as if she was the Pied Piper who had beckoned all the children unto her. She kneeled down with the bowl as flocks of children gathered around her and stared at Sixty. My mouth fell open. Why were there so many children here? Where had they all come from? I felt an arm on my elbow.

'My mom's foster children,' Andrew whispered next to me, as if reading my mind.

I nodded. They fostered a LOT of children. I started counting heads, and was interrupted again.

'Those two redheads are my niece and nephew, from my older sister, Emma. The blond twins over there are from my middle sister,

Shaleen. And that one crawling on the floor, that's my youngest sister, Linda's, child. And the rest are foster children.'

'Ten. There are ten children. I'm not very good with children,' I whispered.

'Don't worry, you can sit at the adults table, with me.'

'Pippa.' Andrew's mom finally stood up with the fish. She was tall and muscular-looking and, I must say, very, very intimidating.

'Yes,' I said in the meek voice I'd been reduced to as she moved towards me. I wanted to step back; there was something in her voice and in her movements that was very authoritative. But I kept my feet firmly planted on the ground.

'Where did you find this fish?' she asked, but it felt more like an interrogation.

'At a pet store. It was all alone in the back. He had a bacterial infection, but don't worry, I've been treating it. But I must warn you, he might not live as long as a normal goldfish, but—'

'That makes it even more perfect!' The serious look on her face faded away as she beamed at the fish.

'Here.' I reached into my handbag and pulled out the fish food. 'Only a tiny pinch a day. Very little. Just a few flakes. Once a day. And don't put the bowl in the sun; it will encourage algae growth. And this is his medication: three drops a day in the water.' She took the fish food and medication and then gently put the bowl down on the table.

'Thank you. This is one of the most thoughtful gifts I've ever received.' And then the muscular woman drew me into her massive arms and hugged me so hard I wondered if I would ever breathe again.

When she walked away, Andrew leaned in and whispered in my ear. 'She's a policewoman. Don't worry, she intimidates everyone when they first meet her, but trust me, she's a sweetheart.'

I nodded. So that's where I knew that voice and pose from. The voice and pose designed to strike fear into your heart at roadblocks and car-licence checks. Police terrified me; if I was ever pulled over, I would frantically scan my mind, trying to figure out if I'd done anything wrong, even though I knew I hadn't.

'The licence disc on my car is about to expire, but I will get it renewed!' I heard myself say, and everyone stared at me again. 'But other than that, I've never broken the law and have no criminal record. Just so you know.'

Becca tipped her head at me. 'Good to know, because I do run a full background check on everyone who comes into my house,' she said, and then headed for the grill.

'She's joking, right?' I asked Andrew.

'I actually don't know,' he replied.

'How did your moms meet?'

'My mom Grace is a social worker, and my mom Becca works in the child protection unit.'

I nodded. That made sense.

'My sister Emma is a dress designer. Shaleen is a librarian, and Linda is a golf instructor. We're very different, but we're all adopted.'

'Really?' I asked, looking from one to the other. Now that I thought about it, they looked nothing alike. 'Are they going to adopt all these children too?'

Andrew's shoulders slumped. 'Unfortunately, they can't. They foster some long term, but most are here on a short-term basis until they find forever homes. It takes a lot longer if they're older though, so some land up staying permanently.' I watched the kids playing. They all looked happy and well taken care of. But even so, sadness filled my chest like a helium balloon being blown up.

'Some of them come from very bad circumstances,' he said softly. 'But they're all great kids.'

'Did you come from bad circumstances?' I asked. Andrew's eyes swept over mine quickly, and then he turned his back on me. *Shit*, my question had been too forward, too inappropriate. 'Sorry,' I said, and tried to reach out and touch his shoulder, but he was already walking away from me.

More feelings filled my chest. Unwanted children, unwanted fish, unwanted Andrew and his siblings. Everyone deserved someone that wanted them. Wanted to know them. Wanted to be there for them. Outside of my parents and Jennifer, I'd always struggled to make those kinds of connections with people. Perhaps that's why I'd felt such an immediate connection with Sixty, and now why I felt like crying in the middle of a sixtieth-birthday celebration. Sometimes emotions overwhelmed me. They pounced on me out of nowhere and made me want to crumple in on myself. Some emotions felt too big to contain within me at times: sadness, anxiety, even happiness. And in moments like this I usually ran for the nearest bathroom, or the nearest quiet space, but that was not an option now.

'So you're an air traffic controller?' one of his sisters asked.

Deep breath. Deep breath. 'Ye—'

'Is that how you guys met?' The next sister cut me off before I could speak.

'That's so cute!' the next sister said.

'And where do you live?'

'Nor—' I was cut off again.

'How long have you known each other?'

'How long have you worked at the airport?'

The questions shot at me from all sides, all at once. I tried to keep up but was soon lost in the rally of words.

'Guys, give her a moment to breathe,' Andrew scolded, with a smile on his face.

'You can't expect us to do that! You haven't brought a girl home in years—' I think it was Linda who said this.

'Years!' Someone else added emphasis to that.

'It's so exciting. We want to know everything.'

'Everything,' someone else echoed.

'Okay, okay.' Andrew walked over to me. 'At least let her have a drink first.' He pointed across at the barbecue. 'If I know my brother-in-law James, there're probably frozen Margaritas in a blender in the kitchen?'

The man named James shot Andrew a thumbs-up.

'Do you want one?' Andrew asked me.

'I don't know. I've never had a Margarita.'

There was silence again. I was sure, if a feather had dropped from the sky, we would hear it as it banged to the ground with a thunderous roar. And then a loud and very resounding group 'What?' rung out. In seconds, it seemed to have become everyone's personal mission to make me drink a Margarita.

CHAPTER 21

'Mmmm, Margaritas are delicious!' I exclaimed as I drank my second one and licked the salt off the rim.

'I can't believe you've never had one,' James said, pouring seconds for everyone else.

'Why not?' Becca asked.

I put my drink down on the table and took a deep breath. 'I don't like cactuses.'

'You don't what?' Becca exclaimed, and a few people laughed, including Andrew.

'I had a bad encounter with one.' I stuck my arm out and pointed to the small red scars.

'What happened?' Linda leaned towards my arm.

'I fell on one. It took the doctor an hour to remove all the thorns.' I pointed to my left leg, which was also covered in small red scars.

'You're kidding?' Shaleen gasped.

'And because you don't like cactuses, you've never drunk tequila?' Grace asked, barbecue tongs in the air.

'Precisely!' I was thrilled she'd gotten it right away and I hadn't needed to explain that thinking about cactuses made my scars psychosomatically itch. Which made me recall how the nurse had had to hold me down as the doctor worked on me with tweezers while I screamed.

'Well, thanks for drinking a tequila with us today,' Andrew said, turning in his chair. He was sitting next to me, and his close proximity made me feel good.

'Hear, hear!' Becca stuck hers up in the air. 'I feel quite honored actually.'

I smiled at everyone. There was something about them that seemed to set me at ease. Not consciously, but on a deep and silent level that was beyond my full understanding. It was in that intangible way that was always hard for me to understand. But maybe intangible ways were not meant to be understood; maybe they were just meant to be enjoyed.

The Margaritas did make me feel more relaxed as the day went on. I hadn't participated much in the conversation, apart from my cactus story; instead I'd sat back and observed the family talking and laughing with each other. They fascinated me, how they finished each other's sentences and knew when it was appropriate to smack each other on the arm in jest, not in aggression. This family unit was a well-oiled machine, each one a cog, a small part of something bigger than themselves but all working in perfect unison together.

'Aaaah!' I gasped when a cat jumped onto my lap.

'Don't worry, that's just Checkers,' Grace said. But I stiffened and looked at Andrew with big eyes.

'You okay?' he asked.

'I'm allergic to cats,' I said, trying to back away from it as much as I could. 'Oh my God! Oh my God! What is it doing?' I winced as it pushed its nails into my thighs. 'Make it stop! Please.' The cat was purring like a machinegun and digging into me with such force that its claws were piercing my skin.

'You really don't like cats at all!' Shaleen laughed.

'Who doesn't like cats?' One of the twins had come over now. A few more children had arrived as I started to shoo the cat away with a napkin. 'Aaah!' I jumped in my chair as the cat attacked the napkin, grabbed it between its paws and dug its teeth into it viciously. It rolled over onto its back and kicked the napkin repeatedly with its back legs while making strange growling sounds.

'Now you've turned it into a game.' Becca walked over to me. 'Are you having fun, Checkers?' She pulled the giant fur ball off, just as my first sneeze came rushing out.

'Bless you!'

I jumped as everyone said that in unison. But it wasn't long before Checkers was on me again. This time he'd sprung up from behind my chair and pounced on me. I screamed, which sent all the children into hysterics. I got up and changed seats, only to find the cat stalking me from under the table. He launched himself back onto my leg and scurried up it and then tried to climb onto my shoulder.

Finally, the cat was gotten rid of and put into another room. I let out three more consecutive sneezes followed by three more blasted-out 'bless you's from what had become a giant audience. I realized that I'd become the center of attention, and this didn't feel as uncomfortable as it usually would have. Maybe it was the Margaritas, or maybe it was the fact that Andrew's family seemed like one big friendly entity. Their smiles looked warm and genuine, and they all talked and joked in happy, relaxed tones which even I was able to pick up on. This was obviously where Andrew got that quality from.

The men barbecued, the children played, and everyone continued to talk as the party got into full swing. This was nothing like my mom's sixtieth. She'd had a formal ball, calligraphic name cards on satin-draped tables, orchids and mood lighting and speeches and a live band. But this was so casual and laid back and, truthfully, I liked it so much more.

'What's your name again?'

I turned at the soft voice coming from behind me. I was met by a small boy hiding behind a huge pair of glasses.

'Pippa,' I said.

'That's a funny name.'

'I hated it when I was young. I always thought of a pip every time I said it.'

'That's what I thought of too,' he said.

'What's your name?' I asked.

'Leroy. I think it's a good name. Much better than Pippa.'

'I agree with you, Leroy.'

'Are you Andrew's girlfriend?' he asked.

'Yes. Why?'

'You look nothing like his last girlfriend.'

'What did Andrew's last girlfriend look like?' I asked.

'She was much prettier than you,' Leroy said, and then turned and walked back towards the pool. I felt a hand on my shoulder.

'Don't take it to heart, dear,' Grace said. 'Leroy doesn't have much of a social filter. He doesn't mean to say things that might hurt people.' I watched him walk away; he was favoring his tiptoes. His arms swung around, as if he had no concept of his body in space.

'He's on the autism spectrum,' I heard myself say.

Grace squeezed my shoulder. 'Abandoned by his birthmother when it became obvious he was different. Such a great kid though, unbelievably smart. But we're having a hard time finding him a family.' She sighed slowly and softly. 'People hear the word "autism" and immediately run for the hills, but I think it's very misunderstood.'

'He looks happy here,' I said, as he sat down at the pool and dangled his feet in.

'He is. We make sure of it.'

A feeling bubbled up inside me. It was anger. It was sadness. It was something else I couldn't name. I thought about Sixty all alone in that tank at the back of that shop. I thought about me, sitting alone on the playground in primary school. Watching from the sidelines. I thought about Leroy on his tiptoes. All he wanted was a family to call his own. I almost opened my mouth right there and then to say something, but didn't.

Chapter 22

'Hey, we're here.' I felt the soft tap of something on my cheek.

'What . . . um . . .' I startled.

'You fell asleep.'

'Did I?' I sat up and looked around. We were in the familiar underground parking lot in the airport again. I had no recollection of falling asleep at all, but I wasn't surprised. After social interactions like that, even though I'd enjoyed it, I was always exhausted. I wiped my face and eyes.

'I didn't mean to. Sorry.'

'Don't apologize. You make really cute noises when you sleep.'

I sat bolt upright. 'What kind of noises?'

He smiled 'Like a squeak.'

'A squeak! That sounds awful.'

'Only on your outbreaths.'

'Every outbreath?'

Andrew laughed. 'No, not every single one.'

'Wasn't that irritating?'

'No, I had the music on, and it blended in.'

I breathed in and out slowly and my nose made a little squeak. I slapped my hand over it quickly.

'It's probably an allergy,' I said, pointing at the offending nostril. 'To the cat.'

'Probably. It's amazing how cats seem to sniff out the one person in the room who doesn't like them. Are you awake enough to drive home?' he asked.

'I'm not going home. I have a shift starting in a few hours.'

'What are you going to do until then?'

'I go to the gym at the airport hotel.'

'Seriously? I also go there. How come I've never seen you?'

'I swim. The pool is on the roof. Different section. I bet you do a lot of weights.' My eyes drifted down to his arms.

He smiled. 'Are you judging me for that? Like I'm one of those guys who wears flimsy vests and films my workouts to post on social media?'

'Do you?'

'No.'

'Well, then I'm not judging you. But if you were one of those guys, then that would be a completely different story and I'd have to break up with you immediately.'

'Well, lucky I'm not then.'

'You have a good physique though. Not that I've seen it properly. Barely seen it at all – not that I'm looking, either – but what I have seen is good so far.'

'Thanks.' He smiled at me; I smiled back. Mine was a natural smile. I wasn't mirroring his facial features to seem more normal, or natural. This was *my* smile, no pretending, no imitating.

'What time does your shift end?'

'Graveyard shift,' I replied, even though I thought that to be one of the oddest expressions yet. I was only saying it because that's what everyone else called it. The expression seemed to imply that graveyards only existed at night. That you couldn't do a shift in a graveyard during the day. Did they magically disappear in the day, like vampires supposedly did? I don't think so. 'I love working at night. It's so much quieter.'

'I'm sure that will be a welcome relief after my house.'

'YES!' I gushed, and then stopped abruptly before offending him. 'I really enjoyed it though.'

'Leroy took a shine to you today. He doesn't usually like people.'

'I don't usually like people either. Like cats who find people who don't like them, we people who usually don't like other people tend to gravitate towards each other.'

'I hope you liked the rest of my family, just a little bit?'

'I like them! But there are a hell of a lot of them, aren't there?'

'I'm afraid human culling is looked down on,' Andrew said, his smile growing.

It took me a while to get it, but when I did, I laughed so hard my shoulders shook. My laugh was so loud that it reverberated around the underground parking lot. And once I started laughing, I couldn't stop.

'That was so funny.'

'I gathered that,' he said, in between his own laughs.

'So dark. So funny. How do you do that? I'm so useless at being purposefully funny. People find me accidentally funny.'

He grinned at me. It was leisurely and long, almost as if the smile was taking its time to fully form on his face. 'I think being accidentally funny is much better than being purposefully funny.'

'Maybe,' I mused, but I wasn't so sure of that. There had been many times in my life when I'd tried to join in with the jokey, witty banter and failed miserably. In fact, all my attempts at purposeful humour were met with very blank stares, and in some cases, people actually backed away from me.

'My family loved you, by the way,' Andrew said, pulling me out of the memory where some girls had all been joking about the hickies on their necks and I'd chimed in and said that a guy that likes sucking on necks should be called a neck-romancer, a play on words that I'd thought was really clever, actually. 'That's so gross,' one of them had said, and then they'd all 'eew'ed together.

'I liked them too.' And I actually meant it.

'Thanks for doing this. It was really helpful.'

'Well, that's what our arrangement is for,' I said, and then gave him a small wave and started backing away from the car.

'Wait!' he called after me. 'You asked me a question earlier today, about my birthmother.'

'You don't have to tell me. I shouldn't have asked.'

'You just caught me off-guard, that's all.'

'Sorry,' I said softly.

He closed his eyes for a moment, or was that a long blink?

'She was young. Really young. Fourteen.'

'Oh my God. What happened?'

'He was the hot, popular guy at school, and he showed her some attention, and one thing led to another.'

'Did she tell you that?'

'No, but I tracked down the nurse who was at my birth, and she told me. Said my biological mother was quiet, and painfully shy; she was flattered that the popular guy took an interest in her. She thought he genuinely liked her and wanted to be in a relationship with her, but I think you can guess the rest.'

I nodded. I'd had a similar encounter once, someone I thought genuinely liked me too, only to find out he'd been dared to kiss the 'strange girl' at the dance by his friends.

'His family and hers wanted her to get an abortion, but she didn't want to. She tried to keep me, but at that age you're a child yourself, and I was taken into care after only a few weeks with her.'

'Shit, that's horrible.' A mass of emotions hit me in my stomach, and I wanted to cry again.

'I was adopted pretty quickly after that though.'

'Do you know where she is?' I asked, trying to push those intense feelings away.

'She's . . . Uh . . . not great. She dropped out of school after she had me, didn't go back. She barely gets by working at a grocery store.

She's got another child, no husband. I don't think her life's worked out the way she would have wanted it to.'

'I'm sorry.' I opened the car door and climbed back inside. This felt like a conversation that needed to be had inside the car, sitting next to each other. He switched the engine off, turned in his seat and faced me.

'Have you met her?'

'No, but I do . . .' He ran his hand through his hair and looked away.

'What?'

'I send her money. She doesn't know it comes from me. I went to a lawyer. It's not totally legal, but I convinced him to tell her a relative had died and left her a monthly stipend. I didn't want to give it to her all at once; she used to have a drinking problem. She goes to AA. It's not a lot. It covers my half-brother's school fees and groceries, and some other things. My moms don't know I do that, though. I don't know why I haven't told them. They'd get it, I know they would. But for some reason I just can't bring myself to tell them.'

'I think that's really nice of you,' I said, my voice cracking a little. 'Don't you want to meet her?'

'Don't know. I chatted to a psychologist about it once. It was a very traumatic part of her life, and I would hate to open up all those old wounds. I'm not sure. Maybe that'll change one day, I'm just . . . not sure.'

Something compelled me to reach out and pull Andrew in for a hug. It was brief, and I let go of him after a second or two.

'What was that for?'

'You're supposed to hug people in moments like this. So I'm hugging you.'

'Thanks, although I would hardly call that a hug. It was a back pat.'

I scrunched my face up. 'I think that's a bit of an exaggeration. It might have been less than a hug, but it was definitely more than a pat.'

'A hat?' Andrew offered.

'A what – OH! Got it. Funny, but corny.'

'Terribly corny.' He nodded his head in agreement.

'A pug?' I said.

'A pug. That's cute. I like it.'

'I like that you like it,' I muttered under my breath.

'What?' he asked, and leaned over.

'Nothing!' My insides did a little something that made me feel off-kilter, as if I was falling forward. I hadn't meant to say that out loud, and now I was embarrassed and certainly didn't want to repeat it. 'I should go!' I climbed out of the car quickly. 'But, that was . . . thanks. And thanks for sharing your story with me, that was also . . . thanks,' I said before scuttling off.

I was just about to dive into the pool when my phone delivered a beep from a number I didn't recognize. I opened the message and was greeted by a photo. It was Sixty. His bowl had been placed on what looked like a bedside table. The message read:

> **Unknown:** Thanks so much for the gift, I'm afraid Leroy has claimed Sixty, though, and he's currently living on his bedside table. Thanks for coming today and celebrating with me. It was lovely meeting you. Hope to see you soon. X Becca

I read the message again. I liked her. In fact, despite the utter chaos of the day, which had at times been utterly draining, I'd liked them all. I put the phone back into my bag and dived, letting the water engulf me. *Envelop*, *encompass*, *inundate*. I loved the way those synonyms sounded, and I loved the feeling of my body sinking into the warm water and gravity disappearing. With gravity gone, you're no longer tethered to anything, you're buoyant. You float freely, weightlessly, through the liquid. I liked to stay under for as long as possible before coming up for air again. Down there, beneath the blue surface, is where I feel most at peace. The world above you fades away behind a rippling veil as water rushes into your ears, silencing everything.

I finally came up for air, took a deep breath and began my laps. But today, because of all the social overstimulation, my brain was not as silent as it normally was. So I moved on to the exercise that helped it simmer down. As I stroked through the water, I focused all my attention on the blue line running the length of the lane painted on the bottom of the pool. I focused on that line as if it was the only thing that existed in the world. And then I began repeating a phrase in my head over and over again; it's hypnotic. 'Blue line, blue line, blue line.' Soon my brain was filled only with those two words and nothing else. Those repeated words pushed everything else out of my head until nothing was left. Sometimes when 'blue line' becomes too much, I'll use synonyms with each stroke.

'Cerulean'. 'Azure'. 'Cobalt'. 'Tanzanite'. 'Sapphire'. 'Navy'. 'Teal'. 'Ultramarine'. 'Turquoise'. And in these moments, when my brain is finally silent, as it had also been in the car when driving with the roof down, I felt utter bliss.

CHAPTER 23

Pippa: What are you doing right now?

It had been a week since I'd seen Andrew. We'd communicated a few times on the radio, but it had been seven days since I'd laid eyes on him. Well, physical eyes, because I had looked at that photo of the two of us kissing from time to time. Not an excessive amount of time, mind you. But there had been times, that's for sure.

Andrew: Honestly, lying on my couch in my pajamas, eating cereal out of Tupperware because I came in late and didn't wash my dishes!

Pippa: Well, I'm being spontaneous. And I might regret it, or I might not.

Andrew: Spontaneous? Wow.

Pippa: I know. Very unlike me.

Andrew: What do you need me to do?

Pippa: I need your expertise. Can you get out of your pajamas, finish your cereal – which by the way holds no nutritional value, even if it does say 'fortified with vitamins' – and come and join me?

Andrew: Where are you?

I told Andrew, and I wasn't surprised by his shocked response; in fact, I was still completely surprised myself, even after a week of mulling it over in my head.

'Seriously?' Andrew's eyes widened. He'd gotten here in record time. I'd estimated that it might take him forty-five minutes to get dressed and drive over, but it had only taken thirty, which was impressive.

'You looked shocked?'

'I am.'

'So it's a bad idea then?'

'NO! Not at all. It's a great idea. A brilliant idea. The best idea ever.' A huge smile parted his lips. 'It's not practical, of course. Or economical, or any of those things that you usually like.'

'I know! And I think that's why I'll like it. Even though I might regret it.'

'Nah, you could never regret this.' He ran his hand over one of them. 'Which one are you thinking of?'

'That's why I called you. I know nothing about classic sports cars.'

'And I do!' Andrew's face lit up as he ran his hand over the beautifully restored gas-guzzling 1981 Mercedes Benz convertible that was so wide and boat-like I wondered how one would ever park it. It seemed to me that if you had to buy this car you would need to take a specialist course in parking.

'What's your budget?' Andrew asked.

I pointed at the Mercedes price tag. I wasn't splashing out, I wasn't going for a ludicrously overpriced collector's item, I was still being price practical, and making sure my trade-in covered at least eighty per cent of the price.

'Oh my God! Look at this one.' Andrew skidded across the floor to the 1989 red Porsche with the square lights that popped out of the bonnet. 'Do you remember that TV show with the talking car, *Knight Rider*?'

I nodded.

'This is so *Knight Rider*.'

'Except it's red!' I replied.

'Well, not literally. But the vibe. The long, square bonnet, the lights. It's badass. It's you.'

'I'm badass?'

'Um . . . You navigated seven planes out of the way to avoid a disaster and guided a plane with one engine down for a safe landing. I would say that makes you pretty badass.'

'How do you know about that?' It had been before Andrew's time.

'Are you kidding? Everyone knows about that. All the pilots talk about it. They say that if they were ever in an emergency, they'd want you on the line.'

I smiled. A little flicker of warm pride moved through me. I liked being told I was good and competent at my job. It was one of my favorite compliments in the entire world.

I walked around the car. It had that eighties retro look that you either loved or hated. It was angular, pointy, boxy and so bloody long and low, and it screamed of Magnum P.I. and big moustaches and women with huge perms and leggings. It was a head-turner, in a good way, or a bad way, depending on how one looked at it. There was no way you could pull up to a stop in the street and *not* have people look at you. It was impractical and old and would probably break down regularly. It was red, a color that showed the dirt, not to mention that it attracted heat and probably bees too – it was a known fact that bees were attracted to bright colors. Mind you, it was also a well-known fact that bright colors in the animal kingdom were synonymous with mating rituals, and the last thing I wanted was to drive this through a game reserve only to have an ostrich hump it! My brain was firing on all cylinders, my thoughts pulling me in all directions, all at once. This happened when I got nervous, and I was nervous now. Nervous, but exhilarated. The tyres also seemed excessively large. I bet they cost a fortune if you happened to get a nail in one or hit a pothole. I took a deep breath.

But the roof came down and I would be able to feel the wind in my face as I drove, the old V8 engine would roar and growl like Andrew's car's did, which made the driving experience so much better. And that's what I wanted, because that night on the open road with Andrew, the wind in my hair, the gearstick in my hand, I'd felt so damn alive. I just had to get the image of an ostrich mounting the bonnet out of my head, and then I would—

'I'll take it!' I shouted to no one in particular, throwing my hands in the air. And before I knew what I was doing my hands came out of the air and landed around Andrew's shoulders, but only for a second.

'You pugged me again,' he said, amused.

'That was more than a pug.' I strode towards my new car, and that's when it happened. My shoes, which lacked grip, began to slip on the highly polished surface of the floor.

'Fuck!' I flapped my arms in the air as my legs involuntarily began doing the splits.

'Got you.' Andrew grabbed me under my arms and pulled me up.

'Thanks.' I looked down at the floor; it was mirror-like. 'They should really not polish it so much. Or they should have a warning sign, at least.'

He grinned.

'What?'

'I don't think I've ever met anyone as clumsy as you. I mean, you fell into a cactus.'

'I've also fallen into a koi pond. Do you have any idea how big and terrifying koi are close up? They are the only fish I don't like – they tried to eat my toes.' I pulled my skirt down, since it had crept up in my gymnastic floor routine. 'I've fallen off a boat, I fell into a muddy pothole once, and I fell flat on my face while crossing a pedestrian crossing in peak-rush-hour traffic.'

'My point exactly: you fall a lot.'

'I have dyspraxia,' I said, without meaning to. 'It's a developmental disorder that affects coordination, so . . .' I stopped. Why was I telling him this? 'Anyway, it makes me trip and fall and knock things over, a lot.'

He looked at me solemnly and nodded. 'Leroy has that too. My moms were saying it's pretty common in kids with an autism diagnosis.'

My body stiffened; it was an involuntary stiffen that I had no control over.

'It's more common than you think,' I said quickly. 'Some people think they're just clumsy, but they're not. That's why I started karate; it really helps with that.'

'Sorry, it must be hard,' Andrew said, his voice low and soft.

I looked away quickly. 'Indeed,' I mumbled, and clapped my hands together awkwardly. 'It's more irritating than hard. I can stub the same toe ten times in a day. It's very, very irritating, and sore.'

'I'm sure.'

'And what have we decided?' The eager salesman with the very big white teeth was suddenly upon me and I startled. I grabbed my chest and let out a little gasp.

'Sorry to creep up on you.' He smiled a full mouth of veneers at me.

I hated it when people came out of nowhere. 'It's fine.'

'Has the lovely lady decided on a car?' he asked, and I looked at him blankly.

'Me? Are you asking me if *I* have decided on a car?'

'Mmm-hmm.' He nodded and showed his teeth even more.

'You know, in the primate kingdom, showing your teeth to that extent is often perceived as a sign of aggression.'

'Oh.' The salesman closed his lips and folded his arms.

'Anyway, since we're very closely related to primates, I just thought it was good for you to know.'

The salesman's lips pulled tightly across his mouth and he looked at me as if he was sucking on a lemon.

'I'll take that one.' I pointed at the red car that I may seriously regret buying a little later today but was going to anyway. I could always trade it back in if I hated it and get a more practical car again.

'Great, let's do the paperwork.' He sounded way less enthused now. The big-toothed salesman started walking away and, just before I turned to follow him, I looked back at Andrew. His eyes were glued to my face with a red-hot intensity that unnerved me. It felt like his eyes had claws that were trying to dig right into me. *What was happening?* Why was he looking at me like that? I was so busy trying to decipher his look that, again, I stumbled. To break my fall, I put my hand against a car.

'Careful, that's a 1967 Ferrari. It costs twenty-two million rand,' the salesman barked at me.

I jumped away from the car as if it were infected with a deadly virus. 'This costs twenty-two million rand?' I pointed at the generic-looking sports car. 'What's so special about it?'

'You're joking, right?'

'I'm not good at joking,' I replied. 'What on earth is it made of?' I continued. 'Surely there's nothing in its manufacturing process that can justify that price tag?'

Andrew looped an arm through mine and started walking me away from it. 'Think of it as a work of art. A Picasso, if you like.'

'I don't get that either. Anyone can paint a Picasso, and certainly a Jackson Pollock. The idea that some paint on a canvas, thrown around in such a haphazard manner, should cost that much money is actually an obscene concept.'

'I think Rothko is the worst,' Andrew said, showing he was knowledgeable in another field outside of aviation. I was impressed. 'Imagine paying eighty million dollars for an entire canvas painted red.'

'How do you know so much about art?' I asked. I only knew a lot because I'd gone through a phase of being obsessed with art theft after I'd watched a documentary about how the *Mona Lisa* had been stolen twice. And so I'd immersed myself in the world of art for a while, until I moved on to the next obsession, which happened to be North Korea. And after North Korea, I'd become utterly fascinated by medieval surgical techniques and, after that, child psychopaths.

'My sister Emma studied art and I often helped her type up her essays. She hated typing and used to pay me for it. I'm also pretty knowledgeable on life orientation and graphic design.'

'I doubt that comes in handy as a pilot,' I said, trying to imagine under what circumstances learning about graphic design would ever come in handy.

'But at least it's equipped me with the ability to have meaningful conversations in order to impress perhaps the smartest person I know.'

'Who's that?' I stopped walking and looked at him.

'You.'

'Me?' I knew I was smart; that was a given. But I was more interested in the part where he'd said he was trying to impress me.

'You're also smart,' I said quickly, because it's always polite to compliment someone back when they compliment you.

'I wasn't saying that so I could get a compliment back, but thank you.'

'Not as smart as me though.' I smiled at him, playfully, teasingly. *I could do this.* I could do witty banter with Andrew, and I loved it.

'By the way, have you told your mom you're bringing a boyfriend to the wedding yet?' I'd told him how I'd been putting this off.

'No,' I admitted. 'I'll do it today though.'

'You'd better, or I'll have to sit on your lap.'

Mmm, that didn't sound too bad, actually. Maybe I could sit on his lap. Perhaps my mom didn't need to know after all.

Chapter 24

I was nervous about calling my mom, even though the entire thing was made up. Still, hearing myself say the word 'boyfriend', out loud, to my mother, would make it real in some other way. I dialled the number and, as usual, she answered on the first ring. That's the thing about my mom: even in an emergency, she always answered on the first ring, even if it's to tell me she's in the middle of a bridal emergency and will call back.

'Pippa, I wasn't expecting this. Is everything okay? It's not Wednesday.' I called my mom on a Wednesday and on Sunday evening, so it was unusual to be calling on a Tuesday.

'Everything's fine, Mom. I just have a question.'

'What is it?'

'The wedding?'

'What about it?'

'Well, you know how I only have one invite . . . I was wondering if I could have two?'

'Why do you want two?'

'Because I'm bringing someone!' I forced the words out as quickly as possible, almost hoping she wouldn't hear them but knowing that she would.

'Is Jennifer visiting? I didn't know she was coming out!'

'No, Mom. Not a friend. A boyfriend.'

'A what?' My mom gasped so loudly that the sound delivered through the phone speaker hurt my ear.

'Boyfriend,' I repeated.

'You have a boyfriend?'

'I do.' God, if she didn't believe me, then no one else in my family would.

'A real boyfriend?'

'As opposed to what, Mom?'

'I don't know! People have these online relationships with AI avatars now. Some guy wanted to know if I could organize a wedding for him in the metaverse with his "girlfriend".'

'It's a human boyfriend, Mom.'

'Wow! That's . . . that's . . . wonderful.' Her voice was an odd mix of notes and inflections – joy and shock, maybe? There was a brief pause, a moment of quiet before the inevitable storm of questions I knew was coming.

'Who is he? How did you guys meet? How long have you been going out? What's his name? What does he do?'

'Slow down, Mom.'

'Sorry, sorry. I'm just so excited.'

'His name is Andrew.'

'That's a lovely name.' My mom always read things into people's names. I thought it utterly illogical, but she didn't. 'Strong name. But not too strong. Classic, but not boring, also very—'

'He's a pilot. We met at work.' I cut her off before she decided to look up the meaning of the name, something she often did.

'A pilot! How wonderful!'

'I know how much you hate it when the seating arrangements at weddings change last minute and how much of a shuffle it takes and how much you complain about it, but—'

'NO! Say no more. For you, for this, I will shuffle the bride and groom around if need be. So how long have you been dating?'

'Two months,' I said. 'He came with me to my school reunion.'

'Wow! He must be someone special then.'

'He's a very good pilot,' I replied.

'I'm sure he is, if you're going out with him.'

'So you can fit him in?'

'Of course, but your dad and I can't meet him for the first time at the wedding. You must bring him around for dinner.'

'Uh . . . I don't think that . . .'

'I insist. Dinner. This weekend. Are you busy?'

I knew it was utterly fruitless arguing with my mother when she 'insisted'. She was one of these formidable people who always got her own way. No matter what.

'I'll have to check my schedule. And his.'

'Check them now and get right back to me!' she demanded.

'Now?'

'Yes, I'll have to plan the dinner. The weekend is only four days away.'

'I'll check and get back to you soon,' I agreed, even though the idea of bringing Andrew to my family home felt odd. Even though I'd been to his.

'I'm so excited to meet this Andrew. And I know your dad will be too. Oh my God, your dad will be over the moon. Finally, someone he can talk to about, uh . . . you know, men things.'

'Men things?' I asked.

'Like sport, beer and wood chopping and . . . *God*, I don't know what men spend their time talking about, but I'm sure he'll be glad for a male energy in the house, since he's constantly surrounded by us and Chi-Chi.'

'Dad doesn't drink beer, and I've never seen him chop wood. True, he does like golf. But that is hardly a particularly manly endeavour and Chi-Chi is a male dog.'

'There is nothing male about Chi-Chi, darling. We had him snipped as a puppy. I don't even think he remembers having balls, so he's basically a she.'

'I don't think that's how gender works, Mom.'

'I suppose it's probably not, but anyway, balls aside, call this Andrew of yours now and then phone me right back.'

'I think he's flying now.'

'Well, call him asap and then get back to me, okay?'

'Okay, Mom.'

I hung up. 'This Andrew of yours'. That expression sounded strange coming from my mother's mouth. I'd never thought of Andrew like that, as if he was an 'of mine'. It sounded somewhat *Handmaid's Tale*, 'Offred and Ofglen'. I wondered if Andrew was indeed an Ofpippa? Or perhaps I was an Ofandrew? Did I want to be a Ofanybody though? And now I wanted to stop hearing the word 'of' in my head. I quickly went through its synonyms – *about*, *pertaining to*, *attributed to* – just to mute the incessant 'of' sound. It did not work.

'How's my favorite ATC today? This is Flightbird Six Zero Zero.'

'You really shouldn't have favorites,' I said with a smile, even though he was my favorite pilot too. 'Go ahead, Flightbird Six Zero Zero.'

'City Tower, we are inbound for Johannesburg Airport, flying over the golf course, dams looking a little empty, we need some rain, requesting vectors for ILS? Flightbird Six Zero Zero.'

'Flightbird Six Zero Zero, turn left heading two seven niner.'

'Copy. Flightbird Six Zero Zero. Turn left heading two seven niner. Have you even played golf, City Tower?'

'Never. My dad does though.'

'You either love it or you hate it. I don't love it.'

'I've never been good with balls.'

He laughed. 'God, I hope no one else can hear this conversation, because if they can, they might have some serious questions for you.'

It took me a while to get what he was saying and, when I did, I blushed.

'Golf balls!' I clarified. 'And tennis balls – especially tennis balls. Soccer, squash. I have no ball–hand coordination.'

'I think it's *hand–eye* coordination. You don't want to say ball–hand. That implies something quite different.'

I blushed again. 'I'm going to stop talking now,' I said, and kept quiet. I dealt with a few other planes while waiting for him again, as well as one of my least favorite pilots, Flightbird Seven Niner. He was always so slow to repeat instructions back to me that sometimes I had to desperately fight the urge not to scold him like a teacher might. Or worse, jump in and repeat my own instruction back to me just to move things along.

Andrew's voice came through again. 'Established ILS. Runway zero seven! It's my lucky day again. I always seem to have luck with you, City Tower.'

I felt something warm and giddy build up inside me, but I tried to shake it off.

'You are cleared to land on your lucky number seven runway, Flightbird Six Zero Zero.'

'Copy, City Tower, cleared to land on runway seven. Flightbird Six Zero Zero.'

I tapped my fingers against the table, feeling nervous about what I was about to ask.

'City Tower, how's the weather down there? Flightbird Six Zero Zero.'

'Wind is two five zero at two knots.'

'Thanks, City Tower. Wind two five zero at a pleasant two knots. Chat soon. Flightbird Six Zero Zero.' I watched his plane guide down once more and, as soon as it had, he was back on the radio.

'City Tower, that was definitely a hundred per cent landing from Flightbird Six Zero Zero.'

'Ninety-nine per cent. Always room for improvement. Please vacate right onto Alpha taxiway, and contact Ground Control on one two one point zero.'

'Copy, vacate right onto Alpha taxiway, and contact ground on one two one point zero. Flightbird Six Zero Zero.'

'Wait, before you go . . . I kind of have a request for you, but I'll tell you after you take your right.' I waited for the plane to take its turn, all the while tapping my fingers anxiously. It felt like the plane took for ever to turn.

'Will you have dinner with me at my parents' house this Saturday evening? I know dinner with my parents wasn't part of our initial arrangement,' I blurted out the second his plane had come to a standstill.

'Sure, I'm not busy.'

'Oh. It's at seven. I'll message later with details.'

'Can't wait. Chat later, City Tower.'

'Okay, Flightbird. Chat later.'

'Chat soon.'

That had been so much easier than I'd thought. In retrospect, I had no idea why I'd been so nervous about it. I suppose, since the dinner fell outside of the parameters of our initial arrangement, it did have a peculiar feeling to it, as if I was inviting him on a real date. I shook my head. It wasn't real dating though. This was fake dating.

CHAPTER 25

It was Saturday night, and I drove to fetch Andrew. As I drove, despite the fact that the roof was down and the wind was blowing through my hair, an anxious feeling rose in my stomach. Introducing Andrew to my parents felt very real – a little too real. And the realness of it all made me nervously pick the side of my cuticle. No, *nervous* was not the right word at all; it would be *agitated*, *afraid*, *skittish* and *shaky*. Those were the words that were making me pick.

Dermatillomania, that's the scientific word for it. The word the psychiatrist always uses, which makes it sound so much worse than just a nervous inclination to pick the skin around your nails. I always felt so ashamed of this habit; after all, isn't nail-picking something only children are supposed to do? Aren't adult women supposed to have gorgeous-colored manicured nails, not little stumps with plasters on because you've picked so hard the cuticle was now bleeding. I hadn't picked my fingers that badly in a long time though – in fact, I hardly picked any more – so this picking I was doing right now was very upsetting.

I dived into my handbag for my fidget toys, and when I found the bag empty panic seized me. *I'd left them at home.* I could see them next to my bed; I'd played with them last night while going to sleep and left them there. The fact that they were not in my bag – where they should be, where they always were – made the need to pick my cuticles even greater.

I would not be able to get through this evening without my fidget toy in my bag – even if I didn't use it once, I needed it to be there. I looked at my GPS. I was almost at Andrew's house; it would not be logical to go back to mine now and collect it. Instead, I should pick Andrew up first and then double back to my house. That would be the most logical and time-saving method of retrieval. I sent my parents a quick voice message informing them that we were running a little late, then pulled up to where Andrew lived. It took him a few moments to appear, and when he did . . .

My God. He got better-looking each time I saw him. Like an ageing red wine – not to imply he was old, or bad for you in excessive quantities and high in tannins – but rather that he improved each time I saw him. And each time I did, I noticed something new too: this time it was his walk. He walked with a confidence and self-assuredness that was most pleasing to behold. It was the kind of walk that you might give when walking up to a podium to receive a prize, or a graduation walk. Long, wide strikes. A purposeful walk.

He was wearing a simple outfit again. Jeans and a white shirt. I liked that. Clean colors, clean lines. I hated patterns; they did things to my brain and eyes that made me need to physically blink. I once went on a date with a man who wore paisley and had intricate tattoos on both arms; by the end of the evening I had a throbbing headache. And when I went to bed that night and closed my eyes those patterns were all I could see, as if their imprint was being projected onto the back of my eyelids. I'd had to tell him I couldn't go on another date with him on account of his clothing choices and tattoos. He'd been offended and called me shallow. But what people don't realize is that I see *everything*.

Every little detail. Nothing is ever filtered out. Everything rushes in. Where most people see a tree, I see all the leaves, branches and bits of bark too. I have enough detail to contend with already, so when someone comes into my space looking like an optical illusion I cannot deal with it. So I was very glad and grateful for Andrew's choice of clothing. He climbed into the car and, without saying hello, I turned to him. 'I accidentally left something at my house.'

'What is it?' he asked.

'That's private,' I said, and pulled off slowly. 'I need to go and fetch it. It's not too much of a detour, perhaps only thirty minutes, so we won't be too late. I've already notified my parents. Are you okay with that?' I asked, but quickly realized I'd done that thing where I hadn't actually asked the other person's opinion but had just told them what I was planning to do anyway, regardless of what they really wanted.

'Sure. Of course.'

We drove in silence for a while before Andrew started fiddling around the car, looking at its various components. Pressing buttons, opening compartments, looking down at the floormat.

'This is in such great condition. Are you enjoying it?'

I smiled. I'd been going out on unnecessary excursions, even if it was just a drive around the block for no other reason than to feel the wind in my face.

'I am,' I replied. That didn't sound quite right, didn't really match my feelings on the matter, so I amended. 'I've been loving it.' Synonyms included *enamoured*, *infatuated* and *impassioned*.

I pulled up to the large gate at the bottom of the enormous walled property I lived in. I pressed the remote control and the gate creaked to life. In my head, I called it the Slowest Gate In The World (™), because it was.

'Wow, this is a slow gate,' Andrew commented.

'I know. The electrician says because it's so old we would need to replace the entire engine.'

Andrew stared at it as we drove in. 'I'll take a look and see if I can't Frankenstein it for you.'

'Frankenstein?'

'Add some new parts to it. Perhaps remove some old ones.'

We drove in and I stopped and waited for the gate to close behind me, as I usually did. The driveway was thin and steep and wound up through the huge forest-like garden.

'Wow. What is this place?' Most people had this response to my house. Not that many people had ever come here.

'You know I told you my mom is a wedding planner?'

'Yes.'

'Ten years ago, she bought this piece of land and wanted to turn it into a wedding venue. She was planning on slowing down in her retirement and running the venue, but that hasn't happened yet. I think she's addicted to all the stress and chaos. So this has been sitting empty until my mom builds her wedding venue.'

'It's enormous!'

'It would've been subdivided and made into townhouses if she hadn't bought it.' The land was on Northcliff Hill, the city's largest hill, with the most amazing views. The properties here were all enormous and steep as it was, but this was a quadruple stand and somehow my mom had found it and bought it. It was beautiful, untouched, full of rocks and trees and wild grasses. Rock rabbits and mongooses inhabited my mini park, as I liked to call it, and I even had some eagles nesting in one of the trees. She'd planned on building the venue at the top of the stand, looking out over the twinkling lights of the city below. It was amazing at sunset here too. And at night, because we were so high up, away from the lights and the smog, you could actually see the stars.

'There was a tiny one-room cottage here when she bought it, so five years ago I asked if I could add to it and moved here.'

'This is incredible,' Andrew said. We reached the very top of the property and parked the car. My cottage was small and rudimentary. I didn't need anything fancy; I lived here alone and a small two-bedroom cottage was more than enough for me. Andrew turned and looked at the view. 'You can see the entire world from here. It feels like you're in the middle of nowhere, but you're still in the city. It's insane.' He looked around. 'You can't even see your neighbors.'

'That's the point. After all those years in boarding school, I needed space.' Boarding school had been challenging for me in terms of personal space, although I had been lucky enough to get my own room for those five years. Well, that's not entirely true, it was actually a small unused storage cupboard under the stairs that I'd moved into of my own volition. There had been an objection raised by the house mistress at first, but when she couldn't give me a logical reason for *not* living in the abandoned storage room, and the school found nothing in their endless rule book to say I couldn't, they allowed me to stay.

'Don't you get worried out here, all alone? It's such a big property, huge perimeter, hard to secure it all.'

I gave him a little wink. 'That's what these are for.' I whistled and immediately heard the thump of the feet. Within seconds my two Belgian Malinois rounded the corner at such a speed that they kicked up dust. Andrew stumbled backwards in fright as they made a beeline for him.

'Sit!' I commanded, and the two dogs stopped dead in their tracks and sat. I walked over and patted them on their heads.

'What on earth are those?' Andrew stared wide-eyed at my dogs.

'My mom was worried about security here too. She did a wedding for a very high-ranking military person and he told her about these military-trained dogs. Instead of paying her with money for the wedding, he paid her with these. They're trained for combat, rappelling out of helicopters, skydiving, detecting bombs, and even performing emergency CPR.'

'Wow! Okay, I always *thought* you were the most interesting person I'd ever met, but now I *know* you're the most interesting person I've ever met.' He took a step closer. 'Can I touch them?'

'At ease,' I said, and the dogs changed immediately, from military dogs to pets that rushed up to you, demanding head scratches and belly rubs. Once they'd raced at me, they raced at Andrew too. Andrew crouched down and scratched their giant faces.

'They're gorgeous! And huge!' he said.

'Zeus and Athena. I didn't name them; they came named. I wouldn't have named them that.'

'I think it suits them.' Andrew stood and looked down at his clothing.

'Sorry, they're huge shedders in summer. Come inside, I have something for that.'

Before going inside, I picked up their favorite toys and threw them down the hill. They waited for me to give the command.

'Play time!' I said, and they ran off to play, until I told them otherwise. 'Some people think it's cruel for dogs to be trained like this, but these dogs are bred to be working dogs. If you don't keep them working and constantly give them activities to perform, they can get bored and become very destructive. Sometimes I'll hide things in the garden for them to find, like they might do in the military. I also have an obstacle course for them here, and they love playing hide and seek, and swimming too.' Truthfully, I loved my dogs. For the most part, they were my only companions, and for the most part, that was really all I needed. But sometimes I did find myself wondering what it would be like if I could find someone to share my life with. I only indulged that thought for a few minutes though, before I packed it away in the part of my mind where I filed those kinds of things away because I knew they were utterly impossible. So far, life had shown me that me and relationships didn't work. They always seemed to go well in the first few weeks, but then something always changed. As if we were attracting magnets that had suddenly been flipped around, and what was once attracting was now repelling. It was my fault for this sudden change, though. I knew that. I'd had too many experiences that had cemented this one irrefutable fact: whenever people got to know me, beyond the mundane and informal 'Hi, how are you?'s, they began to back away. I was too much. Too weird. Offensive. Outspoken. Irritating. Intense. These were the descriptions I'd heard over the years. It was all me: I was not relationship material.

And I was okay with that, mostly, but there were some moments – moments that came late at night, in winter, in a cold empty bed – that made me wonder what it would feel like to be wrapped up in someone's warm arms.

We entered my cottage and I picked up the sticky roller that I kept on the kitchen counter for this exact situation. Thoughtlessly, I started rolling it up and down Andrew's body. His chest first. God, it was hard. I had known it was, but now I had physical evidence of that. It felt like I was rolling over solid marble, not flesh. My rolling slowed down at the unexpected sight of his nipple pressing against the inside of his shirt. The sight made me stare, made me swallow slowly, and I felt a little throbbing deep inside as I traced my eyes over him in a manner that I knew was totally objectifying.

I stopped when it suddenly occurred to me that this might be extremely inappropriate.

'Sorry, is this a little . . .?'

I raised my head. He was looking down at me, and his irises seemed smaller than usual, swallowed by big black pupils.

'Here.' I thrust the roller at him and walked away, feeling a little shaken by the sight of that nipple and the strange effect it had had on me. I grabbed the other roller and rolled it over my dress. I made a mental note to call the mobile dog-groomer. These dogs were not bred for a hot country like ours, and in summer you needed to help them rid themselves of the excess fur. I suppose that's why they were so obsessed with swimming and would jump into any body of water any chance they got.

'This is not what I imagined your house looking like,' Andrew said, doing a full circle in the small open-plan kitchen, lounge and dining room.

'What did you imagine?'

'Something not so . . . full of things.'

'My mom says it's cluttered.'

'Well . . .' He looked around.

'I collect things,' I said, and moved over to my tins. 'These are antiques; I love the pictures on the lids. And these' – I walked over to the row of cups – 'antique teacups. I was really into making my own tea at one stage, but I got over that. And these are vintage stamps.' I picked up a book and passed it to him. 'I told you that I bought everything second hand. It's kind of a hobby to go thrifting on weekends and see what I find. It's like a treasure hunt.'

He opened the book of stamps and began flipping through the pages slowly and thoughtfully. Once he'd finished, he looked around the room. 'I suppose because I know you to be so organized, I guess I was expecting something more minimalist.'

'I like to be a minimalist at work, it keeps me focused. But at home I like to be surrounded by things, it makes me feel . . .' I shrugged because I didn't quite know the right word for how it made me feel. But it made me feel cozy, less lonely. It kept me distracted.

'And what's through here?' Andrew started walking towards the small room that led off the open-plan kitchen/lounge area.

'Wait, don't go . . .' But it was too late.

'Okay. WOW!' Andrew put his hands on his hips and turned one full circle in the room. I felt my cheeks go red, and a little flush of embarrassment tingled through me. I knew that playing a magical card game was perceived as very geeky at my age, but having an entire room dedicated to Pokémon was the height of geek. And, for some reason, I didn't want Andrew thinking of me like others did.

'I also sell rare cards. So it's a business too, not just a hobby,' I said, trying to justify the bookshelves of card boxes. 'In fact' – I walked up to one in particular – 'this one is worth one thousand dollars, so . . .' I paused and then pushed back past him. 'We should get going. I'll get what I forgot.' I rushed into my bedroom, grabbed the handful of spinning, squeezing things and shoved them into my bag so Andrew wouldn't see that I'd returned for what was essentially a bunch of toys. I felt instantly better knowing they were in my bag and, when I came back out, Andrew was standing in front of my tropical fish tank.

My fish tank contained a living, breathing coral reef filled with tropical fish that came all the way from the Maldives. I enjoyed the precise nature and complexity of it all. Checking the water quality, pH, temperature, salinity. Maintaining filtrations, making salt water, scrubbing algae. But, above all, I enjoyed sitting on my sofa and watching them glide through the water effortlessly. The bubbles from the filtration made the soft coral sway back and forth, and the blue UV lights emphasized the bright colors of the fish.

'This is incredible,' Andrew said.

'The water has to stay at a very precise thirty-four degrees and the salt has to be checked regularly. Keeping fish is a very complicated hobby. Let's go,' I said, and walked outside, eager to get going again. I didn't like dwelling in in-between moments like this. That time you spend waiting before you are due to go somewhere, or sitting in a cinema and waiting for a movie to start, and having Andrew here was starting to feel like one of those waiting moments. Waiting to go to dinner with my parents.

Before climbing into the car I called the dogs, patted them a few more times and then gave them their final command.

'Patrol!' They immediately jumped into action, first following me down as I drove towards the gate. They sat and waited for the gate to close, and then they were off, walking the perimeter happily.

Chapter 26

'You didn't tell me you were rich,' Andrew said, staring up at the house at the top of the driveway. I looked at my house and tried to imagine it through Andrew's eyes. I suppose it was completely extravagant and over the top. But my parents had never been subtle. Subtlety was not the way they did things, especially not my mother. If there was a small space to decorate, she would fill it to bursting point with expensive trinkets that she'd gathered. Our house overflowed with gold-framed paintings, large wall-mounted mirrors, luscious cream curtains pulled back by red ropes and an infinite number of scatter cushions! Why my mom thought each sofa needed to be festooned with six scatter cushions was not something I grasped. Nor did I understand why each bathroom had to have a small basket of rolled-up hand towels. There were at least ten hand towels per bathroom.

'Wow, did you really grow up here?' he asked.

'No, I grew up in the tent in the back of the yard,' I said, and Andrew turned and beamed at me.

'Was that a purposeful joke!'

I nodded at him.

'It was a good one.'

'I thought so too,' I said, and pulled my loud car into the driveway. We had a circular driveway, with a huge unnecessary fountain in the middle. I'd never liked that fountain. It was a replica of the Trevi Fountain, but on a much smaller scale. To be more specific, it was a replica of a part of the fountain, the part I liked least: the mythical man wrestling the mythical horse creature. I'd always hated the way he pulled on the horse's mane and the horse looked like it was in pain. But my mom loved that thing. Had it flown in especially. She was obsessed with anything Italian, always had been, and in all her fantasy weddings for me I was getting married in a lavender field in Tuscany, or an old Italian villa on the Amalfi coast, or even on a gondola in Venice.

'You know you're rich when you have a driveway like this!' Andrew remarked when we pulled up.

'Listen.' I turned in my seat to face him. 'My parents and I are very, very different.'

'Okay,' Andrew said casually. Clearly, he was not getting my meaning.

'What I mean is that we are all *nothing* alike. I'm not like them, and they are not like me!' I reiterated.

'I'm sure it's not as extreme as you're making it out to be,' he said, just as my mother's voice could be heard.

'What is that awful sound?' My mother – who looked very similar to me but was absolutely nothing like me at all – rushed out of the front door, dramatically covering her ears. She dripped in diamonds and pearls that sparkled in the lights like comets breaking through the earth's atmosphere and burning up as bright fireballs as they rushed towards the earth. She was also as dramatic as a meteor shower; everyone walks outside to gaze up at one, like you would if my mother entered a room.

'My God! What is that?' She looked at my car and blinked her eyes multiple times. Either she had something in her eye, or she wasn't sure if what she was seeing was real.

'It's my new car,' I said proudly, climbing out and slamming the ten-ton door behind me. I'd learned that in order to close the doors on this vehicle, a hard slam was necessary.

'Where is the Prius?'

'Traded it in.'

'For . . . that?' My mother pointed a bejewelled finger at it.

'A 1980s Porsche!' My dad rushed out behind my mom and ran straight up to the car. 'I used to have one of these. Don't you remember, Wen?' he said to my mom, a massive smile spreading across his face. 'God, I loved that car. It was my first sports car.'

'But it didn't look like . . . that.' My mother stepped closer. 'Surely it wasn't so . . . so . . . long?'

'You're looking at it through today's eyes. Don't you remember, you had a perm back then and I had a huge moustache?'

'I never had a perm,' my mother blurted. 'I have naturally wavy hair.' She looked at me pointedly. 'You would too, if you didn't blow dry it. We have naturally wavy h—' She tapered off, running a hand through her dead-straight hair. 'I had a perm, okay. I had a perm. It's not something I'm proud of, but there you have it!'

'Whose car is this?' my dad asked.

'Mine,' I said, perking up with that feeling of pride again.

'Yours?' My dad's eyes met mine. 'Did you . . . wait, you . . . where's the Prius?' He looked around as if expecting to see it.

'Traded it in. This is my car now.'

My dad's face lit up.

'What, Dad?' I asked.

He shook his head. 'It's just . . . unexpected. That's all.'

'Our daughter has been doing some very unexpected things lately,' my mom said, making a beeline for Andrew. 'I'm Wendy.' She held her hand out for Andrew to shake, but he didn't move. Instead, he gaped at her open-mouthed.

'*Get Wed with Wendy*?' he asked.

'That's me.' She thrust her hand into Andrew's outstretched one. Mind you, there wasn't really that much of a hand left any more. Her big rings and long fake nails swallowed up her fingers, so she was mostly just a moisturized palm.

'*Get Wed with Wendy*,' he repeated again, as if he needed to say it twice in order to believe it. *Get Wed with Wendy* was a long-running reality TV show in which my mom organized weddings for couples in less than a month. It was one of those TV shows that should not have been as popular as it was, but thanks to my mother's personality and her witty one-liners, which had become known as Wendyisms, like, 'You can put a veil on a vulture, but that won't make it a bride' and 'He's only the best man if he sticks to the wedding plan', it was huge. A television staple. Everyone knew it, and everyone knew her, and wherever we went people repeated her one-liners, or asked her to tell their husbands to 'Take the cotton wool out their ears and shove it in their mouths!' Somehow my mom had not only become a wedding planner but also a relationship-advice guru. Counselling the husband- and wife-to-be as they had inevitable fights and melt-downs in the stress leading up to their upcoming nuptials. Strangers stopped her in the street to ask marriage advice. I suppose she's more than qualified, considering she's been married to my dad for thirty-five years.

And then my dad stepped forward and extended his hand for Andrew to shake too. 'Vernon Edwards,' he said.

'Vernon Edwards,' Andrew repeated thoughtfully, letting the name roll off his tongue a few times. 'Why do I know that name?'

'My dad was the first plastic surgeon in South Africa to perform a successful full-face transplant.'

'Oh, right!' Andrew shook his hand and gazed at him in awe. 'I remember that. It was all over the news. The young boy who was trapped in the burning building.' The story had made headlines across the country for years, and everyone had followed the boy's long recovery journey.

'Tragic story.' My mom stepped forward and placed a hand on my dad's shoulder. 'But Vern is such an incredible artist.' With her free hand she pointed up at her nose, gave Andrew a little wink and then pursed her lips together in a 'shhh' sound. I scrutinized my parents;

they were *so* not like me. When I was younger, I'd spent hours wondering if I might have been adopted. I was not flamboyant like my mother, and I was not kind and compassionate like my father, who in all his online reviews is described as having the best bedside manner. But after confronting my parents one night about my 'adoption', they assured me that I was genetically theirs, and even pulled out the VHS birth tape. I declined to watch it though, even if I was curious. I suppose genetics is a role of the dice. You just never know what you're going to get. And they got me, and I got them, and we all couldn't be more different if we tried. Not that I was unhappy, not at all.

As we all walked into the house Andrew leaned over and whispered. 'You didn't tell me your mom was a TV star and your dad was a famous plastic surgeon.'

'I didn't think it was necessary.'

'You didn't think it was necessary to tell me that your family lives in a palace either?'

I stopped and looked at the house. 'I would hardly call this a palace.'

'I think our definitions of "palace" are very different.'

'Well, you didn't think it was necessary to tell me you had two moms and ten thousand brothers and sisters.'

'Fair enough,' he said with a smile.

The further into the house we went, the more I started seeing it through Andrew's eyes. It *was* rather palace-like. The foyer was probably half the size of Andrews parents' house and as shiny as the Taj Mahal. Although my parents were "old money", they both came from wealth, my mother did not believe in being understated, like other "old money" families were. She shined like new money and wasn't ashamed of it; as she always said, 'Why have maple-wood panels, a dusty old library and antique Persian rugs when you can have Italian marble that shines like a mirror?' Her heels clinked on the massive marble tiles as she walked towards the patio at the back of the house that overlooked the garden.

'We'll have a glass of champagne outside before dinner,' she said, turning to us as. 'I have a bottle of Moët chilling out there and ready for us.'

'Fancy,' Andrew whispered in my ear. When we reached the patio, Andrew let out a loud breath. 'Wow, this is gorgeous,' he said, looking out over the pool and gardens that sprawled out in front of us. It was summer, and the gardens always looked amazing at this time of year. And I'll give my mother credit for that; she didn't just palm it off to a garden service. Every weekend, she was on her hands and knees crawling through the dirt. She'd planted every single one of the brightly colored rose bushes that lined the flowerbeds and every one of the purple agapanthus that shot up out of the soil.

When I was younger, I used to sit next to her on the grass while she planted. I never got my hands dirty though. I hated the feel of soil on my hands, and gardening gloves were always too big for me. It was only when my mother adapted a pair of small winter gloves into gardening gloves that I was able to join in. I was the reason for the daffodils that came out every spring, and the clivias that peeped out from behind the oak tree in the corner of the garden.

'My pride and joy,' she said, 'Well, apart from my Pippa, obviously.'

'Mom.' My cheeks flushed with embarrassment.

'I'm so glad you could join us. I just couldn't meet my daughter's boyfriend for the first time at a family wedding. That wouldn't be right,' my mother said.

My stomach twisted when the word 'boyfriend' came out of her mouth. I knew this was what she'd wanted for so long, for me to have a boyfriend, and suddenly I felt bad. It hadn't occurred to me, until this moment, how much our arrangement might impact those around us. At some point, this arrangement would run its course, it would come to an end, and that would affect my parents, and Andrew's family too.

'So Pippa tells me you're a pilot,' my dad said. 'That must be a very stressful job. I imagine it evokes the same responsibility as being a surgeon. Having someone's life in your hands – in your case, many lives?'

'I suppose, like being a surgeon, it can also be equally rewarding. But I never feel too stressed, not when I have Pippa on the line to guide me to safety.'

I blushed again. Everyone was laying it on thick tonight, and I could see my mom was soaking it up, 'oooh'ing and 'aaah'ing at that statement.

'So tell us how you met,' my mom said. 'Pippa hardly tells me anything. It's like trying to get blood out of a stone . . .' She turned to me to qualify. 'I mean, it's hard to get information out of you. You can't get blood out of a stone.'

'Obviously,' I said, and then thought about it for a moment. 'Oh. Got it. Blood out of a stone is like information out of me.' I laughed at this one. It actually did make sense, and I enjoyed it. Andrew shot me a small smile. It made my skin hot. I liked his smiles. I especially liked the way they made me feel. I probably liked them much more than I should like them. I turned my attention to my feet as Andrew launched into the story that we'd told so many times already: radio chatter, coffee shop, recognized each other's voices. We didn't even know each other's names and faces.

But today, for some reason, I was hearing the story through a totally different filter. The story was actually true: that *is* how we met, and if we were a real couple, this would be one of those really cute romantic-comedy stories. The kind you would tell at a wedding, the kind you would tell your kids, and the kind of story that they would tell their partners when they grew up. It would keep going as a story until one day at a funeral someone would tell the story of how Granny and Grandpa met all those years ago. What a true love story it all was. How fate had brought them together.

'Did Pippa tell you how Vernon and I met?' my mom asked when Andrew had finished.

Andrew shook his head.

'It was so romantic too. He saved my life.' I rolled my eyes. I always did, because truthfully, he hadn't technically saved her life, but in my mom's world, he had. The story wasn't as dramatic as life-saving in the traditional sense – a lifeguard plunging into choppy seas, dragging a lifeless body to shore, performing CPR, or a surgeon restarting someone's heart with electrical paddles. My mother had had a botched boob job that my father had fixed; that was my mom's version of having her life saved. And I could see that once she'd told the story, Andrew looked confused but played along and expounded on what a romantic story it was. Then my parents looked deep into each other's eyes and grasped hands. They were so in love! They were Gomez and Morticia Addams, unable to keep their hands and eyes off each other. It had been wildly embarrassing to me when I was younger, but now, it just fascinated me.

I don't think I'll ever be comfortable enough with someone to stare into their eyes for hours and hold hands without feeling like my fingers might fall off and my palms might melt from the hot sweat.

Flutes of champagne were handed out and sipped as we watched the sun sink out of sight. I was silent for most of the time, while Andrew happily chatted to my parents. He was brilliant at it. He was so at ease with people. Relaxed, like one of those huge La-Z-Boy recliner chairs that demand to be climbed into. He asked just the right questions that kept them talking and laughing. He answered all their questions perfectly, thoughtfully, throwing in some jokes as well. The conversation flowed, it was reciprocal, words bounced back and forth and everyone had their chance to speak. I observed it all, again fascinated by the way people intrinsically knew how to wait their turn to talk, how they didn't just jump in, cut someone off, and knew what volume to keep their voice at, and what tone was right for the moment.

And by the end of the hour Andrew and my parents had covered growing up, studying, career, aspirations, thoughts on politics and why fondant was no longer the preferred icing choice for wedding cakes. They'd even found a common link between them; my dad's foundation, which provided pro bono plastic surgery to vulnerable children with facial disfigurations, had worked on one of Andrew's parents' foster children who'd been a victim of terrible domestic violence. My dad and mom expressed a desire to meet Andrew's parents as soon as possible, and dinner arrangements were talked about.

My stomach dropped. We were fake boyfriend and girlfriend. Our parents were *not* meant to meet each other. That was *not* part of the plan. In fact, many things seemed to be deviating from the plan lately, things that were starting to make this arrangement feel too real, which it was not.

'Shall we head inside for dinner?' my mom asked after the last drop of champagne had been drained from the bottle. This was my mother's favorite thing to do, hosting people for dinner parties and events. You could never simply come over for a casual evening at my parents' house, everything was pomp and ceremony, no matter how small the gathering and how insignificant the event. We walked inside and Andrew made some more 'ooh'ing sounds.

'This is a very impressive home you have here, Mr and Mrs Edwards.'

'Oh, please call us Wen and Vern,' my mom insisted, turning to him. 'And thank you. We worked very hard for every inch of it, and I decorated every inch of it too.'

This was true, actually, because despite both coming from money, they'd never used that money to build this house or buy fancy cars; that, they'd done all on their own with their unwavering work ethics. They had instilled the value of hard work in me from a very early age, something I appreciated. Hard work, and a passion for whatever you did, were things I admired greatly in people. Something I admired greatly in Andrew and his family. It dawned on me that our families, despite outward appearances of difference, would probably get on very well. Linda the dress designer and my mom would talk for hours about the latest trends in wedding-dress design. My dad and his moms would chat about his charitable foundation – his true passion. Shaleen the librarian and my mom would probably get lost in books for weeks; my mom had run her book club for over thirty years and, when she wasn't wedding planning, she was reading. And my dad would finally have someone to talk about golf to, another one of his favorite activities. This thought made me warm inside for a second, and then bitterly cold.

As usual, dinner was an extravagant affair. My mom had cooked black truffle and ricotta ravioli from scratch, followed by home-made pistachio gelato. She'd taken an Italian cooking course once and, whether you liked Italian food or not, that was what you were served in this house. In fact, that stretched to most things; whether you liked an Italian interior-design aesthetic, that didn't matter either. It was what you got. Same went for her playing Pavarotti at full volume or putting Parmesan on absolutely everything.

There'd been general chatter throughout dinner but, for some reason, when the port had been brought out and my father suggested 'retiring' to the lounge with it, the conversation changed.

'So tell me, Andrew, what are your intentions with our Pippa?'

'Mom,' I scolded immediately.

'It's a very legitimate question to ask the young man who is dating my only child,' she qualified.

I hung my head and shook it with embarrassment.

But Andrew didn't miss a beat. 'I suppose I'd like to have more fun getting to know her better, enjoying our time together, uncovering more common interests and shared values and goals.'

'And what are your shared values and goals?' My dad was the one quizzing him now.

'I know Pippa wants to manage her own airport one day, and I'd like to be flying internationally soon. A3080s, to be specific.'

'Those are very demanding jobs, a lot of time away from each other. A lot of pressure,' my dad put to him.

'But I think one of the things Pippa and I like most about each other is our passion for aviation. It's part of who we are, and I would support her in her dreams of running an airport, and I would certainly love to land my A3080 there as often as possible.' He turned to me, and something in his tone had changed. *What was it? Why was his voice softer now?* 'That's if . . .' He paused, looked at me for the longest time. 'If she'll allow me to?' He smiled that bloody smile again. The smile that warmed me, even though I knew this was a scientific impossibility. An outside stimulus, like a smile, could in no way change your internal temperature. The room fell silent. I looked around and realized that everyone was waiting for me to say something.

'Uh . . . Yes, well, if his plane had permission to land there, obviously, and also if he has the requisite training to do the specific approach, as well as the permit and—'

Everyone at the table laughed and, for the briefest moment, Andrew touched my arm. The touch was more of a brush, and yet the brush caused my temperature to rise once more. *I was not perimenopausal, was I? What age did that start?* I made a note to google that. I picked up a magazine and fanned my face but realized that had been a bad idea when I caught my mother smiling at me. I dropped the magazine quickly and stole a sideways glance at Andrew.

There was zero logic to it, no explanation, but he looked hotter tonight, sitting there in my parents' home, than he'd ever looked before. Talking, joking and laughing with them. It was as if the environment had somehow affected his appearance. Maybe it was the Italian aesthetic – maybe it was bringing out some kind of irresistible Mediterranean vibe in him. Or perhaps the difference lay in me, in the way I was now perceiving him. I'd never brought anyone home before, and Andrew felt like he fitted here.

'I want to show you something,' Andrew said when we'd pulled up to his house.

'What?'

'It's a surprise.'

'I hate surprises,' I said, because I did. I didn't get the joy that others got in surprises.

'My nerdery,' he said, climbing out the car with a smile.

'Nerdery?'

'You seemed a little embarrassed by your Pokémon room. Well, I have something similar that I wanted to show you.'

'Okay,' I agreed, and climbed out of the car too, slamming the elephant-sized door behind me. Andrew lived in a modern town-house complex. At least, the townhouses were freestanding and did not share boundary walls. I looked down the side to see how big the gap between the buildings were. I estimated four meters.

'What're you doing?' Andrew looked at me curiously.

'I was just looking at the gap between you and your neighbors.'

'Nothing like yours, but it's sufficient for me.'

'I don't think I'd manage here,' I said, looking up at the neighbor's windows and wondering if they could see me right now.

'It's perfect for me, since I'm not here that often.'

'That's true,' I said, watching the next-door neighbor's window while walking to the front door with him.

Andrew walked in and turned on the lights. The place was sparsely decorated, with just the essentials. But the essentials it did have were good quality; you could see that he'd furnished the place well and put thought into it. We walked into the lounge, and I couldn't help notice the massive TV screen on the wall and the games consoles next to it. It seemed very man-cave to me. I followed him into a passage with three doors, all closed, except for one. I immediately peered in. A large bed dominated the room, but what struck me most were the piles of clothes strewn around the place. I stopped.

'I did not picture you as messy,' I said.

Andrew quickly closed the door, as if embarrassed.

'I'm not, uh, messy. Generally. At all.'

I pushed the door back open and pointed. 'Yes, you are.'

'I had some trouble deciding what to wear tonight.' He said this quite softly, and if I hadn't leaned in, I might have missed it.

'Why?' I asked.

He shrugged in a manner that told me he was trying to brush this off.

'Wait, why?' I asked, but Andrew continued walking down the passage. I studied the back of him. He looked so good tonight, but it hadn't crossed my mind that he might have put any effort into looking like that. But clearly he had. Had he put in so much effort because he was meeting my parents? Or had he put in so much effort for another reason entirely?

He stopped at the bottom of the passage and turned to me.

'You ready?'

'Ready for what?'

'A glimpse into my life.' He pushed the door open enthusiastically.

I walked inside but wasn't quite sure what I was seeing. It looked like a toy-plane graveyard crossed with an electrical workshop.

'I make RC planes and race them,' he said. 'I belong to a club. We meet on the last Sunday of every month and race our planes.'

I peered down at the plane lying on the bench.

'I'm trying to make the wings a bit lighter and the engine a little bit more powerful, if I do that, I think I stand a good chance.'

'The last Sunday of the month is tomorrow.' I inspected the complicated wiring and remote control.

'You want to come?' he asked, and I swung round.

'Are there people there that you need a fake girlfriend for?'

'No.'

'So why would I come?'

'Aren't we allowed to hang out outside of our arrangement?'

'I suppose we have had coffee a few times, which is outside of the parameters of the arrangement,' I said.

'Besides, I think you'll enjoy this. We meet at an abandoned runway at a defunct mine an hour out of town.'

'I usually take my dogs to the dog park on Sundays.'

'What time do you take them?'

'Three to five. There's a dam, and they love swimming.'

'Plane flying is from eleven to one, so we could be back at yours by two, fetch the dogs and go to the dog park.'

'*We?* Do you want to come to the dog park?'

'Unless you don't want me to?'

'It's just . . . no one's ever come with me to the dog park before. It's usually something I do alone.'

'You can think about it,' Andrew said casually. 'No pressure. I'd just love to see those beasts running and swimming. I bet they're very impressive.'

'They are. All the other dogs are terrified of them, expect for this one Labrador they always play with.'

'Would you like to think about coming with me to fly the planes too?' Andrew asked.

I nodded. I liked that he didn't push me into making arrangements quickly, like other people did. It drove most people crazy that I couldn't give them an answer in the moment. I needed at least a few hours, a day even, for an idea to marinate and sink in.

Later that night, when Andrew and I had parted ways and I was home alone in my bed, I got a message from my mom that made my blood rather icy.

Mom: I'm so happy. Andrew is perfect for you! Dad and I were just saying so.

Pippa: Mom, stop. It's early days. You can't know that.

Mom: Oh yes I can. I can see it in the way he looks and smiles at you.

Pippa: Really?

This was the second time I'd heard about these smiles that people who supposedly liked each other gave each other. I made a mental note to google them a little later, in an attempt to understand them in more depth.

Mom: Your father smiles at me like that still.
Pippa: Mom, I have to go, I want to sleep.

I did want to sleep, but also, all this talk of smiling was starting to make me uncomfortable. As soon as I put the phone down I typed the following into Google: *Do men smile if they like you?* After reading several articles on the topic, it was indeed confirmed that one of the ways to tell if a person fancied you was through the way they smiled at you. I closed my eyes and tried to remember the way Andrew smiled at me, but I wasn't sure whether they were real smiles or fake-boyfriend smiles. And also, I was too young to be in perimenopause, I'd googled that too.

I lay awake for a while looking up at my airplane mobile. I felt strangely restless, unable to convert lying still into falling asleep. I got up, walked through to the kitchen and poured myself a glass of juice. The evening was summery, so I walked outside and sat on the patio. Zeus and Athena immediately joined me.

They liked to sleep outside in summer, but in winter they slept in my room or next to the fire. I flopped down on the outdoor sofa and my dogs climbed on, each one putting a giant head onto one of my legs. Their heads were so heavy, almost crushing, but I liked the feeling. I sipped my drink and looked out over the city below. I loved being here. It felt as if I was totally removed from the outside world, but still able to access it when I wanted to. It was the perfect set-up for someone like me.

'Dog park tomorrow!' I said, and both dogs put their heads up and looked at me. 'Should we let Andrew come with us?' I asked, even though I knew they couldn't answer. I looked back over the city and focused my attention on each twinkling light. Each light represented a window of a house, or an apartment. I wondered who might be behind those windows. Most people seemed to gravitate together, forming little human clusters, whether it was families, or roommates. People liked being together. I imagined that each of those lights down there represented some kind of union between two or more people; maybe a mother feeding a baby at night, two friends sitting up late and talking, lovers making love, a husband and wife arguing about something mundane. The light from my own window reflected on my feet – one set of feet, not two – and I sighed.

'Okay, fine. I'll message Andrew then, if you two are so insistent about it.' I scratched them again, and fistfuls of hair came away. 'Dog groomers for you both.' They raised their heads again, but not in excitement. They hated the dog groomer. For all their bravery and bravado, bring a pair of nail clippers anywhere near them and they're shaking like baby chihuahuas and screaming like overdramatic huskies! You've never seen such a pathetic sight as Zeus and Athena getting their nails clipped!

I pulled my phone out and opened my message thread with Andrew. I read through it for a while, weighing up my decision. I looked at my dogs again.

'Fine, if you can get your nails clipped, I suppose I can do this.' I put my fingers to the screen and typed as fast as I could, in case I stopped.

Pippa: Yes!

Chapter 27

The abandoned runway looked ghostly. Maybe a better synonym was *eerie*. I liked the sound of that word. The way it sounded like the very thing it was describing. A ghostly moan in the middle of the night. The tarmac had cracked and weeds were pushing their way through them, fighting each other for space. Thick trees and shrubs lined the sides of the runway, which would never be allowed if this was a functional landing strip. I stepped onto the tarmac. I loved standing on airstrips; it wasn't often that I got to do it though. You couldn't just walk out onto a runway and stand there. I imagined how many planes had taken off from here, where they'd all gone and who'd been the ATC.

The broken-down mine had a dystopian feel to it and was the perfect set for a zombie film. Rusty scaffolding that was once a mineshaft stood at an angle like the Leaning Tower of Pisa. Dilapidated miners' accommodation, doors hanging off hinges, shattered glass windows and crumbling brickwork. Abandoned mining equipment lay on the ground, rusting like the bones of a carcass, or long-ago shipwrecks marooned on the rocks. I loved it here. It was mysterious, and I knew I could spend hours exploring it, but that would have to wait, because right now I was being introduced to a group of mostly older men.

Their names all blurred, and because most of them had gray hair their faces blurred too. They were also all wearing the same T-shirt, so no one stuck out. Except Andrew: he was sticking out like he'd never stuck out before.

I was being spun around in a never-ending tornado of introductions. Each time I turned and said hello to someone, another person would greet me and I'd have to turn around all over again. It went on like this until I thought I would fall over from the dizziness. At some stage the 'hello's died down and I found myself standing in front of Andrew again. I let out a relieved breath. It was calm and quiet here, as if I was finally in the eye of the tornado.

'You okay?' he asked.

'Fine. They were just very enthusiastic. In fact, you seem to be friends with very enthusiastic people in general.'

'And that's a bad thing?' he asked.

'It's fine, but I think it needs to be peppered with the opposite of enthusiasm sometimes.'

'And what is the opposite of enthusiasm?'

'I don't really do antonyms,' I said quickly.

'Why?' He looked intrigued.

'I don't like them. I don't like opposites. I don't like things that mean the opposite of something else. I like same things. Similar things. And now I've said the word "things" too many times and I no longer like that word either, and there is not a good synonym to replace that word, in this context anyway,' I concluded.

Andrew slowly leaned towards me, tilting his head to the side as if looking at me from another angle. I tilted my head to match his.

'What?' I asked.

'No*thing*,' he said, placing the emphasis on 'thing'.

'Some*thing*,' I replied, as he began walking away from me. He didn't turn his head though, in fact his eyes were still locked on mine as he walked off, which made him look strange and awkward.

'What are you doing? You're walking like a praying mantis. You should really look where you're going, or you could walk into something.'

He stopped, gave me a small smile and a wave and then turned his head away and walked like a human being once more. I eyed him suspiciously as he moved off. That hadn't been nothing – that leaning and head-tilting and strange mantis-walking had definitely been something. *But what?*

'What?' I called after him as he'd crossed the runway to the other side. He waved his hand in the air and then curled his fingers towards me in a beckoning motion. I was just about to cross over to him when a small plane skidded past me at such a speed that I jumped back. The small yellow plane – a replica of a Cessna Skyhawk – bumped and bobbed down the old runway and then started to lift. It seemed to hover for a while, and I gasped, unsure if it was going to make it into the air. It looked like it was about to tumble straight down again. But it didn't. Shakily, speedily – surprisingly speedily – it launched itself into the air and then shot straight up as if gravity no longer existed. It climbed at a speed and height that I hadn't expected and, as it did, excitement bubbled up inside me. It started in my stomach and then radiated outwards, into my shoulders, down my arms and into my fingers. I fluttered them at my sides a few times and then brought them together and clapped hard like everyone else was.

The next plane caused even more excitement. A fighter jet the size of one of my dogs was suddenly charging down the runway, and when it finally took off it shot straight up in an insane vertical take-off. This time, my feet lifted off the ground as I bounced and clapped for it as the plane engaged in mid-air circus-like maneuvers. I was getting more and more excited and lost in the atmosphere as RC plane after RC plane was launched off the runway. And every time one took off I was shocked all over again by how fast they flew and the noises they made as they cut through the air, with such speed that sometimes you completely lost sight of them. My clapping led to cheering, which then led to me high-fiving two silver-haired total strangers. But I was enjoying it all more than I could ever have imagined. Every so often I looked over to the other side of the runway, where Andrew was, and each time I found myself waving and smiling at him. And then the planes started racing each other, which only added to the building excitement of the crowd, and by the time it was Andrew's turn I felt buoyant. Afloat on an invisible wind of frivolity. Feet hardly touching the floor any more and hands that stung from clapping. Andrew and his opponent lined their planes up, remote controls in hand. A countdown started and then the planes were screeching down the runway and catapulting themselves into the air.

'GO! GO! GO!' I didn't know I'd shouted that until I'd heard my own voice. The plane flew through the air, Andrew running behind it, and I was so caught up in the moment that I too was running and jumping behind him. 'GET HIM!' I screamed over all the other shouting. It was all so damn exhilarating. I felt like I was driving fast with the roof down. I shielded my eyes from the sun as I watched his plane soaring higher and higher, until it wasn't any more.

'Oh shit!' Andrew said as his plane started dropping from the sky. It spiralled towards the ground, riding invisible currents that pushed it further away from us.

'It's headed for the trees,' I shouted as Andrew raced after it, desperately trying to pull it out of its death roll. But it was too late. We stood still, side by side, and watched in horror as his plane tumbled from the sky and finally crashed in the trees at the end of the runway.

'Well, are you coming to help me retrieve it?' Andrew asked.

I nodded, and then, for some reason, squeezed his shoulder. The move took me by surprise. I didn't squeeze people's shoulders. Ever. In fact, I usually never knew what to do in situations like this, when the other person was visibly upset. For the most part, I would just stand there awkwardly wondering if I should try and deflect with something. In this case it would have been a fact about plane crashes. For example, the average number of plane crashes per annum is between seventy and ninety. I might have even blurted out something that I would definitely regret later, an overshare, like 'The first time I ever experienced severe turbulence on a plane I threw up on my dad's feet.' But I did none of these things.

Andrew placed his hand over mine and squeezed back. 'Thanks,' he said, and then started walking towards the crash site.

'Pleasure,' I whispered after him. That had felt good, to offer comfort in what had clearly been the right way.

Chapter 28

'It's pretty high.' Andrew looked up. The plane was lodged in the top branches of a very large, old oak tree.

'I'm very good at climbing trees,' I said.

'Really?' Andrew asked, looking unsure.

I nodded at him.

'But your . . . dyspraxia?'

'Oh no! That doesn't include tree-climbing.'

'How so?' he asked.

'When I was young, I spent a lot of time up trees,' I said, thinking back to the many, many times I spent breaktime, playdates or even birthday parties away from everyone else and up a tree. For some reason, I was always better up high than on the actual ground.

I reached up, grabbed a branch and then swung my legs up and gripped on.

'Besides, I'm also very supple. I'm hypermobile, actually.'

'Right.' Andrew still sounded unsure.

'And swimming has given me excellent core strength, and karate has given me a lot of upper-body strength.'

'No, I can't let you do this,' he said loudly. 'If you fall out of a tree and break something and your parents find out you were climbing it to fetch my plane, I'll no longer be their "favorite boyfriend".'

I stopped climbing and hung on like a koala. 'They said that? "Favorite boyfriend"?'

'That's what your mom called me.'

'I can assure you, that's not much of a compliment, since I don't think I've ever brought a boyfriend home to my parents'.' I continued climbing, and then stopped again. 'That wasn't meant as rude, by the way. I hope you weren't offended?' I peered down at him over my shoulder.

'No offence taken.'

'In fact, I should actually be the one who's offended. Leroy told me that your last girlfriend was way prettier than me.' I shuffled higher up the tree.

'WHAT?! That's crazy talk,' he said from down below. 'You're the hottest real or fake girlfriend I've ever had.'

A little rush of warmth hit me, but I carried on. I climbed quickly and easily.

'You *are* good at climbing.'

'I never exaggerate my talents,' I said.

'What other talents do you have that I don't know about yet?'

'When I was younger, I became very good at ventriloquism.'

I heard a laugh from down below. 'You never cease to amaze me. Military dogs, ventriloquism, black belt in karate, tree climber.'

'I went through a stage where I preferred to speak through a puppet.' I carried on climbing, and he didn't answer back. I didn't expect him to. When I said things like that, revealed something about myself that most people thought was odd, it tended to be met with silence. I now regretted telling him this and wondered why I had. But his response surprised me.

'What did the puppet look like? Was it one of those creepy ones from horror movies?'

'No. Not at all.'

'Well, that's a pity. I think I would pay good money to see you doing ventriloquism with one of those horror-movie puppets.'

I chuckled as I continued the climb. But the tree was thick, and every now and then a small branch scraped against my arms and legs or caught in my ponytail, which was becoming looser and looser with each meter. When I finally reached the top, I was able to see the wreckage properly.

'It's very damaged. Do you still want it?' I called down to Andrew.

'Absolutely. I can always do something with the parts.'

'Frankenstein them?' I asked, now knowing exactly what that phrase meant.

I started loosening the craft. It was tangled badly, and I needed to maneuver it out gently, lest I damage it more. 'Luckily, you're a better pilot than you are an RC pilot,' I said as I finally managed to free the broken-winged thing. I looked down at him; I had a clean gap through the branches. 'Can you catch?'

He nodded, and I carefully dropped the plane towards him. It veered off to the right, thanks to its one broken wing, but Andrew managed to catch it.

I started back down the tree carefully. It's always easier going up than coming down. Mind you, isn't that so for most things in life? Easier getting excited and happy about something, optimistic and hopeful, than the opposite.

I'd bent some of the smaller branches going up and was now worried that putting my foot back down on them might cause them to snap. So I chose alternative branches and a different way down. But when I came to the long trunk, the only branch there that I'd used to get up had snapped. I looked over my shoulder. Andrew had put his hands up in the air.

'I think you'd better jump into my arms,' he said.

'I'll be fine,' I said.

'No you won't. You're the woman who trips over invisible things. You really think I'm letting you jump out of a tree?'

'You'll never catch me.'

'Don't be so sure about that.' And then I felt his hands on my ankles.

'Jump!'

'Are you sure you can catch me?'

'Do you trust me?' The question seemed loaded. *Did I trust him?* Trust him to catch me, or did I trust him with more?

'I do.' I closed my eyes, let go of the branch and fell backwards. I felt like I was falling in slow motion, his hands slipping from my ankles, up my calves, my thighs, my hips. It wasn't really a jump; instead I floated down to earth helped by Andrew's strong grip. I was an air ballerina, doing a *jeté*, held up by my partner. My feet finally touched the ground, I turned around and then found myself standing in front of Andrew Boyce-Jones. Captain Boyce-Jones. I could smell him first. And then feel the warmth coming off his body.

'Your hair,' he said softly.

'What about it?'

He touched my hair. I didn't flinch, or take a step back.

'If we don't clean this up, birds will start nesting in it.' He pulled a twig out of the tangle and held it up for me to see.

I nodded. He moved closer to me and went to work pulling out the small twigs and leaves that had tangled themselves into my hair. He did it slowly. I watched him, fascinated by the intensity in his eyes as they focused on my head, scanning it from side to side. His mouth was slightly ajar, and we were so close that I could feel his breath on my face and lips. I could smell it too. It was not unpleasant. It reminded me of what the world smells like after a much-needed rainstorm.

And then the desire to stand up on my tiptoes and kiss him overwhelmed me. It hadn't started as a thought in my head, like most things do, it had started as a feeling. An urge that had made me shift towards him, even before I was conscious of doing it. *Urge*: *impulse, yearning, craving, compulsion*. Never had a list of synonyms described so perfectly the feeling twisting inside me right now.

'There, all done,' he said, dragging his eyes from my hair and bringing them to collide with mine.

Itching. Longing. Lusting.

I think we both leaned in now. I don't know. I'm not sure if I was imagining it, or not. But we must have leaned, because our faces and lips seemed so much closer than they had been moments ago. Our bodies too. I was sure my weight was now in my toes, pushing me forward, not in my heels, tilting me back. Another warm, pleasant wave moved through me and pushed me forward even more.

'Pippa,' Andrew said in a deep, slow voice.

'Andrew,' I replied. He moved again. The space between us was disappearing quickly.

'Pippa,' he said again.

'Why are you repeating my name?' I asked.

'The thing is . . .' He started and stopped. I raised a brow.

'Thing?'

'I've really been enjoying our time together.'

'Me too,' I said.

'I'm glad.' He smiled at me, but he looked uncomfortable.

'Was that it? The *thing*?'

'It's part of the thing. But there's also more,' he said.

'What more?' I scrunched my face up. 'What do you mean?'

'Do you really not know where I'm trying to go with this?' he asked.

I shook my head. 'You said my name twice, you said you enjoyed spending time with me and that there was a thing, and now I'm lost!'

His eyes scrutinized my face and I wished I knew what he was thinking. I sensed that I was supposed to know – and I felt as if I *almost* knew – but it was just out of my reach. The knowing was on the tip of my lips, but I just couldn't quite access it.

'Am I supposed to know where you're going?' I asked, feeling worried now. Feeling that perhaps there was something wrong with me because I didn't know the direction this conversation was going in.

'No. I mean, I suppose I'd like you to have an idea, but if you don't know, then obviously I got ahead of myse—*Never mind!*'

'Wait, I'm so confused right now!' I shook my head and stepped back.

'Don't be. There's nothing to be confused about.' He forced a smile at me. It was clearly fake.

'Did you find it?' A loud voice made us turn.

'Yup. Found it.' Andrew waved his plane in the air.

'Want to take it for another spin?' the man who'd just appeared around the bush asked.

'Nope. I think I'll have to retire this one.'

Andrew turned and started walking away from me. I wanted to reach out and pull him back. What *thing* was he talking about? And why was I left with a terribly uncomfortable feeling churning in the pit of my stomach? When he was out of sight, I pulled my phone out and sent a message to Jennifer.

Pippa: I find fake relationships just as confusing as real ones. For a moment there I thought it was simple, but now I'm not so sure.

Chapter 29

It was a particularly hot day. I loved hot days. I hated having to wear long-sleeved clothes and anything that covered my legs. I disliked the itchy feeling of fabric brushing against my limbs, and when in the throes of winter, I longed for summer. I put my gym bag down on the bench, pulled my dress off and slipped my cap and goggles on. I dived into the pool. The first lap was always the best, I don't know why, but it was always the lap I loved the most. I reached the other side, and I was about to turn when I swam into a shadow.

'I saw your car in the parking lot and I figured you would be up here,' the shadow said.

'Hi.' I lifted my goggles up to look at him. The sun had created a halo around his body and he was giving off a kind of angelic aesthetic. He'd clearly been working out. His face was red, his hairline wet and his eyes had this spark to them that I hadn't seen before. No doubt a physiological reaction to all those endorphins rushing through his bloodstream. His shirt was tight. I'd never seen him in a tight, form-fitting shirt. It was one of those stretchy, activewear fabrics, and because he'd been sweating it clung to him like he'd been wrapped in cellophane. And, *oh my God*, he was wearing shorts. And his thighs were, well, they were the kind of thighs one might want to sink one's teeth into, if one was so inclined. *Was I so inclined?*

'Am I disturbing you?' he asked.

'You are, actually. But that doesn't mean that the disturbance is a bad one,' I said to his thighs, not his face.

Since that moment by the tree, things had seemed awkward between us. We'd gone to the dog park afterwards, and everything had been absolutely fine, on the surface anyway. We'd chatted and walked and laughed when the dogs rolled in the mud, but there was something lurking beneath the surface of us the entire time. Something that I didn't understand.

Andrew hunched down, his knees gave an audible crick and he reached out and grabbed the concrete floor.

'Shit! My knees are not as young as they used to be.' He sat down flat and then shielded his face from the sun and looked at me. 'How are you?'

'Good. You?'

'Good.' I waited for him to say something, but he didn't. I looked around. The awkwardness seemed to have reared its head again. Maybe I could say something about the weather? Something else? (Not about his thighs though; that would be bad.) It was always the starts of conversations that were the worst for me. I never knew what the correct opening line should be, and especially now, when things were feeling a little off. So I said the first thing that permeated my mind.

'Did you see that they're upping the gym membership fees next month,' I heard myself say, and then cringed. This was possibly the dumbest thing to say, considering they were hardly going up at all. *Why had I said that?* 'They've been over-chlorinating this water lately. Perhaps if they didn't use so much they wouldn't need to up the fees.' And now why the hell had I said that? 'Did you know that the reason chlorine smells like it does in a public pool is from contaminates mixing with it, like urine and perspiration?' I waited for him to say something, but his lips were not moving at all. 'Twenty per cent of adults admit to urinating in a public pool. I've never done it, in case you're wondering, however, I have urinated in the sea, even though you probably shouldn't because of sharks.' I looked at him and waited. Nothing.

'Was it leg day today?' I asked, and immediately regretted it.

He smiled. 'Yes.' He was silent again.

'Are you not going to say anything?'

'I wasn't, actually, I was going to keep silent and just let you continue talking about urination in public pools. Speaking of, is the water warm?'

I pointed at the wall, where a digital thermometer hung.

'Twenty-seven degrees,' he read out loud. 'It's warm, maybe I should get in.'

'You would have to shower first. Like I said, your perspiration would contaminate the pool.'

'Sounds like way too much effort. What if I take my shoes off and put my feet in?'

'Only if you rinse them off under that tap first.' I pointed again.

'Fair enough.' He smiled at me again and got up. He continued smiling at me as he walked over to the tap and rinsed his feet. And he was still smiling at me when he returned and sat back down on the side of the pool. He straightened his legs, his engorged muscles rippling, and then lowered his feet into the water on a long 'aaaahh' sound. I looked down at his feet.

He had really nice feet. I hated feet in general, hated having mine touched, sometimes even hated looking at them, especially the toenails, but his were good. He didn't have one of those disproportionately long second toes that dwarfed the other toes and made everything off balance. Or toes that were so long they looked like fingers. And he didn't have large tufts of toe hair either. His were, like the rest of him, in geometrical proportion.

'Are you staring at my feet?' His question ripped my eyes away from his toes.

'Yes,' I admitted.

'Do you have a foot fetish?'

'No. I was just noting their . . .' I tried not to look at them again, but he'd lifted them out of the water and was wiggling them at me. 'Stop doing that!'

'Why? Is it turning you on or something?' He laughed and reached out one of his toes towards me.

'Stop!' I stuck my head underwater to get away from this conversation, but when my ability to hold my breath failed me and I was forced to come back up he started again.

'Just admit you have a foot fetish.'

'I don't.'

'You can tell me if you do.'

'I don't.'

'It's nothing to be ashamed of.'

'I'm not ashamed of it, not that I have it, but if I did, there's nothing wrong with having a sexual interest in feet, not that I have one.'

'Well, then why are you starting at them so much?' He was still wiggling his toes at me.

'I like the symmetry of your feet, okay?'

'Symmetry?'

'In fact, you are generally a very symmetrical person, which is good.'

'No one has ever told me that I was symmetrical before.'

'Being symmetrical is a good thing. It's a compliment.'

His smile disappeared and his face underwent some kind of shift: his nose crinkled, his eyes narrowed, his jaw stiffened, like he was grinding his teeth. I hoped he wasn't grinding. Grinding was very damaging to the enamel.

'Well, in that case, I find you very symmetrical too.'

'I'm not that symmetrical,' I argued. 'My smile curls up to the left and my shoulders are disproportionately big from swimming. I also think my left leg is a little thinner than my right leg.'

'I don't mean you are *literally* symmetrical.'

'But you just said that.'

'I was complimenting you generally, not symmetrically.'

I didn't get it. I stared at him for a moment until I finally thought I knew what he was saying.

'Aaah, you're trying to say I'm attractive without having to say I'm attractive.'

'I suppose I am.' He leaned back on his hands, stretching his legs further into the water.

'Why didn't you just say that?'

'Because most people aren't as brave as you when it comes to saying exactly what they mean all the time.'

'You think it's brave?'

'What else could it be?'

'Unfiltered. Abrasive. Offensive. Rude,' I offered up the descriptions I'd heard a million times before, but he shook his head.

'No. It's not that. It's brave. Refreshing. I like it. In fact, you've inspired me.'

'How?'

'I told my moms about my birthmother. About finding out who she was, sending her money.'

'And?'

'They were both pretty devastated to learn she was living like that. They also said they would have done the same thing in my shoes. I'm not sure why I didn't tell them sooner. I knew they would get it, but some things are just hard to say out loud.'

I didn't know what to say to him. I felt overcome by those big, powerful emotions again. So I nodded. And nodded some more. And once I'd finished that set of nods, I did another one for good measure.

'I'm getting out,' I said abruptly, after I realized I couldn't nod my head again. I climbed out of the pool and wrapped myself in my towel, all the while trying to work out what the best thing to say to him was. *Well done for doing that?* That sounded wrong. I hadn't planned to have this kind of conversation with him, so I didn't have any pre-made replies I could draw from, so I just opened my mouth and said whatever.

'I think it's amazing how you're looking out for her and your half-brother anonymously. I think lots of people would feel angry and hurt for being abandoned and given away like you were. A lot of people in your shoes might even be glad that her life has turned out the way it has. Resent the fact that she had another child and kept it. But you rose above all that. And that's . . .' I couldn't quite find the right word. Was it *admirable*? Synonyms were *praiseworthy* and *commendable*. But those did not feel like the right words. I didn't have the words. 'I know I've only met them once, but I can tell that you're with your *real* family. You are exactly where you belong.' I walked up to him and quickly put my arms on his shoulders, and then pulled away.

'Did you just pug me again?'

'That was longer than a pug,' I said.

'No, I don't think so.'

'Well, that's all you're getting. Take it or leave it,' I said, picking up my swimming bag.

'I'll take it. I'm taking it. It's taken.' He was smiling at me again. That warm smile. That perfectly symmetrical smile. That smile that had a physical effect on my internal body temperature.

'You're right where you belong too, by the way,' he said, when his smile finally faded.

'What do you mean?'

'Your parents, you told me how different they were to you.' He shook his head. 'They're not.'

'Did you actually meet them?' I asked.

'I did, and I can tell you that you happen to be the perfect mix of all their good qualities.'

'What qualities?'

'You have your mother's charisma and you have your father's kindness.'

'Me, charismatic!' I burst out laughing.

'Not in the same way as your mom, but trust me, you are. When you speak, everyone listens. When you walk into a room, you command it, even if you think you don't. People notice you. You stick out, you don't blend it. Plus, you can also make a very loud and dramatic entrance too.'

I tried to swallow, but I think I'd forgotten how to. *Was that the nicest thing anyone had ever said to me?*

'And you're kind, you give me pugs even though I know they're hard for you.' He looked at me meaningfully. His brows were raised, as if he was trying to ask me a question. Or did he want me to tell him something? I clutched the towel closer to my body, suddenly feeling exposed and naked, even though I wasn't.

'Last time we saw each other things got a bit awkward,' I blurted out with absolutely no warning.

Andrew blinked. My sudden massive conversational segue surprised him. It had surprised me too.

'And I think I know why,' I said, clutching the towel even tighter.

Andrew took a step towards me. 'You do?'

'I think so,' I said, moving towards the bathroom door.

'Wait, where're you going?' He moved closer to me.

'I need to shower,' I said. 'I hate the way I smell if I leave the chlorine on my body for too long. And it's been too long now.'

I turned my back on him and reached for the door.

'Seriously, you're not going to tell me why you know it was awkward between us?'

I stopped, let go of the door handle and turned around again. 'I think we both know the answer to that.' I held his gaze for a moment; it was way too hard to hold it any longer. I turned again.

'Thanks for saying those nice things about me by the way, it means a lot,' he called after me.

'It's a pleasure. It means a lot to me that it means a lot to you,' I said, and then disappeared into the changing room.

I closed the door behind me and then rested my back on it, closing my eyes.

Last weekend, when he'd pulled me out of the tree. When his

hands had touched my waist, my head, my face. When he'd moved closer, when I'd moved closer, when we'd both moved closer, I'd felt it. Even though it had taken me a few days to understand what the feeling was exactly.

I liked him. Perhaps more than a fake girlfriend should like a fake boyfriend.

And I think, *I think*, I suspected . . . that maybe he liked me a little bit more than a fake boyfriend should like a fake girlfriend too.

CHAPTER 30

'Good afternoon, City Tower, this is Flightbird Six Zero Zero.'

'This is City Tower. It's almost good evening, actually, Flightbird Six Zero Zero. Time is sixteen fifty-five.'

'*Tomay-to, tomato*, City Tower. Flightbird Six Zero Zero.'

'What do tomatoes have to do with anything?'

He laughed. I loved it when I made him laugh, even if it was unintentional. The sound of his laughter always came through on my headset with a little crackle. As if his laugh was too big to be contained inside it.

'We are inbound to Johannesburg Airport, heading over the pylons. Request vectors for ILS, please. Flightbird Six Zero Zero.'

'Flightbird Six Zero Zero, turn right heading three five zero.'

'Copy that, City Tower, turn right heading three five zero. Flightbird Six Zero Zero.' I expected him to go, but he didn't.

'Can I wear my pilot uniform to this wedding, or do I have to hire a suit?'

'Don't you own a suit?'

'I don't. Is that bad?'

'I don't think one can assign a moral value to whether one owns a suit or not, but—'

More laughter through the headset. 'Okay, I'll go and hire one then. But only because it's you.'

His voice disappeared again and I turned my attention back to my screen. Amberjet Five Nine Five had to abort its landing due to technical issues, making it impossible for Flightbird Seven Niner, Flightbird Six Zero Zero, as well and Airstreams One Eight and One Seven to land. I made note of all the other flights in the air that would be requesting vectors for ILS soon and getting ready to land. There were twenty planes that would be coming in in the next ten minutes or so, and the knock-on effect that Amberjet would have on them would need a lot of shuffling.

'City Tower, this is Flightbird Six Zero Zero, established ILS, runway zero seven left.'

'Flightbird Six Zero Zero, this is City Tower, abandon approach and hold west on the two seven zero degree radial, right turns, expect further clearance at seventeen twenty-two, time is now seventeen-ten, and maintain five thousand.'

'Copy, City Tower, abandon approach and hold west on the two seven zero degree radial, right turns. Expecting further clearance at seventeen twenty-two, time is now seventeen-ten, and maintain five thousand. Congestion?'

I sighed into the radio. 'I'm afraid so. Let me get this sorted out as quickly as possible.'

'I have no doubt you will. Speak soon, City Tower.'

I put the next five flights into holding patterns while we waited for Amberjet to clear the runway. I diverted two approaching flights when it became clear that it was going to take longer than intended for Amberjet to clear. My brain clicked into that mode it clicks into in moments like these. When factual information is coming at me from all angles, my mind has the ability to sift through it clearly and concisely, and then order and process it in a seamless, unpanicked manner. Why was this so easy for me, when other things seemed so damn hard? Why could I rearrange the entire landing schedule of the airport, and not be able to tell what Andrew had meant when his hand was on my waist and he was staring into my eyes? Within fifteen minutes, I had called the airplanes out of the hold and begun landing them.

'City Tower, you sorted that out quicker than I expected. Flightbird Six Zero Zero, requesting vectors for ILS, again.'

'Flightbird Six Zero Zero, this time turn left heading five nine one.'

'Copy, turn left heading five nine one.' The radio was silent for a while. I took a long, slow sip of iced water. I felt a little warm after all that excitement.

'City Tower, this is Flightbird Six Zero Zero, established ILS, runway zero seven left. Always getting my lucky runway when you're on the line.'

'I hardly think it has anything to do with me but, Flightbird Six Zero Zero, you are cleared to land on runway zero seven left.'

'Copy, cleared to land on runway zero seven left. Flightbird Six Zero Zero. Black or navy?'

'What?'

'The suit? What color are you wearing? Aren't we supposed to match, or something?'

'I'm a bridesmaid. Apparently, the dress is pink. I haven't seen it yet.'

'I'll ask my sister what she thinks will work best with pink. How's the weather down there? Flightbird Six Zero Zero.'

'Flightbird Six Zero Zero, wind two fifty at twelve knots.'

'Copy, City Tower, wind two fifty at twelve knots. Flightbird Six Zero Zero. You know my moms were one of the first legal gay marriages in South Africa. They got married in 2006. I was their combined best man. It was a great day.'

'I would love to have been there,' I said, and his voice disappeared again. I dealt with some other planes, before catching the tail end of his landing. It was not as smooth as I'd thought it would be.

'What happened there, Flightbird Six Zero Zero?'

'City Tower, I think we encountered some wind shear. Flightbird Six Zero Zero.'

'Copy Flightbird Six Zero Zero, I'll check Terminal Doppler

weather radar. Please vacate left onto Alpha taxiway, and contact Ground Control on zero two zero point one.'

'Copy, and vacating left onto Alpha taxiway, and contact Ground Control on zero two zero point one. Flightbird Six Zero Zero. Are pink suits still a thing, or did they go out in the seventies?' he asked.

'Were they ever a thing?'

'I'm not sure, actually. Okay, see you soon, City Tower.'

'Have a good day, Flightbird.'

'You too.'

The wedding was suddenly upon us. I hadn't seen Andrew at all in the week leading up to the wedding, not physically anyway. But I'd spent a bit of time with him, *metaphysically*, so to speak. To my shock, Andrew had been appearing in my dreams with increasing frequency. Usually, the dreams were benign – they involved the dogs and planes – but on one occasion, the dream had not been benign at all.

There had been sex. A lot of it. The sex had been particularly rambunctious; apt synonyms include *boisterous*, *unruly*, *rough* and, my personal favorite, *rampageous*.

We'd had rambunctious sex so many times that night that when I woke up the next day I was utterly exhausted from my nocturnal activities. But it hadn't just been the sex, there had been more to the dream, and these elements unsettled me all day. Later that night I'd googled their symbolism. Not that I put any stock in dream interpretation, but . . .

Finding a four-leaf clover in a dream can be a symbol of falling in love.

I'd wanted to tell someone about all this obvious oddness, so I'd messaged Jennifer and told her that my subconscious might want to have sex with my pretend boyfriend who I seemed to be having some real feelings for, even though the relationship was fake. Unfortunately, given the time difference, I'd only received a message the following day.

Jennifer: Was the subconscious sex hot?

Pippa: It was the hottest sex I've ever had.

Jennifer: Damn! I hate that. When subconscious sex is so much better than real-life sex. Colleen and I are going through a bit of a dry spell at the moment.

Pippa: How long have you been together now?

Jennifer: A year. Is that too soon for the sex to stop? I think it is.

Pippa: I wouldn't know. The sex usually stops after a few weeks in my relationships. That's because I never see them again.

Jennifer: Maybe we just need a break, like a weekend away.

Pippa: Go snorkeling at the Great Barrier Reef.

Jennifer: Because nothing says sexy like goggles, snorkels and flippers.

Jennifer: So what's this about real feelings?

Pippa: I think I'm having them.

Jennifer: Do you think he's having them?

Pippa: I can't say for sure, but I suspect he might be.

Jennifer: Interesting.

I waited for her to write something else, but she didn't.

Pippa: Is that all you're going to say? Interesting?

Jennifer: For now. Let me process this for a while and get back to you.

Pippa: Seriously, is that it?

Jennifer: Got to run.

Pippa: You're not even going to qualify 'interesting'. Just a little bit?

Jennifer: Nope. Hope the wedding isn't too horrendous. Send me pics. Would love to see this bridesmaid dress you complain of.

I waited for Andrew outside the reception hall. The ceremony was over and everyone was making their way there. When I saw him, a realization blinked before my eyes like a neon sign on the Las Vegas strip. It was no longer *only* my subconscious that wanted to have sex with him. He walked closer in this effortless way that made him look like he was gliding on air. God, he looked amazing in that suit and tie. Synonyms included *unbelievable*, *wonderful*, *marvellous*. His hair was styled in a way I'd never seen before, and the dark shadow of stubble across his jaw immediately made him look more masculine, if that was even possible.

'You look . . .' He started and stopped.

'Stop! Don't say it,' I warned him, suddenly aware of what I was wearing.

'It's not as bad as you made it out to be. The other day you made it seem like something out of an eighties horror movie.'

'It is out of an eighties horror movie.' I looked down at the dress. The double, triple, quadruple – who knew how many layers this thing had – dress. 'She calls the color Thulian pink!'

'It is very pink,' Andrew said, tilting his head from side to side.

'I googled Thulian pink. It's in the color family Pastel Crimson. *Crimson!*'

He smiled.

'I look like a life-size Barbie. We all do. What adult dresses her four bridesmaids in bright pink from head to toe, and with so many ruffles?'

Andrew's smile turned into a laugh.

'Even my mom tried to talk her out of this choice, but she was determined. Have you seen my parents?'

'Yes, I saw them at the ceremony. Your mom was wearing an earpiece and yelling commands at people like I've never seen before. She's terrifying.'

'You look nice,' I said, pointing at him, trying to make it sound cool and casual, even though it was anything but cool and casual in my head. I was currently running over synonyms for the word sexy: *sensuous, seductive, provocative, arousing, come-hither, titillating.*

'The man at the shop said that black was out and mid-gray was in.' He held his arms out in a questioning gesture. 'Also said it would complement pink more.'

'Mid-gray?' I eyed the suit, trying to decide what exactly made this gray 'mid', and if 'mid' was referring to middle, then what was it in the middle of exactly? But at least now I was contemplating his suit and not how steamy, racy and inviting he was. Andrew stuck his head around the door and looked into the hall.

'It looks incredible in there. Your mom is amazing at what she does.'

I peered in too. There was a reason my mom was the country's most sought-after wedding planner. She always managed to transform an empty room into something that looked like it had been plucked straight out of the pages of a fairy-tale. Although this sort of thing was not for me – low-hanging crystal chandeliers, hundreds of flickering candles, bowls of floating flowers and bunches of plum-white peonies – I had to admit it was beautiful in its own kind of way. Every detail had been attended to: the elegantly folded napkins, gold hand-calligraphed name tags on the tables, and all the other things that had been painstakingly done behind the scenes that you could not see.

'She really is very good!' I said.

'But is the best man sticking to the wedding plan?' Andrew asked.

'As far as I know,' I said.

'Shall we find our table?' he asked.

I nodded and then quickly shook my head. 'Wait. I just need a minute outside, alone, if you don't mind. That whole service was very . . .' I searched for the word that wouldn't make me sound as crazy as I'd felt standing up there. The sound of the organ had made me want to slither out of my skin and melt into the floor. I'd physically felt everyone's eyes on me, and that had made me nauseous. The cheering at the end and the throwing of the confetti, and it raining down on me, had made me feel disorientated and terrified, as if under attack. I could still feel psychosomatic confetti clinging to my skin. The dress I was wearing had felt prickly and itchy and it had taken all my concentration *not* to scratch myself in front of an entire church full of people. I just needed a moment alone to decompress before I went into the reception and faced yet another sensory circus.

Andrew nodded, as if he understood what I was saying. 'I'll go and find our table. See you inside.'

When I was alone, I circled the lawn a few times, walking in a slow, deliberate manner. I looked around and named the things I could see, then listed the things I could hear and then the things I could feel. I did this for about ten minutes, to bring my hyperarousal down a few notches. This was something that a therapist I'd had many years ago had taught me. It was perhaps the only useful thing the therapist had taught me. I find therapy baffling. So much was said in sessions, and yet nothing was said at all. And everything that was said was shrouded in mysterious terms that made no sense. Did I even have an inner child? And how did I know that child wanted to be soothed? Maybe she wanted to run wild and jump and gallop across the fields? And what age child were we talking about anyway? Baby me, toddler me, teen me? It was all very confusing and impractical, hence the fact she was an ex-therapist, and not a current one. I'd given up on therapy many years back when I realized that it just didn't work for me.

I continued around the garden a few more times, and the silence and the breeze and the cool glass of water I was sipping on did finally do the trick. And when I'd balanced myself out as much as I could under the circumstances, I mustered the courage to go inside.

I found Andrew at the table with all the other pink Barbies and groomsmen. He was draped comfortably and casually in a chair, arm slung over the back as if he'd settled in. Beer in one hand, laughing and chatting away with everyone as if he'd known them for ever. I watched him for a while: the ease and grace he did things with reminded me of an angelfish. The way they glided through the water with such seamless elegance. Synonyms like *refinement*, *sophistication* and *magnificence* were also apt.

'Hey.' I took a step forward and tripped over my foot. Andrew's arm shot out, and he grabbed my elbow and steadied me. I, on the other hand, was not an angelfish. I was a big, bulbous goldfish that had no ease and elegance at all.

'You okay?' he asked as I tried to straighten the stupid dress I was wearing.

'Fine. Just . . . you know.' I sat down and tried to smile at everyone at the table. They were all looking at me.

'We're getting to know your boyfriend here,' Delia chirped.

'We didn't know you were seeing anyone,' Tertia added.

My smile faltered. I wasn't sure why they needed to know whether I was seeing anyone; they were my cousin's best friends, I only ever saw them at functions like birthday parties and graduations. It's not like we rang each other and chatted on the phone. This assumption that they had some kind of right to know about this intimate detail of my personal life struck me as somewhat befuddling.

'And a pilot!' she exclaimed. 'Do you guys work on the same flights? Is that how you met?'

'I'm an air traffic controller, not a flight attendant. I work inside the airport, not on the flights,' I qualified to Delia, *again*. She always seemed to get these two confused, although I never knew why. There was such a large difference between the two it led me to believe that either she was a little slow to catch on to concepts or she was never really listening to me when I talked. The latter was probably more plausible, since she seemed to have grasped what Andrew did perfectly and hadn't needed any prompting there.

'We met because she's one of the controllers that helps navigate my plane down,' Andrew explained. 'We'd been speaking to each other almost every day for about six months before we met.'

Both Delia and Tertia leaned in now. This story always seemed to have this effect on women. I'd noticed this at my reunion too. They leaned, their features going soft, so soft that they looked like they might slide right off their faces, like warm, melted butter. Their eyes usually lit up too, and it had nothing to do with environmental lighting factors.

'And then one day I was buying coffee at the shop and I heard this familiar voice,' Andrew said, continuing with the story that garnered all the soft features and glittery eyeballs.

'That's so cute,' Tertia said.

'It's like a movie meet-cute,' Delia added. She was a self-professed romance junkie and whenever I met her she would always talk about the latest movie or book that I should be watching or reading. I'd tried one of her recommendations once. I'd made it through the first chapter and then given up. The sex scenes had been rather good though, I'll give it that, and I'd skipped ahead to find them. But the majority of the book had left me feeling awkward and uncomfortable. Anything romantic made me feel that way. The way people lay in bed and told each other their most intimate, personal things, or the way they stared into each other's eyes and uttered romantic words in hushed tones. Romance was a strange, cringy creature that I did not understand. Sometimes when a scene got too romantic in a film I had to physically put my hands over my eyes because I was so embarrassed for the actors on the screen. Suddenly this conversation was giving me the same feeling, so I quickly changed the subject.

'Andrew is a very good pilot,' I piped up. Delia and Tertia looked at me as if disappointed. As if they'd been wanting more melty-butter meet-cute stories. 'He has an impeccable safety record,' I added, hoping this additional piece of information might waylay their disappointment somewhat. It did not. 'But yes, it was a very cute meet-cute,'

I said, and their faces instantly softened again. A loud clink of a glass brought the chatter in the room to an abrupt stop. I was grateful for this, and we all turned and settled into listening to the speeches.

The best-man speech made everyone laugh a lot, even Andrew. I didn't laugh. The father of the bride's speech made everyone all teary-eyed. I did not get teary-eyed, but when Delia and Tertia looked across at me I picked up a napkin and dabbed my face in an attempt to fit in.

The whole pomp and ceremony of the thing, all the traditions, seemed silly to me. I'd never understood why smashing cake into each other's faces was funny. It was messy, and just a little bit gross, if you ask me. But everyone seemed to like it, and three glasses of champagne in, I suppose I didn't mind it as much as I thought I would either. The dance floor had been opened up to the father–daughter dance first, and then over to the couple's first dance. They'd chosen one of those songs that you know all the lyrics to but can't name the band or the title of song. It was one of those songs that is only ever played on occasions like these. After their dance, the dance floor was free to everyone. I did not dance. But apparently Andrew did.

'Come on.' He stood up the second the music came on and people began heading for the dance floor. I shook my head.

'I do not rhythmically move my body to the beat of music in a crowd.'

'We could dance in the corner away from everyone?'

'Um . . .' I looked at the corner he was pointing at. I did, from time to time, enjoy flitting around the house with my AirPods in, jumping about to a tune, but the idea of being in a crowd dancing – bodies bumping together, arms touching, sweat beads being exchanged – that thought simply alarmed me.

'Everyone's drunk. No one will care or even notice that we're in the corner,' he said. 'Or is it a case of "you can't put Baby in the corner"?'

'Who?'

'Baby?'

'Who's that?' I asked.

'You haven't watched *Dirty Dancing*?'

I shook my head.

'Patrick Swayze, Jennifer Gray?'

'Who are they?'

'Oh my God, Pippa!'

'Is this a reality-TV thing? Because I don't watch reality TV.'

'Right, you and I have a movie night coming up. My sisters loved that movie! They made me watch it with them and used me to practice that big dance move in the lounge.'

'I'm fine with the corner,' I said, standing up, since I had no idea what he was talking about. I let Andrew take my hand and lead me there. On the way he twirled me around and I laughed.

'I'm a terrible dancer,' I said. 'I only ever dance when no one is looking.'

'Well, pretend that no one is looking, then.' He pushed me away and pulled me close again, repeating that motion a few times as we both laughed. A feeling rose up inside me. This euphoric, happy, giddy feeling. The feeling was colossal and filled every single part of me as we twirled and moved to the music. As the music got faster and louder, so too did the euphoric feeling. It grew so tremendous that I was sure it was going to burst out of me. A discomfort throbbed in my chest and suddenly it was harder to breathe. Andrew stopped dancing and pulled me towards him.

'You okay?' he whispered in my ear. His breath was cool against my hot skin.

'I'm . . . okay.' It was a lie, but I nodded. His face was so close to mine that my cheek slowly dragged against his. His face felt rough and stubbly and prickled against the corner of my lips.

'You sure?' he asked. This was the closest we'd ever been to each other and, before I knew what I was doing, my hand came up and squeezed his elbow.

'I just need to . . .' I started the sentence, but it was impossible to finish when his arm wrapped around my waist. The euphoric feeling was now making me spin, making the dance floor wavy and uneven. The music got louder, his arm got tighter and the feel of his cheek against mine had me at some kind of boiling point. I was afraid I was about to explode.

'Need to what?' he whispered against my ear, and my skin pebbled. A wave of static swept across my body from head to toe. My hairs stood on end, my scalp tingled and a feeling so intense rushed down my spine.

'Need to . . .'

He pulled me even closer, flattening his chest to mine. The euphoric feeling increased, unrelating waves of double dopamine almost knocking me off my feet. Serotonin synapses firing to life.

'Toilet!' I said suddenly, and pushed him away from me. 'I have to . . .' I didn't finish the sentence, instead I turned and walked away, so fast that I stumbled twice, knocking into two different couples as I went.

I was having fun, too much fun. The fun was overwhelming and I needed a moment alone to come down from it before I overdosed on the fun. Sometimes even good feelings were too big to handle. I raced to the bathroom, not the ones that everyone else used but the private ones that we'd used as changing rooms earlier. No one would disturb me there. Once inside, I sat on one of the toilets, closed my eyes and welcomed the sudden silence of the room.

Sometimes it felt as if there was no barrier between me and the outside world. I was porous, the energy of the world rushing straight through my skin and into me. Rushing into my body unfiltered and ready to consume me. Other people's skin acted like a barrier between their insides and the world around them, but mine did not. Everything penetrated me. In moments like these I needed some silence, some stillness to push back the world around me so I could breathe again. This was one of those moments. I sat on the toilet seat, tapping my feet on the ground in a soothing, rhythmic way, the slow and predictable *tap, tap, tap* regulating me a little. The bathroom smelled of lilies, a scent that I liked, apart for the fact that lilies were once used to hide the smell of death at a funeral. But other than that, the smell was sweet and pleasant. The lights in the bathroom were much softer than outside, and all of this helped soften the edges of my jagged senses. That is, until the door flew open with a bang and loud laughter shattered the silence.

'God, I hate this dress. I swear she did it on purpose.' I recognized the voice immediately: it was Delia.

'God, we look awful in them,' Tertia said.

'At least we didn't look as awkward as Pippa. Did you see how much she was scratching herself in it?'

'Sssshhh!' Delia hissed. 'Someone might be in here.'

As quietly as possible, I lifted my feet off the floor, in anticipation for their look under the door.

'No one's here,' Tertia insisted. 'I wish I could take this thing off. I'm not going to get laid in this dress. And I packed condoms – might as well toss them if I'm wearing this thing. Fuck, I can't believe Pippa is wearing the same dress and she's going to get laid tonight.'

'How hot is he?' Tertia asked.

'God, so hot.'

'I mean, I don't mean to be rude or anything' – I've observed that usually when people start a sentence like that, they are about to be rude – 'but how did she get him? I'm not saying she's not hot, she is, but she's never had a boyfriend before, has she?'

'I know. I thought she might be gay once.'

'Seriously, though, I don't think it will last,' Tertia said. It felt like someone had just poked a stick into my side.

'Totally. He seems too nice and normal for her,' Delia replied. 'I can't see them together, you know?'

Another sharp stick in my side.

I had known Delia and Tertia all my life; they'd lived next door to my cousin Bee and whenever we'd gone over, they'd been there. They'd always teased me for being different, for not playing Barbies with them when we were younger, for not wanting to go to parties when we were older. It seemed that no matter what I did, or didn't do, they had a problem with all of it. They had been part of *that* group at school. The group that had teased me for being different.

'I mean, don't get me wrong' – another thing people said before saying something mean – 'I've always liked her,' Tertia added.

'Me too,' Delia jumped in, as if they were both trying to ease their conscience for talking about me like this. 'I've never *not* liked her.'

'It's just that she's so . . . it's hard to put your finger on, you know . . . But I do like her.'

Once more, 'like her' said as if it was some kind of consolation prize.

'But she's always been a bit . . . off,' Delia offered, agreeing with her twin. 'Even when we were young.'

'It's not like she can help it though. She has that type of autism, doesn't she? What do they call it, I can never remember the name . . .'

'Ass something or other.'

They both burst out laughing. And there it was.

The word. The label. The thing that made existing in this world so much harder for me. The thing that made making and keeping friends feel like an insurmountable task sometimes. The thing that made all romantic 'relationships' fall apart. I was on the autism spectrum, and that was the *real* reason I didn't like being asked why I wasn't in a relationship, because then I would need to explain to that person why it was that I was so, so bad at being in relationships and why they never lasted. My stomach flipped. I felt nauseous and then suddenly cold and clammy.

'The whole thing feels a bit off, actually,' Delia added. 'She's just not the kind of girl guys like him usually go for. Seriously, how did that happen?'

'Maybe she's really kinky in bed or something!' They both hooted with such loud and manic laughter that I had to put my hands over my ears.

'Shame, though,' Delia said, once the laughter had faded away. 'It won't last. Bee was saying that she literally goes on five dates with someone and then it's over.'

'God, and Andrew is so fucking hot! I would totally date him if I could.'

'Well, maybe you can. I wonder how many dates they've been on.'

They both burst out laughing again.

'Seems like such a waste,' Delia giggled, and her witchy sister joined in.

A waste . . . the word rang in my head over and over again like a loudly tolling bell. Synonyms for waste included *dilapidation*, *desolation*, *decay*. I was *not* those things. I may be on the autism spectrum, yes, but I was not those things. It had taken me a long time to accept this fact, still, having someone say it out loud like this, it was . . . hard to hear.

'Shame, I mean I hope it works out for her, I really do, but . . .' Delia let the 'but' hang in the air.

'Sure, best of luck to them, but . . .' And now Tertia delivered that dreaded hanging 'but'. Two hanging buts in the air, and my brain scrambled to fill in the blanks.

But no one will ever be able to love her, because as soon as they get to know her, really know her, they leave.

'Fuck, let's get stoned,' Delia said, changing the subject. I heard her rummage in her bag. 'I need something to make me forget that I'm wearing this tragedy of a dress.'

'Lock the door,' Delia said. I looked around in panic. I didn't want to sit in here while they got stoned, and the longer they were in here, the surer their chances of finding me were. I kept still as the lighter flicked, as the sound of inhaling and coughing began. When they spoke again, they voices had taken on a slow, lugubrious quality, punctuated by laughter that seemed more like wild cackling. The kind a jackal might make at night. I tried to hold my breath for extended periods of time; I did not want to get stoned on second-hand smoke. The only time I ever got stoned I had regretted it instantly and then spent the next few hours convinced I was going to die because I was choking on a piece of plastic from a gum wrapper that I'd opened.

'Crap!' one of them exclaimed as something large fell and hit the floor. Suddenly a box of condoms, a packet of mints and a lighter flew under the bathroom door into my stall.

'My fucking bag. I'm so stoned!' Tertia laughed, and then I heard her drop to her knees. I stiffened, positive she was going to catch me when she came looking for her things, only she didn't. 'I don't think my eyes see anymore,' she said, and they both burst out laughing again. How that was funny, I did not know. If my eyes stopped working properly, I would not consider that a good time. But obviously we had different definitions of what a 'good time' was.

'What am I doing on the floor, again?' Tertia asked in a vacant-sounding way.

'I have no fucking clue,' Delia replied as she took another big-sounding puff. She should really stop puffing! It was clear they both needed to stop puffing.

'Me neither.' I heard Tertia get up off the floor again. They spent the next ten minutes talking about all the guests at the wedding, as if doing a post-mortem on the event. They spoke about all the men they wouldn't mind fucking, and Andrew's name came up a few more times, followed by more girlish giggles. They talked a lot about what they hoped they would have for dessert, and whether it was possible to tell if a man was good in bed based on the kind of drink he ordered. They concluded that men who drank Cosmos were not good in bed.

Finally, after what felt like a torturous eternity, they left. I rushed out of the stall, my feet exploding with tingles as the blood rushed back into them. I'd been crouched on the toilet for so long I was sure

I had diminished blood flow in my extremities. I locked the door behind them, pushed all the windows open and paced the room. Their words were still reverberating around my head. I knew what most people thought of me, and most days I didn't care, but on others, like today, faced with my cousin's wedding and my mother's clear disappointment that the wedding had not been for me, I cared. I cared so much that a tear rolled down my face.

I touched my cheek. My fingers came away wet. The fact that salty water poured out of your eyes when you were emotionally upset was such a bizarre concept. I'd googled it once and discovered that in the 1600s people believed that emotions, especially love, heated the heart, which generated water vapour in order to cool itself down. That vapour would then rise, condense near the eyes and escape. And although it was scientifically impossible, I absolutely loved this notion. Because it often felt like my heart was hot and that it needed to cool down. Emotions, good and bad, always felt so intense, so magnified . . . *Like now.*

My mouth was dry, and the packet of mints on the floor caught my attention. I picked everything up, shoved a few mints into my mouth and tossed the other things into the dustbin. My aim was off, so the lighter landed in the bin but the box of condoms missed and fell onto the floor. I was about to pick it up when my phone beeped.

Andrew: Where are you? I've been looking for you. Literally. I've been kicked out of two women's bathrooms. Are you okay?

Pippa: Sort of.

I touched my wet face for a brief moment.

Pippa: Not really.

Andrew: Which bathroom are you in?

Pippa: Downstairs, where the bridesmaids got ready, not upstairs at the venue.

Andrew: Do you want me to come?

I waited before replying; usually, when I was like this, I didn't want anyone around. But Andrew wasn't anyone any more, and his presence always made me feel good.

Pippa: Please.

A few moments later he knocked on the door and I ushered him inside.

'You've been crying.' He came towards me, but I stepped back. 'Are you okay?'

'Fine. Fine. I'm . . .' I clutched the sink and shook my head. 'Not fine,' I admitted.

'Is it something I did? The dance floor?'

I shook my head hard and he looked round the room.

'Have you smoked . . . do you smoke weed?'

'God, no! But Tertia and Delia did, and I was stuck in here with them. I've been trying to get rid of the smell.' I pushed the window open even more, and Andrew pushed open the window that was too high for me to reach.

'Do you want to talk about it?' he asked.

'I don't know. Yes, no. Maybe. It's hard to tell.'

'You can talk to me if you want, you know that.' His fingers brushed over my shoulder, so softly and quickly that I almost missed it. 'I don't like seeing you like this.' His voice had softened to almost a whisper and I felt this overwhelming need to tell him what had happened.

'They said you were too good for me,' I blurted out.

'Who said that?'

'Delia and Tertia. They said it didn't make sense that someone like you could be with someone like me because I was weird and off. And also you're too hot for me, it's a waste.'

'Wait, slow down. What?'

'You and me. Apparently, you're too nice and normal and as soon as you get to know me, the real me, you'll break up with me, which is actually one hundred per cent the truth, if you and I were in a real relationship. But it's not real, so it shouldn't offend me, but I am offended and I don't really know why?'

'I have gotten to know you,' Andrew said.

'No, you haven't,' I whispered. 'Not really, anyway. Besides, this is only technically date number four, so you still find me charming or whatever. But after the next one, if this was real, you won't any more.'

'What are you even talking about?' He looked confused, and I didn't blame him. I felt equally confused, with all these conflicting thoughts and feelings bouncing around inside me.

'It's always the way it works. I meet a guy, often they're quite enamoured with me for a while. They think I'm fascinating and my little foibles are unique, charming even. But there always comes a moment when all of that changes.'

The more time a person spent with me romantically, the less they liked me. My once-endearing eccentricities were stripped of all their appeal and now they were just *weird*, *annoying*, *peculiar* and other synonyms. And it was then that they disappeared. Usually an excuse about it 'not being me' was given. Or not being ready for a relationship, or once, I just never heard from the man again. Ever. This was the pattern that all my 'relationships' had followed. Get to know me well enough, and apparently I was not enough. And apparently this was a known fact about me. Bee had said so, and now Delia and Tertia knew too.

'I disagree. I think I've gotten to know you pretty well.'

I shook my head. 'I'm not relationship material,' I said.

Andrew shook his head. 'I disagree with that too, and besides, who the hell do they think they are, deciding who I should or should not be dating?'

'Fake dating,' I corrected quickly.

'Whatever.' He dismissed what I'd said with a flick of his hand. 'I find that pretty offensive. And what do they mean, I'm the hot one. Have you looked in the mirror lately?'

I tried to wipe away another tear. The wetness was beginning to smudge the black eyeliner that the make-up artist had put on, even though I was sure it made my eyes look smaller.

'Not like this,' I said.

'Just like this.' His voice had changed. A sudden and very distinct change. It was soft now, reticent almost.

'Why is your voice like that?' I asked.

'Like what?'

'All soft and whispery and . . . sexy.'

'You're sexy.' He stepped towards me.

I looked down at the questionable pink dress I was wearing. I'd long suspected, from the few weddings I'd attended, that the bride made the bridesmaids wear ugly dresses on purpose so that there was no question where everyone's attention needed to be. I brushed the pink rayon fabric down and the top layer stuck to my hands like it had been statically charged. I tried to pull my hands away from the fabric, but it followed me. I shook my wrists, and the fabric finally fell.

'Even in this dress?' I asked.

'Especially in that dress.' A smile curled up the left side of his lips. His smiles were usually so symmetrical, but this one was not. I held his gaze and watched him as his eyes traced my face in an anti-clockwise direction. The feeling was palpable, like a feather being dragged across my checks, lips and forehead. The entire room went silent. I wasn't breathing, he wasn't breathing, and the room felt like it had also ceased breathing, because there was a stillness to it that had not been there before.

'The world feels like it's stopped breathing,' I said. I hadn't meant that thought to come out, but it had.

He moved towards me. 'I know exactly what you mean.'

'You do?'

He nodded. His smile grew even more crooked and sexy. An intense, desperate yearning lit me up and I pushed myself off the sink and walked towards him. His proximity felt magnetic, like the dress sticking to my fingers and my skin. I wanted him all over my skin. Not this dress. I wanted this dress to lie crumpled on the floor and for Andrew's smooth hands and lips to be all over my body. And for someone who was not good at reading facial expressions, there was no doubt in my mind that Andrew was thinking the exact same thing.

Chapter 31

I reached for him and waited to see if he would reciprocate. He did. He wrapped his arms around me, pushed his lips against mine and walked me backwards into the vanity. My lips pressed back, then they opened and I sunk into his mouth at the same time that he sunk into mine. Our moans tumbled into each other's mouths, their low vibrations adding to the feeling of floating away on a kiss that was so good it felt like we'd both practiced doing this beforehand. He cupped my face and pulled me deeper. All the want that had been inside me for a while now frothed to the surface. I opened my legs, pushed my pink dress up and let him fall between them. Nothing could stop us now. I had given him a clear signal as to how far I was prepared to go, and he accepted the proposal. He slid his hand up my thigh while the kissing grew frantic. I reached down and scrambled for his pants, for his belt. I wanted to slip my hands in and hold him, like I'd been dreaming about at night.

I hoped my expectations were going to be met, and Jennifer wasn't right about fantasy sex. I slipped my hand over him; it was so smooth and effortless. His body shuddered and he threw his head back, giving me enough time to sneak a quick peek. I hated not knowing what I was working with; I needed to see it. And when I did, I was pleased. It was perfect. It didn't intimidate me like those porn-star dicks did, ripping through their jeans, looking big enough to use as a meat-tenderizing mallet. It didn't underwhelm me either. It was all in perfect proportion. Nothing was bigger or smaller than it needed to be. Soon his hands were reaching for me, but the dress was in the way. He laughed as he attempted to bat the ruffles of the skirt away. But each time he did, the fabric came up clinging to him.

'I take it back. I hate this dress.' He continued to swat at the fabric. 'What the hell is this material and why is it sticking to me!'

I turned around quickly. 'Get it off.' I arched my back, offering up the zip. He took it tentatively at first, but when his fingers came into contact with my skin – hot and blazing – and I moaned, the zip came down so fast and the dress pooled at my ankles in seconds.

'Let me look at you.' He put his hands on my waist and spun me around. The look on his face after he'd traced his eyes up and down my body was also easy to read.

'God, you're hot.'

'Victoria's Secret,' I said.

'What is?'

'My underwear.'

He pulled me towards him. 'I wasn't looking at the underwear.' He kissed me again. I lifted my leg and wrapped it around him, pulling and urging him closer. I pushed my hands under the shoulders of his jacket and worked it off. It fell onto my dress, and then I tackled his buttons until his shirt was open. This was it. The moment I'd been waiting for. I pulled away from the kiss and looked at him.

My sculptural marble expectations had been exceeded. 'Wow,' I said, touching the ten-pack in front of me. He was exactly as I'd hoped he would be. Hard and smooth to the touch, and if I wasn't feeling so desperate for more of him right now, I might have wanted to take my time to admire the physical structure of his body a little more. But I didn't. Because I didn't just want to know how his body looked, I wanted to know how it felt, smelled and tasted too.

I sunk my face into his neck and tried to make my inhalation of him as subtle as possible. He smelled good, and the fact he didn't wear cologne was a plus for me. Strong cologne often made me feel sick, but he smelled clean, like a mountain stream. Curiosity about his scent satisfied, I went back to kissing him. To wrapping another leg around him and allowing him to pick me up and put me on the vanity. We were face to face now, so I closed my eyes. Looking him in the eye would be too intense.

His face moved away from mine. It moved down to my breasts, and I felt his mouth over the lace of my bra. Felt the wet warmth soaking through the delicate lace. I reached down between us again and slipped both hands into his unbuttoned jeans. Gripped him tightly and pulled rhythmically as he took my nipple through my lace bra and played with it in his mouth. His breathing increased, became shorter and sharper, and I knew I would need to ease off soon, especially if I wanted to take this all the way. *Did I want to take it all the way?*

Yes, I did. I felt like I needed a reprieve from my mind and everything that was going on inside it. A break from the reality around me, a way to silence and block out the chaos from behind that door, and also . . . *I just wanted to be close to Andrew.* I wanted to have all of him. Sex was not often about the other person for me, but this time, it was.

'Do you want to have sex?' I pulled away and asked, just in case some signals were getting mixed here. I'd once assumed that the guy I was with had wanted to have sex, but apparently, he didn't have sex on first dates. This had led to an embarrassing moment for me. So now I always made sure I asked.

Andrew didn't speak. He just blinked.

'So, do you? Sex? With me?'

'Um . . .' Andrew ran a hand through his hair, looking unsure.

'I mean, I feel like it's headed that way. You're clearly ready for it, physically.' I looked down at the hard bulge in his pants. 'I'm obviously ready for it.' I looked down at my nipples and waited for him to respond again, but he didn't. 'Shit, was that too forward? Should I not have asked? It's just that this one time I climbed onto a guy's lap while we were kissing, thinking that he wanted to have sex, but he didn't, so I don't want to assume that—'

'I want to.' He cut me off. 'A lot.' He smiled at me and closed the gap between us once more. 'A lot.'

'Me too.' I smiled back at him, pleased with his answer.

'But . . .' Andrew looked around the room and then back to me. 'Here? In a bathroom? I thought you said you would never have sex with me in a bathroom.'

It took me a few moments, but when I got it I laughed and clapped my hands together in utter delight. Andrew laughed too, and when I tried to clap my hands together again, he grabbed them. He held on to them tightly, but not too tightly, just the right amount of tight. And then he guided them back to his body.

'I love it when you touch me,' he whispered.

'I love touching you,' I said, tracing the lines of his torso with my fingers. His body was a map, and all the lines on his torso were roads, and all the roads seemed to lead to the exact same place. I slipped my finger into the elastic of his underwear and pulled at it.

'You should take these off,' I said, letting the elastic go.

'So should you.' His eyes moved to my purple panties.

'Okay.' I took a step back so he could watch me. I was awkward in social situations, awkward in most other places, but I'd never been awkward here. In moments like these. I slowly pulled my underwear down and stepped out of it. His eyes went straight there, and stayed there.

'What about you?' I pointed at his underwear and clicked my fingers.

'Impatient?' he asked.

'Very!'

'Well, then . . .' He pulled them down in one quick move. I tilted my head back and forth, taking him all in, and then I started nodding.

'Good!' I closed my one eye. 'Good proportions. Perhaps a bit more girth than I'm used to, but good.'

'Wow. Did you just review my dick?'

'It was a good review though.'

'I know, but seriously, *out loud*!'

'Should I have done it in my head instead?'

He didn't respond; instead he hung his head and shook it for a while.

'What?' I asked, worried that I'd offended him. But it had been a good review. 'It's one of the nicest penises I've ever seen!' I added quickly, in case he needed the review to be glowing, not 'just good'.

He looked up at me again, His head-shaking continued.

'Honestly, it is. It's very—'

'Stop!' He held his hand up to cut me off, just as I was about to launch into the theory of penis size and the size of your index finger in relation to your ring finger.

'Okay,' I said, putting my hand over my mouth.

But he didn't look upset with me. On the contrary. His smile was even more crooked and unsymmetrical now. 'You,' he said, coming towards me.

'Me what?'

'I honestly don't know, actually. I don't know what it is about you, but . . . just, *you*.' He started kissing me again and my body reacted instantly. But I pulled away despite this.

'What does that even mean?' I asked.

Andrew shrugged. 'Does it matter?'

'No.' This time I kissed him. My body was slowly melting into his now. I wasn't sure I could tell where my lips ended and his began. Which tongue was mine and which tongue was his.

'I don't have condoms,' Andrew whispered into my ear.

'Look down,' I whispered back.

He stepped back and looked down. 'Condoms. Did you bring them tonight because you thought we might—'

'No. They're not mine. But I'm glad they're here.'

'So am I.'

CHAPTER 32

He slipped inside me with a sense of urgency. As if he'd been waiting for this moment as much as I'd been. The sex quickly became a strange blur of body parts and movements. A hunger that I'd felt deep inside made me lose myself like I hadn't lost myself before.

'Sssshh!' Andrew slapped a hand over my mouth with a chuckle.

'What?'

'You're being very loud!' He laughed when I took a finger into my mouth and then pushed his hand away. I hadn't realized that I was being loud. I pursed my lips together tightly and tried to concentrate on *not* making noises, but there was an intensity to the sex that was making it very hard. I slapped my hands over my mouth when loud, sharp breaths started pushing their way out of my lips. I looked at Andrew and shook my head. My face felt like it was going to explode if I couldn't make any noises. Because the more tightly I clamped my hands over my mouth, the deeper and harder and faster he thrust.

'I thought you said we were having mediocre sex,' he said through a tightly clenched jaw. 'It doesn't sound like it, does it?' he asked, and thrust so deeply into me that I thought I was going to break, in the most delicious way possible.

'I said you were improving,' I managed in between gasps for air, and then let out a loud moan as he drew slowly out of me, stopped completely for a moment, and then drove back in.

'Shhhh!' he said, gripping my waist tighter.

'I CAN'T!' I half shouted on an outbreath as I wrapped my legs around him even tighter. 'Fuck it, let them hear me.'

Andrew gripped the back of my head. 'Maybe this will help.' He pulled me into an open-mouth kiss, his mouth resting over mine. I panted and moaned into his mouth, and it dulled the sound a little but it wasn't enough to stop the moan I let out as I came. I buried my face in his shoulder and clung on to him as I waited for my body to go limp. And when it did, and I finally pulled my face away, I found him looking at me.

'What?'

'That was the hottest thing I've ever seen,' he said, and then leaned his face close to mine. 'You're the hottest thing I've ever seen.' He kissed me slowly and softly this time. The kiss stayed slow and deliberate, and his thrusting now matched it too. Slow. Shallow. Then deep. We got into a perfect rhythm and my skin prickled and I shivered under his touch.

Shit. What was happening? Something was happening. To me. To us. To everything around us. To the fabric of spacetime itself. This feeling was new and intense and I could not quantify and catalogue and understand it, and I didn't much like that. It left me feeling uneasy and off kilter and totally out of control. But a part of me liked it. And that part of me was trying to convince the other part to just let go and succumb to the feeling, even if it was utterly terrifying. My brain started whizzing, which was not supposed to happen during sex. I was not supposed to be thinking right now, but an internal war was being raged in my head. A war between the part of me saying 'let go to this strange new feeling' and the other part telling me to hang on tightly and not lose myself in this moment. Because if I lost myself in this moment, I wasn't sure I'd ever be able to find my way out again. There was no GPS or map to navigate me out of a moment like this. And the idea of being lost in it, for ever, terrified me.

Let go, the voice in my head seemed to urge.

I wanted to scream back at that voice. That voice that seemed to be ignoring all rationality. But I didn't, and the voice was getting louder and louder until I finally let go.

I allowed myself to fully fall into Andrew. I lifted my head and sought out eye contact. I wanted to feel even more connected to him. I'd always thought eyes said too much; that's why I didn't like looking into them. He stared straight back at me, his arresting eyes made even more arresting by the difference in color between them. This was the only non-symmetrical thing about him, and I think this was my favorite part of him too. I couldn't see his lips, but if I did, I bet they were smiling. Because his eyes were smiling, I tried to make mine smile back at him. But soon, the smile was gone. They clouded over, as if he was leaving this place and looking into a far-off world that only he could see. That far-off gaze, his sexy, hooded eyes that looked almost drugged, threw me over the edge. I felt my entire body responding to that look as another orgasm began to build. His built, too, as if our bodies were telling each other what to do.

And when I couldn't handle it any more, because the physical feelings were just too much, I closed my eyes. It wasn't black behind my eyelids though. There were colors, bright and intense. I was watching a fireworks show projected onto the back of my eyelids, and the show got more and more explosive and impressive as I raced towards my orgasm. And then it all went white.

We clutched on to each other like that for I don't know how long. I felt euphoric wrapped in Andrew's arms. As if being wrapped in his arms provided me with that barrier to the outside world that I lacked. I sunk deeper into him, smiling and basking in the glow of the strange but wonderful feeling, but then . . .

The feeling became too much. His arms began feeling itchy around me, the warm glow became sticky. The euphoria became terrifying. I pushed him away and slipped off the counter. The spell was broken. Maybe I had broken it. Which was fine, I shouldn't have let go like that. Letting go was not safe. It exposed me in a way that I didn't like being exposed. It exposed that part of me where my feelings were too big, too uncontainable, too everything. I needed to reel it in before I let him see me like this.

'I . . . uh . . .' I raced into one of the toilet cubicles, pulled my clothes back on, peed and wiped myself clean.

'You okay in there?' he called from the stall next to me.

'Fine. Just . . . cleaning up.' We flushed at the same time, and then emerged from our respective toilets at the same time.

'You okay?' he asked again.

'Mmmm,' I mumbled, nodded and tried to arrange my features into a 'fine' look, whatever that was.

'You sure?' He looked worried now. Everything around us that had previously been out of focus and almost non-existent rushed back in. Cold, hard reality seemed to settle in around us, pushing away the magical moment that had existed seconds ago. And the reality was that I'd shown Andrew too much of myself. And that was terrifying. He was sure to disappear now. Like all the others had at that moment when I revealed a little more of myself. The part of myself that seemed so unpalatable to others.

'Should we *not* have done that?' he asked, trying to make eye contact with me. I dodged it.

We should not have done it like *that*, is what I wanted to say. But instead, my words came out coldly. 'We did do it, though.'

'This will complicate things between us,' he said softly. 'Unless . . . you want it to complicate things? Do you?'

I frowned at him. 'What do you mean?'

'You and I. Maybe you want to . . .' He looked at me as if hoping I would fill in the blanks.

'To become complicated?' I asked.

'Well?'

'Why would I want something to be complicated?' I said, and his face crumpled.

'I thought you said, the other day at the pool, that you knew why it had been awkward under the tree?'

I had said that, hadn't I? But I didn't answer that question. 'I don't want things to become complicated between us,' I said. 'Our arrangement is proving so successful, I would hate anything to come in the way of that.'

'Sex always complicates things.'

'Why?' I asked.

'Because it's sex.'

I was about to open my mouth and argue with him, but I think I knew what he meant. I didn't agree with him that sex in general complicated things. I'd had uncomplicated sex before, but with Andrew I wasn't sure that was possible. Something felt like it had fundamentally changed between us. I could feel it in the way that my body was now hyper-aware of him. As if I had tuned into his radio frequency and was receiving transmissions.

'So, let's decide not to complicate it,' I said. Synonyms for *complicate* included *impede*, *muddle*, *convolute* and *perplex*. I didn't much like this.

'You can do that?' he asked.

'Can't you?' I turned to face him now.

He nodded. 'Sure. Why not? Click my fingers and uncomplicate things.'

'Are you being sarcastic?' I asked.

He shrugged. 'I just thought that maybe this was starting to evolve beyond our "arrangement".' He did that thing with his fingers in the air. I never knew what that meant. It always implied that words had other meanings, hidden meanings that I was not privy to. But I had understood the part where he'd said 'beyond'. Synonyms included *above*, *apart from*, *beyond the bounds of*, *over and above*, *in addition to*. I inhaled sharply and then put my hands on my ribcage. Thinking about what our relationship could be outside of the confines of this arrangement was terrifying. It was the unknown. The drop off the cliff when you couldn't see the bottom. I had not prepared myself to think about that. Panic seized me.

'We'd better get back to the wedding,' I said, walking towards the door.

His face had a deadpan quality to it now. As if he hadn't bothered to arrange his features into any kind of expression, which seemed even more confusing to me than an actual expression. And then his face changed again; I think it was sadness, or anger. I often found those two emotions hard to tell apart. They seemed to do the same things to people's lips, pulled them tighter and then bent them down at the edges. He finally shrugged after looking around a little, as if trying to find an answer on the walls or the carpet.

'Okay!' he said. 'Let's get back to the wedding.'

Chapter 33

I found a quiet spot outside at the wedding and pulled my phone out. I hoped Jennifer was awake, because I really needed her advice.

Pippa: I had sex with Andrew.

I typed and waited for a response. Thankfully, it came.

Jennifer: You had sex with your fake boyfriend?
Pippa: Exactly.
Jennifer: That's going to complicate things.
Pippa: That's what he said.
Jennifer: Do you want things to get complicated?
Pippa: That's exactly what he asked me! What does that even mean? Who wants complicated?
Jennifer: I don't mean literally ☺, I mean, do you want this relationship *not* to be fake?
Pippa: So real? Real relationship?
Jennifer: Do you?

Do I? The big question. The question that didn't seem to have an easy answer.

Pippa: I don't know.

Jennifer: Well, how do you feel about him?

Pippa: I've been thinking about him a lot.

Pippa: And I get excited to hear his voice on the radio.

Pippa: But I also worry that he'll get to know me better and then leave.

Pippa: And I think I might have already shown him too much of myself.

Pippa: And I also don't think he's the kind of guy who would go out with me, in real life, anyway.

Jennifer: What does that even mean?

Pippa: He's too perfect. And normal. And nice.

I almost said 'for me', but didn't. *Maybe Delia and Tertia were right?*

Jennifer: That's a ridiculous reason.

Pippa: Okay, what about this reason? My relationships always go wrong.

Jennifer: Maybe they go wrong because you always choose the wrong guy?

Pippa: And Andrew is the right kind of guy?

Jennifer: When did you last look forward to speaking to someone? You barely speak to me or look forward to speaking to me.

Pippa: That's true!

Jennifer: I take no offence, obviously.

Pippa: I know. And that's what I love about you.

Jennifer: Did you just say you loved me?

Jennifer: Oh my God, you must like him. That, or the sex was so good you're high on endorphins and have no idea what you're saying.

Pippa: How's your sex life?

Jennifer: Dismal. I'm not sure if Colleen and I are going to make it.

I stared at the phone awkwardly.

Jennifer: Don't worry, no pressure to say something profound and perfectly consoling to me.

Pippa: God, I do love you!

Jennifer: I know.

Pippa: I'm sorry.

Jennifer: I'm okay, actually. She's great, I really like her, but I don't think we're compatible. You, on the other hand, seem very compatible.

Pippa: Well, I did have two orgasms.

Jennifer: Hahah! I wasn't meaning just sexually, but thanks for the visual.

Jennifer: Wait, aren't you at the wedding? Where on earth did you have sex?

Pippa: The bathroom.

Jennifer: Whoooaa!

Pippa: I know. It was very thrilling.

Jennifer: I bet.

I paused for a while and shuffled from side to side.

Pippa: Do you think I'll ever get this being in relationships thing right . . . you know. With my . . .

I stopped typing.

Jennifer: With being on the autism spectrum?

Pippa: Yes.

Jennifer: Look, relationships are hard for anyone. Take me, for example, I'm grumpy, an extremely negative person, I'm very blunt (and I don't have an excuse like you do), which means I'm probably just a rude bitch, and I'm very set in my ways. That makes dating hard for me. Dating is hard for you in other ways.

Pippa: I overheard Delia and Tertia talking about me. They said it would never last with Andrew. That I was too odd for him.

Jennifer: Delia and Tertia barely have two brain cells between them.

Pippa: Delia still thinks I'm an air stewardess.

Jennifer: My point exactly.

Jennifer: Right, listen to me, because I am wise and am a psychiatrist, even if my specialty is forensic psychiatry.

Pippa: Okay.

Jennifer: You're on the spectrum. It makes relationships harder; it does not make them impossible. It's only going to hold you back in relationships with someone that isn't right for you and doesn't appreciate *all* the parts of you. One day you'll find a person that loves all those quirky little things about you, that doesn't run from them, and even thinks they are the best things about you. You can never show a person like that too much of yourself. In fact, the more you show of yourself, the more I bet they'll fall in love with you.

Pippa: That is a terrifying prospect.

Jennifer: Life is terrifying.

Pippa: We agree on that!

Jennifer: That's why we're friends.

Jennifer: And on that note, I don't think you're as bad as you think you are with relationships. How long have we been friends?

Pippa: Fifteen years.

Jennifer: Exactly!

Pippa: My relationships usually fall apart around date five. And this was fake date four with Andrew.

Jennifer: So then don't let it fall apart. Go and talk to him.

I looked around, I actually hadn't seen where he'd gone.

Pippa: Okay. I will.

But when I got back to our table and found him talking animatedly with Delia and Tertia and the other men, as if nothing had even happened, I didn't say a word to him. I also didn't say a word to him when we bid each other a very awkward goodbye at the end of the evening, after having spent the rest of the wedding not talking and deliberately not looking at each other.

CHAPTER 34

'City Tower, this is Flightbird Six Zero Zero.'

His voice came through cold and unfeeling. It was the first time he hadn't said hello to me. In fact.

'Good morning, Flightbird Six Zero Zero. How's the view?'

I tried to insert our usual banter into the conversation, but it didn't work.

'Inbound to Johannesburg Airport, heading over the golf course. Request vectors for ILS. Flightbird Six Zero Zero.'

'Flightbird Six Zero Zero, turn left heading two niner zero.'

'Copy, City Tower, turn left heading two niner zero. Flightbird Six Zero Zero.' His tone was so different today, and I didn't like it. Everything felt different since the sex.

'City Tower, this is Flightbird Six Zero Zero, established ILS, runway zero seven left.' He didn't even comment about the runway.

'Flightbird Sex Zero Zero, you are cleared to land on runway zero seven left.'

'What did you just say, City Tower?'

'Flightbird Sex Zero Zero, you are cleared to land on runway zero seven left.'

Silence.

'Did you hear me?'

'Copy, City Tower. Cleared to land on runway zero seven left. Flightbird Six Zero Zero'

Barry, who was sitting next to me, shot me a peculiar look.

'What?' I asked.

'You just called him *Sex* Zero Zero.'

'I did not. Did I? Oh my God, I did.'

'Flightbird SIX Zero Zero, this is City Tower, apologies for using the wrong call sign there. I didn't mean to . . . it was . . . I . . . it's not like I was thinking about sex, or anything. It was just a mistake, a mispronunciation, sorry.'

'A mistake?' he asked after a pause.

'Definitely a mistake. One big mistake. Sex, it was a mistake.'

'Copy, City Tower. Loud and clear. *So loud and so very clear.* Flightbird SIX Zero Zero. Can I have a weather report?'

'Wind two fifty at ten knots.'

'Wind two fifty at ten knots, Flightbird SIX Zero Zero.'

I watched his plane land on my screen, not in real life this time. I couldn't look at his plane today, for some reason.

'Flightbird Six Zero Zero, this is City Tower, please vacate left onto Alpha taxiway and contact Ground Control on zero two zero point six.'

'Vacated left onto Alpha taxiway and contact Ground Control on zero two zero point six. Flightbird Six Zero Zero.'

No goodbyes, no banter. I had a deep feeling of regret in my stomach.

Christmas was coming. It was splattered across the entire world for all to see. Every shop, lamp post, billboard and poster in the parking lot told you Christmas was on its way. Snowflakes and Santa faces and lights that twinkled. There were more cars on the streets, more people in the malls and more planes in the sky.

Andrew and I hadn't been very chatty in the weeks following the wedding, and the tension on the radio between us continued. With Christmas just around the corner, we'd communicated once via WhatsApp to iron out our respective arrangements. But other than that, nothing. Despite adhering to my regular routine, which I liked,

I felt miserable. Lonely even. I never felt lonely. Even things like walking my dogs and Pokémon were no longer making me happy.

'You're off tonight,' Sheila said to me.

'You've never lost to Zane before,' Orion added.

The table was looking at me expectantly. I put my cards down and held my head in my hands.

'I had sex with my fake boyfriend,' I said. No one gasped in shock and horror. This is what I liked about being in a crowd of neurodivergent people: we said facts out loud as they were, as they came to us. And most of us here didn't filter them either.

'Mmmm.' Zane rubbed his hands together thoughtfully. 'Sex always complicates things.'

'That's exactly what he said!' I looked at him as he reached over for Sheila's hand and pulled it into his. The gesture was so odd, and not at all expected, that it took me a while to register.

'That's exactly what happened when Sheila and I had sex, anyway.' They smiled at each other and I saw it!

'Are you guys . . .'

'Yes! We're together.' Sheila put her arm around his shoulder. 'Turns out he was a better fake boyfriend than I ever anticipated.'

'I knew I would be a good fake boyfriend,' Zane said. 'Although, I actually don't think people can be fake, when it comes to dating. I don't think you can pretend to be fake with someone in those kinds of situations – romantic situations. Feelings inevitably come into play.'

'What do you mean?' I asked.

'It's like when your opponent plays bosses' orders and takes one of your Pokémon off the bench and slams it into the active spot.'

I paused to contemplate this.

'Clearly, you have feelings for him,' Orion chirped up. Everyone at the table nodded in unison, even silent Abe.

'How do you know?' I asked.

'You're distracted,' Anele said.

'You never lose games, and you're also no fun at the moment,' Orion jumped in. 'In fact, you've been no fun for the last few sessions.'

'You're not giving fun vibes,' Jono said, and they all nodded in agreement.

'You should talk to him,' Sheila said. 'He was really good-looking too.' Everyone nodded in agreement again. There was a lot of nodding going on tonight, and suddenly I found my head bobbing up and down too.

'Sooo good-looking,' Orion agreed. 'And I'm not even into men. But I think I might be persuaded to be into him, if push came to shove.'

'You'd better not be.' Anele smacked her on the arm playfully.

'He looks like Henry Cavill,' Sheila declared.

'No, he does not,' Orion spat, almost with disdain. 'He looks nothing like that. He looks more like Tom Cruise.'

'Tom Cruise! No! Stop!' Sheila burst in. 'He looks nothing like that. Tom Cruise is too short. And old. And weird.'

'Harry Styles,' Jono offered.

'He does not look like Harry Styles – you wish he looked like Harry Styles,' Anele said. 'You wish everyone looked like Harry Styles.'

'That is true,' Jono said wistfully.

'He looks more like Idris Elba.' Sheila clicked her fingers at us all.

'Idris . . . Ha!' Orion argued back. 'Idris Elba is black.'

'But he has the same teeth. So perfect. So white,' Sheila said, and everyone stopped. I imagine they were trying to picture it, like I was.

And then everyone nodded again. 'He does have his teeth,' Orion confirmed.

'But definitely Henry Cavill's hair,' Anele added.

They carried on like this, piecing Andrew's looks together one celebrity feature at a time. I zoned out as they continued to debate who Andrew looked liked. Honestly, that seemed to be the least important and interesting thing about him. His good looks seemed irrelevant when you weighed them against all his other qualities, of which there were many. I'd even made a list of his qualities, trying to figure out why I was thinking about him so often. Andrew had become something that preoccupied my mind. At work, I even found my thoughts drifting from the screen to him. I'd never had drifting thoughts at work before. He had many qualities that I admired: honesty, promptness, intelligence and excellent conversational skills. He was also kind, understanding and made me feel so much more at ease in the world when I was with him.

I thought about Andrew on the drive home. I thought about him in the shower, while brushing my teeth, while feeding the dogs and climbing into bed. I was thinking so much that while my brain was completely distracted by it, my fingers found their way to my phone and started sending messages.

Pippa: Hey.

I lay and waited for the response. I waited for over half an hour until the two blue ticks appeared. I then had to wait a further ten minutes before the typing dots appeared.

Andrew: Hey.

Pippa: I was just messaging you to tell you that you were right about Zane and Sheila.

This wasn't actually why I was messaging him; it was just an excuse. I waited another minute before the jumping dots started again.

Andrew: Are they together?

Pippa: Yes.

Andrew: Told you . . .

Pippa: You were right about that.

Pippa: You were also right about something else too.

Pippa: Sex does complicate things.

Andrew: I know it does.

I took a deep breath and held my fingers over the keys, trying to figure out whether it was appropriate to say it, or whether it was too much. *Fuck it.*

Pippa: I miss how things were between us.

Andrew: Me too.

Andrew: I miss you.

My heart practically soared.

Pippa: So how do we go back to the way things were?

Andrew: Do you want them to go back to the way they were?

Pippa: Of course I do.

There was a really, really long pause. He finally replied.

Andrew: I don't know then.

Pippa: We should probably not have sex again. No matter how good it was.

Andrew: Well, then how about *not* highlighting how good it was right off the bat.

Pippa: But it was. Perhaps the best sex I've ever had.

Andrew: Pippa! Stop!

Pippa: Wasn't it good for you?

Andrew: It was good. More than good.

The typing paused.

Andrew: Best sex I ever had.

Every single nerve, fiber and cell in my body flushed with heat.

Andrew: Seems like it might not be possible to go back to the way things were between us . . .

Pippa: Unless we both go out and have better sex with other people.

Andrew: Hahaha! I'm not sure that's the solution.

Pippa: Sure it is, you can't be the best sex I'll ever have for the rest of my life, can you? There've got to be hundreds, maybe even thousands of men on the planet that are better in bed than you.

Andrew: Wow! I'll try not to take offence at that.

Pippa: I'm sure there are many women who are better than me. Porn stars – they have sex for a living. They're probably far better than me.

There was a really long pause in the conversation again. The dots started bouncing, as if he was typing, and then they stopped abruptly and didn't start again. It was as if he'd just deleted what he wanted to say. *What had he wanted to say?*

Andrew: So you think I should go and have sex with a porn star?

Pippa: Exactly!

Andrew: Maybe I don't want to have sex with a porn star.

Pippa: Who doesn't want to have sex with a porn star?

Andrew: Me.

Andrew: I don't think having sex with other people is the solution.

Pippa: Then what is?

Andrew: Don't know. You're the one with all the unconventional yet strangely genius ideas.

I thought for a moment.

Pippa: We need to have sex again, and it needs to be bad. Thus, it will erase the memory of the good sex and we will never want to have sex with each other again.

Andrew: Um . . . can't tell whether you're joking or being serious? Besides, how on earth do you propose having bad sex?

Pippa: I hate it when men talk dirty. You could call me things like 'naughty girl' and 'dirty slut', and I hate the word 'pussy'. If you used that in bed with me, I would never sleep with you again!!! Ever. What about you?

Andrew: Oh my God, you are being serious?!!!

Pippa: And I also hate it when men call their penises cocks! It makes me think of a big, feathery rooster and then I get very put off. Who wants to think about poultry while having sex?

Pippa: And I'm not a fan of anything anal. A guy once tried to stick his finger up my bum and I had to use the Gedan Barai on him.

Andrew: The what?

Pippa: It's a downward block, very standard karate move.

Andrew: Oh my God! I actually don't know if I want to know all this.

Pippa: You're the one that wanted a solution.

Andrew: I didn't think the solution for NOT having sex would end up being us talking about sex. And certainly not you telling me about the sex you've had with other guys.

Andrew: I really, *really* don't want to hear about your previous sexual encounters.

Pippa: You had previous sexual encounters too though. What's the problem?

Andrew: The problem is you telling me the details about them. Strange as it may seem, I don't want to imagine you having sex with anyone else, if that's okay with you? It's not an image I want stuck in my head.

Pippa: He wasn't nearly as good as you, if that makes you feel better.

Andrew: NO! No that does not make me feel better. In fact, that somehow makes me feel worse.

Pippa: How?

Andrew: Because now I'm thinking about how good the sex was again.

Pippa: So we're back to square one again?

Andrew: I don't think we ever left square one.

Pippa: It would be great if someone had invented a time machine by now. Scientists have used a quantum computer to show that time travel is theoretically possible by changing a simulated particle back into an ordered state from its original entropic state.

Andrew: Would you want to go back in time and not have sex with me?

Pippa: Yes.

Andrew: Well, since that is impossible, I'm afraid it's not the solution.

Pippa: Then what is?

There was another long, long pause now. The pauses were so physically painful. I waited, desperate for him to come up with a solution to the issue. But he didn't, so I typed back.

Pippa: I don't think the problem was the sex per se, well, not from my side anyway. It was rather the type of sex we had.

Andrew: And what type was that?

Pippa: I'm not sure, because I've never had that type of sex before.

Andrew: Me neither.

The pause that stretched on after that was endless. Ten minutes passed, another ten, and then, before I knew it, an entire ninety minutes had passed and no one had said a word. But it became too much to take.

Pippa: You there?

Andrew: I am.

Pippa: So what do we do?

Andrew: Okay. No more sex. No more sex talk. No more referring to sex ever again. The word 'sex' shouldn't come out of our mouths when we are together! Definitely no calling me SEX Zero Zero at work.

Pippa: I can do that.

Andrew: Me too.

There was another pause and I wondered if he was thinking what I was: *how impossible that task was going to be.*

Pippa: So are we friends again then?

Andrew: I was never not your friend.

Pippa: Good, because I don't have many friends.

Andrew: Well, you have me as one.

Pippa: Thanks.

Andrew: Speaking of friends, remember that school reunion I mentioned?

Andrew: I was going to go alone, since we weren't really talking, but now that we are, not sure if you are still keen? Or is it too soon for something like that?

Pippa: Do you still need a fake girlfriend?

Andrew: I suppose I don't *have* to have one, but it would be nice to have one. I enjoy having one. It's this Friday night.

My cheeks felt a little hot and sticky. I reached up and touched them: my hands felt cool against my skin.

Pippa: I need to think about it, is that okay?

Andrew: Sure, take your time. But not too much time, since it is in seven days.

Pippa: Sorry, I'll try. It's just that sometimes, when things are sprung on me that I'm not expecting, I need to take some time to think about them.

Andrew: ☺ I know.

Pippa: You do?

Andrew: I probably know you better than you think I know you.

I only half believed that.

Chapter 35

The intense masculine energy that was oozing off this event was palpable. I could feel the thick, sticky masculinity in the air. From the moment I'd parked my car and begun the walk across the car park to the restaurant, I could feel it. I could hear it too, the big, loud 'Bro' talk, the backslaps, and what sounded like clapping high-fives, or something equally ridiculous. I could also hear women's voices, high-pitched laughter, and lots of 'Oh my God's rang out. This event was my worst nightmare. If I thought my reunion was going to be bad, this, I could tell, was going to be worse. At least I'd known the people at the reunion. I didn't know anyone here, apart from Andrew. Nerves made me physically itchy, and I tried not to scratch myself.

I walked up the stairs that led to the restaurant and stopped at the entrance. The noises were louder from here; not that they hadn't been loud before, but now they were obscenely loud. Testosterone-infused. That was the only way to describe the beefy, buff laughter and voices I was hearing. Guys like this made me nervous. The very sound of them collecting together in groups like this gave me horrendous high-school flashbacks to dances I'd been to where the popular guys had looked at me like I was a weirdo. One to avoid. Maybe I was making assumptions though. Andrew wasn't like that. And I'd judged him incorrectly at first, so perhaps – despite the hearty manly laughter coming from the restaurant – these guys were also like him. I took comfort in that thought.

I walked in tentatively and immediately scanned for Andrew. There were a lot of people. A lot of broad shoulders and muscular arms. Thick heads of hair, tight-fitting shirts, big belt buckles on equally fitted jeans. Lots of healthy, tanned skin. What the hell kind of school had Andrew been to? One where everyone worked out and had white teeth and clearly bench-pressed elephants. And then I finally saw him.

God, he was dazzling. Every time I saw him, a new synonym jumped to mind.

Striking.

Wondrous.

Splendid.

There didn't seem to be enough synonyms for this man. The thesaurus was too small a book, despite the fact that the latest *Oxford Thesaurus*, my thesaurus of choice, was over five hundred pages long. I began my walk towards him. He was surrounded by a group of these big-shouldered men, all clutching beers in one hand, the other hand in their jeans or stationed on their hips. They stood as if it was their objective to take up as much space as humanly possible. Man-spread legs. Elbows that jutted out, creating a kind of radius around their big bodies. I continued walking, and with each step I tried to muster courage for the inevitable introduction. But the other inevitable came too. *Shit!*

As I reached the group, as I reached out and tapped Andrew on the shoulder, as I stepped back to give him space to turn, I lost my footing. It wasn't an elegant slip this time, if you could ever call a slip elegant. My entire body was involved. As I fell back I flapped my arms in the air and they connected with a table of beers. The beers fell and I was sure I was about to fall on top of the now broken glass when an arm came around my waist and stopped me. I hung there in the air, suspended by Andrew's arm. And then slowly he pulled me back up.

'You okay?' he asked.

I nodded, but my face was burning with embarrassment as the entire group of men moved their eyes to me.

'You sure?' he asked.

I nodded, and then turned my attention to the beers on the floor. Well, they were no longer beers. They were shards of glass floating in a river of hops.

'Sorry about the beers. I'll pay for them, obviously,' I said quickly into the silence that had fallen around us. 'They broke. Well, I broke them. Not on purpose. I don't fall on purpose. But they are broken. I would be careful with all the glass on the floor, though. Glass is actually sharper than a razor blade. Most people don't know that, but it is. Injuries caused by glass can be much worse than injuries caused by a knife, and then of course you need to be careful of the infection – a floor is the most bacteria-ridden part of any building.' I tried to smile at them. They did not smile back. Instead, they were all looking at me with something that resembled confusion, and I wished I hadn't carried on, but I did. It was regrettable. 'Especially when most people don't clean the soles of their shoes often or well enough. The soles of your shoes can be filthy.' I looked down at everyone's feet. 'Yours are probably all filthy.' I stopped talking and flapped my fingers quickly by my sides. It felt like a physical energy was building up inside me, and that if I didn't let it out I was going to explode like the bottles of beer.

'Don't worry about the beers,' Andrew said, now rubbing small circles into my back.

'Yeah, don't worry about them,' one of the men said, but he was still looking at me in that odd way that I didn't like at all. In fact, I didn't like the way that any of them were looking at me. I shuffled from side to side and clenched my fists.

'Oh my God, what the hell happened here?' the pack of lionesses – because that's what they looked like, as they stalked across the floor towards us – said.

'Jesus,' another lioness said. 'Looks like the party really got started.'

'I broke their beers. Sorry. Not on purpose, obviously. I don't break things on purpose,' I said to the lionesses. 'Well, except for that one time I had to break my car window because I locked my keys in – that was obviously before car immobilizers.' *Stop talking, stop talking!* I internally begged myself. 'You can't lock your keys in your car any more, not with modern technology, unless you drive an older one like me, when you still can.' *Stop talking, stop talking.* Two of the lionesses shot each other sideways glances. I did not miss them. Then they smiled at each other in that conspiratorial manner that I'd seen many, many times before. *What is it about people like me and people like them?* They always seemed to sense that I was different, before even having a conversation with me. Granted, I had knocked over an entire table of beers, rambled about floor bacteria and the modern car immobilizer, flapped my fingers and accused everyone of not cleaning the soles of their shoes regularly, or well enough. But even so, I recognized that familiar look in their eyes. It was that knowing I'd seen so many times before. That knowing that I was different from them.

'Sorry, guys, I haven't introduced you. This is my girlfriend Pippa. Pippa, these are all my old schoolfriends.'

His hand left my back and I felt its absence acutely. I wanted it back there, because so far, in these disastrous few minutes, it had felt like the only good thing. I tried to do what Andrew did, when he casually put his hand in the air and gave people an effortless wave accompanied with a slight head tilt and an understated 'Hi'.

'HI!' My hand shot into the air. This was not a wave; this was the hand of an overly enthusiastic student who sat in the front of the class jumping in to answer all the questions first. This was not going well. No matter what I did, or said, I seemed to be stuck in a loop of disastrous happenings. It was probably best to take my hand out of the air – it was starting to feel like it had been there for too long – and keep my lips sealed.

CHAPTER 36

'That wasn't good,' I said to Andrew when I had him alone at the bar.

'It wasn't that bad,' he said, ordering us drinks.

'I knocked over a tray of beers and then spoke non-stop about stuff I don't even quite remember now.'

'You spoke about having to break into your car once,' he said with a smile.

'It's not funny.'

'I thought it was.'

'I think you were the only one who found humour in it,' I replied flatly.

'Maybe their sense of humour is not as sophisticated as mine then.'

'Or strange,' I added.

'You did accuse them all of having filthy shoes.'

I covered my face with my hands. 'I did.'

'You make loud and dramatic entrances,' he said. 'It's part of your charm.'

'Are you using the word "charm" as a euphemism,' I asked, taking my hands off my face and looking at him.

'Not at all,' Andrew said in a voice that was so serious I was taken aback. The seriousness of his voice seemed totally out of place in this establishment. It seemed like the kind of voice one might use in a court of law, or a politician might use when delivering a state of the nation address, not here slouched over a bar counter, and not a very clean one, if I do say so myself.

'Oh.' I straightened myself formally. The moment seemed to call for it.

'You seem surprised by that?' he said, looking at me. The light was rushing through the window in such a way that a golden sliver had fallen over his face, highlighting that perfectly imperfect eye of his.

'Your eye is the only non-symmetrical part of you,' I said.

He blinked it at me. 'Sorry. I know how you like your symmetry.'

'NO!' I gushed quickly, and stepped forward. 'I think your non-symmetrical eye is my favorite part of you.' I stepped closer to him, and something familiar happened. Our eyes locked, for the longest time they had ever locked before. But Andrew broke the moment and, when he looked away, I felt a rush of shame. This was exactly the thing we were *not* supposed to be doing. He reached into his pocket and pulled out his wallet, and his phone crashed to the floor.

'Crap,' he said as he bent to retrieve it. 'This pocket is way too small for my phone. This is the second time I've dropped it today.'

I held out my hand. 'I'll put it in my bag.'

Andrew handed me the phone, but as I closed my fingers around it he closed his too and locked my hand in place. I looked up at him, and his fingers uncurled.

'I'm going to go back out there and chat to the guys. You want to come with me?' he asked.

'No. I think I'll lurk at the bar, if you don't mind.'

'You okay? I know stuff like this is hard for you.'

'It's okay.' I tried to muster up a confident look but wasn't sure I'd nailed it. Andrew walked back to the group, and I sat nursing my drink for longer than it should have taken. I drew the sipping out to such an extent that I was sure I looked like I was moving in slow motion. When the drink was finished and I knew I couldn't sit there any longer I headed off to find Andrew. I walked outside, rounded a corner and saw him standing with the one they called Gee. I was about to walk up to them when a snippet of their conversation floated over to me. It made me stop.

'I'm just saying, she's hot, but she's a bit weird. I don't know why you didn't go on that blind date with Ashley, man. She's also hot, but she's also recently divorced, and you know what those recently divorced chicks are like.'

'I don't want to go out with Ashley, and Pippa's just shy. She's not good at meeting new people and—'

'That shit went beyond shy. Seriously.' He slammed his hand down on Andrew's shoulder and squeezed it. 'Or is she amazing in bed? Is that it?'

I slapped my hands over my mouth to stop the gasp from escaping. The gasp had started deep in my belly, where it had just felt like I'd been punched. Punched right in the gut, and the pain was almost too much to bear. I wanted to physically bend over and cradle my stomach as it throbbed and churned. I needed to get out of here and go to a place that was noisier than this place, so that it would drown out the noise in my head right now.

I sat in my car, the roof down, watching the runway in front of me. A small Piper Arrow lined up on the runway, its single propeller rotating as it waited for its turn to take off. The sound of the engine was already loud, but I knew that as soon as it reached the end of the runway and took off it would fly directly overhead and, for a few moments, I would not be able to hear anything else but the screaming of its engines as it tried to gain altitude. I watched and waited for it to start moving, but it didn't. The pilot was probably still running their checks, possibly waiting for airspace to clear. Maybe the ATC might be keeping them back because of congestion, or maybe they were waiting on a delayed landing. I understood this world right here in front of me and all its complexities and nuances, but the world that I'd just left behind at the bar I didn't understand at all. I heard a door slam and turned.

'What are you doing here?' I asked as Andrew climbed out of his car and began walking over to mine at speed.

'What are *you* doing here? You just vanished. I looked everywhere for you.' He was walking so fast he was almost running.

'How did you find me?' I asked.

'You have my phone in your bag, I checked its location on my friend's phone.'

'Oh,' I said flatly. I'd forgotten about that.

'Seriously, what are you doing here?' He stopped at the side of my car and put his hands on my door with a bang. His hair was messy; he looked flustered and sweaty. 'I tried to call you. About ten times!'

I reached into my bag and pulled out my phone. 'Silent mode.'

'Jesus,' he hissed, and ran a hand through his messy hair.

'You sound angry,' I noted.

'I'm not angry, I was worried. I looked everywhere for you, and when your car wasn't in the parking lot I panicked a bit. I didn't know if something had happened to you, or . . . You can't just leave without telling the person you're with.'

'Really? Is that so?' I swung around and glared at him.

His head jerked back. 'You look like you're angry with me.'

'I am.' I stared and folded my arms.

His face softened, his eyes met mine and he let out a long out-breath. 'Sorry, that was awful. That whole event. I shouldn't have made you come.'

'That's not what I'm angry about,' I said.

'What's wrong then?'

'I heard you and Gee-Man – or whatever gross name you call him – talking.'

'Heard what?' he asked, looking genuinely confused.

'But you're *not* one of those guys, right?' I was throwing out sarcasm now, and if I wasn't so upset, I would have been seriously impressed by my sudden sarcastic skills.

'What guys?'

'Maybe you *should* be dating Ashley.'

Andrew sighed and lowered his head. He stayed in that position for way too long, and the longer he did, the worse I felt. He finally looked up.

'Can I climb in?' He pointed at the passenger seat.

I shrugged my shoulders. I didn't want him so close to me, but this standing over me that he was doing was probably worse. I tapped my hands on the steering wheel as he climbed into my car, the car he'd helped me choose. There were signs of Andrew all over my life now. He'd infiltrated it and left his mark on so many parts of it, on so many parts of me.

'How much did you hear?' he asked.

'Apparently, I must be really good in bed for you to date me.'

'You didn't hear more?'

'Why, did it get worse? Did you tell him you fucked me in a bathroom at a wedding?'

'No, I actually told him he was an asshole.'

I stopped tapping my hands.

'I think my exact words were "You're a small-minded asshole." And then if you had stayed around, you would have heard me tell him that I never wanted him to say your name again, and then I left and went looking for you so we could get out of there.'

I looked at the plane. I wanted it to fly overhead so it would kill this conversation we were having.

'Maybe I used to be one of those guys,' Andrew said after a long pause. 'No, not maybe,' he went on, '*yes*, I was one of those guys for a while back in high school. But when my moms started fostering kids, I think that changed. You get exposed to types of people and situations that you would normally never be exposed to. Your worldview is opened up, you have to be less selfish, you have to learn to have empathy for others and not be so self-absorbed. Yeah, I probably was one of those dickheads that teased people like you at school.'

'That's a very dickhead thing to do,' I stated coldly.

'I know. But I'm not like that any more. I wasn't lying to you about that when we first met. That's not me any more.'

I kept quiet, but the silence was so awful. It was loud and thundered in my ears like an approaching storm. I turned the engine and radio on quickly just so there was some kind of noise to drown out the silence.

'How do I know you're telling the truth? It's pretty convenient that I didn't hear the things you supposedly said to him.'

A phone started beeping frantically from inside my bag. I stuck my hand in and pulled it out. It was Andrew's. I passed it over and watched as he read what was clearly a long string of messages. When he was done, he passed the phone over to me and gestured for me to look at it. I cast my eyes down.

Gee: Hey, where are you?

Gee: I've been looking for you.

Gee: You're right, I was a dickhead.

Gee: Fuck man, that was a seriously dickhead move.

Gee: Don't know what to say other than sorry.

Gee: Call me when you can so we can chat.

Gee: I'd really like to do that over again and not screw it up.

Gee: If you like her, which you clearly do, I'll like her too. We all will.

Gee: You've always been the good guy in the group. You probably have better taste in women than all of us put together anyway.

Gee: I'm a small-minded asshole. What can I say!

I put the phone down on my lap after I'd read the string of messages.

'Generally, they're good guys, they just haven't had those life experiences that change people for the better. Like I've had. That maybe you've had too?'

I handed him back his phone and as I did, his hand locked on to mine.

'I'm sorry about what happened,' he said, tightening his grip a little, but not too much.

'I've always been . . . different,' I heard myself say.

'I know,' he said.

'No, I don't think you do.' I pulled my hand away, even though it felt good to be touching him again.

'Tell me then.' He turned in his seat and faced me, but I couldn't face him, so I looked straight ahead, locking my eyes on something that felt familiar and comforting: the plane, the runway, the air traffic control tower.

'I've never fitted in. Even if I've tried to. And for the most part, that's okay. I've created this life around me that doesn't require me to fit in. I live away from people with my dogs, I do a job that doesn't require much friendly office banter, I don't really go out, except for Pokémon and the dog park and to swim alone in the pool. I have my parents, I have one friend, Jennifer, who I speak to intermittently but who doesn't care that we aren't in constant communication. And that's how I like it. I've created my own little bubble and I was pretty happy in it, and then you came along and ripped me out of it, and suddenly I'm going to family functions, and dinners with friends, and bars, and it's, it's . . .' I flapped my fingers together on the steering wheel and didn't care that I know he'd seen that. 'And then I hear your friends saying the kinds of things that I know people say about me, usually behind my back, though, like Tertia and Delia, and it was all just . . .' I lost the words. I think I had them in my head; all the synonyms were there lined up and ready to use: *crushing, paralyzing, agonizing, burning, gut-wrenching.* But even those didn't seem big enough. My breath caught in my throat. The feelings inside me were starting to become big, too big. Big and messy, and I didn't want him to see me like this. With my big, messy emotions oozing out of my eyes as my heart heated up.

He reached out and put his hands over mine on the steering wheel. 'You don't have to explain it to me.' His tone was sympathetic, and that only made me feel worse. I needed something right now that would obliterate this moment. Obliterate these feelings and the rampaging thoughts in my head. I needed something bigger than me to overpower and overwhelm all the awful feelings I was having right now. And that's when the plane started racing down the runway. The noise the engine made was so loud that it felt like it was shaking the ground. I stood up in my seat. I always did this when they flew straight above me. I liked to be as close to them as possible. I held my hands in the air, reaching up, and shouted for Andrew to do the same. He stood up and put his hands in the air too.

'OH MY GOD!' I screamed as loudly as I could as the plane flew directly over our heads. The noise was deafening and the wake turbulence from the small plane pulled at my loose strands of hair and blew them around. I closed my eyes and held my hands up until the noise of the plane, finally, finally, disappeared. When I opened my eyes, I found Andrew sitting back in his seat staring at me. I looked down at him and smiled. He smiled back.

'I'm sorry,' he said softly.

'Sorry for what?' I asked.

'I'm sorry for everything bad that ever happened to you.'

I sat back down in my seat next to him. 'You don't have to feel sorry for me.'

'I don't feel sorry for you,' Andrew said quickly. 'Not at all.'

'Good, because you don't need to. I can take care of myself.'

'Oh, I know you can,' he said, his smile growing.

CHAPTER 37

Christmas Eve at Andrew's house, with Andrew's family, was utter chaos. Maybe 'chaos' was the wrong word for it. It definitely needed a word bigger than 'chaos', and I searched my internal thesaurus.

Pandemonium! That was it. That was the correct word for the scene playing out in front of me. Christmas with my parents would mean fancy table settings, food under silver cloches and probably some instrumental music in the background that my mother was sure would aid in digestion. But Andrew's house was none of those things. If anything, it was the opposite.

His mom and sisters were packed into the small kitchen, shouting commands at each other about correct oven temperatures and how best to stuff the turkey and roast the potatoes. Children were chasing each other around the room while his other mom tried to set the table, the scattered remains of Christmas crackers that had already been pulled strewn across the carpet like bits of debris. It was bedlam. A madhouse.

'Hey, guys,' someone shouted from the kitchen. There were so many people in the kitchen I hardly knew who was doing the shouting.

'Pippa, do you know how to cook?' Grace shouted.

'Uh . . . no. I do not.'

'Pity, we could do with some extra hands in here.'

'Mom, seriously. No one else can fit in this kitchen,' Linda shouted over what sounded like a hot frying pan being placed into cold water.

'Mom, how long did you say the butternut needed to roast for?' Emma's head appeared over the counter she'd been crouching behind. 'Hi, guys! Mom, butternut?'

'I don't know, it's on the packaging,' Becca replied.

'I threw away the packaging.'

'What? You never throw away the packaging! Not until after you've cooked.' Becca threw her hands up in the air.

'Well, I'm not digging it out of the bin!' Emma said.

'Move over, everyone, I need to blend the Margaritas.' James pushed his way into the kitchen now too. 'Hi, Pippa. Hi, Andrew!'

'Make it a very strong Margarita,' Grace called from the living room, where the table was finally set.

The arguing over the packaging then continued, made a million times worse by the sound of the blender being turned on and Grace shouting at the twins for running inside.

'Is it always like this at Christmas?' I asked.

'Always. Come on, let's get you out of the noise,' Andrew said as he led me outside.

I was about to tell him that he'd read my mind, but . . . I stopped walking and looked at him curiously. 'How did you know that I needed to get out of the noise?' I asked. Only my parents and Jennifer knew when I needed to get out of the noise. In fact, now that I thought about it, whenever I told Andrew that I needed a moment, or a break, he seemed to understand.

'I told you, I know you better than you think I know you.' He walked outside and I followed behind him.

'What do you know about me?' I asked.

He turned around and looked at me, seriously. Synonyms include *earnestly*, *resolutely*, *purposefully*. I stood up straight. This moment had a gravitas to it, as if Andrew was about to deliver an important speech from an invisible podium. I waited for his mouth to open.

'I know everything I need to know about you, Pippa.'

'You . . . what?' He held my gaze with an intensity that threatened to knock me off my feet. 'What does that even mean?'

'It means exactly what I said.'

I shook my head, fast. 'Well, that's the thing, I don't know what you said.'

Andrew smiled. That gigantic, warm smile that always made me want to climb up onto his lips and hug them. His lips looked as soft as my favorite pillows. They smelled and tasted nice too. They would be the perfect place to lay your head after a long day. His lips vanished though, when he turned and walked into the garden.

The sounds outside were almost as bad as the sounds inside. There was a large bouncy castle on the grass, and it was perhaps the noisiest thing outside. The fan powering it, combined with the noise of the many, many children jumping on it, was a lot to take in. Jumping children, laughing children, children jumping into the pool – everywhere you looked, something was going on, something loud, and a hell of a lot of jumping.

'This is . . . it's so . . . um,' I stuttered, looking around me.

'I'm coming to get you!' Becca shouted from my left, and I swung around in fright. She raced out of the house, hands in the air, her fingers claw-like, and sprinted towards the bouncy castle. The kids screamed at the top of their lungs, as if they really were being chased by a claw-handed monster, when it was clearly not one. I had no idea kids had such high-pitched screams. I was sure, if they continued, they would shatter all the glass windows in the house.

'Loud?' Andrew offered.

'Understatement,' I replied, trying to think of the correct synonym. But as I ran over the words in my head – *thundering*, *rowdy*, *deafening* – they didn't seem quite right. Because although this was loud, overwhelming even, it wasn't unpleasant.

'Hi, Pippa!' Leroy screamed. He jumped off the castle, rushed towards me on tiptoes and then grabbed my hand. 'Come on.' He tugged at my arm and began pulling me towards the bouncy castle.

'I'm not sure I like bouncy castles,' I said.

'I used to hate them. I didn't like the noise and the bouncing made me feel sick. But you get used to it. And then it's fun. Take your shoes off.' He pointed at my feet.

'Okay,' I said tentatively. I hated being barefoot.

'You can leave your socks on if you don't like the way the ground feels,' he added.

'I don't like the way the ground feels.'

'Me neither. Especially grass.'

I smiled. 'I hate the way grass feels.'

'And cotton wool,' Leroy added.

'Me too!' We smiled at each other for a while and, when my shoes were off, Leroy pulled me onto the bouncy castle.

'Whoaa!' I almost fell. I hadn't imagined it feeling this soft and unstable.

'It takes some getting used to.' Leroy jumped up and down, causing me to lose my balance. Clumsy people and bouncy castles were probably not a good combination.

'Here. Take my hands.' Leroy reached out and took my hands. We jumped together like that, getting into a steady rhythm. At one point I almost fell, pulling Leroy with me.

'My OT says bouncing is good vestibular and proprioceptive input.'

'Wow, okay. Do you know what that means?' I asked. I knew what it meant, because my OT had said something similar to me. I'd also been in OT for years.

'No.' He shook his head. 'I just remember everything people say, even if I don't understand it all.'

'Your OT means that it's probably good for developing better balance and stability,' I said, continuing to jump.

He rolled his eyes at me. 'Why do people never say what they actually mean?'

I smiled back at him. 'Tell me about it. Bouncing is really good for people with dyspraxia, like us.'

'Do you also have it?' he asked.

I nodded. I held on to his hands as I jumped. When I was his age, I'd longed for someone to tell me it was okay to be different, or to tell me they understood. I squeezed his hands a little. 'Can I tell you something else?'

He nodded.

'I'm also on the autism spectrum, like you.'

He smiled at this but didn't say a word. We just continued to jump. My jumping got better as my confidence increased and I became more comfortable on the uneven surface.

'This is so fun,' I screamed across the garden at Andrew. 'You should join us!'

'Yes! Yes!' all the kids shouted together.

'If you say so,' Andrew called. He bent down, took his shoes off and then raced towards the castle. Everyone screamed, including me, as he launched himself onto it, sending small bodies flying off in different directions. The children collapsed in fits of laughter and happy squeals as Andrew grabbed them by the ankles and brought them back down once they'd gotten back up.

'Do it again! Do it again!' one of the kids shouted. More 'Do it again's rang out, and Andrew put up a big show of not being sure if he wanted to and having to be convinced.

'I'll stay on the ground,' I said. I folded my legs underneath me and braced myself by putting a hand on the wall, which really provided zero support, since it was about as wiggly and shaky as this entire contraption was. Andrew jumped off the castle, ran all the way to the other end of the garden, and then turned.

'Ready or not, here I come!' he shouted, and then started an exaggerated run towards the castle. He launched himself onto it and, once again, sent small bodies flying into the walls. But this time, something else happened. He landed on his stomach, bounced once, twice and then went flying towards me. I tried to stop his approaching body, but it was impossible. Seconds later, he was on top of me.

'You okay?' he asked, raising himself up onto his elbows and looking down at me.

I nodded, because I couldn't speak. My heart had decided to somehow start beating in my throat, thus allowing no words access to my mouth. He felt so good on top of me like this. As if he was meant to be here.

'Andrew and Pippa sitting in a tree, K. I. S. S. I. N. G.,' someone sang, and my face went red.

'We're not kissing,' Andrew shouted over his shoulder, sounding amused.

'First comes love, then comes marriage, then comes Pippa with a baby carriage,' the singing continued.

'That is highly unlikely,' I called out from under Andrew.

'But one can only hope,' Becca shouted from the lawn. 'Although, I do want more than one, please. Preferably.'

'Three, even,' Linda shouted.

'Guys,' Andrew chided them, and climbed off me. He pulled me up, which elicited another round of 'OOOOhh's from the kids.

'Oh, everyone just keep quiet,' Andrew playfully warned.

'K. I. S. S. I. N. G.,' the singing continued.

'Fine, have it your way then,' Andrew shouted, and then, with no warning, leaned in and planted a soft kiss on my lips. My entire body reacted. As if it had just been fired to life like a rocket engine.

'Happy now, everyone?' Andrew swung around and faced the kids. 'And if I hear that one more time, I'm going to start throwing people in the pool! Including you, Mom.' The kids jumped off the castle and raced around the garden as Andrew chased them. But I didn't move. I couldn't.

My legs were gelatinous lumps. My lips burned as if they were being incinerated. And my heart was beating inside my skull now. Such a short, small kiss and yet . . . It had the power to make me feel like this.

This. *What exactly was this?* I couldn't name it, but all I knew was that I really, really wanted Andrew to kiss me again.

But we weren't doing that any more. Kissing led to sex, and sex complicated things. I had to remind myself of that over and over in my head, especially when he whipped his shirt off and dived into the pool.

I walked around the side of the bouncy castle and pulled my phone out.

Pippa: I know we agreed to not have sex again, but he just kissed me, and now all I'm thinking about is sex again. Which seems highly inappropriate, because I am at a Christmas lunch and there are lots of kids here. But I also think I am thinking about more than sex with him . . . I think I like him. I do like him. I like him a lot. But last time we discussed things, we agreed that we weren't going to go there. This is all so confusing. Why does it have to be like this? Why can't it be simple. I know you're not awake now, but I just needed to say that.

'Hey, I was wondering where you went!'

'Aaah!' Andrew's voice frightened me, and I dropped my phone on the grass.

'Sorry, let me.' He bent down and started reaching for the phone. The message from Jennifer was still plastered across the screen. I lunged.

'No! No. That's fine, I'll get it.' I practically pushed him out of the way, and he smiled at me.

'Something you don't want me to see on that?' he asked, as if he already knew the answer.

'No, not at all . . .' I wiped the grass off my screen. 'Actually, yes.'

'What is it?' he asked.

'None of your business.' I straightened up and folded my arms, but this only caused his smile to grow.

He raised his brows up and down at me, so I raised mine back, because I wasn't totally sure what he meant. He chuckled softly.

'I'm going to get back to the party, but you can stay here and send more secret messages if you want.'

I looked down at my phone and then slipped it into my bag. 'No, it's okay. I think I've sent all the secret messages I need to for now.' I walked past him, but as I did, he moved left and my body brushed against his. I stopped moving. I let my arm dangle like that, touching his.

'Are the secret messages about me?' he whispered.

'You're very presumptuous.' I turned my neck and looked at him. His asymmetrical eyes seemed to be glinting now with his own secret.

Chapter 38

'OH MY GOD!' Grace screamed from inside the house, and we all ran. It was one of those screams that you couldn't ignore; it had an urgency to it that made your hairs stand on end. We all burst into the house.

'The turkey. It's burning!' She opened the oven and a massive plume of smoke billowed into the room. I coughed several times and then saw, to my horror, that the turkey was engulfed in flames. Hysteria broke out. Children were pulled back and people started screaming.

'Who the hell put it on three hundred degrees?' Grace shouted.

'You said three hundred degrees, Mom,' Shaleen barked.

'I said two hundred. Two!'

'No, you didn't. You said three hundred degrees for two hours.'

'I said three hours on two hundred degrees!'

'Can we stop arguing about who said what?' Linda shouted over everyone. 'The whole house is catching fire!'

'Crap!' Becca rushed forward, grabbed a dishcloth and started hitting the turkey. She beat the turkey over and over until Emma's ear-piercing scream brought her to a stop.

'Mom, the dishcloth is on fire!'

Becca looked at it. We all did. For a second, the entire audience, including her, went still. And then she snapped back to life and tossed it at the sink. It missed and hit the curtain, which also caught on fire.

Andrew pushed past me and ran out of the house. He returned seconds later, pulling the garden hose with him.

'Stand back, everyone,' he said, aiming the hose at the oven. 'Turn it on, Leroy,' he shouted into the garden. The sound of the water rushing up the hose made us all turn and look. The anticipation of the moment when the water would gush out made everyone hold their breath. The hose stiffened in Andrew's hands, it spluttered, a drop came out, and then it exploded. Water raced out of the hose, soaking everyone in the kitchen. Andrew moved the hose from left to right, soaking the curtains and then the dishcloth, and swinging it back to the oven. The whole kitchen made sizzling sounds, until, finally, it didn't.

'You can turn it off, Leroy!' Andrew shouted again, and then the hose went limp in his hands. We all stood there in shell-shocked silence, surveying the damage. Emma was soaked, Linda was soaked, Shaleen was hiding behind an open cupboard door and Grace and Becca were soaked. Water gushed out of the oven, and the burnt turkey lay on the floor, legs in the air, marinating in a blackened pool of water.

'Shit!' It slipped out of my mouth, and everyone looked at me, including the kids. I searched the children's faces. They were all trying to hold back smiles.

'Kids, don't swear.' I wagged a finger at them. 'Swearing is very bad. It's rude and crass and very offensive . . . well, unless you have Tourette's syndrome, in which case it can't be helped and no one would judge you if you swore. So, if you have Tourette's syndrome, please, go ahead and swear, but if you don't, then you shouldn't say things like "shit!"' I threw my hands over my mouth and shook my head. I looked at the adults in the room this time. 'Sorry, I didn't mean to say it again, and I don't have Tourette's.'

'Shit!' one of the kids whispered, which caused an almost fall-to-the-floor fit of giggles to erupt.

'No, no!' I moved towards them. 'There are plenty of other

synonyms one can use, like *damn*, *oh dear*, *dammit*, *poop*—' I stopped talking when I realized I was making the situation worse by saying the word 'poop' to a bunch of children. They giggled louder. I looked at the adults again, expecting displeased faces, but that's not what met me.

Becca smiled at me and then threw her hands in the air. 'Well, shit!' she exclaimed.

'I second that,' Grace said. 'Double shit.'

And then we were all laughing. Not just the kids.

We sat outside on a giant picnic blanket that we'd made by carting out at least six blankets from the house. There was silence. The sun was setting, and it was casting a warm glow over everyone and everything. I looked up at the sky, bright orange and red. The rest of the day had been spent inside the house, trying to rectify the mess in the kitchen. We'd all mopped and wiped until there was no trace of the disaster.

'I'm sorry that we're eating toasted cheese sandwiches for Christmas dinner,' Grace announced.

'Don't be!' I said quickly. 'This is the best Christmas Eve dinner I've ever had.' I felt Andrew's arm come up around me. He pulled me towards him and planted a soft kiss on the side of my forehead. I caught his eyes before he looked away. His eyes looked beautiful in this light. His face looked beautiful in this light. He was beautiful.

Chapter 39

We buckled ourselves in. The flight was fairly empty, so luckily we had two free seats next to us. I was exhausted and needed sleep in order to recuperate before tomorrow's festivities with my family, which I was sure would be just as chaotic, but in a totally different way. I had no idea what my mom had planned yet, but the day was sure to be filled with a lot of eating and more eating. I put my head back and closed my eyes. Andrew's shoulder pressed into mine and I was acutely aware of the warmth radiating off his body.

'Tired?' he asked.

'Exhausted.' I wiggled my head in an attempt to get comfortable.

'I'll move over to the end seat so you can stretch out,' he said, and immediately moved. I inspected the available space between us, measuring it in my mind.

'There's not enough space to spread out,' I said.

Andrew took a jersey out of his bag, rolled it into a ball and put it on his lap. 'You can put your feet up on my lap.'

'I've been wearing these sneakers all day. My feet will stink.'

'Your head won't smell,' he said, and a peculiar, impossible silence filled the plane, as if the pilot had turned the engines off and we were now gliding through the air.

'Put my head in your lap?'

'If you want,' he said casually, as if this was no big deal. *Was it a big deal?* Wasn't I just stretching out and grabbing a quick nap in my friend's lap? My fake boyfriend friend's lap. But it didn't feel like that at all. His lap felt like an entirely different kind of invitation. It wasn't his shoulder, it was his lap! There were things in laps, his thing. The last memory I had of the thing in his lap had been a very, very pleasant one, and I wasn't sure I would be able to relax, knowing that his penis was poking my ear. Literally.

He quickly pulled the jersey off his lap, as if he'd just thought the exact same thing.

'On second thoughts, maybe that's not the best idea.'

My heart dropped and, before I knew I was actually going to say it, it flew out of my mouth. 'It's a great idea!'

'It is?' He eyed me, his pupils bigger now, or maybe it was because they'd just turned down the overhead lights.

I loosened my seatbelt so I could stretch out but still have it on – in the unlikely event of an emergency – and then very slowly put my head down on the rolled-up jersey in his lap.

I closed my eyes. It felt good here. Safe. As if I was wrapped up in some kind of cocoon. Maybe I was, an Andrew cocoon, and in an hour I would emerge a beautiful, rested butterfly.

'This is comfortable,' I mumbled happily.

'I'm glad,' he said, and then I felt a sensation that almost catapulted me out of the emergency exit and into the sky. He pushed a strand of hair off my cheek and tucked it back into my ponytail. I let out the tiniest of moans, I hadn't intended to. Clearly spurred on by my moan, he did it again. This time, there was no hair on my face though; instead he brushed his fingertips across my cheek and ran them up to my ponytail. He started playing with it, running his hand down the length of my hair and then twisting it between his fingers when he reached the bottom. The gesture felt absent-minded, as if he wasn't even aware he was doing it. Or as if this was the most natural thing in the world to be doing.

'When I was young, my sisters taught me how to braid their hair. They said they needed a fourth so they could do it faster. So in the mornings before school, I used to help them. I can do a

French braid, a fishtail braid, a Dutch braid and a four-strand braid.'

'Would you braid my hair?' I asked, his fingers still trailing through my hair, making every nerve ending in my scalp tingle.

'What would you like?'

I rolled over and looked up at him from his lap. He looked down, our eyes met, and my insides constricted.

'Whatever you think will suit me.'

'They'll all suit you.' He smiled at me, and I turned to melted, rubbery mush.

'You choose then,' I said.

'Fine, but you'll have to sit up and turn around.'

Although I was reluctant to leave the warmth of his lap, I sat up in my seat. I loosened my seatbelt even more and turned my back to him. I felt him turn in his seat and, as he did, his leg came into contact with mine. I wondered if it was an accident. Wondered if he was going to move it when he adjusted himself, but he didn't. It stayed there, pressed into mine.

'Here.' I pulled a hairbrush from my handbag and passed it over. 'You might need it.'

He took it, gathered all my hair into his hand and then I felt the brush. *Did you know that the scalp has thousands of nerve points which connect to the amygdala, which is the pleasure centre of your brain?* 'Melted, rubbery mush', was no longer the right description. But what on earth was the description for this moment? It was all-consuming and intoxicating; it put me into some kind of altered state where the only things that existed were his hands, the brush and my scalp. I no longer felt my body, my extremities drifted away to another dimension and all that was left was the brain-smelting sensation on my scalp.

Intoxicating: synonyms included *rousing*, *heady* and *stirring*. And I was being stirred. And when the brushing was over, an even better sensation started. The pulling and twisting and threading.

I could sense his concentration, his focused precision. He took his time. Either that, or the plait was so complicated that it took an infinity to create. Or maybe he could read my mind, which never, ever wanted this feeling to end. Maybe that's why it felt like he would let strands of hair go from time to time, and then re-braid them all over again. I closed my eyes and pressed my leg into his. I shuffled back to be closer to him. I could hear his breathing and feel his breath on the back of my exposed neck. Without making a conscious decision, my breathing synced with his. I experienced a full bodily connection to him, even though we were barely touching. There was a magical intimacy to this moment that I hoped would never end. But all good things *do* eventually come to an end.

He finished the braid, but neither of us moved.

'How does it look?' I asked.

'Perfect.'

I touched the back of my head. My fingers landed on what felt like a perfect pattern. I ran them over the grooves of the plait, up and down the length of it, tracing all its intricacies. Andrew finally moved away, and I was instantly aware of a drop in temperature around me, especially on my leg. I peered over my shoulder. He'd sat down in his seat and pulled the jersey back onto his lap. I didn't need a verbal invite. I stretched out again and lowered my head onto his lap.

'I hope I don't mess up my hair,' I said.

'I do,' he replied.

'Why?'

'Because then I would have to do it again.'

I looked up at him again. His eyes probed mine ferociously. Was that the right word? Well, even if it wasn't, his probing look made me want to sit up, put my arms around his neck and kiss him. He smiled. Small. Only the left corner of his lip moved.

'I would like that,' I replied, and settled back into his lap. Moments later, his hand was on my head again. He dragged his fingers over the plait and twisted the end of it around his finger once more. I sighed, a long, loud contented one. I placed my hand on his knee, giving it a small and encouraging squeeze. One that said 'Please don't stop.' He didn't stop. He got into a slow rhythm of stroking my head in a way that reduced me to a puddle of pure relaxation. I started rubbing my thumb in small circles, tracing the curve of his kneecap. The circles were slow. But each time I reached his thigh I dared to rub it with my thumb just a little too long.

And that's how we stayed for the next forty minutes, not talking, running our hands over each other's bodies in a way that didn't feel sexual but also didn't feel friendly. This felt like the kind of thing two people in love might do. After making love, they curl up together to sleep, each touching the other in a nurturing way that showed just how much they cared. I could feel his care in every single touch, and I hoped that he could feel mine.

Chapter 40

We disembarked, and I walked past a pane of glass in the airport. I was finally able to see my hair.

'I love it.' I moved closer to the window. I'd never worn a braid in my hair before and I didn't know why, because I loved the precision of it. I loved the way it scooped all my hair back and pulled it away from my face. 'You'll have to teach me how to do it.'

'Or you could just keep me around to do it for you,' he said, and gave me that same strange smile he'd given me on the plane, where only the left-hand corner of his lips kicked up.

'But where would I keep you?'

'Don't know. Where would you like to keep me?'

'Where would I like to . . .' I mulled it over for a while. The concept of keeping him to do my hair seemed odd. 'Wait, that was a joke, right?'

He stood up a little taller. 'Not necessarily.'

I squinted my eyes. Maybe if I looked at him like this I would understand what he was trying to say.

'Sometimes you confuse me,' I finally said, relaxing my eyes.

He smiled, the right side of his lips kicking up too, so it was now a full, symmetrical smile. 'I know.'

Because it was relatively late, there were a lot of available taxis. We climbed into one and started the forty-minute drive that took us out of the city and towards the coast.

'So what's the house like? A beach mansion?' Andrew asked.

'What do you think?'

'A beach mansion.'

'Unlike the Italian vibe of our other home though, she went with a Greek feel.'

'Really?'

'It's so Greek you would think you were walking into Santorini. She's whitewashed everything and even had old tiles flown over from Greece to complete the look.'

'Of course she did. I wouldn't expect anything less from her.'

I gave Andrew a sideways glance. This was new. Talking to someone about my parents as if they knew them too. I imagined this was something a real couple might do, and I liked it. So I carried on.

'She had a statue of Poseidon made that stands at the front door.'

'She what?' He sounded amused.

'It's hideous,' I added. 'And very disproportionate. Remember what I was telling you about Greek and Roman sculpture? Well, this one is really a very good example of that. It has the tiniest penis!'

Andrew laughed, and the Uber driver craned his head and looked at me in shock.

'Not that there is anything wrong with a smaller penis,' I quickly added, in case I'd offended him and our Uber driver was indeed in possession of said smaller appendage. 'Unless of course it's a micro penis, which is an actual medical diagnosis. But that is very, very rare. Most men fall within the perfectly average five to six inches, but even if you're a little outside of that, it really doesn't—'

Andrew cleared his throat and placed a hand on my leg. 'It's okay. I'm sure he didn't take offence.'

'Should I stop talking?' I asked.

'I think you should,' he confirmed.

'Please, don't stop on my account.' The Uber driver smiled at me in the rear-view mirror. 'This is by far the most interesting conversation that anyone has ever had in my Uber before.'

Andrew squeezed my leg. 'When Pippa's around, you'll only ever have interesting conversations, trust me!'

'Really?' I turned to him, and he to me.

'My all-time favorite conversations have been with you,' he said in a hushed tone, too soft for the Uber driver to hear, but just loud enough for my ears. This was something that he wanted only me to hear.

His hand moved across my leg, and I gazed down at it. He'd turned it palm up, his fingers open and extended, almost as if he was expecting something to land in his hand. He wiggled his fingers at me, and that's when I knew. I took my hand off my bag and slowly brought my fingertips down to his. We stayed like that for a while, me running the sensitive tips of my fingers over his in small circles. But when the feeling became uncomfortably ticklish and unpleasant, I slid my fingers into his. Skin against skin. My warm hand in his. Andrew let out a loud breath and my ribcage constricted around my heart.

I wanted more than his hand. I wanted his arm too. Both arms. I wanted to press my face into his chest. I wanted him to lie me down, lie on top me, so I could feel the weight of his body on mine. *How heavy would he be?* Heavy enough to push all the air out of my lungs? Would I survive with him on top of me, physically and emotionally?

I held Andrew's hand for the entire drive. And didn't let go, even when the moisture gathered between our palms.

Andrew stared slack-jawed at the statue by the front door.

'Isn't he exquisite?' my mom gushed, gazing at her statue with such reverence you would have thought it was a religious icon.

I could see Andrew was holding back a smile. 'He's very . . . symmetrical and proportionate,' he said, and I stifled a laugh.

'Isn't he?' My mom beamed at Andrew. 'I'm so glad you like it.

Vern and Pippa absolutely hate him. But I think he really brings a special something to the entrance of the house, don't you?'

'Gives it a sense of grandeur,' Andrew agreed, and my mom gasped.

'It does!' She looped her arm through his. 'Since you're so interested in sculptures, and clearly have an eye for aesthetics, you must come and have a look at my patio. The pillars are identical replicas of the Parthenon, and then I must show you my collection of ancient Greek crockery.' And with that, my mother whisked Andrew away.

'Looks like your mother has found an ally,' my dad said, pulling me into a hug.

'Seems like it.'

'How was the flight? You very tired?' He pulled out of the hug; my dad knew exactly how long to hug me for.

'Exhausted. I was thinking of climbing straight into bed.' My dad picked my bag up off the floor and started walking it, and me, up the massive marble staircase that led to the bedrooms upstairs.

'Let's hope she doesn't bring out the Greek wine! Or you'll be sleeping all alone in that bed tonight.'

'Alone in the be—' I was about to ask why that would be the case, when it dawned on me. He thought that Andrew and I would be sharing a bed tonight! I hadn't expected this. I hadn't thought about it, planned for it; it hadn't even crossed my mind that we would actually be sharing the same bed. I tried not to let my dad see the strange mix of panic and excitement I was experiencing. My dad stopped outside my bedroom door.

'Well, goodnight, honey. So glad you're here. And I suggest getting an early night. Your mother has planned a full day for us.'

I walked into the familiar room, opened the windows that looked on to the patio outside and lay down on one of the loungers. The house was right on the beachfront. It had been my grandparents' house, and I'd come here for holidays as a child. I'd played on the beach for hours, hunted for shells in the rock pools for days on end and drawn patterns in the sand with a piece of driftwood. I loved it here. I loved the sound of the waves. Soft, and repetitive. I closed my eyes and settled into my new environment happily: the smell of cool, salty air, the sounds of the waves and a breeze rustling the giant palm leaves. I was so relaxed that I drifted off to sleep.

'Hey.' A soft caress on my cheek made me open my eyes. 'Wakey, wakey,' Andrew said. He was lying on the lounger next to me, propped up on an elbow.

'I thought that would never end,' he said, rolling onto his back. 'And by the way, that crockery is obscene! Your mother said it depicted images of the early Olympic games. Men's wrestling and athletics. That was *not* wrestling! And they were *not* holding javelins either.'

I chuckled and sat up. 'She brought it out at a family function once. My dad and I had to quickly whisk it away. She refuses to believe it depicts a giant orgy.'

'Well, what Poseidon at the entrance lacks, those wrestlers definitely make up for.'

I stretched my arms above my head. 'I'm exhausted.'

'It's very comfortable on this lounger. I could sleep outside.'

I pointed at the sky. 'You can't sleep outside. Wind at twenty-one knots with a forecast of rain on the way.'

'Then where should I sleep?' He looked into the room.

'I didn't know we would be sharing a room, by the way,' I said quickly.

'Well, we are boyfriend and girlfriend.'

'I know, but for some reason, bed sharing didn't even cross my mind.'

'That's usually what boyfriends and girlfriends do, or so I'm told,' he teased.

'I could pull those two wingback chairs together and sleep there. If I curled my legs up, I think I'll fit,' I offered.

'My mothers and sisters would kill me if they found out I'd made you sleep on some chairs while I slept in a big bed.'

'Your mothers and sisters would never find out unless you told them.'

'But *I* would know,' he said.

'So then it has nothing to do with your mothers and sisters, does it?'

'No. It's got nothing to do with what they would think, and everything to do with what I would think.'

'What would you think?'

'That I wasn't being very gentlemanly.'

'Mmm.' I considered this for a while. 'I guess you could sleep in another room.'

'And what would your parents think?'

'We could tell them you came down with a sudden case of snoring and I kicked you out in the middle of the night.'

'Or . . .' He paused. Raised his eyebrows and let the 'or' ruminate in the air around us.

'Or?' I asked, wanting the 'or' to stop ruminating.

'We could . . .' He paused again and then looked at the bed. This time it was the 'we could' that hung in the air.

'Okay, you're making no sense. We could what?'

'You know.'

'I know what?' I asked.

'Share the bed.' The words rushed out of his mouth.

'Well, why didn't you just say that?'

'I didn't want you to think that I was deliberately trying to get you into bed.'

'You are, though,' I pointed out.

'Well, not in *that* way.'

'What way?' I asked.

He laughed. 'God, you're really bad at getting hints.'

I rolled my eyes. 'Yes, I am! But I also don't see why I should have to always be trying to get hints. I don't understand why people can't just say what they mean. It would be so much easier and simpler, and certainly less time-consuming. Do you know how much time we've just wasted playing this unnecessary guessing game?'

'Okay, fine then.' He took a deep breath. 'I don't want you thinking that I'm suggesting we share a bed so we can have sex.'

'Obviously! We said we weren't going to be having sex again.' I paused briefly. 'Didn't we?'

'We did. Indeed, we did.'

We both paused, as if we were both waiting for each other to say something, only neither of us did.

I inspected the room. There really wasn't anywhere else for someone to sleep. And the separate room would raise too many questions, and I was terrible at lying.

'Sleeping in a bed together doesn't need to lead to sex,' I said.

'Um . . . but sometimes it kind of does,' Andrew replied.

'Why?'

He shrugged. 'The proximity, I guess. The connotation. I think it's harder not to have sex when you share a bed, don't you think?'

'I'm willing to take that chance.' I got up and headed for the bed. 'What's so special about a bed anyway? It's not like we're lying on top of each other. I don't see how it's any different to sitting next to each other on a plane, expect we're horizontal, not vertical.'

But it was different. The second he climbed into bed I knew *exactly* what he'd meant. We lay on opposite sides, as far away from each other as possible, but it felt like the mattress between us was indented. A huge valley ran the length of it, and the slope was pulling us towards each other. I clung on to my side of the bed with my hands, battling this strange gravitational force that was being exerted on me. Battling this building desire to roll towards him. The room was still and quiet, so incredibly still that I think the waves must have stopped. Every shuffle he made, every slight adjustment to his pillow, blanket, movement of his feet against the fitted sheet, I felt through every fiber of my body. Warmth radiated off him as if he was the bloody sun. The warmth found its way to me across the mattress valley, and at first it was pleasant, but soon it made me so hot I had to throw off the blanket.

'Fan!' I jumped out of bed and turned the ceiling fan on. I lay back down and stared up at the blades as they started to build up their circular rhythm. The wind from the fan rushed at me, but it didn't cool me down. Nor did it do anything to quell that idiosyncratic electric energy that was building in my fingertips. The energy made me want to reach out and touch him, even just let my fingertips graze his arm. His shin. His big toe. Anything. I would graze anything right now if I could.

Andrew also turned onto his back. The move brought his body closer to mine. I gazed to my right and calculated the distance between our hands: ten centimeters. Maybe a little more. But it wasn't so much that if I had to brush my hand against his he wouldn't think it wasn't an accident. But as I was weighing this 'accidental' brush up in my head, the sheets crinkled and I felt something touch my baby finger. Andrew had put his pinky finger over mine. Not an accident. That was intentional. Pinky fingers didn't get tangled up accidentally. Not that I knew of anyway.

I wrapped mine around his and squeezed, to let him know that I knew. Knew that his finger had made deliberate contact with mine and that I was okay with this. More than okay. We lay there, pinky fingers clutched together as if we were kids making a pinky promise about something important. The blades flew round in a blur and the wind on my body felt good now. Fresh. Then his pinky finger started moving. It rubbed itself up and down the side of my hand. I inhaled sharply; I had no idea I had so many nerve endings there! And I had no idea that those nerve endings seemed to be wired directly to a very specific place between my legs that was now throbbing.

He was right. Andrew was right. The chances of us having sex were greatly increased by the act of sharing a bed. The throb became uncomfortable, borderline painful, when he slipped his fingers through mine. I wanted to take his hand and put it on my body. Slip it over my breasts, put it between my legs and trap him there with my strong swimmer's thighs until I was thoroughly satisfied. Thoughts of him and me and our naked bodies and hands and tongues started to consume me. Started to sweep me away on a fantasy rollercoaster. The rollercoaster climbed and climbed to the highest point, before it dived down, then it twisted and turned and gained speed and momentum until it became almost too much to bear—

'What if we have sex?' I asked, breaking the silence. 'Why can't we be, what do they call it . . .'

'Friends with benefits?'

'Exactly.'

'But we're not friends. We're fake boyfriend and girlfriend. And remember what happened last time we had sex.'

'Complicated,' I sighed and pulled my hand away from his.

'Complicated,' he echoed on an equally long sigh.

We lay in silence again, looking up at that stupid fan together. I think my mind was whirling as much as the fan was. 'What about heavy petting?'

'WHAT!' Andrew burst out laughing, and then the whole bed moved as he got up on his elbows and looked down at me. 'Did you just say "heavy petting"?'

'What would you like me to call it?' I tilted my face towards his.

'Not "heavy petting".'

'Fondling?'

'That sounds even worse!'

'Stroking?'

'Oh my God, stop. Please. They get worse and worse each time you open your mouth,' he said on a chuckle.

'Sorry,' I whispered into the silence that had fallen over us when his laughter tapered off.

'So . . . um, hypothetically, of course.' Andrew's voice was low and sexy as hell. 'What would this proposed petting involve? Hypothetically, again. Not really.'

This time I sought his eyes out. And once I had them, I held on to them. 'I don't know, some touching.'

'Touching where?'

I brought my hand to my face and ran it over my cheek. 'Here.' I traced my hand down my neck and across my collar bones. 'Here.' I dragged my hand down my chest slowly. I hesitated for a moment, letting his eyes catch up to my hand before I ran my fingers over my breast. Slowly. My nipple hardened against my T-shirt and I traced its outline. 'Maybe here,' I whispered. I ran my hand down my stomach and paused when I reached my sleep shorts. I paused at the elastic and watched him. His jaw clenched. His eyes were fixated on the spot between my legs, so I parted them a little. His response was instant, a rapid inhalation of breath. Then I slipped my hand into my shorts. It felt good and I jerked at my own touch.

'Fuck, Pippa,' Andrew growled next to me. 'What are you doing to me?'

'I thought that would be obvious by now,' I said, sliding my fingers over myself. I gasped.

Andrew moved closer to me. 'Keep doing that,' he whispered, eyes still watching my hand as it moved under my shorts, my fingers finding all the places I liked to be touched.

'We don't even have to touch each other,' I said, and looked down at Andrew's hand, trying to convey my meaning. My eyes moved from his hand to his shorts. He was clearly hard. That much was *very* obvious. His eyes widened and, for a second there, I worried that my suggestion was too unconventional for him, but clearly not. He lowered his hand and slipped it into his shorts. I watched, fascinated, and more turned on than I'd ever been in my life before as he pumped his hand up and down under his shorts, his eyes still fully locked to my hand as I increased my own speed and pressure. This was the hottest thing I had ever done in my life! It was hotter than sex, so, so much hotter!

And then I think we lost ourselves. At least I know that I did. I didn't feel like I was a part of the bed any more, but floating above it, riding an invisible wave of pleasure, made even better by the fact that Andrew was moaning next to me. I matched mine with his, until we were perfectly in tune with each other. Like two instruments in an orchestra, playing the same melody in the same key and sounding like perfection. Not once did I stop to think about what we were actually doing. Instead I just went with what my body was telling me I *needed* to do. My moans turned to panting. The pants came out short, sharp and clipped.

'Jesus, that's so fucking sexy,' Andrew said, his words only spurring me on, and with one last move, I came. The intensity surprised me. I grabbed the bedsheet in an attempt to steady myself as my legs shook and my stomach contracted. Andrew's moans were getting louder now too. I watched him. His eyes were closed, but as if he'd sensed me, he opened them and looked straight at me while he came. It was the most intimate moment of my life.

Chapter 41

I sat on the toilet, cleaning myself up in shock. I couldn't believe we'd just done that. If sex made things awkward, then surely mutual masturbation made things just as awkward, if not more so. I washed my hands thoroughly and splashed water on my face. What had I been thinking? The answer to that very rhetorical question was of course that I had *not* been thinking. We'd just shared something with each other that was usually intensely private. We'd laid ourselves bare in the most vulnerable way possible. *How the hell was I going to look him in the eye again?*

I walked back into the bedroom, hoping he'd turned the lights off. He hadn't. He was sitting on the bed with his back against the headboard in what looked like a pose that signified he was waiting for me.

'You okay?' he asked.

'Mmmhmmm,' I mumbled. It did not sound convincing.

'What happened—' he started, but ended abruptly.

'Sorry, it was my suggestion, I was, I don't know, caught up in a moment, or whatever. Something.' *That was articulate!* I mentally chided myself for that lack of fluency.

'You might have suggested it, but I was a *very* willing participant.'

'I could see that!' I said, loosening up slightly when it was obvious that Andrew wasn't feeling as awkward as I was.

'I've never . . . with anyone. That was a first for me,' I said quietly.

'Me too.' His voice matched mine in tone and volume.

I walked over to the bed and sat down on it. 'Virgins,' I muttered.

'Not any more.'

I patted the bed with my hands. They felt like they needed to do something productive. Not that they hadn't been engaged in something very, *very* productive a while ago, but I was not looking for that kind of productivity right now. On the contrary.

'It's late,' I said randomly. Commenting on the time or the weather was one of those things you did when you had no idea what to say, when you needed to drop some kind of conversation into a very silent space, and the space between us had just become very, very silent.

'Are you tired?' Andrew asked.

'Are you?'

He cleared his throat. 'Well, usually after, *that*, I'm a little tired.'

'Tha—' I cut myself off mid-word when I registered what he meant. 'Yes. That.' I patted my hands on the bed again.

'Should I go and sleep in another bedroom?' he asked.

'No. Why?'

'It's clear you're feeling awkward,' he offered.

'No, it's okay. I'll stop feeling awkward. In fact, why am I even feeling awkward, now that I think about it?' I sighed and flopped down on the bed. 'Actually, we really shouldn't feel awkward about what just happened. Masturbation is a very normal and natural expression of sexuality. Many animals masturbate too: primates, walruses, even rodents and lizards.'

'Oh my God. I really don't want to imagine walruses masturbating right now, thanks. How does that even happen?'

'They have flippers.'

'Stop! Please. You're killing me!'

'I am?' I sat up and looked at him.

'Figure of speech. But if this conversation carries on down this particular path, I might die of embarrassment.'

'Okay, no more walruses then.' *Did they do it with their flippers, though?* I needed to google that. 'You know what, we are adults. Fully developed sexual beings. We should not be embarrassed to talk about masturbation!' I declared loudly. 'In fact, we should embrace it as part of who we are! We should even celebrate it! We don't celebrate masturbating enough, actually. No wonder there's so much shame and stigma attached to it. We should talk about it more openly.' I turned my head and looked at him. 'Like this! Don't you think?'

'Think that we should celebrate masturbating? What, with a National Masturbating Day?'

I thought about it for a second, but then cut my thoughts off. 'A joke. Sarcasm,' I said.

'Sarcasm,' he echoed. We seemed to have found ourselves right back where it had all begun. Lying next to each other, on our backs, looking up at the fan.

'I think I'm going to try and sleep now,' I said, rolling onto my side.

'That's a good idea,' Andrew replied, and did the same thing. 'Should I turn the light off, or do you like to sleep with it on?' he asked.

'Oh. I forgot about that. Off, please.'

I heard him get up, heard his footsteps on the floor as he walked over to the switch. The room was then plunged into total darkness, which I was happy about. The light was far too exposing. And then a loud bump, followed by a piercing scream.

'What! What!' I jumped out of bed at the sound of agonizing moans emanating from Andrew's mouth.

'I stubbed my toe,' he wailed.

'You sound like you amputated it,' I walked across the room, feeling my way towards the light switch.

'I think I did,' he moaned.

'I doubt that very much.' I flicked the lights on and glanced at the bed. Andrew was spread out across it, clutching his foot and rolling from side to side as if he'd been impaled.

'Let me see.' I sat next to him and held out my hand. Perhaps he'd done real damage to it. Judging by the way he was acting, I was sure his nail would be hanging off. He winced as he passed me his foot.

'Is that it?' I asked.

'What do you mean, is that it?'

'There's no blood, the toenails are intact, the tendons and ligaments aren't flapping around outside your body, there's barely a red mark.'

'There is!' He sat up and pointed to the red mark on his toe.

'It's pink. Flushed. It's hardly red.'

'Do you know how much this hurts? I bet I'll have a black bruise under my toenail tomorrow.'

I leaned in and looked closely. 'That's doubtful.'

'Do you know how painful stubbing your toe is?'

'Yes, I do, actually, or have you forgotten who you're talking to.'

'Oh, right,' he nodded.

'It's sore. But you're acting as if you snapped it in three places. No wonder men aren't the ones who give birth. Honestly, the population would have died out a long, long time ago if we'd left it up to males to have the babies.'

'Childbirth is *nothing* compared to this agony, I can tell you that.' He moaned again, this time with a small smile playing on his lips.

'Shall I wake my father up? Maybe you'll need emergency surgery. An amputation, crutches – hell, maybe you'll need the entire leg removed.'

He chuckled between his moans. 'You seriously have zero sympathy for the agony I'm in?'

I looked at his foot again. 'The most I'll do is get you some ice, but that's it!' I stood up and started walking towards the door.

'Hurry!' he said as I exited the room.

Moments later, I was back and found Andrew sitting on the bed with his leg propped up on a pillow.

'You're not being serious,' I eyed his foot.

'You're supposed to elevate it.'

'Yes, if you have a sprain or a pulled ligament. Not if your toe brushed against something.'

'Brushed? It smashed.'

'I would hardly call it a smash, but be that as it may, I shall ice it for you.'

I sat down on the bed by his elevated foot with a bag of frozen peas in my hand. My dad was a big believer in the power of frozen peas. And being an incredibly clumsy child, our freezer had always been stocked with them, even though they were never eaten. Mother insisted that they were inferior to fresh peas.

I lowered the bag, and he winced again. I rolled my eyes very deliberately at him. He smiled back, clearly unoffended by my eye-roll. The bag was getting too cold to hold, so I put a hand towel over it, which allowed me to keep it in place. We sat in silence as I watched the bag of peas become softer and softer. Droplets of water slid down his foot and fell onto the bed. I looked up from his foot, for the first time since I'd put the peas on it, and found Andrew staring at me.

'What?' I asked.

He shook his head and looked down.

'What?' I said, louder this time.

'It's just, this feels, you and me, you icing my injury, it feels . . . *real*.'

'Well, it is happening in real life, if that's what you mean.'

'No, I mean it feels like the kind of thing you would do if you were a real couple,' he said, and continued to look at me.

'I suppose it does,' I said softly.

And that's where we left it. The conversation did not continue, not out loud anyway. But it continued in my head, and I could tell it was happening in his head too. Synonyms for *real* include *authentic*, *true* and *undeniable*.

Was this authentic, true and undeniable?

'There,' I said, as the last of the ice melted off the peas and the bag turned to mush. 'I'll put this back in the freezer.' I stood up and walked to the door.

'Thanks,' he said, and I turned.

His 'thanks' sounded loaded with extra meaning. It was bigger than just a 'thanks'. I could tell.

'It's a pleasure,' I said, and my 'pleasure' was also loaded with meaning. It was bigger too.

Chapter 42

'Merry Christmas!' I flew out of bed at the loud knock on the door.

'Merry, merry,' my mom crooned again. She loved Christmas. She lived for occasions: Easter, holidays, Valentine's Day. My mother could make an occasion out of a total non-occasion; that was her gift. And I was sure there was a giant Christmas occasion downstairs waiting for us all.

'Presents and breakfast downstairs!' She walked away, humming a Christmas tune.

'Morning,' Andrew said, stretching his arms above his head.

'Morning. How's your toe? Is it still on?'

He pulled the bedsheets back and raised it in the air.

I scoffed. 'Not a single mark.'

'There.' He pointed to the corner of his toe. 'A bruise.'

'Tiny, barely a bruise.'

'Bruises are relative,' he said.

'No! No, they are absolutely not,' I chuckled. 'A bruise is a bruise, or else it is not a bruise.' My eyes drifted down his leg and then stopped.

'Um . . .' I pointed, and he shot up.

'That's just . . . it doesn't mean anything, it's just—'

'A morning erection!' I helped him along, since it was clear he was floundering.

He put both of his hands over his crotch, and I could see he was trying *not* to look at me.

'I've seen it before, you know. Twice. No need for this modesty. Even though, apparently, modesty is a virtue.'

'I think the saying is "chastity is a virtue", which really doesn't work at all under these circumstances either,' he said, still cupping himself.

'Because we haven't exactly been very chaste.'

'No, we have not.'

'In fact, we've been doing the opposite of chaste.'

'I thought you said you hated doing the opposite of anything?' He smiled at me, and I felt a warm rush up my neck.

'Seems that I was wrong about *certain* opposites,' I said, smiling at Andrew in a way that could not be misinterpreted.

'You're making this so much harder – UH, NO, *worse*, I mean so much *worse*!' he said, now crab-walking sideways along the bedroom wall. 'I'm going to stop talking and shower now,' Andrew said, disappearing into the bathroom. Moments later, the water turned on, and a few moments after that, all I could think about was his naked body standing under the water. And when he emerged ten minutes later with nothing but a towel around his waist I was nearly apoplectic. I shot up off the bed and dived into the bathroom myself. I peeled my own clothes off, only too aware that he'd probably dropped the towel and was also naked in the other room. The warm water rushed over me, and it felt amazing on my skin, as always. I loved the feel of water, but I think I would have loved the feel even more if Andrew had joined me. After the shower I got dressed, did my hair and we headed downstairs.

Cousins, aunts and uncles had all started arriving by the time I was there, and soon I was caught up in a Christmas cyclone. Greetings, presents and baked goods, lots of cinnamon-flavored things, and paper being ripped off presents. Ribbons littered the floor and bits of tape that had once held presents together stuck to the bottom of your foot wherever you walked. It was loud and busy, but not as unpleasant as I usually found it. And I think that had everything to do with the fact that Andrew sat next to me the entire time and, every now and then, as if he knew when I needed it, he made that slow, soft circle on my lower back.

'That was a lot,' I said, when it was finally all over.

'At least nothing caught fire,' Andrew replied.

I looked at the time on the wall. 'I need to get out of this house and go for a walk on the beach.'

'Alone?' he asked.

'No, you may come, if you want.'

'Why thank you,' he said in a formal tone. 'I feel honored.'

We walked onto the beach; it was late afternoon. The sun was lower and the weather was cooler. Nonetheless, I had saturated my porcelain skin with SPF100+ anyway, and was wearing the biggest beach hat known to mankind. We walked up the beach towards the rock pools in relative silence. Andrew commented on the flora and fauna a few times, and on the temperature of the water, and pointed out a crab. But other than that, we'd fallen into this glorious, comfortable silence. A silence that I didn't feel the need to fill with something completely unnecessary, and a silence that felt like the ultimate palate cleanser after a day that had been filled with so little silence.

We arrived at the rock pools, my favorite part of this beach. These pools were their own unique ecosystems and a treasure trove of shells and other interesting finds. I could spend hours exploring them, getting lost in pleasant thoughts and enjoying the wonderful sensations of cool water on my hands, or sea anemones tickling my fingertips.

'When I was a kid we didn't go on that many holidays, what with my moms' jobs and finances, but my favorite holiday was by the coast. My sisters and I spent all our days catching these little crabs in the rock pools.'

'What did you do with them after you caught them?'

'Put them back so we could come back and catch them again the next day.' He smiled at the memory.

'I like collecting shells,' I said. 'They wash up onto the rocks and collect in the pools and crevasses.'

'You like collecting things full stop,' he said, walking onto the rocks and looking around. 'Lots of pools to look for shells in.'

'Come on, I know the best one.'

I walked over the rocks; I knew them so well. I knew exactly where to put my feet and where not to. Where the barnacles congregated in clumps, ready to pierce your soft sole, and where it wasn't slippery. I made it to the large, shallow rock pool and, as always, the floor was covered with shells. I walked over to the edge, sat down and lowered my feet into the cool water. I ran my toes through the sand and shells, a feeling that I loved. I didn't like the feeling of grass prickling my feet, or soil, or a sticky floor, but I loved this feeling. Cool and comforting and reminiscent of so many holidays well spent. Andrew lowered himself onto the rock next to me and also dangled his feet into the water.

'And now what?' he asked.

'And now dig.' I stuck my hands into the shallow water, ran them through the shells, taking in all the textures. Most of the shells were broken, so you needed to be patient and thorough when looking. Andrew's hands also moved through the shells on the floor. He methodically searched a grid, like a crime scene, pushing broken shells off to the sides once he'd inspected them. Our hands worked close to each other and, every so often, they would brush together as they went. But soon shells were forgotten and our hands simply tangled together. He pushed my palm into the shells and ran his hand over the back of mine. I spread my fingers, letting his slide between mine. He closed his fingers around my hand tightly and squeezed until it was almost sore. And then he was gentle again, picking up a pointed cone shell and tracing the palm of my hand with it.

We became transfixed by this little game of ours, hardly noticing that the tide was creeping in. Not noticing that the water lapped higher and higher up our legs, climbing our calves and reaching for our knees. The spray from the waves wet our hair and faces, but still, our fingers tangled together in a dance that was slow and soft and so, so intimate.

Chapter 43

I woke up in the middle of the night and the bed was empty. I turned the bedside light on and noticed that the curtain to the outside patio was open. But the patio was empty.

I walked downstairs, looking for Andrew, and when I got to the lounge I noticed that the patio door had been slid open wide enough for a person to exit through it. I walked out of the door, across the lawn towards the beach. The gate at the bottom of the garden, the one that led onto the beach, was open. I walked through it, walked up and over the sand dune until I reached the beach. And there he was. Sitting alone on the sand, lit only by the light of the moon that was wrestling the clouds for space in the night sky. I sat down next to him in the sand.

'It's really beautiful here,' he said, not looking at me.

'It is.' I pushed my hair behind my ears. The cool breeze coming off the waves was pulling at the strands.

'I always think a beach looks better at night, don't you?' He looked at me. His hair was ruffled, his eyes were lazy and hooded from sleep. God, he looked so sexy right now with that sliver of silver moonlight cutting his face in half. I leaned towards him.

'Most things look better at night,' I said. 'It's the play of light and dark, shadows.'

'Like what?'

'Like you,' I said, running my eyes over his features.

'You too,' he said, almost a whisper.

We gazed at each other for an infinity. As the clouds moved over the moon, so did the silver light flicker across his face.

'I'd really like to kiss you,' I said, looking at his lips.

'I thought we weren't supposed to be doing that?' he asked, but also leaned in.

'I think, perhaps, it's too late for that.'

'Especially after last night,' he replied, still leaning in.

'Definitely after last night.'

He closed the gap between us and brought his lips to mine. The kiss was quick, short and soft. We pulled away and looked at each other.

'That wasn't really a kiss,' I said with a smile.

'You didn't specify what kind of a kiss you wanted.'

'I want the big kind of kiss.'

His smile faded. He shuffled closer to me, took my face in his hands and brought his mouth down onto mine.

His lips tasted salty from the sea, and my lips felt like they were dissolving into his. He pushed my mouth open with his and his tongue found mine. They pressed together like long-lost friends embracing, they danced with each other, twirled around the dance floor and then came together for a slow dance. The slow dance was so, so slow. Deep and soft and slow. Until it wasn't any more. Until it was a raging storm. The kiss became lip-biting, hair-pulling and fingernail-digging-into-shoulder. It became so hungry and ravenous that I didn't think I would ever get enough of it, or him. I never wanted it to stop.

'Th—that was big,' I muttered when the kiss finally ended.

'But was it big enough?' he asked, that kicked-up-corner-lip grin on his face.

'I don't see how it could get any bigger if we tried.'

Andrew pushed me back. I landed in the sand. He brought his body down onto mine, pressing me into the cool beach.

'I think we can.' He brought his lips to mine again, and this time, he took his time. His lips and tongue explored every inch of my mouth, and then my neck, my earlobes, and then my hands and fingers. The sensations were different in each place but no less erotic. I was traveling from one sensation to another; they built on each other until my entire body was screaming out for him, screaming out for new sensations. I reached for his pants, simple pajama pants; all that was holding them up was an elastic band. I slipped his pants down, his erection sprung out and I wrapped my hand around it.

I watched his face in a mixture of awe and fascination. His eyes closed, his lips parted and he winced every time I completed a full up and down stroke. I did it slowly; I wanted to watch him as I took him on this journey. As I moved faster, his lips opened wider; when I moved slower – so slowly that I was almost not moving my hand at all – he bit his bottom lip so hard that I thought he might puncture it with his teeth.

'Wait, wait!' he said, clamping his hand over mine so it was impossible to move it. 'You're going to have to slow down there.' He scrambled to his knees and pulled away from me.

I sat up and faced him. 'What happens if I don't want to slow down?' I asked, pushing the straps of my nightie down. My breasts reacted instantly to the coolness of the air as the thin nightie pooled in my lap. His eyes travelled down there, but only for a second, because it wasn't long before he covered them with his big, warm hands, then his warm tongue, mouth and lips. He cupped them in his hands, pushed them together and tried to take both nipples into his mouth at once as if he couldn't get enough of them, as if he wanted to devour them both at the same time. I cried out as he pulled at them with his teeth, put a hand up my nightie and cupped me between my legs. He squeezed me there and my legs shuddered and twitched.

'Don't stop,' I said, lust and need dripping from my lips.

'I don't have condoms.'

'I'm on birth control.'

'Aren't you worried about anything else?' he asked.

'That would have shown up in our annual medical exams,' I said, sucking on his earlobe now as if it was the best lolly I'd ever tasted.

'We're in the sand,' he said. 'Not to mention on a public beach.'

I opened my eyes and looked around. I'd totally forgotten where we were. I'd been so caught up in the moment that it hadn't even crossed my mind.

'Come on,' I got up, holding my nightie over my breasts, and started running for the house. As I ran, Andrew reached out and grabbed my ass and squeezed. I was forced to stop running as he did that. Forced to stand still, rest my back against his chest as he palmed my ass and squeezed it in a way that was not conducive to walking. I pulled his hand away, shoved it between my legs and dragged myself across it. I held his hand there tightly, ground down into it, moaning as he reached around and squeezed my nipples.

'At this rate, we're never going to make it,' he said, and then gave me a small smack, like someone smacking a horse to make it go faster. I got the message, and started running again. But when I stopped to unlatch the gate, Andrew pushed me into the fence and slipped his fingers under my panties and dragged them over me. I stopped fiddling with the gate, I grabbed on to the fence and pushed myself backwards, giving him better access to me. But when he slipped a finger into me, I knew we needed to get back to the house. We fumbled with the gate some more and then ran across the lawn. We reached the patio outside, and as soon as I saw it I threw myself down onto the massive day bed and held my arms out for him. He flopped down on top of me, crushing me with his weight.

'You sure your parents are asleep?' He rose onto his elbows and looked down at me.

'They are. Besides, they're literally on the other side of the house.'

He looked around. 'You're very loud though.'

'I'll try and be quiet.'

'And just how are you going to do that?' He slipped a finger into me again and I gasped loudly. 'See, you're very loud.'

I slapped my hand over my mouth again as he moved his finger in and out. I shook my head at him desperately as he went a little faster and harder. I was struggling to hold back the noises that were building inside me.

'Ssshhhh!' he hissed, looking amused.

I shook my head again and he grabbed a pillow and pushed it over my hand and mouth. I wrapped my arms around the pillow and then bit on it as he moved faster and faster. I raised and dropped my hips, matching his rhythm, but I needed to make noises; my body told me to.

'Fuck the pillow.' I tossed it on the ground and let out a loud moan as Andrew laughed and brought his mouth down to me.

'You're going to make me scream,' I panted, getting closer and closer, his tongue and fingers working some kind of magic on me that made me feel like a wild animal that could not be contained.

'Time it with a very loud wave,' he said, and then laughed against me. The words falling from his lips, his breath rushing over me, the steady rhythm that was so perfectly timed, almost like a ticking metronome, all helped me come faster. Soon, I could no longer contain the noises falling from my lips, no matter how I flattened my hands over them. Finally, I let out that shout that I knew would inevitably come. My body shuddered for a few moments, and then stopped.

'That was very loud.' Andrew smiled at me.

'Was it?' I sat up and looked around. 'Do you think my parents heard?'

'I think the neighbors might have heard.'

'No! Are you being serious?' I looked towards their house to see if any lights had come on, but it was still dark.

'It's possible that the people of Australia heard too.'

And now I recognized he was teasing me so I slapped him on the arm. He grabbed my hand, raised it to his lips and kissed my fingers one by one, and then he kissed the soft, sensitive skin on my wrist.

'You know I've fallen in love with you, right?'

'What?' I pulled my hand away in shock.

'I've fallen in love with you, Pippa.'

I crossed my legs and shuffled away from him. I had not been expecting to hear this declaration right now, and it shook me.

'Um . . .' I mumbled. I hated it when conversations took a surprise turn, and this was definitely a surprise turn.

'You okay?' he asked.

'Okay? I don't know, I mean . . . You just blurted out that you've fallen in love with me, so I'm a little . . .' I fanned my face with my hand frantically as my cheeks warmed up.

'You need a moment, I get it.' He stood up and walked over to the chair opposite the daybed.

'Needed a moment' was an understatement. I needed ten moments. I needed . . .

'Fallen? Not falling?' I asked. 'Past tense. As if it has already happened, and not currently happening?'

He nodded.

'So already in love with me, not going to be in love with me.'

'Already.' He smiled and crossed his legs casually.

'Wow, okay.' I continued to fan my face. Even though there was a breeze this evening, I was still hot, and now it felt like sweat might be forming in my hairline. 'And when exactly did you fall in love with me?' I asked.

He shrugged casually. 'I think there were a few times that I fell in love with you. Like when we were looking at the Vampire together, or when I saw you with your dogs, when I saw you winning your card game, when I saw how scared you were of cats, when I first heard your little snoring noises, when I saw you with your family, saw you with my family, when we danced at the wedding, when I unzipped your dress, saw how good you were at swimming, how good you look naked, when you told me about ancient Greek penile sizes and wondered where merpeople's sex organs were, and when you call me Flightbird Six Zero Zero.'

'I call you that all the time. I've called you that for months.'

'I know.'

I closed my eyes. I fluttered my fingers together a few times, trying to take this information in. Trying to readjust the picture I had of Andrew in my head. Because fake boyfriend Andrew, the picture I had in my head, was no longer the same as the Andrew sitting in front of me telling me he was in love with me. Mind you, if I really considered it, I don't think he'd been *fake* boyfriend Andrew for a while now. Maybe even from that very first weekend together. I sat in silence and bit my lips, chewing on them while I mulled on his words.

'I want the frozen peas with you, Pippa,' Andrew said softly, leaning forward in his seat. 'I want it to be real with you. No more faking it.'

'The frozen peas,' I echoed softly, knowing exactly what he meant.

'Or the frozen sweetcorn, if you prefer.'

'I hate sweetcorn. It always gets stuck in the back of my throat.'

'Peas it is then.' We both went silent. I didn't know what he was thinking, but I knew what I was thinking. I had not prepared for this kind of a conversation. I had not practiced it in my mind, so I didn't know what to say.

'You don't have to say anything back to me. And certainly not now. I know you need time when it comes to things like this.'

'So then why tell me now?'

'Because I couldn't *not* tell you any more. It's been on the tip of my tongue for months now. Every time I see you I have to force myself to hold it back. When we talk on the radio, I have to pinch my leg to stop myself from blurting it out while I ask you for the vectors for the ILS. I had to say it.'

'That would be inappropriate,' I said.

'It would be.'

'And I would also hate that,' I said. 'I don't do public displays of emotion. I could think of nothing worse than laying all my private feelings and emotions out there for everyone to see and hear.'

'I know that about you too.' He chuckled quietly.

'You keep saying that you know me, but you don't know everything about me.' I picked at my cuticle nervously.

'So tell me then.'

I scratched at my cuticle more. 'I'm not good in relationships. I've never been good in them. I don't think I know how to do them properly.'

'You've been doing this one properly,' he said.

'But this one is fake.'

Andrew let out a half-scoff, half-laugh sound. 'This relationship hasn't been fake for a very long time, possibly even from the very beginning,' he replied.

'When people get to know me well, they usually don't like me,' I added quickly.

'That's just not true. The more I've gotten to know you, the more I've liked you, *no* . . .' he paused and looked straight at me. 'No, *loved* you.'

'I'm on the autism spectrum.' The words rushed out of my mouth, and for some reason Andrew burst out laughing.

'I'm not trying to make a joke,' I said. 'I'm being serious.'

'I know you are.' He stood up and walked towards me.

'Then why are you laughing?' I asked as he sat down next to me.

'I'm laughing because I can't believe you thought you needed to tell me that.'

'You knew?'

He put his hands on the sides of my face and pulled me into a soft kiss. 'Probably from the first time I met you.'

'You knew?'

He looked at me incredulously. 'You can't handle the feel of sweaty palms, you're a walking thesaurus, you flap your fingers when you're nervous, or happy for that matter, jokes go over your head, you mix up your idioms, you can't take a hint, you sometimes say the most inappropriate things in public at the top of your voice, like talking about mermaids' genitals in a room full of schoolchildren, you get overwhelmed with noise and crowds easily, you're hysterically funny without knowing that what you said was funny. I've never met anyone that collects as much stuff as you do, you play Pokémon with a group of some of the most neurodiverse people I have ever met, you say exactly what you mean all of the time, you need time to think about things and process them, don't like spur-of-the-moment arrangements, or changes in plans, and you're the only person that Leroy lets hold his hand . . .'

'Oh.' I was flabbergasted. 'And, you're . . . It's . . .'

He kissed me again. 'And those are literally all the things I love most about you.'

It felt like a bomb had dropped. There was an imaginary explosion in the air around us as he said those words, but when the exothermic reaction stopped and the mushroom cloud dissipated, *silence.* Horrid, vacuous silence. My brain continued to race, and the silence continued to drag. It started feeling like one of those moments where I needed to just say something, anything. Drop any word vomit into this silent space between us, or the silence was going to overwhelm me.

'Did you know that an octopus can lay up to eighty thousand eggs at one time?' It flew out of my mouth.

'And you're also a treasure trove of the strangest yet informative facts.'

'Octopuses often eat themselves after mating.' That also flew out of my mouth like an unstoppable word bullet.

'That's awful,' he said, pulling my hand up to his mouth and kissing the back of it.

'Basically, they self-destruct after sex.' His kisses were slow and soft. They moved down to the crook of my elbow. The feeling was so torturously ticklish yet erotic all at once that a shiver ran the length of my body. And when he was back at my hands, drawing each finger into his mouth, I let out a breathy whimper and shuffled closer to him.

'So, you know I need time to process all this information, right? It's taken me by surprise!' I whimpered as he started kissing my neck.

'I know.'

'I might need a few days for this one, it's very . . .' I moaned as he kissed my jawline, working his way to my chin. 'Very big,' I murmured.

'It is,' he said, running his lips over mine.

'Fuck. I think I'm going to self-destruct if we don't have sex,' I said, climbing onto his lap and wrapping my arms around him.

'You read my mind.' He drew me into another kiss. A kiss that didn't stop until we were covered in sweat and gasping into each other's mouth as we rode our orgasms together there on the patio furniture.

Chapter 44

In the blink of an eye, the holiday was over and Andrew had to fly to Cape Town for work. I would stay on at my parents' house for a few more days, while he would be up there in the skies above my head. I stood at the front door looking at him, my parents behind me, the Uber behind him. I didn't want him to go. And neither did my parents. In fact, during the holiday, they'd already organized that his family would come over to our place on New Year's Day. When Andrew had warned them just how big his family was, my mom had said that she would hire caterers and butlers. My dad had pointed out that perhaps butlers was taking it a little too far, and after a playful argument she agreed to only hire one. We all said our goodbyes at the door, but as Andrew walked up to his Uber, as he was about to climb in, I pulled him back and threw my arms around him. I didn't let go straight away like I normally did, instead I allowed my body to fold into his.

'I see we've moved on from pugging,' he whispered against my ear.

'I think we have,' I whispered back. 'Just give me a little more time to think about what you said, okay?' Andrew hadn't said he loved me again after we'd made love last night, or when we'd fallen asleep holding each other. Or in the morning, when I'd opened my eyes to find him watching me. Not during breakfast either, when we'd held hands so much that it had become difficult to eat our pancakes. Not when I'd openly kissed him in front of my parents, something I don't think they'd ever seen me do. And not after lunch, when I was feeling so full that I had to lie down and he'd come up behind me and stroked my head while I closed my eyes.

He nodded against my face. 'I know you, Pippa. I really, really do.'

I was back at work a few days later, and I'd run Andrew's declaration over in my head so many times. I had concluded that there was a ninety per cent chance that I loved him back, but I wasn't entirely sure, since I'd never been in love before. I needed someone to talk to, and Jennifer had taken Colleen away on a romantic trip as a way of trying to salvage the relationship. I was not going to disturb her. But I needed to talk to someone else.

'Blessing, are we friends?' I asked, walking straight into the business class lounge. Blessing leaned across his reception desk and looked thoughtful for a moment.

'I would like to be friends with you, and I've tried to be friends with you, but I've noticed that there's a certain line with you that you don't really let people cross. But I enjoy the friendship that you've allowed me to have.'

'You once said you were good at understanding people, right?'

'That's true,' he said.

'Can you give me some personal advice then?'

'I can try.'

'It's about Andrew.'

'Aaaah,' he nodded. 'And your budding relationship.'

'How do you know about that?'

'You make social plans with him over the radio, in front of other airline pilots. Everyone knows that you're dating.'

'We're actually *not* dating. Not in the real sense of the word, anyway. We're fake dating.'

'Fake dating?'

I nodded.

'Like, *fake dating*? As in "rom-com trope" fake dating?'

'I suppose you could put it like that.'

'For what purpose are you fake dating?'

'My parents are always going on about me getting a boyfriend and settling down, and his friends and parents are always asking him when he's going to settle down, so we solved each other's problems by being each other's fake partners.'

'You know, in all the romcoms, the fake relationships eventually all turn real, right?'

I lowered my head. 'I suspect that might have happened somewhat.'

'Have you fallen in love?'

'I've never been in love. I wouldn't know.'

'Oh honey, you'll know if you're in love. Tell me how you feel?'

'How I . . .' I paused, and then closed my eyes, trying to get in contact with the feelings that I knew I'd been having. 'I have this constant feeling inside me – in my stomach, specifically – when I see him and talk to him. It's like an itch I can't scratch. He's all I can think about, and being near him and talking to him is the best part of my day. And when I have to say goodbye to him I miss him, physically, like someone might miss a phantom limb.'

Blessing burst out laughing and I flicked my eyes open. 'You're in love.'

'Am I?'

'One hundred per cent, head over heels in love.'

'Head over heels is a forward roll. I've never understood how you can be "forward roll" in love.'

Blessing walked around the reception desk and stood in front of me.

'When you do a forward roll, there's a point at which you can no longer stop your forward momentum. There's a tipping point that, if you cross it, you're going to roll, and at that stage, there's no stopping it from happening. That's like love. You can't stop love from happening either. And it can sneak up on you too, believe me.'

'Love can't sneak,' I quickly corrected.

'You're wrong. Love does it all. It does your head in.'

'Sounds awful. Why do we want to be in love if it does our heads in?'

'Because it's also the best feeling in the entire world,' he said, looking into the distance as if he was now thinking about someone he loved too.

'He said he's in love with me,' I added.

'What did you say back?'

'Not much. But we did land up having sex, so there wasn't that much talking.'

'YOU HAD S—Hi, Welcome to Middle East Air business lounge, how may I direct your call?'

'What?' I blinked at Blessing, and he pointed to the headphones that he was wearing.

'That is correct, open twenty-four hours a day.' He pointed at me, and I think he mouthed something that looked like 'Don't you dare go' when I took a step back. I stopped walking.

'See you soon, sir. YOU ARE HAVING SEX WITH YOUR FAKE BOYFRIEND.'

'We've only had sex twice,' I defended myself. I felt like I was under attack. 'Mind you, the one night, *God, it was hot*, the one night we also—'

'Whoa, whoa, whoa! I don't need all the ins and outs, so to speak.' He folded his arms and seemed to regard me with real purpose. 'There is one thing I know about sex for sure, though. When it comes to sex you *shouldn't* be having, once is too many and twice is never enough.'

I ran that line over in my head, trying to make sense of it.

'It means that you probably shouldn't have had it once, but now that you've had it twice, you're just going to want more and more of it.'

'I do want more.'

Blessing suddenly stiffened and looked over my shoulder. 'Hello, welcome to Middle East Business Class Lounge. Can I see your boarding pass, please.'

I straightened and grabbed one of the complementary magazines and started flipping through it, trying to convey the message that I was *not* here talking about sex. Which I was. And I was sure it was written all over my face too. I was not good at hiding what was happening in my head at all, so I buried my head in the magazine even more.

The man handed his pass over and Blessing escorted him into the lounge. He returned moments later to continue the conversation.

'Okay, so you've had sex twice and done something else one night that was very hot that shall remain unnamed. But under what circumstances did the sex occur?'

'The first time was very unplanned. In a bathroom at my cousin's wedding.'

He shook his head and tutted. 'In a bathroom.'

'It was more of a changing room, and I wasn't bent over a toilet or anything . . .' I paused and felt my cheeks get hot. '. . . I was perched on the vanity.'

'And the second time?' he asked.

I sighed when I thought about the second time. There were hardly any words in the universe to describe what the second time had been like. I had thoroughly run through my internal thesaurus but was yet to find a word that described with any level of accuracy what that night had been like. I touched my hands to my face; I could feel it getting hotter.

'You're so in love with him.' Blessing slumped across the reception desk. 'I'm jealous. He's gorgeous!'

I started nodding my head. 'I think I'm in love with him,' I finally said.

'You should tell him. Say it back. The guy went out on such a limb there, telling you how he felt.'

I smiled for a moment, and then my shoulders slumped. 'But even if we are in love with each other, is that enough to make a relationship work? I've never been in a relationship that made it past the fourth date.'

'Oh God, now you're just depressing me. You think too much.'

'What if—'

'Oh my God, stop it!' Blessing held his hand up. 'You have two choices here – it's not that complicated. Tell him you're in love and give the relationship a real go. You've been fake dating for almost half a year already, so it's not like you're starting over. Or don't.'

'That's your advice?' I asked. I had expected more. 'What would you do?'

'I think if I never told him how I felt and gave the relationship a chance, I would regret it.'

I looked at the clock above Blessing's head. It was almost time for my shift.

'I have to go, but I'm not entirely sure that any of that was helpful.'

He laughed. 'It was helpful. You just haven't realized that yet.'

'Thank you then, I suppose.'

'Any time,' he said.

I started walking away, but stopped when I reached the doors. I looked at my feet awkwardly before speaking again. 'Would you like to have coffee sometime? In the airport?'

'I'd love to have coffee,' he said.

'Good. I'll confirm a time and date with you at a later stage.' I walked towards the door again and then stopped once more. 'Thank you for your advice.'

'Any time,' he said again, and answered another call.

CHAPTER 45

'City Tower, this is Flightbird Six Zero Zero.'

Even though I'd been expecting to hear his voice, I physically jumped in my seat, sending my coffee cup flying to the floor with a splash.

'Sorry, sorry,' I said to my colleague Barry, who'd turned to look. I grabbed the box of tissues on my desk and started shoving them on top of the wet patch, and then stood on them.

'Sorry, what, City Tower?'

'No, not you, Flightbird Six Zero Zero. I spilt my coffee. I'm saying sorry to someone else. Never mind. It's not relevant. Hello. I mean, good morning.'

'It's technically just gone twelve p.m., so I think that makes it the afternoon, City Tower.'

I looked at the clock on the wall. 'You're right. Good afternoon, Flightbird Six Zero Zero.'

I heard a breathy chuckle come through the radio and I imagined his smile.

'Hello there. We are inbound for Johannesburg Airport, approaching pylons, requesting vectors for . . .' He paused for the briefest second, and someone that didn't speak to him all the time and didn't know his speech patterns intimately might not have noticed it, but I noticed. And I also knew why. '. . . ILS. Flightbird Six Zero Zero.'

'Flightbird Six Zero Zero, turn left heading two niner zero.'

'Copy, City Tower, turn left heading two niner zero. Flightbird Six Zero Zero.'

There was another pause.

'How was the rest of your holiday?' he asked.

I wanted to say that I missed him, that it wasn't the same without him, but didn't.

'Good. Sunny. Warm. Beachy. You know.'

'Sounds good. What's the weather like down there?'

I scanned the automated weather information system.

'Visibility is perfect, wind two fifty at ten knots.'

'Copy that, City Tower, wind at two fifty knots, Flightbird Six Zero Zero.' He disappeared for a little while. I landed two more planes before I heard from him again.

'City Tower, this is Flightbird Six Zero Zero, established ILS, runway three zero left.'

'Maintain the approach, Flightbird Six Zero Zero. You are cleared to land on runway three zero left.'

'Copy, City Tower. Maintain approach and cleared to land on runway three zero left. Flightbird Six Zero Zero.'

I looked out of the window, waiting for his plane to come into visual range, and when it did an icy feeling crept through my body. I'd seen him fly so many times before that the second I saw the plane, I knew something was off. There was nothing particular that stuck out; it was more of a feeling in the pit of my stomach. And I was right.

'Pan-pan, pan-pan, pan-pan,' he said, and I sat bolt upright.

'Flightbird Six Zero Zero, did I hear you correctly? Can you confirm a pan-pan?'

'Yes, confirmed.'

At the sound of those words, which rippled through a slight moment of silence in the room, the atmosphere around me changed as all the other air traffic controllers turned and looked at me. 'Pan-pan' indicated that something was wrong.

'This is Flightbird Six Zero Zero, we have a problem with the undercarriage. Landing gear will not extend. We do not have three greens. I repeat, we do not have three greens.'

The ATCs all looked at each other. This wasn't an emergency, yet. Pilots were trained for this, but for me this felt like an emergency and it was taking all my calmness and coolness to respond accordingly.

'We copy, Flightbird Six Zero Zero. Please switch over to emergency frequency one to one decimal five.'

'Copy, City Tower, switching to emergency frequency one to one decimal five.'

I looked around the room as I waited for him to switch to the other frequency. I closed my eyes and pulled out the emergency file from my memory banks. I read over it quickly in my mind.

ASSIST. Acknowledge, Separate, Silence, Inform, Support, Time.

'City Tower, this is Flightbird Six Zero Zero on emergency frequency.'

'We copy, Flightbird Six Zero Zero. Please state your intentions.'

I waited for what felt like ages before his voice came through again.

'This is Flightbird Six Zero Zero. We're going to go around and request entry into Signal Hill VOR holding pattern. Requesting flight level six thousand and will troubleshoot the problem and get back to you.'

'Copy that, you have permission to enter Signal Hill VOR holding pattern. Hold east on the two seven zero degree radial, right turns, and maintain six thousand.'

He paused, and I was sure he was going to say something else to me, but he didn't. Everyone in the tower stood up and watched as the approaching plane started going back up into the sky. I put a pencil between my teeth and bit down until the plane disappeared above the clouds. I looked at the clock. How long would it take them to troubleshoot? And how much fuel did they have? How long could they remain in the holding pattern for? At speeds of two thirty knots, the inbound leg would take a minute, outbound leg another minute, two right turns into fix end and outbound end, two more minutes. I bit the pencil again and stared at the clock, willing time to move faster, but it didn't. And after the longest four minutes of my life, I heard him again.

'This is Flightbird Six Zero Zero. We have troubleshot the problem and are still unable to confirm landing gear down.'

My stomach tightened and the atmosphere in the room became tense.

'Copy. What are your intentions?' I asked. I waited again, and another minute passed in deathly silence, as Andrew was no doubt discussing with his co-pilot. The second hand dragged around the clock in the most painstakingly slow manner. And then he came through again.

'City Tower, this is Flightbird Six Zero Zero. We would like to do a low approach for visual inspection of landing gear.'

'Copy that! We will stand by for visual inspection.' As that was said, just about everyone grabbed their binoculars and rushed to the window. We lined up shoulder to shoulder, waiting to see the plane. And when it finally appeared we all leaned in, straining to get a visual on his landing gear. And when we finally did, an icy pit formed in the very bottom of my stomach.

'And do you see them?' he asked. At this point, the usual script for procedure went out the window; pilot and air traffic controller no longer had to communicate in a formal manner, repeating each word and phrase. In these situations, we were allowed to talk in a casual manner. It helped ease the tension of the situation.

'No. Sorry, Andrew. I can't see them.'

'Shit,' he whispered.

'Can you confirm your intentions?' I asked again. The ball was always in the pilot's court when it came to emergencies. They had trained for them, and it was up to them to decide what to do. There was a pause. It wasn't longer than thirty seconds, but it felt like for ever.

'We will return to Signal Hill holding pattern to burn off fuel. Please can you stand by for emergency landing.'

I looked at Barry, the air traffic controller next to me, and clicked my fingers at him. He immediately jumped into action and called the emergency ground crew. I clicked my fingers at Pier, the ATC in charge of Ground Control, and he started clearing the runway, and now it was up to me to start clearing airspace, putting other planes into holding patterns and diverting the ones that I could to other airports.

'How long do you think it will take to burn off enough fuel?' I asked, desperate to know. The longer he was in the air, the worse the situation was. We needed him on the ground as soon as possible. But we also needed him to do his emergency landing with as little combustible fuel in the aircraft as possible.

'Estimate one hour.'

'AN HOUR! That long?'

'Short flight, full tank.'

'Okay. I have to divert air traffic. Give me fifteen minutes, twenty,' I said, and then jumped into action. Even though there was so much to do, my brain went into a hyper-focused state and I managed all the other planes quickly and efficiently. When I was done, I returned to Andrew.

'You've tried normal system, back-up system and freefall, right?'

'Yes,' he replied.

'Hydraulics?'

'Nothing wrong with them.'

'Electrical control circuits?'

'Nope,' he replied. I closed my eyes and scanned my mind for all the information I had stored in my brain about his aircraft.

'What was your take-off weight?' I asked.

'A hundred and ten thousand pounds.'

I started doing the maths in my head, subtracting the weight of the fuel and accounting for a deviation in accuracy of passenger weight.

'I want you to land on runway zero seven,' I said. 'It's longer.'

'And it's my lucky runway,' he said humorously, but I could hear for the first time that there was a little quiver in his voice. Nerves?

'Is there anything you need from me?' I asked him.

'No. I'll speak to you in thirty minutes when I've burnt off all the fuel.'

'Emergency services will be standing by,' I assured him.

I gripped my hands together tightly and looked up at the clock. The ticking hand was torturous, but still, I kept my eyes glued to it. I tried to focus all my attention on the second hand, because if I didn't I was replaying scenes from *Airplane Investigation*: planes crash-landing without landing gear, skidding to a stop, sparks and flames blazing on the undercarriage, fuel leaking, plane igniting. *Boom!*

'It's all over the TV,' a voice said, and I turned towards it.

'What is?'

'Look,' Yvonne, one of my fellow ATCs – the only other woman who worked here – switched the TV on, and there it was. Live coverage from right outside the airport. How on earth had they found this out? Someone must have tipped them off, or maybe a passenger had sent a message when they'd passed low and she momentarily had cell phone signal. And that is exactly what had happened. Not just one message, but tens of messages sent to loved ones telling them about the problem and saying emotional goodbyes in case they never came back. We stood in stunned silence as the newsreader read the various messages, the camera fixed to the clouds, waiting to see the circling craft. Pier pulled out his phone and looked down at it. 'It's all over Twitter,' he said.

'Facebook too,' Barry confirmed.

My stomach dropped when my phone started lighting up. It was a message from Andrew's mom.

Becca: Is it true?

My fingers shook as I typed back to her.

Pippa: Yes. But it's going to be okay. I'm the ATC in charge of the flight. And he's an excellent pilot.

But I wasn't sure I quite believed that. It didn't have much to do with his skill, or mine for that matter. Once that plane was on the ground, skidding across the tarmac, it was really up to the forces of nature to determine what damage would occur to the undercarriage. If there was a fuel leak, or not. What did or did not get damaged on touchdown. There were so many variables it was impossible to know if this would end happily or in a ball of fire. I was just about to put my phone down when a string of beeps made it vibrate in my hand.

10-Year School Reunion WhatsApp Group

Katie: @pippa, I just saw the news. Is it really Andrew?

Emily: OMG! I can't believe it! How is he?

Larissa: WOW. This is unbelievable. How are you holding up?

Palesa: Sending prayers. Thinking about you. I hope everything will be okay.

A string of praying hand emojis lit up my screen.

Yanilla: I've asked my church friends to pray for Andrew too.

Nobuhle: Sending love! I'm sure everything will be okay.

And then lots of heart emojis lit up my screen.

Sasha: Keep strong! We're all thinking about you, guys.
Katie: Reach out if there's anything you need!

I quickly silenced the notifications from the group. I couldn't have any distractions now. But it had felt nice to have so many people reach out to me like that. I needed to focus now. But my mind was jumping between things. Between images of fiery plane crashes and Andrew and I kissing.

Andrew and I laughing. An exploding fuselage.

Andrew and I collecting shells. Andrew hanging out of the window, his plane in flames, a long drop to the concrete below.

Andrew lying on top of me on the bouncy castle, an inflatable emergency slide.

'City Tower, this is Flightbird Six Zero Zero.'

His voice pulled me back to reality. Everyone in the room leaned in. The sense of anticipation was palpable.

'This is City Tower. How are you? How are all the passengers? Crew? What do you want to do?'

'Crew are having to deal with some pretty panicky passengers but, other than that, they've been briefed for emergency landing procedure and crew is standing by.'

'How many souls on board?'

'One hundred and four.'

One hundred and four people! My blood ran cold again.

'We've burnt off sufficient fuel and we are ready for approach. Intend to make a full stop landing on this approach, but it could be a go-around.'

'Try a gravity drop one more time. Please.' I sounded desperate, and a small laugh came through again.

'I've done it about a hundred times. The gear is not coming down today. But at least I'm landing on my lucky runway.'

'You are cleared to land on runway seven,' I said softly, wishing that runway seven would suddenly grow grass, or carpeting, soft padding to absorb the force of his landing.

'Acknowledge that, City Tower, cleared to land on runway seven, and—'

'And what?' I asked.

'I'm glad it's you, Pippa.' His voice was soft, and I didn't care that everyone around us had leaned in to listen.

'I'm glad it's me too, and I, I wanted to . . .' I looked left and then right. Too many people here. Too many pairs of eyes. Too much of an audience.

'Your moms wanted me to tell you that they know you can do it,' I said softly. 'And I know you can do it too.' Everyone in the room was nodding.

'Thanks, Pippa. Wish me luck.'

'You don't need luck!' I shot back. 'You've got this. I know you do!' And I wanted to say something else too, but didn't.

'I'll see you on the ground. Vectors for ILS, please.'

'Turn left heading two niner zero, Flightbird.'

'Thanks, City Tower.'

'My pleasure.'

I sat back in my chair and looked out the window, desperate for his plane to come into view. As illogical as it was, I felt that if I could see his plane, it would be safer. If I was watching it, maybe everything would be all right. Or was I just telling myself that? I ran through the possible worst-case scenarios in my head, and each and every one of them ended in a ball of flames and Andrew *not* coming back to me. The pain I felt in the pit of my stomach at that thought was physical. I ached. Right in the centre of my body. In the centre of my being. I had never felt such an awful feeling before. Or so I thought . . .

'Mayday, Mayday. This is Flightbird Six Zero Zero.'

The words that everyone working in an airport dreaded.

'What's wrong?' I jumped out of my seat and looked to the sky.

'We have an electrical failure. We do not have reliable airspeed indicator.'

A combined gasp was taken by every single person in the room. This was the worst-case scenario. If the pilot did not know how fast the plane was traveling, he might travel too slow and stall mid-air. But if he travelled too fast, the plane could rip apart. Without a reliable airspeed indicator, the pilot wouldn't know how much to speed up or slow down for the landing and, worst of all, if Andrew missed the landing, there was no reliable way of climbing back up if he was having to guess the aircraft's speed. I took a deep breath and calmed my voice.

'Acknowledged, Flightbird Six Zero Zero. What are your intentions?'

'Uh . . . Uh . . .' He stumbled over his words.

'Andrew. Take a breath.'

I heard him do as I asked.

'Right, what are your intentions and what do you need from us?'

'We are committed to landing on runway seven. We have one chance to get this right. Evacuate anyone in proximity of runway. Have emergency services standing by.'

'Done,' I said quickly. 'You can do this, Andrew! I know you can.'

'That means a lot, coming from you,' he replied.

'I want the frozen peas with you too!' It flew out of my mouth.

'Really?' I could hear a smile in his voice.

'I want all the frozen things with you. I'll even have the sweetcorn, even though it gets stuck in the back of my throat – wait, that didn't sound right – what I'm trying to say is I love you too. There, I said it! I love you.' I knew everyone in the room had heard me, but I didn't care, and so I carried right on. 'I love you, and I'm sorry I didn't say it before. I just needed some time to think it over and get used to the idea that you loved me. Get over the shock of you saying it. But now I'm over it, and I love you, and I'm sorry that I need these moments to think things through like this, but that's just me.'

'Don't apologize. I like it. I know that when you finally do say something, you really mean it. But I also need to tell you that your timing is terrible.'

'I know. I'm terrible at a lot of things, but I think you know what those are, and if you want to, because I want to, I really, really want to, we could make this thing between us real.'

'It's been real to me for a long time now, Pippa.'

'Me too. I just took longer to realize that.'

'I love you too,' he said. Out of the corner of my eye, I could see my colleagues watching me as if I was the most entertaining daytime drama. 'Pippa, I have a visual of the runway. Stand by for emergency landing.'

'Copy! Standing by for emergency landing.'

'I need silence, now. Please don't contact me until I'm on the ground. I love you.'

'I love you too. Good luck!' I said, and heard that familiar chuckle.

'Luck! I don't need luck.'

But this time it wasn't true. He did need luck. He needed all the luck in the entire universe to get this plane onto the ground. The line went dead.

'Look at this,' Pier said, turning up the volume on the TV as South Africa's biggest news station started broadcasting from right outside the airport.

'Over the skies of Johannesburg, Mzansi Airways, with one hundred and four souls on board, are minutes away from attempting an emergency landing here at South Africa's busiest airport, without any landing gear. Across South Africa, viewers have been watching the drama unfold and holding their breath as the plane, piloted by Andrew Boyce-Jones, circled in a holding pattern for over an hour, burning off fuel for the imminent emergency landing.'

'Turn it off,' someone shouted.

'Fucking media, turning a real emergency into fucking entertainment,' Barry said, and then I felt a tentative hand on my shoulder. I turned. This was the first time that anyone at work had ever touched me.

'He's an excellent pilot. He'll do this.' He squeezed my shoulder and then moved towards the window. I followed.

'What if the plane does crash and it's broadcast live on TV to the entire country?' Yvonne said. We all looked at her. The implications of her words rung in my ears.

'That would be . . . awful,' Pier said.

'No one is going to crash,' Barry said firmly.

Awful. I repeated the word to myself. It was not the right word though. Synonyms included *horrific*, *shocking*, *gruesome* and *ghastly*. Those words were more apt. *Awful* sounded too benign and pedestrian to describe the horror that was playing out right now. In a few minutes, Andrew was going to bellyflop – either too fast, or too slow – one hundred and ten thousand pounds onto a concrete runway. Skid along the runway with no brakes to slow them down and hope that they reached a full stop by the end of the runway and in the process did not burst into flames. Andrew's plane came into view. I pressed my face up against the window like I'd done at the aquarium, but this time under very different circumstances. I felt nauseous. Dizzy. But the closer the plane got to the runway, the closer it came to the inevitable belly flop.

Please let him be safe.

Please let him be safe.

He was going too fast!

'Slow down,' I said to him quickly. 'You're coming in too fast.'

'Slowing down,' he said, sounding so unbelievably calm.

'As soon as you hit the ground, wing spoilers and reverse thrust.'

'I know.'

'Keep your nose up for as long as you can.'

'I know.'

'Sorry, I know you know. I love you.'

'I know you know I love you too. I have to go,' he said, and the radio went silent. I could see he'd slowed the plane somewhat, but he was still coming in fast. Andrew was controlling the plane now by instinct alone. Keeping the nose up at just the right angle, judging the speed and rate of descent based purely on what he could see and feel, without any electronic equipment to guide him, and he was about to touch down. I gasped as the back of the plane hit the runway. White smoke exploded from the tail and the sound of the metal grating against the concrete was so loud I was sure the entire world could hear it. And when the engines came into contact with the concrete, sparks lit up the runway like firecrackers. I hoped the fuel tank was bone dry. Let it be dry! But the flames that suddenly appeared told me that it wasn't, and worse than that, they were not slowing down fast enough.

'Come on, come on! Slow down!' Barry said next to me. I think every single person watching this was willing the plane to slow. And the willing worked, because the plane started to slow and finally stop, just at the end of lucky number seven. But none of us clapped or celebrated yet. I felt someone grab my hand, I didn't know whose hand it was, but I squeezed it tightly as I watched the flames and smoke growing bigger by the second. The doors opened, inflatable slides flew out of the plane, and people began climbing out. The fire trucks raced to the plane, and soon it was being doused.

'Come on, come on!' I was trying to count the heads running across the tarmac. The pilot could only leave the plane once the last person had exited. The wait was almost impossible to bear, but finally, finally, the last of the passengers exited and I saw Andrew and the crew jumping out onto the inflatable sides. A massive cheer rose up around me, but I slumped down in my chair and held my head in my hands. I was shaking. My heart was racing and I realized that tears were streaming down my face.

I no longer cared that I hated big romantic displays of public affection. I no longer cared that romantic reunions made me cringe and that crying in public felt like the worse thing in the world. I no longer cared about anything else but running as fast as I could, through the airport, tears streaming down my face, pushing people out of the way and looking for Andrew. I'd never run so fast in my life, and when I saw him round the corner I'd never been so happy to see anyone before.

'ANDREW!' I screamed. People looked, and I didn't give a fuck. 'I LOVE YOU!' I screamed again. Andrew put down the bag he was carrying and held his arms open as I streamed ahead. I flung myself at him, and the second he wrapped his arms around me *I knew.* I absolutely, utterly, wholly, without exception, no reservations, categorically, definitely, unquestionably, undoubtedly, positively and every other synonym *knew* that I loved him and this was where I was meant to be.

Chapter 46

Four months later

'We should just get married,' I said, looking down at Andrew as he took the lid off the engine on the gate.

'What?' He stopped what he was doing and peered up at me.

'Yes, I've been thinking about it a lot, and I think it would be a good idea to get married.'

He stood up, sweat glistening on his brow, his hands dirty and covered in oil. Why he persisted in trying to fix this gate was beyond me. We'd been together for four months by now, and in that time he'd tried to fix it at least six times. Each time, the gate had not sped up at all. Even Zeus and Athena looked exasperated as they sat next to him watching.

'And I also think you should stop trying to fix this gate and just let me buy a new motor for the engine.'

'No!' he said, in that same stubborn voice he used every time I mentioned buying a new motor.

I rolled my eyes. 'You're obsessed with this gate engine.'

'I know I can fix it though.'

I shook my head at him. 'You cannot fix it. You've tried and failed multiple times.'

'Did you say you think we should get married?' He leaned against the wall and folded his arms.

'I did. We've been living together for four months already, and we still love each other, and it seems like we're just putting off the inevitable. Also, financially, it makes so much more sense for you to sell your place. We could build an extra room here, or even a cottage for your RC planes. That's really the only reason you go back home anyway. Also, we could file joint taxes, which would save so much time and money, and tax season is coming up.'

'This is all very logical and practical of you,' Andrew said with a smile.

'I know. I told you, I've thought about it quite a lot.'

'Are there any other reasons you'd like to get married?'

I smiled at him. 'Not really. Just that.'

He pushed himself off the wall and walked towards me. 'Are you asking me to marry you?'

I shook my head. 'No, just pointing out the benefits of marriage, if that is what you wanted to do . . . Is it, what you want to do?'

He walked all the way up to me, placed his hands on my shoulders and tangled his fingers through the pigtail braids that he'd done on me earlier. 'The thought had crossed my mind, once or twice. But I wasn't going to bring it up for a while. I didn't want to freak you out.'

'It doesn't freak me out. Nothing that I thought would freak me out has freaked me out so far.' This was true. From the moment Andrew had gotten off that plane and I'd fallen into his arms the relationship had moved very quickly. I'd thought that living with him would have freaked me out, but it hadn't, because he was flying internationally now, which meant that he was away for almost two weeks a month, which suited me perfectly. I got to have my own time, which was important for me, and best of all, when he came back we were so in love with each other and had missed each other so much that the never-ending sex was amazing.

'Good to know,' he said, and his hands moved off my shoulders and down to my hips. 'But you have kind of taken the romance and the surprise out of this moment, you know that.'

'I hate surprises. If you ever decided to drop down on one knee in front of me and pull out a ring, I would never, ever marry you. I'd probably break up with you right there and then, in fact.'

He laughed and pulled me into a hug. A real hug. We no longer pugged. 'I would never dream of surprising you with an engagement. And I know you don't like wearing rings either. They make your fingers feel claustrophobic.'

'Like they're being strangled.' I pulled out of the hug and looked up into his eyes.

'So?' he asked.

'So what?'

'So are we doing this? Are we getting engaged?' he asked.

'I think engagements are stupid, don't you? Why do you have to get engaged first before you get married? It makes no sense. You only do that if you're buying time so you can organize a big wedding.'

'So you want to jump ahead to the getting-married part then?' he asked.

'Tax season is right around the corner.' I smiled at him.

'Very funny.' He ran a hand down my cheek, stopped under my chin and then tilted my face up. 'Seriously, though. Do you want to get married?'

'Yes. But can we elope and not tell my mom about it.'

'I don't think that would be very nice.'

I sighed. 'But let's give her as little time as possible to plan the wedding so she can't make it totally over the top.'

He rolled his eyes. 'Your mother's job is to create over-the-top weddings for people in days.'

I groaned. 'She'll make it huge, won't she?'

'But do you know how happy it will make her?'

'I suppose.' I looked up at the sky. The sun was creeping lower now.

'Shit, what's the time? I need to get to work.'

'Better run along, Miss Supervisor.'

'What are you going to do?' I asked.

'I'll probably take the dogs for a walk.'

'Good idea, they'll love that.' I started jogging up the long driveway. Zeus and Athena did not follow me though. In the last few months, I'd come to realize what fickle animals they were. Instead, they stared at Andrew with their big brown eyes. I was not the only one who'd fallen in love with him.

'Hey,' Andrew called out, and I stopped. 'Did we seriously just agree to get married?'

'Yes.'

'Are you going to take my surname?'

'Pippa Boyce-Jones?' I said it out loud and instantly liked the way it sounded. 'I think I will.' I turned and started jogging, but then stopped.

'Andrew.' I turned and started walking back down towards him.

'What, wifey?'

I laughed. 'No. No pet names. Please.'

'What, Pippa?'

'If you don't manage to fix the gate engine this time, I am calling the electrician.'

He smiled at me. 'I'll fix it.'

'That's what you said the last six times.'

'Well, lucky number seven then.'

Chapter 47

I stood in my bedroom and looked at myself in the mirror.

'I cannot believe I allowed my mother to organize a wedding for me,' I said to Jennifer, who was spread out across the bed playing with the dogs.

'How bad do you think it will be? How many people do you think she's invited? How many ice sculptures and water fountains and marching bands will she have there? She won't even tell me where it is, just to be ready for the limo to fetch us at five. God, an evening wedding and a night-time reception. There'll be fireworks, won't there? Lots of fireworks.'

Jennifer sat up on the bed and crossed her legs. 'Are you seriously asking me these questions? You do know that they are totally rhetorical, because we both know the answers to them.'

I put my face in my hands. 'It's going to be bad, isn't it?'

'It's your mother,' Jennifer said flatly. 'Cirque du Soleil has probably been flown in from France and she's probably uprooted the Leaning Tower of Pisa and put it in the middle of the garden as a centrepiece. She's probably resurrected Pavarotti from the great beyond to have him sing the wedding march.'

I grabbed my stomach. 'I feel sick!'

'At least you look amazing!' Jennifer walked up behind me and looked at me in the mirror. 'This dress is incredible.'

I blushed a little. 'It's inspired by Skyler, the Pokémon trainer card.'

Jennifer laughed. 'Of course it is. At least your mom let you choose what you wanted to wear and didn't make you dress in a meringue and make me dress in teal.'

'Yes.'

'And she let us do our own hair and make-up too. She didn't call that guy – what's his name, that dramatic one from her show? – to do it.'

'His name is Angus.'

'Well, I for one am very happy that Angus is not doing my hair and make-up right now. And who in this day and age is called Angus anyway? Isn't that a type of beef.'

'He's Scottish,' I replied, looking down at my white sneakers, feeling very grateful that I hadn't been made to wear heels.

'You know what,' Jennifer said, pacing the room now, the dogs hot on her feet. 'You just have to get through this. Your mom has been wanting to throw you a wedding since before you were born. Just let her have this moment, and when it's over you're off to the Maldives to have sex for ten days. Think about the sex and the snorkeling and all the tropical fish while you're walking past the faux-gold pillars lining the hundred-meter aisle covered in red, velvety petals.'

'Okay! Fish, snorkeling, sex.'

'Exactly. Although I would not have put them in that order necessarily, but whatever.'

'Fish, sex and snorkeling!' I repeated.

'Nah, not that order either, but the sentiment is there.' Jennifer placed her hand on my shoulder quickly and then pulled away equally quickly. She knew exactly how long to touch me for.

'Thanks for being here.' I turned around and then reached out and gave her shoulder a little pat too.

'I wouldn't have missed this for the world, seriously.'

'I'm sorry things didn't work out with Colleen.'

Jennifer shrugged. 'One of the upsides to this wedding is that I'm sure, among the one-thousand-plus invited guests, I'll find someone who won't mind sharing a *bathroom* with me.'

'It was more of a changing room,' I corrected her again.

'You were pressed up against a bathroom vanity, Pippa. I think that says "bathroom" loud and clear.'

I smiled at her. Jennifer was, and would always be, my best friend. Even if I didn't communicate with her all the time, even if we didn't connect for months on end, it just worked.

'You're my best friend,' I said.

She sighed dramatically. 'I know. I feel sorry for you.'

'You're not that bad,' I joked back.

We looked at each other awkwardly. We weren't the kind of friends who got gushy and sentimental with each other. Jennifer was naturally dark and somewhat gloomy – at school they'd called her Wednesday Addams – and I was on the autism spectrum. As such, neither of us was comfortable with big shows of emotion and sentiment. But this felt like the right moment.

'You know I love you, right?' I said to her.

'Me too,' she said, and grimaced. 'Are we done now?' she asked.

'Totally done!'

'Great!' she said, and then we gave each other the quickest of hugs and pulled away.

'Right!' I looked down at my dogs. I wished they were coming to the wedding with me. But I was too afraid that, had I expressed an interest to bring them, my mom would have had doggy bridal outfits made for them and had them walk down the aisle with the ring. They would have been mortified. 'Come on, I'll throw the ball for you outside for five minutes before we go!'

At the word 'ball', they jumped and raced for the door. I walked out of the front door and stopped when I saw everyone standing in the driveway. Andrew was there, Andrew's entire extended family was there and so were my mom and dad.

'Hi!' I said, looking around, startled. 'Don't you always say what bad luck it is to see the bride before the wedding?' I asked my mom.

'This is not a normal wedding.' She smiled and walked over to me.

'What do you mean?'

Zeus and Athena were panting at my heels, staring at the ball in my hand. I threw it for them and they raced off.

'Where's the limo?' Jennifer asked, clearly as confused as I was.

'It's not coming,' my mom replied.

'Well, how are we all getting to the wedding then?' I looked at my watch. 'We're going to be late soon, and then all the guest will have to wait and it will all be doubly embarrassing when I arrive.'

'We're at the wedding.' My mom gestured with her arm to the wooded section at the highest part of the property.

I looked at Andrew. He was smiling at me. Best bloody smile in the world.

'Dad?' I said, looking for someone logical who could explain what was going on.

'This is your wedding.' My mom looped her arm through mine and started walking with me. 'Come on. Let's go.'

'Where? Nothing is making sense right now!' I swivelled my head around, trying to extract clues from this moment that I could piece together to create the full picture. But I was stumped.

My dad took me by my free hand. 'Consider this your mother's wedding gift to you. That there is no wedding.'

'Wait.' I stopped walking when it clicked.

'No wedding?'

My mom nodded.

'No wedding?' I asked again. It was met with another nod.

'No Tuscan ice sculptures and two-storey chocolate-fondant cakes?'

She nodded again.

'No crystal chandeliers and orchids and meters of draped lace and calligraphy name places and an orchestra?'

Another nod.

'So I'm getting married here? At home? With the dogs and you guys and *not* one thousand guests?'

'Well, I did need to get hold of a priest, or it wouldn't be legal, so he's here too.'

'Are you serious, Mom?' I gasped, overcome with so many emotions.

'Totally serious,' she said, tearing up.

I threw my arms around her, drawing her into maybe the biggest hug I'd ever given her. 'This is literally the best wedding present you could ever have given me.' I pulled away and found that my face was wet from tears I hadn't known I was crying. My mom reached up and wiped the tears away. I turned to my dad. 'This isn't a joke, right? We're not going to walk around the corner and she's created the Venetian canals and has a gondola ready and waiting for us?'

'No, no gondolas, no one thousand guests. Just us and the dogs and, well' – he swung his arm out over the view – 'this view.'

'I always intended it to be a wedding venue one day, so here we are,' my mom said.

'Oh, thank God!' Jennifer exclaimed from behind me, sounding as happy as I was feeling. 'I can't tell you how much I've been dreading the walk down the aisle, Mrs E. And, knowing you, I was expecting a landing-strip-length aisle.' My mom smiled over at Jennifer, who'd called her Mrs E for ever.

I craned my neck around and looked at Andrew.

'Did you know about this?' I asked.

'No, I'm as surprised as you are.'

'Well, I think this is perfect,' Becca declared from next to her son. 'Laidback, relaxed, and just with the people who really matter.'

'Exactly,' Linda said, and the other sisters all agreed.

'And don't forget the Margaritas are waiting for us,' James added.

The sun was dipping lower and the sky was starting to darken. We walked up the old stone steps that led to the wooded area at the very top of the property. This was the area where my mom had wanted to build the chapel.

'I did do one thing, though,' my mom said, stopping me before we walked into the shaded area. 'But it's the only thing I did, and I just had to! I couldn't not do anything.'

For a moment, my heart sank, I imagined people jumping out from the shadows to surprise me. Only that didn't happen. My mom flipped a switch and the trees lit up with thousands and thousands of tiny dots of light.

'WHOAAAA!' Leroy shouted from behind us, and ran forward.

'Careful,' I pointed to a rock in front of him just before he tripped over it.

'Remember what I said: always watch the ground.' I gave him a firm nod. The other kids all ran behind him, equally taken aback by the lights.

'It's like STARS!' Leroy shouted, and clapped his hands together in an excitement that could not be held in.

'It's beautiful, Mom,' I said to her.

She took my face between her hands and planted a kiss on my forehead. 'Not nearly as beautiful as you look today.'

We walked into the woods. I looked up: it was magnificent. Fairy lights wrapped around and between the trees like hundreds of intricate spiders' webs. I felt an arm come around me and I knew exactly who it was. I knew the feel of his arm as if it was my own.

'Shall we get married then?' he whispered against my ear, and I felt my whole body go weak and crumbly.

'I can't wait to marry you,' I said, taking hold of his hands.

'Well, if that's the case, we'd better get this started,' a priest said, walking up to us.

And that's how we got married, Zeus and Athena running around our feet, some of the kids playing with them, my mother-in-laws and parents standing around us casually, no pomp and ceremony. Leroy still looking up at the fairy lights as if he was oblivious to what was happening and Jennifer trying to hide the fact that she was actually shedding a tear!

'I love you, so much,' Andrew whispered as the priest started talking.

I met his eyes.

Over the months I'd gotten good at holding eye contact with him. In fact, I'd come to like it. Because when I looked into his eyes, it felt like I was looking into my future.

One year later

'Come, come, it's on!' I shouted from the TV room.

'Coming!!!' Andrew came running through the door, Zeus and Athena behind him. He jumped onto the couch next to me and we clutched each other in unadulterated excitement as we waited for the show to start.

'I'm so excited!' I flapped my fingers a few times. It was almost impossible to contain the excitement and I no longer did when I was around Andrew. I no longer hid things like my finger flapping or playing with a fidget spinner. And then the familiar voice came on and we both screamed together.

This week on Airplane Investigation, *Mzansi Airways flight one one two narrowly escapes disaster when it experiences not only a landing-gear failure but also an electrical one. But what exactly happened to cause this? our investigators ask. How was it that a plane carrying one hundred and four souls on board was forced to make an emergency landing at the busiest airport in Africa?*

Mayday, Mayday!

'Oh my God! I can't believe this!' I bounced on my knees as the actor playing Andrew spoke in a dramatic cutaway re-enactment.

'It's you.' Andrew pointed at the screen as the actress playing me spoke in another dramatic enactment.

Flightbird Six Zero Zero, this is City Tower, what is the nature of the emergency?

I sat back on the couch and gripped Andrew's hand as we watched our love story unfold in front of our very eyes. Our *real* love story that was only just beginning.

Don't miss Jo's hilarious and heartfelt Starting Over Trilogy!

Available now!

HEADLINE
ETERNAL

Don't miss Jo's glorious standalone office rom-coms!

HEADLINE
ETERNAL

For laugh-out-loud,
swoonworthy hijinks,
don't miss Jo's
Destination Love series!

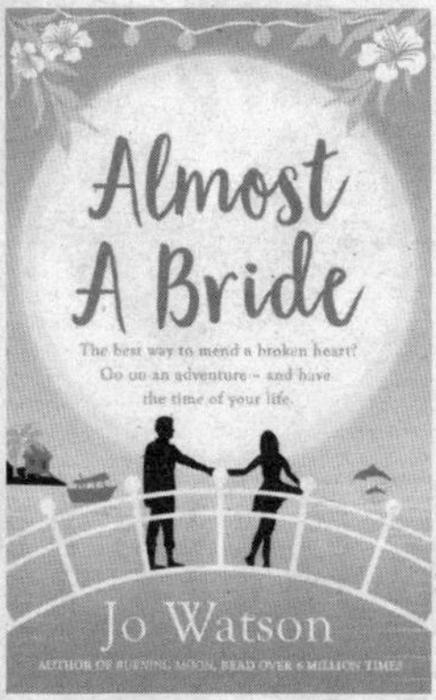

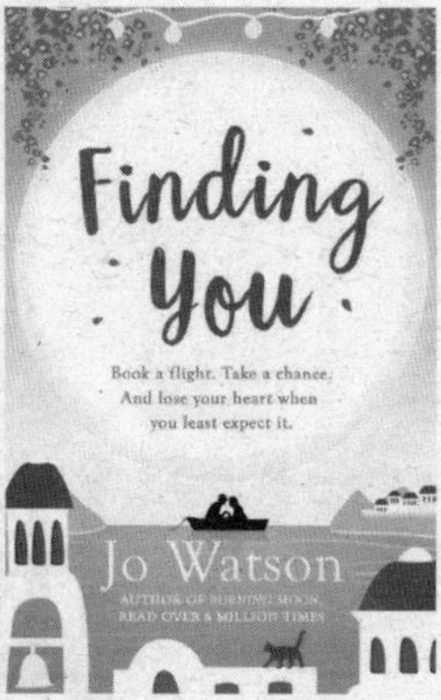

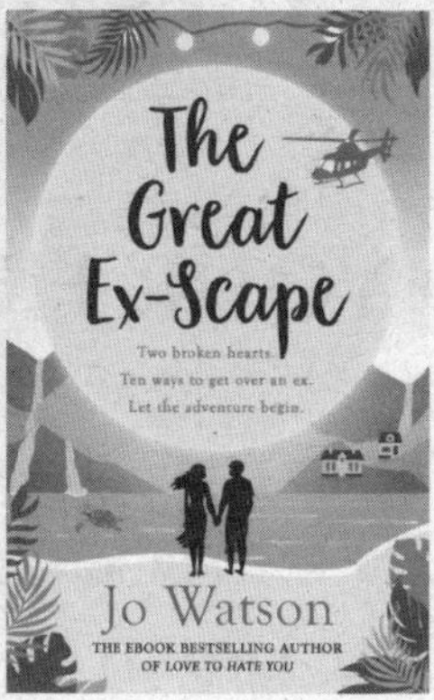